GIRLS NIGHT

GIRLS NIGHT

I.S. Belle

Tiny Ghost Press

Copyright © 2023 I.S. Belle

www.tinyghostpress.com

All rights reserved

The characters and events portrayed in this book are fictitious. Any similarity to real persons, living or dead, is coincidental and not intended by the author.

No part of this book may be reproduced, or stored in a retrieval system, or transmitted in any form or by any means, electronic, mechanical, photocopying, recording, or otherwise, without express written permission of the publisher.

ISBN:
E-book 978-1-915585-11-0
Paperback 978-1-915585-12-7
Hardback 978-1-915585-13-4

Cover Art by: Bhavna Madan

ALSO BY I.S. BELLE:

ZOMBABE

The BABYLOVE series:
BABYLOVE
SUGARSNAP
SWEETHEARTS

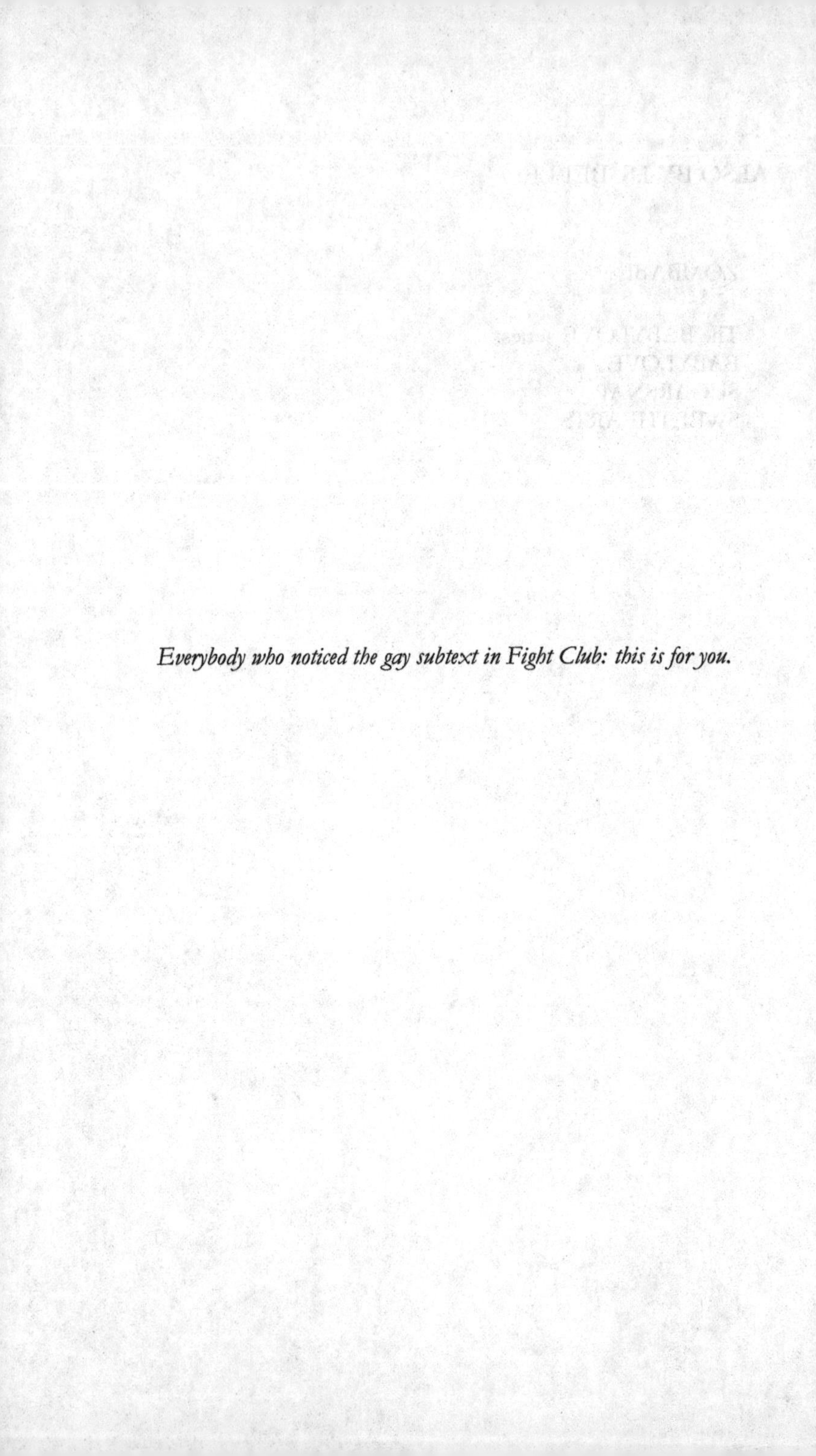

Everybody who noticed the gay subtext in Fight Club: this is for you.

Content warning: Violence, gaslighting, emotional abuse, biting, parental abuse, and mentions of sexual assault.

Sometimes eating makes you
hungrier
like violence
and love.

—Sara Sutterlin

CHAPTER ONE

Alex didn't notice the crowd until she was already in it. As she was about to open a text sent by her faithful gossipmongers (which, she would later learn, was about this very fight), she looked up to see the new girl's fist catch Olive's cheek hard enough to knock her sideways. Another punch and she hit the floor.

Continuing to walk to chemistry was never an option. Alex stopped and stared at the first fight she'd seen that wasn't on cable.

Clementine, she remembered, watching New Girl climb on top of Olive and keep punching. *Clementine R-something.*

It was hard not to remember the girl who showed up a month late to junior year. On her first day, Clementine showed up to school in jeans that were ripped in a way that seemed accidental rather than purposeful like the fashion statements of the other girls, her face stark and clean, her eyes heavy-lidded and aimed straight ahead.

Clementine reminded Alex of a bomb: a colorless, odorless gas bomb nobody noticed until it took out the entire city. She was always sitting in class by the time Alex walked in, dark hair buzzed to the scalp, staring straight ahead at the board. She hadn't met anyone's eyes since she'd started coming here.

Alex watched as Clementine's gaze burned into the eyes of everyone's favorite class president, fists cracking into her face one after the other, a steady drum of hurt.

A crowd had gathered in the wide hallway. It wasn't like crowds on TV—there was no yelling, and no one had their cellphone out to record it. Instead, everyone stood in stunned, appalled silence as Clementine broke Olive's nose with her hard hands.

A snap and a scream, then Clementine stood, barely out of breath. She did not look at the damage she had done to Olive or at the wreckage of her own knuckles. She did not look at the girls who had gathered around her.

She did not, despite Alex's unexpected and inexplicable need for her to, look at Alex.

Clementine kept her gaze on the linoleum instead as she moved through the gap in the crowd. Girls pressed themselves against lockers to get out of the way in case she took a swing at them.

Clementine turned the corner into a hall. It didn't lead to an exit. Where was she going?

Alex stared at the corner where Clementine had disappeared as students started forward to help Olive up off the floor. When she zoned back in, she realized three things: one, her phone was going crazy with texts; two, she was getting strange looks; and three, she was grinning hard enough to hurt her cheeks.

Alex forced her lips into a more appropriate shape. She could already hear phantom whispers—*she must hate Olive, she was so happy to see her get punched*—when it wasn't that at all. Still, she didn't want people discussing how excited she was to see someone get the shit kicked out of them.

A hand on her shoulder. Alex turned.

"Oh my *god.*" Cady tugged fretfully on her pink hair. "*Right?*"

"Oh my god," Alex agreed. Her phone buzzed in her hand. Girls were already glancing her way, expectant.

Cady giggled nervously. "I can't *wait* to hear what you dig up about this."

"I'll get right on it."

"I'll make sure I have something to trade for it." Cady tugged at her pink necklace, which was a shade darker than her hair. She was trying to be polite, which Alex appreciated. It didn't stop the undeniable truth: once the rumors stopped, no one had a single word to say to gossip queen Alex Veck.

Alex searched desperately for a way to keep the conversation going. What would Cady be interested in? A senior was dropping out due to bulimia. Another was off to rehab. No, Cady liked *fun* rumors, nothing too dark. Alex was surprised she was talking to her about a fight.

Alex tried, "Did you hear about—"

Cady talked over her. "We should probably—"

Girls streamed around them. Class was almost in session.

"Right," Alex said. "I'll keep you updated!"

Cady waved in thanks and vanished into the crowd.

As Alex turned to leave, a darkness caught her eye. She paused to stare at it. On the linoleum where Olive's face had been were spots of blood, still hot enough to smear.

Her gaze zeroed in on Clementine the moment she got to chemistry. Everyone else was following suit, staring and whispering and trying to be subtle. It wasn't working, but Clementine didn't seem to notice. She was staring at the blank whiteboard.

Alex sat down in her seat two rows over. Her phone vibrated again and again, an annoyed wasp in the cage of her hand.

A security guard came in, and the class went silent. The guard marched up to Clementine's desk and stood next to it. "Come with me, please."

Clementine didn't move.

"Ma'am," the guard said, "come with me." He took a step forward into her field of vision.

Clementine startled—a small thing, a twitch in the line of her shoulders. She looked over as if just noticing him and reached up to her ears to switch on her hearing aids. They were purple.

"Ma'am—"

Clementine stood. She let the guard put a hand on her arm, though she didn't look happy about it. Then she followed him out of the classroom.

A collective sigh rushed around the class as everyone relaxed.

Everyone except for Alex. She stayed clenched, hands curled into fists, eyes fixed on the door where Clementine had vanished into the hall.

Her phone vibrated in her fist. Alex swallowed, then started to scroll.

At the end of the day, Alex squeezed into a bus seat made to fold up for wheelchairs, staring down at her phone in frustration. No one had any dirt. No one had any information, period. Clementine didn't have any social media accounts, which made things ten times harder.

"You wanted info on Clementine Rady?"

Alex jumped. Sterling's head cheerleader, Quentin Scarhill, stood in the aisle, red hair a gleaming pile on her head. It looked queenly. It suited her.

She sat down next to Alex. Their thighs grazed. Alex fought the urge to squirm, inexplicably guilty about her leg spilling over into Quentin's seat. She had big legs. She had big everything.

"I noticed my cheerleaders were getting texts, so I got in touch with some old flames." Quentin raised a devastating eyebrow. "Do you still need information, or have you already—"

"No!" Alex cleared her throat, tucking her phone into her skirt pocket. "I'm still looking for—yes, I'd love some information. What do you have?"

Quentin gave her an amused look. "You first."

Alex ran through her mental catalog of gossip. When that didn't work, she got out her phone and pulled up her favorite Excel spreadsheet. "Uhhh . . . Someone heard one of your cheerleaders puking in the second-floor bathroom."

It was weak. She didn't even have a name. Besides, if a cheerleader was pregnant or bulimic or even just hungover, Quentin would know. She ruled that squad with an iron fist.

Quentin rolled her tongue in her mouth, unimpressed.

"One second," Alex tried. "I can find something. Um . . . "

Quentin cut her off. "You can make it up to me later."

"Really?" Alarm bells pinged in Alex's head—it wasn't a great idea, being in debt to Quentin Scarhill—but they faded away with Quentin's smooth smile.

Quentin leaned in, an excited glint in her green eyes. "Our resident psycho got kicked out of two schools for fighting."

"Shocking," Alex replied. Clementine had hit Olive like she did it for a living; like her entire purpose in life was to transfer to Sterling and bloody up their class president's face. Alex wouldn't be surprised if she started having dreams about it.

"Someone from her old school says she got legally emancipated. Her legal guardian's her big brother. They moved here to get away from their parents." Another devastating eyebrow raise. "Yikes."

"Yikes," Alex agreed. Then: "Thank you. You didn't have to."

Quentin wasn't one of her informants. They'd only talked directly to each other once: last year, Alex had tripped in the hall, and Quentin, close behind and walking fast, had had to step over her to avoid stepping *on* her.

Oh my god, she'd said, not breaking her stride. *Careful, Alex!*

Thank you, Alex had called after her. What else could she have said?

"You'll just have to pay me back someday," Quentin said. She smiled blandly and got out her phone. Conversation over.

Alex swallowed her disappointment and went for her own phone. This was when she noticed Sunju Park sitting across from her.

Sunju was hugging her backpack like a lifeline. Her dark hair hung limply down the back of her neck, contrasting with the tightness clenching the rest of her body. Until today, Alex had had no reason to talk to her.

"You're Sunju, right?"

Sunju jerked. She'd been staring out the window, too deep in her head to recognize anything blurring past. Her eyes were nice, Alex noticed—light brown and kind. Alex's mom said that her eyes were kind, but Alex had never seen it, despite all those hours staring into the mirror. In Sunju's the kindness was obvious, even if it was almost obscured by nerves.

"What?" Sunju asked, caught between nervous and suspicious.

Alex didn't blame her. If gossip queen Alex Veck started talking to you out of the blue, you were either about to receive some great gossip or about to be the subject of it.

Alex crossed her legs, trying to make herself fit better into these tiny seats. "I heard you gave Tulsi Ortiz an essay. What's she got on you?"

Sunju's jaw was locked. A muscle fluttered.

"Tulsi didn't tell me," Alex tried. "Someone walked in as you were leaving the essay with her. I'm sure you noticed—you seem like the jumpy type."

Sunju's gaze dropped to the floor.

Alex's smile shrank. "Tulsi wouldn't blackmail you if it were that important. She only does petty stuff."

Sunju's eyes darted up again. Incredulity flickered over her face and quickly washed out into neutral.

"Or maybe she's changed," Alex tried. "I haven't hung out with her since middle school."

She looked over to check if Quentin was going to add anything—Tulsi was her second in command, after all—but Quentin was still scrolling through her phone, looking like she hadn't heard any talk about her cagey squadmate.

The bus jerked into motion.

Familiar yelling. Cady was standing on a stepladder outside MeatLovers, her sign decked out in the same hot pink as her jacket, pumping her fist as she chanted. Every day she didn't have cheerleading practice, she'd park herself across the road from Sterling with her usual band of protestors.

Quentin turned to Alex. "Are you going to Cady's party on Saturday?"

"Yes!" Alex beamed. "Sunju, are *you* going?"

Sunju's grip on her backpack eased, just a little.

"Yes," she said. Then, sounding surprised at her own voice: "Tulsi invited me."

"It'll be good to see you at one of those."

Sunju went red at the top of her cheeks. It was cute.

Quentin didn't look at her. "I'll see you there," she told Alex, and smiled.

Alex clung to that image for the rest of the bus ride. She often did this, holding onto moments that implied people wanted her somewhere. It was for gossip, but Alex would take that over nothing.

When she got off the bus, she glanced back at Quentin to find her examining her ruby nails. Sunju met her eyes instead. She had no friends, Alex was pretty sure.

Alex imagined sitting down and saying, *me too*. She'd tried confiding this to a few girls over the years, and everyone had said the right things and then ignored any text that wasn't the latest scoop.

Did Clementine Rady have friends? Alex was betting not.

Alex nodded goodbye.

Sunju nodded back. Then she gathered up her dark bob and put it into a ponytail with the same grim determination you'd lay your head on a chopping block.

The apartment was quiet when Alex got home.

"I'm back," she said. She couldn't yell—her dad was asleep. He worked night shifts. Her mom worked twelve-hour day shifts, so there was no time in the Veck household to be anything but silent.

Alex stood in the front hall for a while, thinking about making a snack—gently opening the fridge, tiptoeing to the cupboard for a plate.

Before she could decide on a snack, her parents' bedroom door opened.

Her heart leapt in her throat as her dad emerged from the bedroom, bleary-eyed in boxers and a ratty shirt. A late-night bathroom visit at 3:30 p.m.

Alex smoothed her skirt down, smiled wide. "Hi!"

He grunted. It had been a hard shift—she could tell from how aggressively he slumped.

She stepped aside to let him past as he moved sideways to give her room. Then he continued on to the bathroom. The door closed.

Alex waited, not moving, and eventually the door opened again. Her dad came back out.

Alex smiled hard. "Hey, Dad!"

He walked past her, nodded in her direction, not taking his eyes off the floor.

Alex nodded back, watched the hallway door close, then eased her backpack off her shoulders. She wanted to throw it, break something, but she put it carefully down on the floor, her shoes following it, so she could walk in socked silence to her bedroom.

It took Alex longer than usual to organize her gossip texts into a spreadsheet. She kept getting distracted by the memory of Clementine's gaze, huge and all-encompassing; by Sunju's small smile as she admitted she was going to the party; by Tulsi Ortiz, who never talked to Alex anymore unless it was to toss out an insult, and who everybody avoided in the hallway so as to not cut themselves on her sharp edges.

Alex stared at her phone for a long time before pushing CALL. It rang a devastating seven times.

Click.

"Tulsi, hi! It's Alex. Um, Veck."

A pause. "What do you want?"

"Wow, okay. You know you used to be friendlier?"

"Lies. Tell me what you want so I can get back to my life."

Alex lay back on her bed, eyeing the old celebrity posters she had plastered up there—James Dean, Kristen Stewart, Halsey. "Are you getting Sunju Park to do your English essay?"

"How dare you," Tulsi said mildly. No venom yet. She was obviously in a good mood.

"What do you have on her?"

"Nothing I'd tell you about."

When Alex pictured Tulsi, she pictured her ears. Both of Tulsi's ears glimmered with five scarlet studs, courtesy of Quentin at a freshman house party. She looked like she'd been freshly hole-punched.

"I heard there was a fight," Tulsi continued. "Who the hell would want to hurt Olive Barnes?"

"It was this new girl. Clementine Rady." Alex shivered, remembering Clementine's intense gaze. *Like a laser beam,* she thought. *Cutting through clear and fast to the important bits.* "She looks like a dark-haired, sturdier version of Leonardo DiCaprio circa 1996 in *Romeo + Juliet.*"

"No clue who that is," Tulsi said.

Alex reached up, rearranging her pillows in a color gradient: purple to red to pink to blue. "I'm thinking of getting her number."

Tulsi snorted. "Why, you putting out hits on people now?"

"I might be," Alex said, and sucked in a deep breath. Now or never. "Hey . . . Are you driving to the party on Saturday?"

Another pause.

"I might be," Tulsi said warily. "Why?"

CHAPTER TWO

Clementine waited until Joseph was taking his last bite of dinner to say, "I got suspended on Monday."

"You got—" Joseph cut off, choking. Clementine leaned over the table to clap him on the back. It wasn't much of a stretch: their "table" was a box left over from moving in. This was the first time Joseph had been home early enough for dinner in weeks.

"*Thanks*," he signed. Out loud, he said, "You're telling me now? I thought you were heading off to school after I left for work."

She shook her head. "Sorry for not telling you earlier."

He sighed, motioning at her scabbing knuckles. "It didn't have anything to do with . . . ?"

Clementine flexed her hand around her spoon. It was plastic— she'd stolen it from the Sterling Girls cafeteria.

Joseph scraped the last of his cereal from his bowl, picked up his microwaved potato. "Thought you weren't having that kind of fun anymore."

"This wasn't for fun," Clementine said, ignoring the wistful ache that came with it. "There was this girl." She reached reflexively up to her ear. The aid curled around the back of it. "She touched my ears."

Joseph nodded. "You bluescreened."

This was what Joseph called it when Clementine's brain went offline and the only thing that existed was the fight. Clementine did this when she was backed into a corner. She wanted to remember the good fights, the ones that left her bright and satisfied, but these kind of fights—desperate, lost—she did her best to bury.

Joseph finished his potato. Signed, "*You're OK*," folding his fingers into her sign name: CLIP-CLOP-CLEM.

Her mouth twitched as she imagined those fingers galloping. *"How was work?"*

He groaned during all five steps it took to get to the sink.

"Yeah," Clementine said. She reached up and took off her hearing aids. The world fell into comfortable semi-silence. When her brother's mouth started moving again, Clementine clicked at him until he glanced back and nodded in acknowledgement. He rinsed his dish and plastic spoon and came to sit back at the box-table.

"Was wondering why you were wearing them after coming home," he signed. *"Usually, they're the first thing to come off."*

"I'm trying to get better at talking to people."

"You talk to people."

"I talk to you." Clementine scraped her bowl with her spoon and imagined the noise.

"I mean talk to people at school," he said.

Before coming to Sterling, she had briefly entertained the fantasy she always had before a new school: that she'd somehow slot herself into a group of friends. Not even a group—she'd settle for one friend. An acquaintance, even. Someone who asked about homework. A reason to use her voice. Since she usually spoke to Joseph in ASL, Clementine would go for days without talking aloud. Sometimes she'd speak into thin air just to check her voice box hadn't rusted shut.

It would be even nicer to find people to sign with, but she didn't have high hopes of that. The two deaf kids at her old school avoided her like the plague, and she'd long since lost touch with the people in the ASL courses Joseph had taken her to as a kid.

Clementine had hoped that all the work she'd done in therapy would make her into someone people wanted to be around, but the song remained the same: no one wanted to sit with the freak with the shaved head and bruised knuckles. It was a bitter pill, and it only got more bitter the longer Clementine didn't have anyone to talk to.

Then that girl—*Olive*—had tapped her shoulder. For a second, that hope had risen again, and Clementine envisioned a friendly conversation. She'd even have taken a *polite* conversation.

And then Olive had reached up to touch the skin above Clementine's hearing aid. Her words were lost in a red haze, but Clementine didn't need to know what she said—the cruel twist of her mouth said enough.

Clementine ran a gentle finger over her hurt knuckles. Joseph eyed them worriedly.

"They'll heal," she told him.

He met her eyes. Clementine didn't usually speak when she couldn't hear herself.

She watched his mouth move around, "Yeah. They always do."

He drummed the cardboard table and signed, *"How's your weekend looking?"*

Clementine shrugged. She had a poster for a party crumpled up in her pocket. She'd been thinking of going before she got suspended. She'd be less welcome now, but the idea of that sparked something old inside her—maybe someone would pick a fight, and she could open up her healing knuckles on their face. She clenched her hand around her fork, her scabs tingling with potential, everything narrowing into the adrenaline of it all.

If she couldn't have friends, then she could at least have a fight.

At 8:44 p.m. on Saturday night, Clementine's phone rang.

She looked up from a YouTube tutorial on rust repair. Once she turned 18, there was a job lined up for her at the mechanics shop Joseph worked at.

The phone rang again. She stared at it. Joseph was the only one who called her, and he was eating store-brand ice cream in the kitchen. A lawyer would call her sometimes, but that had mostly stopped since they'd moved here with Joseph as her legal guardian.

It was an unknown number, someone in the same area. The school? Someone threatening her for punching a girl who turned out to be a beloved class president?

She fumbled her hearing aids on and held the phone up, letting frustration bleed into her voice. "Yeah?"

"Hi, Clementine? This is Alex Veck."

The name niggled. Clementine had no idea who that was. "Hello."

"From Sterling," the girl continued.

Clementine braced herself.

"Sorry for calling you out of nowhere like this," Alex continued, shockingly polite for a threatening call. "I was just wondering if you needed a ride to the party tonight?"

It took a second to sink in, another second for Clementine to remember the poster crumpled up in her jeans pocket. She'd been considering it, just for the chance of a fight, but her old therapist's disapproving face and Joseph's worried looks kept popping up in her head whenever she pulled up Google Maps to check bus routes to the house.

"Uh," she said.

"Are you going? It's at Cady's house," Alex continued. "It's uptown."

"I know," Clementine said. She got the poster out of her pocket and smoothed it out in front of her on her mattress.

"So, do you need a ride?"

Clementine's knee-jerk answer was no, she didn't need a ride because she wasn't going. Someone would sneer at her for beating up their favorite class president, for wearing hand-me-downs, for forgetting to wear deodorant for the fifth day in a row, and Clementine would lose control again, and as much as she wanted a fight, she didn't want to invite more trouble into her life.

Parties weren't Clementine's vibe even when she hadn't turned the whole student body against her. Her hearing aids worked well one on one, but if she was in a crowd, sound became a blur. It was hardly worth wearing the aids at a party unless someone had the patience to lean in close and talk slow.

Clementine made her voice gruff. "How did you get my number?"

"Oh, you know," Alex said. "I have my ways."

This was when it clicked. That voice—Clementine had heard that voice in class. Alex Veck, gossip queen of Sterling Girls. Offer a secret, get one in return. Alex Veck, who had been one of the many girls gathered around when Clementine beat Olive Barnes's face in. She'd been staring, Clementine remembered. Not in horror, like most of the others. There had been a bit of horror, but mostly, Alex had been . . . entranced. Like Clementine was something spectacular.

Clementine didn't know how to react to that.

"If you don't need a ride, that's fine," Alex said. "I just wanted—"

"Is this a prank?" Clementine asked. "Is . . . if I show up, will I get tied to a goalpost or something?"

"What? No!"

"Because if it is, it's not smart. You know how hard I can punch."

Alex laughed, then tried to cover it up. What was *with* this girl?

"No punching will be necessary," she said.

"Then why call me?"

Alex hesitated. Clementine could feel the weight of it.

"I'm just calling around," Alex said finally. "Tulsi has one free seat, and I . . . thought of you."

"You thought of me."

"Yes."

Something shy and hopeful reared in Clementine's chest— something she'd tried to beat down, no matter how much her therapist said to embrace it.

She sucked in a breath, worrying the wrinkled poster in her hands. "If this is a prank—"

"It isn't," Alex said. Nerves didn't suit her. "I wouldn't . . . it isn't a prank. I just . . . I wanted . . . um. I wanted you to come."

Clementine's nails met through the paper, stinging her fingers. "Okay."

The ETA gave her time to put on her best jeans and shirt, pick the lint off her least-ripped leather jacket and slide it on, and get into her sturdiest boots.

It was an underwhelming outfit. A teacher had once told her that her dress sense hinted at a past in juvie and a future in jail, but Clementine thought that was just her face, her body, how she always stood stiff and guarded, ready to hurt and to be hurt.

She went into the kitchen.

Joseph was washing dishes. *"Hey."* He did a double-take. *"Why are you dressed?"*

"I'm going out," Clementine said.

He raised his eyebrows, but his skepticism quickly gave way to a hopeful smile. "Yeah?"

Clementine dipped her fingers into the dishwater. "A party," she said, dabbing wet fingers on a stain on her jeans. "I'm getting picked up in 10."

Joseph seemed more excited than her, though he didn't know what to do with it. His hands went from resting on his hips to bracing on the counter. "Who's picking you up?"

"Some girls from school," Clementine said. She tried to remember the others. Tulsi Ortiz, a cheerleader who was loud and mean and wild. Sunju Park—Clementine had no reference for her. Alex had mentioned she was quiet, which was a relief: Clementine didn't want to be the only quiet one in the car.

Joseph nodded. "What are they like?"

"I don't know."

Joseph rocked back and forth on the balls of his bare feet. "I feel like I should be giving you advice."

"It's not a big deal."

"Don't drink too much—"

"You know I hate drinking—"

"—and give me a call if you need me. I'll come pick you up." His voice softened. "Seriously, call if you need me."

"I will," Clementine assured him.

He sat with her on the floor beside the door for the next eight minutes.

Clementine's phone vibrated.

"They're here?"

Clementine nodded, pulling on her jacket. She glanced out the kitchen window. The moon was full, and it filled Clementine with thin hope.

"Have a good time, Clip-Clop."

Clementine nodded again. She was sweating. Why had she forgotten to buy deodorant again?

She nodded goodbye to Joseph and headed down the apartment stairs, into the hot night air.

A car idled at the curb. It was shitty, which made Clementine relax a little.

"Don't put your feet up on the headrest," the driver told Clementine as she climbed into the backseat. She didn't turn to look at Clementine, who took in her silhouette in the dim light: brown skin, arched eyebrows, broad shoulders. Both ears were pierced many times over, red gems that made her look like she was bleeding. Her left eyebrow was studded with stick-on plastic rhinestones.

Alex twisted around to wave at her, polished and large and lovely, all pastel tones. She seemed genuinely pleased Clementine was here. The other girl in the backseat, a mousy girl in a baggy blue dress, looked just as anxious as Clementine felt.

"Guys, this is Clementine," Alex said. "Clementine, this is Sunju and Tulsi."

"You missed Sunju's neighborhood," Tulsi said. "It was gnarly. The houses were so fancy, everyone glared at us from their windows, ready to dial 911 if I dared to rev the engine."

"They had a pond," Alex added. "And garden gnomes."

Tulsi barked a laugh. It made both Clementine and Sunju jump, though Clementine was more subtle about it.

"Garden gnomes," Tulsi said. "God. I forgot about the gnomes. Fishing in the goddamn pond. Hey Sunju, does the pond have fish in it?"

Sunju cleared her throat. Heavy mascara made her eyes stand out like a bushbaby's. "Yes, it has fish."

"Gnarly," Tulsi repeated, and gunned it.

CHAPTER THREE

Tulsi made it two steps into the party before two cheerleaders tried to drag her off. She had resigned herself to being dragged when Alex's hand closed around her arm.

"She's with us tonight," she said, all sunny bullshit smile.

Yazmine and Cady whined.

Yazmine started, "But Quentin—"

Tulsi tugged Yazmine's nose ring. "How about *you* amuse our captain for a few minutes. *Go*, jesters—amuse!"

Yazmine twisted her nipple. Tulsi smacked her. Cady backed off, giggling nervously, dragging Yazmine in her wake.

"She won't wait long," Yazmine called as she vanished into the crowd.

Girls spilled out of hallways, lounged on couches, leaned in doorways. Nary a boy in sight. This was Tulsi's kind of party.

Alex dragged them to the beer pong table. Tulsi allowed it, waiting for Alex's actual motivation to show itself. No way she called Tulsi out of the blue to go to a party. Maybe she just needed Tulsi for her car and was stringing her along. One thing Tulsi knew about Alex Veck: there was always an ulterior motive.

"You take the ball," Alex explained to a clearly reluctant Clementine and Sunju, "throw it at the other team's cups—"

Her arm arced. The ping-pong ball dropped into a cup in front of Clementine, who stepped out of the splash zone.

Alex cheered. "Okay, now that cup is dead, and you have to drink it."

Clementine watched Alex hard, as if trying to read a sign from a distance. It took her a moment to respond. "I don't drink."

Tulsi rolled her eyes towards Sunju, who, if possible, looked even more uncomfortable than Clementine. Clementine was hiding it under a layer of badass and threat; Sunju was clearly miserable, hugging herself around the middle of her baggy dress so hard that Tulsi wanted to walk over to that side of the table and drag her arms back to her sides.

It's fine, she imagined telling her. *Just fake having fun until it sticks, like everybody else.*

"You can just take away the cup," Alex said. "Or . . . juice? Do we have juice?" She looked hopefully towards the kitchen. This was Cady's house party, which meant the juice had been spent in mixers hours ago, and the only thing left was shitty beer and worse vodka.

Clementine was still staring at Alex, brow wrinkled. Were her hearing aids malfunctioning? They looked cheap.

"Never mind." Alex's smile was getting desperate. "Play ball! Sunju, you go first."

Sunju picked up a ping pong ball like it might bite her.

Alex whooped. "Go Sunju!"

Tulsi rolled her eyes again.

Sunju shrank under her gaze, and Tulsi almost felt bad. *I wasn't rolling my eyes at you—I was doing it at Sunny McGee over here.*

Sunju's lips thinned. Her arm wound up. The ping-pong ball sailed through the air and zapped Tulsi right in her razorblade cheekbone.

Sunju yelped loud enough to drown out Tulsi's gasp.

"Nice . . . shot," Alex said hesitantly. "Um, let's say that doesn't count—"

Tulsi couldn't hold back her laugh. She touched her cheek. The sting was already fading.

A chorus of apologies spilled from the other end of the table.

"I'm so sorry," Sunju said, mortified. "Oh god, I'm so sorry, I didn't mean—"

Tulsi swallowed her disappointment. She'd half-hoped Sunju had done it on purpose. Tulsi had been a dick enough to deserve it.

Sunju hugged herself even tighter than before. Clementine scanned the crowd, looking for exits, or maybe someone to punch.

"Just like old times." Alex held out a ping pong ball. "Remember your 11th birthday? Juice pong, with the M&Ms and the apple juice? Kind of a weird game to play with middle schoolers—"

Tulsi smacked the ball out of her hand. "What the hell are you trying to do?"

Someone shrieked and fell. The ball had slid under a girl's high heel.

Alex blinked rapidly. "What would I be trying—"

"Is this about me getting Sunju to write an essay? It's *one* essay. Is this about baldie over there beating the shit out of Olive Barnes? Don't drag me into that shit. What're you planning?"

"Planning . . . " Alex's blinking increased. "I'm not *planning*. I just wanted to go to a party."

"With *us*?" Tulsi flung out an arm at the friendless losers on the other end of the table. "We've never had a conversation together before we got in my car. I don't know what you're up to—"

"Since when do I have *plans*?"

"—but leave me out of it."

Alex swallowed. Her eyes were very shiny. Her cheeks shone with gold glitter; Tulsi hadn't noticed it until she bent close to hiss at her.

"Um." Alex tried another smile. This one was almost see-through. For a moment, she almost looked like the blushing kid who'd cornered Tulsi on the swings to ask how she made her braids so pretty. *You were my first real friend*, Alex told her once. Then she'd betrayed Tulsi the first chance she got.

Tulsi turned away, ready to storm off.

An arm closed around her neck, Quentin's voice low in her ear. "You two look like you're having fun."

Tulsi pushed her off. Quentin rolled with it, flashing her tongue. Her right eyebrow was bedazzled with silver rhinestones, the exact number and width apart as Tulsi's. They were mirror images: one bedazzled eyebrow each, a series of ruby studs in their ears, the same dark lipstick. Once upon a time, it made Tulsi feel like they were the warm center of the world.

Tulsi scrunched up her face. She had a very expressive face, and she mostly used it to react to things she thought were stupid.

"Let's just go," she said.

Quentin slinked sideways, pulling Alex under her arm. "One second! I have *gossip*."

"Oh," Alex said thinly. "Okay."

Quentin nodded across the table at Clementine. "Hey, Rady. Killed anybody tonight?"

"No," Clementine said. Her wide jaw flexed. "But the night is young."

Sunju made a noise in the back of her throat. She was still folding in on herself, drawing away from the crowd behind her, not daring to jostle her beer pong buddy. Like she was trying to vanish into the floor.

Alex cleared her throat. "Quentin, this is Sunju! She's in our lunch period and . . . English class?"

Sunju gave the smallest dip of her chin.

"Right." Quentin flicked her bright red hair, almost catching Alex in the eye. "Anyway, I just wanted to tell you Tiara puked in the dog bowl, and grab my favorite teammate."

Tulsi snarled. "Eat me."

"*Mean* today," Quentin gasped. "*Rrrow.* Maybe I won't come and grab you. Maybe I'll grab Alex instead." She dug her pointy chin into Alex's shoulder, beaming.

Alex smiled back, nowhere near wary enough. Anybody on the end of that look needed to be careful. Quentin used to give Tulsi that look. It didn't end well; they both had the scars to prove it.

"What do you say, gossip queen of Sterling? Want to come hang with the cheerleaders?"

"Um," Alex said. She glanced at the others, reluctant to leave the losers to the lawless jungle of the house party, but also . . . *eager*.

Tulsi frowned. Alex had dirt on everybody. She had to know Quentin was trouble.

"You wouldn't want to hang out with Alex, anyway," Quentin continued, all faux innocence, like she didn't know about the knife she was twisting in Tulsi's gut. "You guys haven't hung out in a while, right? Not since—"

Tulsi stomped over to the other end of the table. Clementine and Sunju both stiffened as Tulsi slung her arms around their shoulders, but Sunju didn't run, and Clementine didn't swing at her, so Tulsi was counting it as a win.

"I don't know," she said. "She's kicked up a fuss all night about sticking together. Might have to drag all of us."

Quentin rolled her tongue in her mouth, expression changing from one Tulsi didn't like to another she hated: a look of *interest*. Sly, bright interest in her toys who were doing something she hadn't predicted.

Her mouth opened. "How about—"

"I want a drink," Alex blurted.

Quentin flinched. Alex's mouth was right near her ear.

"Sorry," Alex said. "I just . . . could you go and get it for me? I'm pretty big, and it's a tight squeeze to the drinks table. Always takes me forever."

Quentin cocked her head. Alex squirmed under her gaze, and Tulsi remembered freshman year, her stomach swooping whenever Quentin pinned her with the powerful scope of her all-seeing eyes.

Then she relented, flicking her hair so it slapped Alex in the cheek. "Alright! One Vodka Coke, coming up."

Alex rubbed her cheek, obviously pleased. Tulsi thought about slapping her to her senses as Quentin pushed through the crowd towards the drinks table.

Clementine was a rock in a leather jacket against Tulsi's arm. "You can let go now."

Tulsi did. "Thanks for not decking me."

Clementine shrugged.

Sunju's shoulder was a bony point in Tulsi's armpit. She felt even shorter tucked into Tulsi's side. Tulsi hoped she wasn't sweating on Sunju's baggy blue dress—it was awful, but this was the only time Tulsi had seen her in anything but jeans.

Tulsi's arm dropped. Sunju immediately stepped away, and Tulsi tried to tell herself she was relieved to be the kind of person people were always stepping away from.

"Good work with Q," she told Alex. "I thought we'd have to start biting you."

Alex gave her a bewildered look.

"Staking our claim," Tulsi explained.

"You didn't seem very invested in *staking your claim* before."

"I'm not. I just want to ruin Quentin's day."

"Aren't you guys friends?" Sunju rubbed her baggy dress strap. Shit, maybe Tulsi *had* sweat on her.

Tulsi laughed. "Nobody's *friends* with Quentin. We're all just—"

A shout from the front hall. The crowd squished tighter as an ever-growing throng of girls all tried to move at once.

"What's going on?" Alex craned her head. "What's—"

A yell went up. "COPS! SCATTER!"

"Damn," Clementine whispered.

"Shit," Tulsi spat.

Sunju's eyes were so wide and dark that Tulsi forgot about her panic for a second. "Run."

They forced themselves into the mass of people cramming through the living room. Alex concentrated on moving forward and not falling over, but the jostling had changed since they'd gathered around the beer pong table: where that had been incidental and soft, this was desperate and pointed.

An elbow caught Sunju in the side. She made a gurgling noise.

"Watch it, shitbrick," Tulsi snapped at the elbower, who quickly disappeared into the crowd. She twisted towards the others (she'd taken the front since she was the tallest). "The back door has this huge line—"

"Bathroom window!" Alex called. She grabbed Tulsi's hand.

Tulsi considered shaking her off, but they were on a time limit: she could see a cop's hat through the crowd. She tugged Alex down a side hall, Alex dragging Clementine and Sunju behind them like kids trying not to get lost on a field trip.

They spilled into the bathroom, Clementine pulling the door closed behind them. The toilet was full of vomit—classic Cady party.

Alex slammed the lid shut and gestured at Sunju. "Come on! You're the smallest!"

Sunju stared at her. The harsh bathroom light revealed a dark smudge on her dress strap—Tulsi had definitely sweat on her.

Tulsi pushed her towards the closed toilet. "What are you waiting for? Crawl!"

Sunju jerked into motion.

The window above the toilet was one of those half-sliding windows with a wooden divider down the middle. Sunju pulled the left half open and clambered out into the yard.

Next was Clementine. She bolted through the window, with no curves to hinder her.

Tulsi climbed up. The window was . . . smaller than she had hoped. Her broad shoulders caught on the wooden divider.

"Shit," Tulsi said. "Come on . . ."

Thrashing and swearing did nothing to help. She yanked herself back into the bathroom.

Alex clapped her hands together. "Okay. Let's—"

Tulsi yanked off her jacket and wrapped it around her hand, bashing at the wood.

"Sure," Alex said. "That works."

Alex climbed up onto the toilet with her. It creaked worryingly. Tulsi gave another punch, and the wood split, turning two sections into one big hole. Glass showered the yard. Clementine and Sunju stepped back.

"Thanks," Alex said, and paused. "Um. Can I go first, in case I—"

"Go!"

Alex was halfway out when her stomach caught on the window's limits.

Tulsi swore. "Somebody pull her!"

Clementine and Sunju bent and tugged. Tulsi couldn't help thinking of Pooh Bear stuck in Rabbit's hole after eating too much honey.

"Alex!" Tulsi yelled. "I'm gonna put my hands on your ass—don't freak out."

"No promises!"

Tulsi braced her hands on Alex's butt, then her forearm.

A man shouted in the hallway. It wasn't locked. Why the hell hadn't they locked it?

There was a rip, a flash of skin through the hip of Alex's dress, and Alex slipped into the yard. "Tulsi, are you okay down there?"

"Shut up." Tulsi heaved herself up through the window. Shoulders, torso, waist—

The door burst open behind her. Tulsi didn't look back, still crawling. A pair of meaty hands closed around her ankles.

Tulsi yelped. "Some asshole is grabbing my legs!"

The girls reached for her, but Tulsi was already on it: one swift kick and the man behind her grunted, grip slipping. Tulsi spared a glance behind her and saw a cop with blood and tears streaming down his face—she'd caught him in the nose.

She crawled onto the dead grass. "I kicked a cop!"

"Don't shout about it," Clementine said, helping her to her feet.

Alex's hair and eyes were wild. "We should—"

"Yes," Sunju said.

They ran.

CHAPTER FOUR

Alex didn't look back, too busy listening for sirens over the din of her thundering heartbeat.

Please, God, she prayed as she ran, *don't let them catch us. I want to go to a good college. Thank you, God.*

By the time they came to a stop in an alley not far from Sterling, Alex felt sober enough to take a breathalyzer test. She hadn't drunk much at the party, but she was a lightweight: one beer was enough to get her giggly.

She braced her hands on her knees and wheezed, trying to convince herself she wasn't actually dying. She crossed herself in case the cops were still coming, then looked up to check on the others. Tulsi was pushing her thick hair back from her forehead, Sunju was trembling against a wall, and Clementine was . . . bending down to examine the garbage stuffed in the side of the alley.

Right.

"Is everybody okay?"

Tulsi made a noise like a dying whale.

"I'm fine," Sunju said, clutching at her sleeves. "Sorry."

Alex sighed. "For what?"

Sunju blinked, shook her head.

Alex looked towards Clementine. "Clementine?"

No answer. Clementine knocked a can aside with her shoe.

What the hell, Tulsi mouthed at Alex.

Alex shrugged and moved forward to touch Clementine's shoulder. Before she could make contact, Clementine jerked and whirled around to face her.

"Hi," Alex said. "You good?"

It took a second before Clementine nodded.

"Okay." Alex cleared her throat. "What're you looking for?"

Clementine's voice was slow and clunky. "My hearing aids fell off."

Sunju moved her hands hesitantly. It took Alex a moment to recognize it as sign language.

"I only know the alphabet," Sunju said apologetically, moving her fingers painstakingly around each letter. Finally, her hands stopped.

Clementine nodded. "They're purple."

"Purple," Alex said. "Got it."

She gave Clementine a thumbs up. Clementine's mouth twitched in what might've been a bemused smile before she turned back and resumed her search through the alleyway trash.

Alex turned to the others and said, "Purple hearing aids."

"Yeah, we got it," Tulsi snapped. "*We* aren't the deaf ones."

Sunju shot her a cross look. Alex was surprised at its severity, and that Sunju actually held Tulsi's gaze for a second before glancing away.

It took a few minutes of rummaging through varying levels of grossness before Tulsi let out a triumphant whoop. "Purple, assholes!" She stood, brandishing two lumps of plastic. She waded through the trash to drop them into Clementine's hand.

Clementine fitted the devices back onto her ears. Some of the stiffness bled out of her shoulders. "Thanks." She looked towards Tulsi. "You get that cop good?"

Tulsi let out a surprised, fearful laugh. "I think I broke his nose."

Clementine jerked her head in a nod. "Cool."

The four girls traded looks, waiting. All eyes gravitated towards Alex, who swallowed.

"So," she said. "Food?"

There was something about sitting in a fast-food restaurant as nighttime adrenaline faded. Fluorescent lights took over. Nothing existed outside of four girls crammed into a peeling red booth, shoveling four orders of MeatLovers fries into their wordless mouths.

Alex glanced through the window. Sterling lay across the road, shadowy and unassuming. She looked back at the girls hunched over the white table and ached: a short, sharp throb. In the middle of it and missing it already.

She bent her head and sent up a brief prayer. *Please, God, let this continue. Let me have them. Thank you, God.*

When she looked up, Tulsi was narrowing her eyes.

Alex made a face. *What?*

Tulsi narrowed them further.

Still buzzing with leftover adrenaline and the echoes of friendship, Alex kicked her under the table.

Tulsi snorted, dusted salt off her hands. She was the first one to finish her food.

"So," she said, and burped. "What was with you beating up Olive Barnes?"

Clementine went rigid.

Alex let out an anxious laugh. "You don't have to answer that."

"We were all thinking it." Tulsi scowled, stealing a fry from off Alex's plate. "You're telling me Alex Veck, gossip queen of Sterling, was just gonna"—she bit into the stolen fry—"let that go?"

Clementine looked over at Alex, who floundered. Distrustful and worried was *not* how she wanted Clementine to look at her.

"I mean . . . yes, I want to know." Alex swept a curl behind her ear. "But if you don't want to tell us, that's . . . fine."

Clementine blinked, looked back at her fries. She was eating slow and measured, but every so often, she'd speed up and have to slow down again, as if it required effort not to take the Tulsi route and cram ten fries into her mouth at once.

"Do I get something for it?" Clementine asked. "Rumor for a rumor, right?"

"If you want."

Clementine's expression was unreadable. Her jaw worked.

Alex wet her lips, tasting salt. "You looked like you were trained for it."

"No training," Clementine said after a moment. Her mouth twisted wryly. "Just a lot of experience."

Later, Alex would believe it was the fluorescent lights. It was Tulsi, whip-mean with sweat glistening on her upper lip. It was Sunju, small Sunju, not hunching into her shoulders for once, as if too tired to bother.

But mostly, it was Clementine. She was looking down at the shiny plastic table, her face almost blank. It was nothing like her face when she was on top of Olive, fists raining down. Alex shivered to think of it: that burning gaze, everything else falling away except the girl underneath.

She cleared her throat again.

"Hey," she said. "You should fight me."

Clementine's head jerked up. Haloed in the diner light, she really did look like Leonardo DiCaprio in *Romeo + Juliet*. She checked over the others—Tulsi pretending not to be interested, Sunju openly confused. "You want me to fight you."

"Yeah!" Alex's smile wobbled into a grin. "There's . . . there's this abandoned parking lot a block away. We could . . ."

She mimed a few punches. Bad ones. Kitten punches.

"Pow," she finished weakly.

Tulsi snorted.

Clementine glanced back towards the door, like she still wasn't sure if tonight was a prank. "Why would I fight you? You haven't done anything to me."

"'Cause I want you to," Alex said. She clapped her hands together quietly—no matter what the lights made her think, they weren't the only ones eating bad diner food at 11 p.m. "Come on, this isn't fighting because someone upset you—this is just . . . for the heck of it! For fun!"

Clementine stared at her. "Have you ever been in a fight?"

Alex opened her mouth.

Tulsi beat her to it. "She knocked my tooth out during gym in eighth grade."

Alex squeaked. "That was an accident!"

"*That* was a vicious volleyball foul you pulled because you were mad your team was losing," Tulsi replied, plucking a rhinestone from her brow and flicking it across the table at Alex.

Alex batted it away and turned back to Clementine. "For fun," she repeated, head still swirling with the image of Clementine's gaze burning all the way into her. "Isn't it fun sometimes?"

Clementine blinked. She glanced at all of them, still wary, but it was being overtaken by something else: a hopefulness Alex could recognize in the mirror.

"Yes," Clementine said softly.

The abandoned parking lot was behind an equally abandoned warehouse. Alex still remembered the sweet smell that used to spill out when she walked by it as a kid. The old name was still there, faded and chipped on the outer wall: HARTBURN CANDIES.

"Wrap your hands," Clementine said.

"What with?"

Clementine turned to Sunju and Tulsi. "Do you two have something sharp?"

Sunju dug in her pocket and came out with a tiny pair of nail clippers. Tulsi did the same and held out a pocketknife.

Clementine took it. "Thanks."

"That's . . . big," Sunju said as Alex was busy watching Clementine slice a strip off of her shirt.

Tulsi hummed in agreement. Then: "You don't carry a knife with you?"

"What? No."

"Right, I forgot where you live—garden gnome central."

Clementine held out the T-shirt strip. Alex valiantly kept her gaze off of Clementine's toned stomach.

"Hold out your hands."

Alex did.

Clementine cut the strip in half. Alex kept her hands still as Clementine wound it around her fingers, her knuckles, circling down to her wrist to keep it all in place. Clementine's fingers were long and dry and calloused. It shouldn't have been soothing.

Alex flexed her newly bandaged hands. "Wow. You have to show me that later. How do you say 'later' in ASL?"

Clementine paused. She shot Alex a single finger-gun.

Alex copied it. "Is that right?"

Clementine nodded. She looked charmed. Alex tried not to feel too proud about it.

"Your hands aren't wrapped," Tulsi said from beside Alex. "You're gonna bleed on Alex when you hit her."

Sunju made a sound that turned over on itself.

"She can handle a bit of blood," Clementine said, tying the strip off.

Alex grinned again. Clementine's answering smile was shocked in the best way.

"Yes," said Alex, who had never been punched in her life, "I can."

Clementine reached for her hearing aids.

"Wait," Alex said. "Won't you—"

Clementine paused, one aid off. "I don't want to break them. New ones are expensive."

She took a case out of her pocket and slipped the aids in. Alex watched the case disappear back into her pocket and imagined the parking lot plunging into muffled quiet.

The other girls stood back. Alex settled into a fighting stance she'd picked up from action movies. It felt flimsy and awkward.

"You ready?" Clementine asked. She was looking at Alex warily, but behind it . . . behind it, there was the start of that look she'd given Olive: the world narrowing down into one girl. Into *her*.

Alex grinned and swung.

CHAPTER FIVE

A particularly hard punch made Sunju gasp. This one, surprisingly, was from Alex.

Tulsi rolled her eyes. "Unpucker."

Sunju rubbed her arms. "I really feel like we should stop this before someone gets hurt." This wasn't the first time she'd said this, but it was the most insistent. She was shaking with leftover adrenaline.

"They're fine," Tulsi said. Tulsi did the occasional wince, but mostly she stared. *Gazed* was probably a better word. Her eyes glinted, mouth twitching like she wanted to cheer: *Coming at you whirling! Look out for those girls from Sterling!*

Clementine kicked into the back of Alex's knee. Alex's legs crumpled out from under her.

"Good god," Sunju said. She brought her hand up and bit her palm.

"They're fine," Tulsi repeated. Her nose scrunched. "Did you just say *good god?* Who says that?"

"I say that."

"People over 80 say that."

Alex brought her knee up into Clementine's stomach.

Tulsi whooped. "See? Everyone's doing great. Chill out."

Sunju averted her eyes and started humming.

Tulsi asked, "Is that the theme song to *Star Rangers?*"

Sunju stared at her.

"What?" Tulsi arched one sharp eyebrow, now home to just a single rhinestone. "Everybody watched that growing up. Saturday morning, watch *Star Rangers.*"

Definite lie. Only a couple episodes ever aired in America; you had to order the rest of it as a DVD from overseas. Sunju thought about bringing this up to Tulsi. She also thought about telling her she had brought all five seasons and watched them religiously until her mom threw them out.

In front of them, Alex wheezed. "I'm done. I'm out. *Phew.*"

Sunju allowed herself a look. Clementine immediately took her foot off Alex's back and bent down to help her up.

"You alright?" Clementine's gaze stuck on Alex's mouth as she replied.

"I'm good." Alex laughed. There was something off about her voice, something that didn't seem to have anything to do with her swelling cheek. She was giggling, Sunju realized. Shoulders shaking, eyes scrunching in between small gasps of *ow*.

Clementine fit her hearing aids back on. "She *did* say she was good, right?"

Sunju nodded.

"That was fun," Alex said brightly. She spat blood onto the asphalt.

Tulsi ghosted her shoe over the blood spot. "If *this* was your plan for tonight, you're even weirder at sixteen than you were at eleven."

"There's no *plan*, jerk." Alex grinned, blood wedged between her teeth.

It wasn't aimed at her. But Sunju felt herself grin back, her breath catching in her chest. When she glanced over, Tulsi was grinning too, brimming with that gleaming energy she'd been vibrating with during the fight.

Tulsi took a step towards Clementine. "Do me next, psycho."

Clementine hesitated. "Never call me that again, and okay."

Tulsi plucked the last remaining rhinestone off her brow. "Done," she said, and crushed the shining plastic under her shoe.

Alex wrapped Tulsi's hands. Clementine talked her through it.

Tulsi flexed her fingers against the layers. The material was streaked with red from Alex busting Clementine's eyebrow open.

Alex came to stand next to Sunju, radiating the usual friendliness that bewildered the heck out of her. "Feeling alright?"

Sunju nodded, distracted. She cupped her hands around a yell. "This is a stupid idea, and you're dumb for suggesting it!"

Tulsi flipped her off.

Sunju hesitated, then did it back. It was the first time she'd ever done it, and she glanced around nervously. Neither her mom nor dad appeared to scream at her.

Clementine tucked her hearing aids in her pocket. Then she paused, took them out, and walked over towards Sunju with a cautious look.

Sunju did two of the few signs she knew as words instead of individual letters: ME-TAKE. She felt like a caveman. At least it made Clementine's caution melt into something like fondness.

"*Thanks*," Clementine signed.

"*You're welcome*," Sunju signed back, hearing aids held carefully in one curled hand.

Clementine returned to Tulsi, who immediately punched her so hard she stumbled.

"Oh," said Sunju and Alex in unison.

Clementine grunted. Tulsi threw back another fist, but Clementine caught it fast, using the momentum to yank Tulsi off balance. Tulsi's face caught on a freeze-frame of *nope*. She brought her arm up just in time to hook an elbow around the back of Clementine's neck and drag her down onto the ground with her.

"Whoo!" Alex said, sounding like she had at the one pep rally Sunju had attended. "Go girls!"

Sunju eyed her shoes again. Black suede, her best pair. She'd debated for an hour whether to wear them—if she spilled anything on them at the party, her mom would have conniptions.

"You're really not into this," Alex said brightly.

Sunju checked. Alex wasn't glaring. Her face was as bright as her tone, even with fresh bruises.

"Not really," Sunju admitted.

Alex nodded. Her eyes lit up as Clementine caught Tulsi with a punch. She whooped, then seemed to gather herself. "You don't have to stay. You seem uncomfortable."

Sunju hunched into her shoulders. She opened her mouth, ready to say, *Sorry, I'll go.*

Alex cut her off. "You should stay, though."

Sunju laughed incredulously. She couldn't stop herself.

Alex let out a little laugh in return, uncertain. She seemed unsure if she was being laughed at. It was strangely comforting to Sunju, who was never sure either.

In front of them, Tulsi tackled Clementine to the ground. They lay there for a moment, both of them panting, Tulsi waiting with clenched fists.

Clementine tapped out on the concrete. "I'm done," she said, loudly so everyone could hear, or maybe because Sunju had her hearing aids.

Sunju laughed, bending at the middle with the force of it. They'd run from the cops, they'd never make it home before Sunju's curfew, Sunju's shoes were probably scuffed, and they were fighting in a parking lot a block away from their high school. Sunju was holding onto the hearing aids of a girl she barely knew who'd been suspended. The gossip queen of Sterling Girls was bleeding next to her, and Tulsi Ortiz and Alex Veck had invited her to a party.

You need to let loose, Tulsi had said, and had to reassure Sunju twice that no, it wasn't a threat. Sunju still hadn't believed it in the car, hadn't believed it until they were running.

Tulsi pointed at Sunju, who was still laughing. "What's with her?"

Alex shrugged. "I have no idea."

When Sunju uncurled from her laughter, Clementine was looking at her with her fists held up half-heartedly.

Sunju shook her head.

"Okay," Clementine said, and held out an open hand.

Sunju gave back the hearing aids.

Clementine fitted them in. "*Thank you.*"

"Aw," Tulsi said. It was slurred: her cheek was swelling. Skin must have burst inside her mouth. "Come on, loosen up a little!"

"I don't like being hit."

It sounded very loud in the silent parking lot. Sweat dampened Sunju's armpits.

She expected Tulsi to push, like when she'd invited Sunju to the party. But Tulsi just turned to Clementine. "You couldn't fight her even if she wanted to—your knuckles are shredded."

Clementine turned them over in the streetlight to examine them, and Sunju winced. They needed to put something on them, sharp and stinging.

"Plus," Tulsi continued, "I beat you up pretty bad."

Clementine chuckled.

"What? I did."

"Uh-huh," Clementine said. She rolled her shoulders. After two fights, she had a bleeding nose, a busted eyebrow, and a bruise splotching down her chin and neck. She looked more relaxed than Sunju had seen her all night. Some girls, Sunju supposed, ran a gossip empire, some girls blackmailed people into doing their homework, some girls tried to be as small as humanly possible, and some girls got into fights for fun.

"Hey," Tulsi said, slurred over the swelling cheek. "Why is there blood on Sunju?"

"What?" Sunju's voice cracked mortifyingly as she checked herself up and down.

Tulsi pointed at the thick strap of her dress. A smudge of blood sat plainly against the pale blue.

Sunju's face collapsed.

"You can get it out if you wash it with bleach," Tulsi tried.

"I'm sorry," Alex told Sunju, looking genuinely apologetic. "Must've happened when I touched your shoulder during their fight . . ."

But Alex's voice was becoming distant. She rubbed the spot on her dress. It smeared.

Idiot, idiot, idiot. Why hadn't she just taken a bus when they stopped running from the cops? She was going to, but then Alex had suggested food. Sunju hadn't hung out with anyone in years, not really. And look where that had gotten her.

Sunju rubbed some more. It continued to smear. *I could bleach it before I go to bed. But they'll be waiting up for me; I won't get the chance—*

Tulsi said something. Sunju's world was small enough now that she didn't hear it.

A hand moved close to her bloody shoulder. Sunju looked at it, looked at Clementine, who had reached out but not touched.

Tulsi repeated, "I know a laundromat we can break into."

Whatever Sunju's face did, it was enough to make Tulsi continue: "Jesus, calm down. I mean *metaphorically*. I work summers there; I know where the key is."

Sunju's alarm twitched into something incrementally calmer.

"Come on," Tulsi said. "You got any other choice?"

Sunju checked with the others. They were approving, but they'd also just had a fistfight in an empty parking lot at 11 p.m.—not exactly bastions of judgment.

Sunju looked towards her dress. Being home after curfew would be bad; being home with scuffed shoes and a stained dress—stained with blood, no less—would be another matter.

She sighed. "Alright, I guess."

"Awesome," Tulsi said. "Let's go."

Tulsi waved at them to stop in the alleyway. "I'll go find the key. Wait here."

Sunju decided against making small talk as Tulsi vanished around the corner. They were all too keyed up on a cocktail of nerves and weariness and, for three-fourths of them, pain.

The sound of breaking glass reached them. They looked at each other. None of them had the energy to be surprised.

Tulsi re-emerged around the corner in the middle of shrugging her jacket back on, shaking one of her hands.

Sunju said, "You said you knew where the spare key was."

"I do," Tulsi replied. "It was on the window in the back room."

"The wrong side of the window."

"I mean, yes."

Sunju thought about pressing the issue, then thought about her parents, who hadn't sent any texts, which was more menacing than if they'd barraged her phone with calls. They were definitely waiting in the living room. Maybe her mother was trying to read a magazine, her frustration making her flip through the pages, unseeing. Her father would be dozing in his armchair.

Alex spoke up. "Let's get cleaned up, okay? If we don't do it soon, I'm going to take a nap on one of the washing machines."

Sunju followed them inside and then had a miniature aneurysm when they started taking off their clothes. Tulsi strutted around like she walked mostly naked through laundromats all the time; Alex surreptitiously adjusted her bra and sucked in her stomach; Clementine shucked her shirt with soldier-like efficiency.

Sunju stared hard at the wall and cursed herself for not thinking about the stupidly obvious fact that washing clothes involved taking them off. *Idiot, idiot*—

"Shit, it's cold," Alex said.

Sunju gripped at the waist of her dress. She should've worn tights, anything else, so she wouldn't have to stand here in her underwear, so they wouldn't see—

"Sunju?"

She looked up to see Clementine dropping her shirt into a washing machine. She was wearing a sports bra that flattened everything out. It suited her.

"You can use this one," Clementine offered, which was pointless: they were all putting their clothes in that one. Sunju appreciated it anyway.

She nodded and pulled off her dress in one hasty move, moving forward and throwing it into the washing machine without taking her eyes off it. Then she sat on the ground and stared at it, thinking of her new goosebumps and the cold of the floor under her. She tilted her shoes. A barely-there scuff mark sat on the right heel. Damn.

Above her, the girls were silent.

"Jesus," Tulsi said finally. "I thought you didn't like to fight."

Sunju didn't bother following their gazes: a big purple splotch on her shin; a more vicious one on her back they wouldn't see unless she leaned forwards; a smaller set going green over her left shoulder—five green lines. Finger marks.

Clementine's voice was strangely blank as she said, "You must've banged yourself up when you climbed out the window."

Sunju nodded, traced *don't ask* into the linoleum with her finger.

Someone put a capful of bleach into the machine, and it started vibrating against Sunju's spine. Bruises twinged over her back and shoulder. The laundromat filled with the wet, circular sounds of a washing machine working.

The girls joined her. Alex and Clementine sat across from Sunju, Tulsi beside her, dangerously close to touching her knee.

Tulsi's tongue eased around her cut cheek. "Guess I should say thanks *for* decking me this time," she told Clementine, who looked at her blankly. "At the party, I said—"

Clementine's face opened in realization. "I can't hear great in crowds."

"Even with . . . ?" Tulsi gestured at the aids.

"Even with," Clementine confirmed, touching their purple curves.

Alex asked Sunju, "So, you know ASL?"

"Just the alphabet."

Alex pulled her legs up in front of her. Her stomach squished against her thighs. She pulled them back down. "Um, what's 'you're welcome' in ASL?"

Sunju signed it, looking over at Clementine to check.

Clementine nodded. "Same as 'thank you'."

Alex copied her.

"What's 'asshole'?" Tulsi asked.

Alex snorted.

Clementine held up the universal signal for "OK" and turned it upside down.

Tulsi mirrored it triumphantly. "Cool. Sunju, do 'asshole'."

Sunju held up her hand towards Tulsi, who looked absolutely delighted to get called an asshole in ASL. Her knee grazed Sunju's. Tulsi's was a little stubbly, which was a surprise—she'd assumed Tulsi had a strict shaving regime. All those cheerleading skirts.

Tulsi's smile cut off, a hiss escaping her injured mouth. She felt her bruised cheek. "Okay, it'd be bad if I showed up at home with my face all busted. Any tips, psy—uh, Clem?"

"Tips," Clementine repeated.

Tulsi waved impatiently. "Makeup, or whatever people do to hide that they've just been hit in the face a bunch of times."

"Tell people you fell."

"A fall that messed up the side of my face along with my eye?"

Clementine pocketed her hands. She hadn't put her jeans in the washing machine, despite them having specks of blood on the thighs. "I don't wear makeup."

Tulsi sighed and rolled her head around so she faced the ceiling. "Shocking. Whatever. Everyone will be asleep when I get back; I'll look up YouTube tutorials tomorrow morning. Ugh, this bruise will be even worse on Monday."

"You could say you got mugged," Alex suggested. "Or someone decided to let you know just how tired they are of doing your schoolwork for you."

Tulsi aimed a kick at her.

Alex kicked back, then tilted her head to admire her face in the shiny washing machine. "My face doesn't look *too* bad. I think I could cover it up."

"Your bruises haven't set in fully," Clementine reminded her.

Words caught in Sunju's throat. It took two tries to get them out. "I . . . I . . . could show you. I mean, I know how to cover things with makeup."

She brushed letters against the linoleum with her finger, getting to the A in *don't ask* before Alex said, "I'd like that."

Sunju pressed a nail into the linoleum hard enough to hurt. She lifted her finger to find a dent in the floor.

The washing machine rumbled against her back. Sunju leaned into it, exhaustion hard and heavy in her bones. It was as if she had just landed on the ground after skydiving, or ran a mile, or . . . or got into a fistfight.

Sunju closed her eyes. Their clothes would be washed and dried, and they'd head to a drugstore. They'd buy appropriately-colored makeup, and Sunju would show them how to cover bruises, and if anyone *did* ask why she knew how, Sunju would say something about YouTube and boredom. As if they'd buy that now that they could see the finger marks on her shoulder.

After another minute, it was as if the rumbling at her back was the only thing keeping her awake.

Distantly, she heard Tulsi tell Alex that she had a weird face on.

"What kind of weird?" Alex asked.

"You've got the same face you had on when you came up with that fundraiser that stopped the library closing down," Tulsi told her. "No plans, my *ass*."

Alex was quiet. Then she said, "I'll let you know if it comes to anything."

Sunju spared a thought to wonder what she meant, opening her eyes to do so. Her gaze caught instantly on the bareness of the girls' stomachs, which ranged from the muscled hardness of Clementine's to the small pouch of Tulsi's to Alex's pillowy folds. Sunju lingered on Tulsi's belly button piercing for a heart-stopping moment: a red jewel catching the light. The image sank deep inside Sunju, who knew she would remember it for the rest of her life.

When she tore her gaze away, Tulsi was examining her nails— red, like her piercing. She'd chipped a nail on Clementine's face.

Sunju tried not to feel grateful. Yes, Tulsi had taken them to the laundromat so Sunju wouldn't have to go home with blood on her dress, but she'd also blackmailed Sunju into writing an essay for her.

Please don't tell anyone, Sunju had begged when Tulsi showed her the drawing she'd found, the one Sunju had dropped on the floor in the library. *I'll do anything, however many essays you want.*

Tulsi had looked surprised, like she was going to leave the drawing on Sunju's desk and walk out, no essay required.

It was just a sketch. Sunju had only drawn it because she'd found a private corner in the library with no one at her table. In the sketch were two girls from the torsos up. Their eyes were closed, smiling into a kiss.

Tulsi had agreed to one essay done by next week. Sunju had thrown the drawing into a trashcan across from her bus stop.

She took a deep breath, then she leaned forward and pulled her dark hair up in a ponytail.

CHAPTER SIX

Tulsi trembled at the base of the pyramid. Her shoulder throbbed. There was a foot on it: Cady, straining above her with the effort of holding up Quentin. Quentin, head cheerleader, top of the pyramid, and the girl who had, during a practice last year, stomped on Tulsi's shoulder hard enough to mess with the muscle.

Yazmine adjusted herself, leaning her full weight on Tulsi for a moment. Tulsi winced.

"Keep smiling down there," Quentin called. It meant, *I see you, Tulsi.*

Tulsi gritted her teeth, locked her legs. She preferred Quentin drunk. When Quentin was drunk—which she only was every second weekend at parties—she would let the "nice" mask slip, and out would come all the nasty stuff she couched under well-meaning comments.

Quentin was a good head cheerleader. She was even a good teacher, so long as you didn't get a move wrong too many times. But you couldn't trust her.

"Okay," Quentin said. "One . . . two . . . three!"

Yazmine shifted her weight. Tulsi's shoulder throbbed again, a hard stab of pain. She ignored it. The next part was her favorite.

Quentin came down first, crouching and then falling into one teammate's arms, then another's. Around her, the mid-base was disassembling, but Tulsi didn't pay attention.

Quentin fell into Tulsi's arms. For that one moment, Tulsi was surrounded on all sides, warm and solid. Then everybody found the floor.

Quentin brushed her red hair back into place. "Good job, Cady."

Cady startled. She'd been mid-base, next to Yazmine. She lit up in a shocked smile. "Thanks!"

Quentin smiled back.

Tulsi waited.

Sure enough, a sly leg snaked out to trip Cady on the way to her backpack. Cady hit the floor with a shriek.

Quentin turned to Tulsi, smile still fixed in place. "Your uniform's getting a little smelly," she said. "How often do you wash it?"

Tulsi squeezed the meat of her shoulder. It twinged. "I wash my uniform, Q. Jesus."

Quentin hummed, eyes roving over her. She was shorter than Tulsi by two inches, but she still managed to loom over her.

"Oh well," she said. "Must just be you."

Over on the bleachers, untying her sneakers, Yazmine laughed.

She wasn't the only one, but Tulsi zeroed in on her anyway. "Yaz, you can't talk. How's that prescription deodorant going? You know, the extra strength one that stinks of pine needles?"

Yazmine struggled with her nose ring. "I don't know, are people still avoiding you in the hallways 'cause you're such a bitch?"

Her nose ring slid into place. A trickle of red dripped off her nostril. If she left it off for more than 45 minutes, the process was bloody.

Tulsi stalked over to her backpack, bending to dig for her water bottle.

Quentin came over to lean on the wall beside her. This time, she really did loom. "Didn't see you after getting out of Cady's party. Too busy running away with Alex Veck?"

Tulsi snorted. Quentin had been wary of Alex ever since she rose to fame as gossip queen of Sterling in freshman year, which was exciting, since it meant Quentin had dirt she was afraid Alex could find. So far, Alex hadn't said anything, but that didn't mean she was clueless.

"Yeah, we got married. Didn't you hear?" Tulsi busied herself with her backpack. Where was her water bottle? If one of her teammates had stolen it again, she was cracking skulls.

Quentin hummed. "I could help you out if she has leverage over you. Some sneaky information. Just say the word."

Ah-ha! Water bottle. Tulsi uncapped it and drained half of the water in two large gulps. "*I* do leverage," she said.

"Right. Your five whole essays you've blackmailed people into writing for you. What a criminal empire, Tulsi." Quentin reached out, touched Tulsi's arm right below her injured shoulder. "Seriously, just say the word."

"We weren't *conspiring*," Tulsi snapped. "Would you get out of the way? I have things to do."

Quentin took a step in front of her. "Like what?"

A chin dug into Tulsi's back—Cady, trying to be cute. Now Tulsi was trapped on both sides.

"Marrying Alex, duh." Cady beamed. "Can't believe you found somebody to put up with your sharp elbows."

"Sharp mouth," Yazmine called.

"Sharp heart," Quentin whispered, too close. Tulsi could feel her breath on her cheek. Once, it would've been exciting. Now it made her think of Red Riding Hood and the wolf.

Tulsi shoved them out of the way. She'd pay for that later, she was sure, but she was too tired of all this cheerleader crap to care.

She glanced back as she escaped into the empty hall. Quentin was still staring, her expression unreadable. Tulsi hated that.

As she went into the locker rooms, she thought back to that parking lot, then the laundromat; how refreshing it had been. Bickering with the cheer squad was biting, ruthless, humiliating. The laundromat girls were *fun* to bicker with. Sunju was a surprisingly good time if Tulsi paid attention and ignored the awkwardness.

Clementine was the same, if a little stiff and definitely dangerous. Alex, though . . .

Alex should just drop the nice act, Tulsi thought as she strode down the deserted hallways of Sterling High. She got enough of that shit from Quentin.

The parking lot was empty apart from Tulsi's car, plus the three girls leaning on it. Clementine was showing Alex and Sunju signs.

"If I do it from here, it's rude?"

"Yeah, it means 'screw you'."

"But it's so close to—Tulsi, hi!" Sunju dropped her hands at Tulsi's approach, stepping away from the car. She wiped the place where she had been leaning, like she was still covered in sweat from fleeing the cops and not clean as a newborn baby, as always.

"*Relax*," Tulsi told her. She dragged her keys along the roof, laughing when everybody winced. "This car's a piece of shit; you can't hurt it any worse than it's already been hurt. Get in."

Alex took the passenger's seat. Of course she did. "My house is on—"

Tulsi cut her off. "Oh, your house? The house I dropped you off at two days ago? The house I went to a million times in middle school? *That* house?"

Alex clenched her teeth in a smile that meant *look at how nice I'm being even though you're being an asshole.* Tulsi found she'd almost missed it.

"Yes," Alex said. "That house."

The car jerked into motion. Tulsi watched Sunju clutch the car door and grinned.

"Speaking of," she said, "nobody's paid me gas fare yet. What gives?"

Alex's house was the same. She tiptoed around, offering them water and juice, apologizing for having to be quiet.

"My dad's asleep," she explained.

Tulsi grunted. "Still working that shitty night job?"

Alex hummed and busied herself with straightening a dishtowel. Had she been this anal as a kid? Tulsi didn't think so.

"Are you sure you don't want juice? I got all the kinds you liked." Alex pointed at Clementine and Sunju. "Apple, orange . . ." She paused on Tulsi. "I just assumed you still like that pink passion fruit drink; I should've asked—"

Tulsi sighed. "None of us want juice, Alex! We want to get in that garage and start throwing punches like you promised, you big weirdo."

Alex led them out into the garage. Tulsi couldn't remember if she'd ever been inside. She hadn't come over to Alex's much, since they needed to be quiet 24/7 for one of her sleeping parents. Tulsi remembered thinking it must've been nice, all that quiet. Now it felt . . . a little stifling.

The garage door rumbled shut. A workbench had been shoved aside, allowing for a concrete space big enough for Tulsi to shove her car into and have room left over. Enough room for a fist fight if they were careful.

Alex waved towards the workbench. It was empty except for a roll of bandages sitting proudly next to scissors and three pairs of towels. She asked, "Sunju, did you bring—"

Sunju placed a makeup bag on the bench. It was overflowing with shiny new products. "I tried to remember what foundation everybody got at the drugstore. I can buy other ones."

Tulsi picked up a tube of foundation. *Bronze Princess.* It was the same cringey brand she'd picked up at the drugstore after the four of them had trailed out of the laundromat. Tulsi hadn't thought Sunju was paying attention.

She bonked Sunju on the forehead with the foundation tube. "What'd I say about relaxing, Park?"

"To do it," Sunju said slowly. She rubbed her forehead. "If I got your makeup right, do I still have to pay you for gas?"

A giggle bubbled up Tulsi's throat. She dug her teeth into the inside of her cheek, hissing when it threatened to open the healing cut. Tulsi Ortiz did not *giggle*. Had anybody noticed?

Sunju definitely had: the little shit looked far too smug. Tulsi glanced behind her. Clementine was on the other end of the table, rolling out a strip of bandage. Alex was . . . also looking smug. Smug and surprised, like something good had just happened. *Shit.*

"Dibs on the first fight." Tulsi snatched the bandages from Clementine, but Clementine was holding onto the end, so the roll just extended between them.

Clementine looked annoyed. She raised the scissors and snipped a long line of bandage, twisting it quickly and efficiently around her hand.

Tulsi snipped her own line and tried to look like she knew what she was doing. Her bandages ended in bows under her thumbs.

Clementine eyed them.

"Fashion statement." Tulsi waggled a thumb, making the bow shift. "Isn't it pretty? I think—" she stopped. Alex had a notepad out, scribbling fast. "Alex, are you taking notes on the fight club?"

"We need to learn how to wrap our hands properly," Alex said, frowning in concentration. "And we need to cut our nails. And take our earrings out. And—"

"Of course you'd drag us down with *rules*," Tulsi jeered. Just like Quentin—the cheer captain *loved* rules. She loved to pull them out from under your feet or use them to hit you around the head. Alex didn't seem the type. Selfish? Sure. *Malicious?* Not really.

"They only had two rules in the movie, and none of them had anything to do with personal hygiene," Tulsi continued, walking to the middle of the floor where Clementine was waiting, hearing aids safe on the bench, feet bare.

Tulsi winked at her. "Let's go, psycho."

She bent low, almost a crouch. Clementine paused, frowning at Tulsi's mouth. Lipreading, Tulsi realized. She'd forgotten.

She was trying to remember the sign for P when Clementine said, "Tulsi?"

"Yeah?"

"Not a good idea to piss off somebody you're about to fight." Clementine lunged.

Tulsi hit the floor laughing. She'd never thought she could feel so elated with a girl on top of her with her fist raised. Tulsi twisted. Clementine's fist hit her shoulder. Tulsi reached up and covered Clementine's face with her hands.

"No eye gouging!" Alex shouted, scribbling.

"I'm not gouging!" Tulsi screamed back. On second thought, she hooked her thumbs into Clementine's mouth. The next punch faltered as Clementine reared back, trying to free herself, her face a delightful mask of annoyed confusion.

Tulsi kneed her in the stomach.

"Bath-tard," Clementine slurred, and chomped down on Tulsi's fingers.

Tulsi howled, half pain, half laughter.

"I don't know if we should allow biting," Alex called.

"Ignore her," Tulsi hissed.

Clementine's mouth stretched in a grin around Tulsi's fingers as Tulsi pulled with increasing desperation. Clementine really wasn't letting up.

"Okay!" Tulsi gritted as the pressure mounted into dangerous territory. "Maybe don't ignore her!"

Clementine spat her fingers out and cracked her fist across Tulsi's face.

Tulsi's head rang. The inside of her cheek was bleeding again, blood running down her throat. Clementine's eyes were so bright, and so were Sunju's and Alex's behind her, even if Alex kept glancing down at her notepad and Sunju was watching through her hands.

Near the end of the fight, they veered too close to the other girls. Clementine shoved Tulsi to the ground, and Tulsi, not knowing what else to do, reached out and grabbed Sunju and Alex's ankles.

Sunju yelped. Alex kicked Tulsi's head—not hard; more of a love tap.

"Two girls to a fight," Alex said, and the rest of what she was going to say was swallowed in a four-girl shriek as Tulsi *yanked*.

They surrounded her. Like the end of a cheer pyramid, everybody falling down into her, except she didn't have to worry about anyone's sharp edges but her own. Cheerleading used to feel like this sometimes, before Quentin had let her true colors shine through.

Somebody's hair was in her mouth. It was dark, which meant it was her own or Sunju's. It wasn't glossy enough to be her own—had to be Sunju's. Tulsi turned her head, and her mouth grazed Sunju's cheek.

"Oh my god." Alex rolled away, onto her hands and knees. "Sunju, are you okay? I fell *right* on you."

"You're not *that* big," Tulsi laughed. "And Sunju's not *that* small."

Sunju wobbled to her feet. "I'm fine. Just . . . surprised. Did anyone bleed on me?"

Shit. Tulsi's gaze roved over Sunju's jeans and blue button-down intently. Both baggy as hell. Why did Tulsi find that endearing?

"You're fine," Clementine announced. She was still on the floor, her leg stuck under Tulsi's butt. She looked at Alex consideringly. "You could use that to your advantage more, in a fight."

"What? Crushing people?"

Clementine nodded, tugging her leg free from Tulsi. "And putting more weight behind your movements."

Alex cast a thoughtful look down at her own body, as if someone had just told her she had opposable thumbs for the first time and she was considering a world of thumb-filled possibilities.

Clementine scratched at a scrape on her forehead. Tulsi's ribbon-bandage had caused damage after all—not just a fashion statement.

Tulsi thought about apologizing for calling her a psycho. How did you say *sorry* in ASL? Sunju would know—it was probably the first thing she learned.

Clementine asked Alex, "Are you next?"

Tulsi pushed herself up on her elbows. "Hey! Did I tap out? This fight is still going, baby."

Clementine took a beat to reply. She probably couldn't hear, Tulsi remembered, and had to guess what was being said based on mouth movements and vibes.

"You forfeited when you dragged the others in. Two girls to a fight."

"That rule didn't exist until *after*—"

Sunju stared at the small window above the work bench. "Guys."

Tulsi talked over her. "—I pulled them in, and I haven't gotten you back for biting me yet—"

"GUYS." Sunju wilted as everyone turned to her at once. "Um."

"Um?" Tulsi repeated, expectant.

Sunju shook her head. "I thought I saw . . . no, never mind."

Tulsi stretched out and tweaked the cuff of Sunju's jeans. Of course she cuffed her jeans. Probably *ironed* them, too. Probably hired a cleaner to iron her cuffed jeans and buff the garden gnomes so it shined in the moonlight.

"Can't get us all riled up then disappoint us like that," Tulsi said. "Very rude. GUYS! Sunju's being rude!"

Clementine fitted her hearing aids back in. "What is it?"

Sunju shook her head. A smile flinched across her face. "I thought I saw someone. It's nothing," she added when Alex turned, alarmed, towards the tiny window. "It was probably leaves. Or a bird."

Alex peered anxiously out the window. "I can't see anyone. I don't know who would come back here other than my parents, and if they saw two girls tussling in the garage, they'd *definitely* be banging on the door right now."

Sunju worried at her sleeve. "Sorry. I'm a little nervous."

"Aren't we all," Tulsi said, beaming when Sunju shot her a look that meant *you've never been nervous in your life*. She closed her hand once more around Sunju's leg.

"Don't," Sunju warned.

"Not doing anything," Tulsi said. She rearranged her shoulders against the concrete. "Actually, I think I'm good here. Alex, you can have the next fight."

Alex stepped out of her shoes, lining them up neatly near the door.

Sunju dropped to the ground and curled an arm around her legs, which Tulsi regrettably had to let go of.

"You're an only child, right?" Tulsi asked as Alex and Clementine stepped into the middle of the floor.

Sunju frowned. "Yes, why?"

Tulsi tapped the ankle she'd just had in a vice grip. "Didn't even threaten to kick me. Only child behavior right there."

Sunju ducked her head in a smile. She was always ducking her head when she smiled. Tulsi was struck with a powerful urge to see her eyes and her smile at the same time, then came to the conclusion that it was better if she didn't. Tulsi didn't like being speechless.

"You have siblings?"

"Two brothers. One sister." Tulsi pulled her plait over her shoulder. "I'm the youngest."

Sunju laughed. It was small and fluttery, but it was the biggest laugh Tulsi had heard out of her since the laughing fit in the parking lot that night.

"Youngest child behavior," Sunju said.

Tulsi elbowed her. "Shut up."

Sunju rubbed the spot Tulsi had elbowed, still smiling.

Something throbbed in Tulsi's chest. It joined the chorus of her aching cheek, her stinging fingers, her bruising back. Not *pain*, exactly—just sensation, deep and dangerous.

"Hey!" Alex clicked her fingers at Tulsi. "We haven't fought yet! We need to do that next!"

"You got it." Tulsi leaned back against the leg of the work bench and waited. The brightness that had started to recede as the girls got up from the pile Tulsi created began to flow back in force as she watched the girls circle each other, waiting.

Sunju's leg brushed hers, denim against Tulsi's bare knee.

This is what I was missing, Tulsi thought as Alex rammed into Clementine with all her weight, slamming her into the ground.

CHAPTER SEVEN

"Is everyone still looking?"

Tulsi rolled her eyes and twisted to check. Sterling Girls' cafeteria was the same as the last time she'd looked over her shoulder—girls avoiding the meatloaf, showing each other exciting TikToks, and today's special: yet another girl stealing a glance, maybe a double take, then leaning over to a friend and whispering, *Why the hell are those girls hanging out?*

The corner table wasn't helping. Neither was the way they were all hunching together, the opposite of subtle: Clementine's shaved head almost grazing Sunju's dark bob, Alex's fake blonde curls fluttering against Tulsi's sharp cheek every time she breathed.

Tulsi turned back, sipping a juice box. "Same as the last time you asked me. And the time before that. *And* the time before that."

She started to lean back in her chair, then stopped when Alex gave her a warning look. She'd tried it earlier, but Alex had hooked a foot around her chair leg and dragged her in.

So we won't be overheard, she'd hissed. Like that wasn't going to make people want to listen even more.

Alex said, "I've been color-coding the rules into two groups."

Tulsi groaned.

"Physical safety," Alex listed as if Tulsi hadn't made a sound, "and secrecy. I think those are our two pillars."

Sunju traced shapes onto the table. Words, definitely, but too fast for Tulsi to make them out.

Sunju asked, "Are you sure your parents don't suspect?"

Behind her, Yazmine sent up a bewildered peace sign. She'd stopped at the end of the lunch line, tray in her hands, to stare at Tulsi's strange seating arrangement.

"I'm sure," Alex said. "I mean, neither of them has looked me in the face for longer than two seconds since I started having to cover bruises, but if the teachers can't tell, no way they're going to!"

Tulsi held up a middle finger. Yazmine flashed her tongue and headed over to the cheerleader's table, where everybody was waiting with delighted, menacing anticipation. Every time Tulsi looked over, it sent a wave of dread through her gut.

This is a loan, the dread told her. *These girls are borrowed; you'll have to slink back eventually, tail between your legs. What will Quentin have you do to make it up to her?*

Clementine frowned. "Your parents haven't looked you in the face for a week?"

"What? Not like . . ." Alex chuckled. "That sounded weird. They're busy! Anyway, do we have any ideas about what we'll tell our parents? I think we should have a *thing.* Like a book club."

"Girls Night," Tulsi said absently, chewing her juice box straw, scanning the cafeteria again. More stares. More whispers. Yazmine got up to say something in Cady's ear. Thank God Quentin wasn't here yet.

Uncharacteristic silence. Tulsi turned to find all eyes on her.

Alex asked, "What?"

"Uh." Tulsi spat out the straw. "Girls Night? It's what I told my auntie about yesterday."

Clementine tilted her head, considering.

Sunju hummed.

"Girls Night," Alex repeated, rolling it around her mouth like a piece of candy. "I like it."

Tulsi's teeth worried the straw, trying to hide her stupidly pleased smile. "I mean, it's no *book club.*"

Alex laughed. It was almost a snort; none of the sleek cuteness she'd adopted since freshman year. She shoved a hand over her mouth, but the damage was done—Tulsi was charmed. She was charmed by all of them: Clementine watching Alex laugh with strange wonder, like a birdwatcher who just discovered a species thought to be extinct; Sunju ducking her head against a smile and tracing words into the table: *Girls Night.*

I want to keep them, she realized. It wasn't as bitter as she'd expected. Something swelled in Tulsi's stomach, almost drowning the dread. Maybe she could . . . get out? Maybe these girls could be *her* girls. No more cheerleaders tripping her up or grinding a heel on her injured shoulder, no more tossing barbs back and forth. Maybe Tulsi could file down her sharp edges. Maybe—

Quentin strode into the cafeteria. Every bounce of her red hair against her camisole made Tulsi's dread flow back in force. For a moment, Quentin headed for the lunch line, oblivious. The cheerleaders waved, and some of them called, but Quentin was already slowing. She stopped, heels squeaking on the linoleum. She turned, slow and precise, and Tulsi had an irritated moment to think, *Is the bitch actually goddamn psychic?* before their gazes locked.

Quentin's lips parted. Dark red lipstick. She and Tulsi used to share the same tube before homeroom.

Those dark lips twitched—incredulous, threatening, a little impressed—and Tulsi had to fight down a weary, self-hating swell of pride.

Quentin raised her hand. Her nails were the same shade as her lips. She waved, jerked her head. *You've had your fun. Come on back now.*

There was an empty chair next to her: the seat Tulsi had sat in every lunch period since freshman year. She was always going to have to go back.

Tulsi's chair screeched against the linoleum. She shot a tight grin to the occupants of the corner table, who were all watching with puzzled expressions as Tulsi stood up.

"Back to our regularly scheduled programming," Tulsi said. She rapped the table goodbye, *bang bang,* putting on a show for the people watching. Because everybody was. Some people were more careful about it, but everybody wanted to know what the hell Tulsi was doing hanging out with the gossip queen, the bruiser, and the wallflower, and why the head cheerleader's smile looked, more than anything, like she was baring her teeth.

Alex called after her, "See you later?"

Tulsi risked a glance back. Alex looked expectant—she was checking if Tulsi was coming to Alex's garage tonight.

Tulsi nodded.

Alex nodded back, expression going sunny again, like that was the problem here and not the gallows Tulsi was walking towards.

The cheerleader's table was dead silent. An anxious titter broke out at the other end as they sat down.

Quentin looked up.

The laughter died.

Quentin set her tray down. Pried the lid off her yogurt. Dug her spoon in. Ate it slowly as Tulsi sat next to her, chewing the end of her straw to a pulp.

Halfway through her yogurt, Quentin finally relented. "So, things *must* have gotten interesting after the cops broke up Cady's party."

"Not really." Tulsi stared determinedly out the window. You could see MeatLovers across the street. Somebody was hanging up a sign above the door: IF YOU'RE CAUSING A DISTURBANCE, WE WILL CALL THE POLICE.

Tulsi leaned over to Cady. "Look, they made you a sign."

Cady frowned. "They can't stop the truth. If we—"

Quentin cut her off. "What's that bruise?"

Tulsi went still. Maybe if she didn't look over . . .

Quentin's fingers closed around her chin, jerking her to meet those inevitable green eyes. Even now, after the shoulder and the fights and the endless manipulation . . . Tulsi was entranced. She could never trust Quentin, but she would always be captivated by her. She would always make her breath catch, even if it was from a thumb digging into a bruise.

Tulsi shook her hand off. "It's from practice. *Some* people need to get better at not smacking me in the face with their massive *feet*."

She directed this last part at Yazmine, who shopped for shoes in the men's department.

Yazmine raised her middle finger and kept eating her tuna sandwich.

Trying to drag other people into the conversation wouldn't deter Quentin, but it could delay her. Tulsi would take what she could get.

Quentin stared at her. Tulsi squirmed, then forced herself to be still. Quentin was the one to teach her that. *If you act unaffected, people will respect you more.*

Quentin kept staring. She didn't blink. Her red lips thinned, a flicker of hurt running through her expression. "What happened to us not having secrets?"

Tulsi snorted. A thing Quentin never had to teach her: how to make someone feel small with a single sound.

"You never played by your own rules," Tulsi said, and stood up.

She didn't look at the corner table, or even at the cheerleader's table, as she strode out into the hall, found the closest bathroom, and hid in a toilet stall until the bell rang.

Almost nobody dared to speak to Tulsi for hours. *Sharp heart,* Quentin had whispered. Anyone who dared come close to Tulsi got cut, and Tulsi made sure everybody that afternoon goddamn *knew* it.

Girls swung out of her way in the hallways. Ms. Kitch went to call on her in history, got one syllable into her name and then switched hastily to the girl next to her. Alex tried to meet her eyes in English until Clementine wisely distracted her.

Only two people were stupid enough to actually try it.

The first was Sunju. Clementine was too busy walking Alex out of class to stop her, and as Sunju stopped in front of Tulsi's desk, Tulsi couldn't stop the anger that swelled behind her ribs. What the hell was Sunju doing? She couldn't even smile at people head-on. Somebody needed to protect her from Tulsi's sharp heart.

Tulsi riffled through her backpack for five seconds longer than she needed to, waiting for the class to empty, hoping Sunju would leave. Her shadow stayed stubbornly on Tulsi's table, covering the heart shot with an arrow Tulsi had carved in the last half hour of class.

Tulsi jerked her backpack onto her shoulder and stood, snarling, "*What*, Park?"

Sunju flinched. Just a little.

All of Tulsi's fight drained out of her, replaced by a howling self-hatred. What the hell had Sunju ever done to her? Tulsi *knew* she was going through shit; there was a *reason* she was so timid; of course she wouldn't react well to someone looming over her and yelling—

Tulsi tried pulling herself in, making herself less scary, but the overbright sheen in Sunju's eyes was already gone.

"I know what I'm going to write about for your essay," Sunju said quietly.

"What?"

"*The Tempest*. Is that okay?"

Tulsi blinked. "Why would that not be okay?"

Sunju shrugged. Her shirt was less baggy today; it showed off her collarbones. Tulsi had never seen them outside of that night at the laundromat.

"Maybe you've written on it before."

"I haven't." Tulsi tried to remember which play it was. The one with the witch? She hated Shakespeare unless it was being performed in front of her, and even then, she had to rely on the actor's reactions to understand what was going on.

Sunju nodded, fidgeted with her sleeve. Light purple today, no blue in sight.

"Well, see you tonight."

Tulsi nodded back and watched Sunju weave around the desks and then step into the hallway.

"Sunju," Tulsi blurted.

Sunju leaned back in, expectant.

Tulsi's mouth moved mortifyingly around thin air. She coughed. "Um, nothing."

Sunju nodded again. She waited a moment, with Tulsi standing there like an idiot.

"See you," Sunju repeated, then she ducked back into the hall.

Tulsi waited until her footsteps faded. Then she took her backpack off, stuck her face into it, and shrieked.

They should've scheduled it after school. Then Tulsi wouldn't have to pace around her bedroom with her headphones on as loud as they would go. But Clementine was doing something with her brother, and Sunju had something with her parents, and Alex had said something about homework, so Tulsi paced and screamed along until all her siblings were pounding the walls and it was time to go.

No pickup necessary this time. Clementine lived closer to Sunju than Tulsi, and her big brother was apparently so delighted she was making friends he offered to drive them to Alex's. They even offered a ride to Tulsi, but since Alex's house was only a few blocks away, Tulsi had turned them down.

Probably a good move. Tulsi didn't want to be in anyone's company until she was allowed to punch them.

She walked the three blocks to Alex's house, hair a dark stream behind her, teeth clenched as tight as her fists. She took a detour into a gas station, sifting through the chocolate bars. The old lady behind the counter gave her a judgmental look. Tulsi sneered.

Sharp heart. Tulsi was one big blade. Alex would cut herself on her razor edges, because tonight was *the night*—Alex and Tulsi's first fight together—and maybe Tulsi was a little sad it would be vicious and not the joyous thing she'd imagined, but it was hard to care when she was walking so fast with her music so loud that everyone in the gas station knew to give her a wide berth, everyone except—

A hand on her shoulder. Tulsi ripped out her headphones and turned to face—

"Tulsi," the man said. "How've you been?"

She froze.

Mr. Keener's gelled hair was as smooth and shiny as ever. He had a pocket protector tucked neatly against his chest and a narrow face suited for smiling. He was thirty years old but looked younger, and once upon a time, Tulsi had thought he was the cutest guy in the world.

Mr. Keener raised his thin brows. "Tulsi? Cat got your tongue?"

She swallowed. Her tongue felt thick and slow. It was ten steps to the cash register.

"Move," she mumbled.

"I'm sorry?"

If it were anyone else, she would've shoved them out of the way. But this was Mr. Keener, so she waved the chocolate bar she was holding towards the front of the store.

"Right." Mr Keener didn't move. "I feel like we haven't seen each other in forever. How long has it been?"

"A few years," Tulsi mumbled. She stepped to the side.

"Tulsi, wait—" He moved for her, but she was too fast. He let out a huff as she passed, not quite blocking her but not *not* blocking her, either. To anyone watching, it would've looked like an innocent shoulder brush caused by an overeager teenage girl.

Tulsi threw the chocolate onto the counter and fumbled for her purse.

Footsteps behind her. "I thought we agreed to call me John."

Tulsi didn't look at him as she left. She ran the last block to Alex's, sprinted down the driveway and into the backyard, where the garage door was already open.

Clementine, Sunju, and Alex were chatting on the concrete. They trailed off as Tulsi burst in, chocolate bar half-gone in her hand.

Sunju stood. "Tulsi, what's wrong?"

"I really—" Tulsi jammed the last of the chocolate into her mouth. Her next words were garbled: "I *really* want to punch something."

Five minutes later, Tulsi lay wheezing on the cool concrete. Her cheek throbbed. Her knee ached. She was covered in sweat—her own and Alex's, since Alex had taken Clem's advice and was throwing her entire weight at people. At one point, she'd sat on Tulsi, and Tulsi'd had to pinch her thighs to make her move.

"You're better than I thought," Tulsi panted.

Alex beamed, wiping her shiny face with one of the towels she'd lined up on the work bench. "Thanks! You're already so good. Like, Clementine's efficient, but you're *vicious*."

Tulsi laughed, trying to hide the complicated swell of emotions that brought up. Pride, obviously, but also a deep weariness. *Vicious* was getting old.

Alex dragged Clementine into the ring. Tulsi shuffled over to the wall where Sunju was leaning.

"Hey," Tulsi said, with only a bit of the self-loathing left from the classroom earlier. The fight had done a lot to wash that shit out of her system, and talking with Sunju was easier with adrenaline in her veins.

"Hi." Sunju clutched a sketchbook. Tulsi hadn't noticed her getting it out; it must've happened during the fight.

She leaned over. "What're you drawing?"

Sunju pressed the paper into her knees. "It's not finished, and none of your business."

"My business if you're drawing me."

The silence stretched on long enough that Tulsi gasped in delight. "Wait, *were* you? Holy shit, I need to see this."

"No!" Sunju trapped the sketchbook between her chest and thighs, keeping it away from Tulsi's prying hands. "It was just a muscle study; you can't even tell it's you!"

"I have *muscles*?" Tulsi held up her arms and flexed, as if she didn't do this every morning, marveling at the small bulge in her upper arms. "Come on, show me!"

"No!" Sunju ducked her head. She was smiling, but she looked unsure about it, like it could dissolve at any time.

Tulsi relented. She didn't want to get sweat on Sunju's shirt.

Sunju uncurled, eyeing Tulsi suspiciously.

Tulsi closed her eyes, waiting for her heart rate to come down. It wouldn't calm all the way, not with the background noise of Alex and Clementine's fight, but it was slowing to a reasonable rate.

Fighting Alex had been . . . surprisingly *fun*. Even with all their baggage, even with the shaky rage Tulsi had shown up with, after the first few punches, Alex had laughed, blood in her mouth, and something about it had set Tulsi off, and the two of them had had to stop fighting until the laughter stopped. Like they were 10 years old again, wrestling on the playground.

Soft scratching. Tulsi looked over to find Sunju turned away, holding her sketchbook so Tulsi couldn't see it, glancing up at the fight, her eyes lingering on Clementine's back muscles. Did Tulsi have back muscles? She kept meaning to check.

"It's cool you can draw," Tulsi offered.

Sunju hummed. "I'm not good at it."

"Better than me."

"You haven't seen—" Sunju cut herself off. Tulsi *had* seen Sunju's drawings—she'd stolen a look at those two girls in a sweet embrace. It was a good drawing. Tulsi mostly remembered the girls' faces, so tender and vulnerable she'd had to look away.

"You're good at capturing expressions," she said, watching Alex kick Clementine's foot out from underneath her.

Clementine hit the ground, rolled out of the way as Alex tried to pin her down.

"Thanks," Sunju said, so quietly Tulsi barely heard it over the wet sound of a punch: Clementine's fist against Alex's chest.

It was a solid fight, and they could have sat there in silence, Sunju sketching, Tulsi watching, until it ended. But Tulsi couldn't leave it like that—not with the reminder of how Tulsi had screwed Sunju over.

"Hey. What'd you see the other day that made you think someone was watching?"

Sunju's pencil paused. It was one of those fancy artist ones with expensive lead or whatever. "It was nothing; I just—"

"No, tell me."

Sunju sighed. "I don't know. I saw . . . red? I thought it was a scarf, or hair, or something."

Sweat rolled down Tulsi's forehead. "Red hair."

"Or leaves," Sunju said, as if it was the time of year for it. "Tulsi, what—"

"Shit," Tulsi spat. She stood, hissing when her hip flared. When the hell had she hurt her hip? It was like cheer practice all over again: waking up to find mysterious bruises. When had someone hit her in the shin? Did she fall on her tailbone? Why did her chest hurt?

Gravel crunched outside.

"*Shit*," Tulsi repeated, louder. She marched to the door—to do what, she didn't know. She reached out towards the handle—

The door rumbled open. Standing in Alex's backyard, smirking like she hadn't just brought Tulsi's new world down around her ears, stood Quentin Scarhill.

The fight stopped. Alex pushed herself to her feet. "Q-Quentin! Hi!"

Quentin waved. Cady and Yazmine stood behind her, Cady nervously twisting a strand of pink hair around her finger, Yazmine flashing a peace sign, cool as a cucumber.

"Tulsi," Alex said thinly. "Um, did you—"

Tulsi whirled on her. "I didn't say shit!"

"You know how word travels at Sterling." Quentin stepped inside, and Tulsi stepped back automatically, wanting to shove her outside and lock the door, to scream at her, to grab her new girls and yell something stupid, like, *I called dibs! You can't have them!*

"Cute digs," Quentin said, eyes roving the garage hungrily. Her smile grew as she saw a spot of red on the concrete—Tulsi's. Fresh nose blood. Alex had clocked her in the face.

"Thanks!" Alex twisted her hands. She kept glancing at Tulsi, like there was an inside joke she wanted Tulsi to let her in on.

Quentin's hungry eyes kept going: the shoes lined up at the door, bandages, water bottles, towels, everybody bruised and bloody except for Sunju standing in the corner.

"My first mate keeps showing up bruised," Quentin said. "Couldn't have that. Not unless it's for a good reason."

She nodded at Clementine. Clementine didn't nod back.

Quentin reached into her pocket and came out with a rubber band. She gathered her crimson hair in one hand, slowly twisting the rubber band over it. "So . . . what, you get together and throw each other around?"

Tulsi glared at Yazmine and Cady, who were too busy being bewildered by their surroundings to notice. It was better, Tulsi figured, than Quentin's fervent eagerness.

"We have rules," Alex said. "It's not just . . . brawling. There's no shoes, no jewelry, no biting—"

"Uh-huh." Quentin pushed out her earrings. Red diamonds dropped into her palm. "And no telling."

"Of course! No one's finding out about Girls Night."

Quentin's green eyes flashed. For the first time since she'd walked in, her attention focused entirely on Alex Veck. "Girls Night?"

Alex's breath caught. "Yes."

Tulsi's heart sank. She knew what Quentin's undivided attention could do, and what girls would do to make it continue.

Alex cleared her throat, and Tulsi knew the words before they came.

"Do you want to join?"

CHAPTER EIGHT

Everyone was sweating, even Sunju and Cady and Yazmine, who hadn't fought. Watching a fight was tiring in itself.

Alex lay on the ground, chest heaving. She'd flopped down on her back after Quentin had tapped out.

Tulsi had pulled her aside after she'd accepted Quentin and the other two into the club, hissing, *I thought this was just us?*

I never said that, Alex had told her, flushed from the intoxicating intensity of Quentin's gaze. *Look, she gave me gossip, and I gave nothing back. I owe her.*

Jesus, are you an idiot? Never be in debt to Quentin goddamn Scarhill!

Tulsi, come on. What's the harm?

At first, Alex had thought she was about to be strangled. Then Tulsi had sagged, rubbing her face like she'd just been told the worst news of her life. *Your funeral,* she had muttered.

Alex lifted her arm. She'd had to remind Quentin about the no biting rule halfway through the fight, but by then, it was too late: a small bite mark sat on the soft skin of Alex's upper arm, just a line, where the bottom teeth had started to sink in.

Alex wiped at it. Red smeared over the crook of her elbow.

A bottle appeared next to her ear: disinfectant.

"You're a genius," she told Sunju.

Sunju crouched, dabbing disinfectant onto a cotton pad and pressing it to Alex's bite. The sting was shocking and bright. Alex whined.

"Yikes." Quentin giggled, hair falling over Alex's shoulder, as red as the blood Sunju was clearing away. "I really took a chunk out of you."

"You did!" Alex laughed, giddy with Quentin's closeness. The other girls didn't stay this close after a fight. Now that she thought about it, Alex didn't really touch people unless they were punching her. Weird.

"Sorry," Quentin added. She gathered up her hair away from her sweaty face, curling it into a bun. "Tulsi! You sure you don't want a go?"

"Next time," Tulsi said, sounding incredibly bitter about the idea.

Alex didn't know what had happened between Tulsi and Quentin, but Tulsi had been even more unfriendly than usual to Quentin this past year. She didn't keep close tabs on them, but she could sense potential gossip. Whatever had happened between those two, (a) it was big and (b) no one was talking.

Clementine and Tulsi joined their little cluster. They'd lingered in the corner with Sunju during the fights, with Yazmine and Cady sitting against the opposite wall.

Quentin handed Alex her towel. It was damp with Quentin's sweat. Alex turned it over and used the clean side to dry her face.

When she lowered it, everybody was looking at her. At first, Alex looked at her laundromat girls—an instinct that felt older than a week, like it already had roots—but Quentin's gaze was so magnetic, so captivating, like she wanted to open up Alex's brain and scoop through the soft bits.

Quentin smiled. "So," she said. "Food?"

They attracted glances, a group of girls bruised up and laughing as they walked across the street. Alex paid them no mind. She was on another plane of existence, buzzing, too high to care about a mother of two stopping to frown at them in worry. Two Girls Night rules already broken—number 3: no biting, and number 7: always hide the evidence.

The cheerleaders led the way, arms linked. Alex's laundromat girls hung back, chatting quietly. Alex was relieved, if not a little disappointed about the lack of linked arms. She'd been worried adding more people would make this like Cady's party, with Alex trying desperately to make them talk and getting awkward silence in return.

Suburbia gave way to cityscape until they reached the fluorescent lights of MeatLovers across from Sterling Girls.

Cady stopped. "I think we should go somewhere else."

"You can get fries," Quentin said, and unlinked their arms.

Cady's arm dropped to her side, bereft, and Alex eyed the new bared skin of Quentin's elbow.

They squeezed into a booth. Alex was shored on both sides, with Clementine and Tulsi at her right and Sunju pressing against the window at her left. Alex pulled her legs in as close as they would go, but they still pressed uncomfortably against the girls on either side. It felt rude, like she was intruding on their space.

"Sorry," she whispered.

"For what?" Sunju whispered back. Both she and Clementine appeared genuinely confused.

Alex shook her head. Fighting had made her feel good about her body for the first time in . . . years. Not just accepting, not just tolerating, but *good*. But now she was back in the real world.

She tried to feel good about her size, body positivity and all that, but it was difficult when clothing stores didn't have her size and strangers watched her eat with their judgy little eyes. Alex would feel fine about being fat when other people stopped being so *weird* about it.

Alex tried once again to pull her body in. Taking up this much room in an already-small booth made her feel exposed, and it didn't help that Quentin was leaning towards her on her elbows, looking at her like she knew everything Alex had ever scribbled out in her diary.

"So," Quentin said. "How did this happen?"

She waggled her fingers at the four of them—Sunju, Alex, Clementine, and Tulsi, jammed into one side of the table.

"Uh," Alex said. "We hung out at a party."

"We ran from cops together," Tulsi added. "Did some light breaking and entering."

"Right," Alex said. "Can't forget about the breaking and entering. Thank you, Tulsi."

"And . . . what?" Quentin put her chin in her hand, twisting a strand of red hair around her pinkie. "You decided to fight each other for fun, just because?"

She turned her gaze to Clementine, who stared back until Quentin broke out in a grin. *That* made Clementine look away.

"Yes," Clementine gritted. "That's about it."

A waitress came up to their table. "What can I get y'all today?"

"Oh, may I have . . . " Alex trailed off as Quentin slid her plastic menu over.

"Order for me?"

"Um. Sure." Alex turned to the waitress, suddenly panicking. "Two . . . number fifteens? With cherry milkshakes."

She checked. Quentin was examining her nails. Was that good or bad?

Tulsi rolled her eyes, leaned back as far as the booth would allow. "The pancakes for me. With bacon."

Quentin hummed, peering at the underside of her nails. They were long and painted, like Tulsi's had been last week. They'd come close to poking Alex's eye out earlier. Alex made a mental note to equip Sunju's makeup kit with a pair of nail scissors.

Their food arrived. Alex sliced her pancake into tiny pieces so she could bide her time and monitor Quentin's reaction. So far, there was nothing, just Quentin eating a pancake with a neutral expression.

"So," Quentin said finally, cutting into a conversation Sunju and Clementine were having about Saturday morning cartoons. "You can't keep it in your garage, obviously."

"*Obviously*," Tulsi muttered, cutting savagely into her bacon.

Had she known about this after all? Alex couldn't tell. One second, Tulsi seemed shocked, not knowing anything about it, but she also seemed . . . strangely unsurprised. Maybe Quentin was just the kind of person who showed up unannounced to a secret fight club and started making suggestions about where it should be held.

Alex sucked on her milkshake. "Why do you say that?"

"Because it'll grow," Quentin said. "That's what you want, right? I can't see gossip queen Alex Veck starting up a club without wanting it to go global."

"I don't know about *global.*" Alex looked down the line at her laundromat girls. She *hadn't* thought about expansion. It surprised her to realize she hadn't considered it. Isn't that what she'd always wanted: more people in her life? More people *looking* at her?

A soft kick in the leg. Alex glanced over to find Tulsi giving her a death stare, motioning at the bathrooms.

Alex turned back to Quentin, who was sipping delicately at her cherry milkshake. The fight had rubbed off her lipstick, and the drink colored her lips a familiar red.

"Good thing I'm on board," Quentin said. "*I* have an idea."

"What—ow!" Alex bent to rub her shin, glaring back at Tulsi. "One second."

Tulsi dragged the bathroom door shut behind them.

Alex took the opportunity to fix her hair in the mirror, picking it away from her sweaty forehead. "Wow, you *really* don't like your friend groups mixing."

"Shut up."

Tulsi spoke with her usual sharpness, but she also sounded tired enough to make Alex turn around. She looked strangely exhausted, like she'd taken every fight back there and then gone out to find some more.

She bit her lip. Alex hadn't seen her do that in years.

"I'm warning you," Tulsi said. "So don't come crying to me later. 'Cause I *warned* you."

"Warned me?" Alex hid her disappointment behind a peppy smile. She'd really thought they were becoming friends again. "Okay, hit me with a . . . a good old Tulsi threat. Haven't had one of those in a few days."

"Not about—" Tulsi rubbed a hand down her face, wincing when it pressed on her bruised cheek. "I'm warning you about *Quentin*, asshole. She's not good for anybody."

"She isn't?"

"No, she's a raging tire fire. You don't want to get too close."

Alex waved at Tulsi, a laugh escaping. "*You're* close with her!"

"Nobody's close *with* her. I'm close *to* her. There's a difference." Tulsi squeezed her own shoulder, wincing. Had she hurt it during a fight? Alex didn't remember her landing badly on it.

Tulsi's jaw clenched unhappily. There was no jealousy there, just . . . resignation, like she didn't want to be having this conversation. And there was a crease in her brow, an uncharacteristic look of worry, like she genuinely wanted Alex to get away, for her own sake.

"Look," Alex said. "I get that you guys are going through . . . whatever you're going through. But that doesn't mean *I* can't be friends with her. She's cool."

"Oh, if she's *cool.*"

"She seems nice."

Tulsi's expression morphed into disgust. "She's not nice."

"She's *interesting,*" Alex tried, which was true. She wasn't about to tell Tulsi the truth: she'd put up with a lot of weird friendship weirdness if it meant Quentin would look at her like she had in her garage.

"She is," Tulsi admitted grudgingly. "Just . . . don't say I didn't warn you. And I won't be there to pull you out if things go bad. Which they will."

"Wow, thanks."

Tulsi rotated her shoulder, grimacing.

"Did I . . . in the fight, did . . . " Alex hovered her hands over it, dropping them when Tulsi shot her another glare. "How did you hurt your shoulder? I didn't hear anything about it."

Tulsi's face twisted, just for a moment. Then it smoothed out into the cool, unaffected, mean, familiar face of Tulsi Ortiz.

"Old injury," she snarled.

Alex opened her mouth to ask what the hell had *happened* between them . . . then closed it. Tulsi would just come up with some stupid retort, and Alex would only annoy her more. She could be so *defensive* sometimes. Defensive and rude and viciously barbed, all sharp edges. Even when they were kids, Tulsi could take offense at something Alex didn't mean anything by or say something terrible out of nowhere. Maybe Quentin *had* done something awful, but she wouldn't have done that for no reason. Tulsi would've done something to deserve it.

Tulsi dug her fingers into the meat of her shoulder. Nail marks stayed in her skin, a painful reminder of whatever she was hiding.

"Come on," she said darkly. "We should head out before she poisons my pancakes."

CHAPTER NINE

"This is so illegal," Joseph said.

"Only a little bit." Clementine leaned around him, the legs of her plastic chair squeaking against the linoleum. "He's freaking out again."

"I'm not freaking out," he insisted, but Sunju had already gotten out of her seat beside him to let Alex take it.

The school hall was empty. The end-of-day bell had rung 15 minutes ago. Clementine was trying not to be skeeved out, but empty schools always gave her the creeps. They made her feel like something terrible was about to happen.

The feeling was strangely lessened by her girls and her brother lined up in the plastic chairs beside her, but still. Skeeved.

"You'll be lying about your qualifications," Alex said as she sat down beside him, "which is illegal. But you aren't *actually* teaching."

"But this"—Joseph waved a hand at the line of chairs up against the wall of the principal's office—"is still illegal."

"Yes. But not a lot," Alex told him. "Compared to, like, murder."

"Oh, compared to murder," Joseph said. "That's fine, then."

His hands twisted together in his lap. They were blunt and stubby like Clementine's, and one of two things that made him and her appear related. The other was their eyes. Joseph was rail-thin, fair, and nonthreatening, in stark contrast to Clementine, with her dark hair, strong features, and menacing stance. Hands and eyes: apart from those, Clementine didn't look very much like her brother.

"And everything else?" he asked.

Clementine looked to Alex, who obliged. "So! At first, I thought a fight club couldn't be assault, since everyone will be consenting, but it turns out to be more complicated than that. It can technically be called mutual combat, which is . . . sort of illegal in this state depending on how you swing it, but there's a lot of leeway to move around in that definition, so I'm not sure how bad it is. I think as long as we don't let anyone get hurt too bad, and we don't gamble, we should be set!"

"And don't get caught," Clementine interjected.

"And don't get caught. Obviously."

Alex's blonde hair bobbed prettily with her nod, and Clementine's gaze caught on the pearly sheen. Alex looked like the kind of girl with a haircare routine. Clementine imagined a dozen tiny bottles lined up on her bathroom sink, waiting to be rubbed through her shiny hair.

At the end of the chairs, Tulsi blew out a mouthful of air. "The meeting was supposed to start ten minutes ago. She's always on time when I screw up, but when I finally have something *constructive* to help the *school*—"

Alex said, "Tulsi. It's a front for a fight club."

Tulsi smirked. "Man, say that louder, why don't you?" She craned her head, but the hallway remained empty.

The principal's office door opened. Ms. Ryans stepped out, patting her messy brown hair and adjusting her glasses. Clementine had only talked to the woman twice—once when she was accepted into Sterling and again after beating up Olive—but she'd passed her a few times in the halls, and she'd never seen the woman not look stressed. Alex told her Ms. Ryans was young, maybe thirty-five, but she looked older. Running an all-girls public school scraping the lowest deciles had to take its toll.

Ms. Ryans looked the wrong way down the hall.

"Howdy, Ms. Ryans," Tulsi called.

The poor woman startled, whipping to face the girls lined up neatly against the wall. "Girls! And Mr. Rady. Sorry, I had a call run long."

She paused, her face doing something complicated, a look Clementine was coming to recognize as, *Why the hell are these girls willingly spending time together?* Clementine and the others had received it countless times since they'd started hanging out.

Would the reaction have changed if Quentin had tagged along? She'd seemed eager enough to suggest the gym, but when Alex had invited her to the meeting (ignoring Tulsi's glare), Quentin had told them she was sure they'd do a great job.

Quentin Scarhill was trouble—of that, Clementine was sure. The only question was whether she was *worthwhile* trouble. Alex definitely thought so, and Clementine tried to stem the wave of worry that swelled at the thought.

Ms. Ryans stood back, smoothing her pencil skirt. It stayed creased. "Come in."

Joseph went to sit in the chair in front of Ms. Ryans's desk, and the girls took the couch. It was a small couch wedged into the corner of the room, and Sunju was last to sit down. She eyed the thin space next to Clementine dubiously.

"It's fine," Clementine told her. "Just . . ."

Sunju sat. One butt cheek rested on Clementine's lap.

Sunju whispered, "Sorry."

"It's fine," Clementine lied. Sunju was pokey and rigid. It probably didn't help that Clementine wasn't a good choice of seat, her legs too wiry. Clementine looked longingly at Alex's pantyhose-covered thighs, which would absorb Sunju's bony butt like hers never could.

She looked up to find Tulsi glaring. Clementine blinked, but before she could wonder what she'd done to incur Tulsi's wrath, Tulsi had turned away, watching Ms. Ryans shake Joseph's hand. Clementine hoped they weren't as sweaty as they looked.

"I have to admit, I was surprised when Tulsi approached me about using the gym for a new group." Ms. Ryans wiped her hand surreptitiously on her skirt. Damn. "But I must say, I'm glad to see my students being proactive. I think a self-defense course is a wonderful idea."

Clementine's jaw unclenched. Now all they had to do was convince Ms. Ryans that Joseph was a certified instructor and not a mechanic whose only teaching experience was showing his little sister how to fight dirty.

"That's great," Joseph said. The strain was clear in his voice, but she hoped Ms. Ryans would chalk that up to the stress of a sort-of job interview. "I think it's very important that young girls should have the necessary tools to defend themselves."

Ms. Ryans beamed. "Exactly. What did you say your name was, again?"

"Joseph Rady, ma'am."

Her smile shrank. "Rady? You aren't related to . . ." Her gaze flicked over to Clementine, with her fading bruises and scabbing knuckles. (She wasn't good at makeup.)

"She's my little sister, ma'am." Joseph's voice went firm, sincerity seeping in through his thin veil of professionalism. She could always count on him to stand up for her. He hadn't been able to stop any of the bad shit when they were kids, but he'd gotten out as soon as he could, and he'd dragged her with him.

I'll come back for you, he'd promised the day he moved out of their parents' house. And he had. He'd come back with lawyers and restraining orders and a rickety old car that took them to safety.

Ms. Ryans folded her fingers in front of her. "Well. At least we know you're effective at teaching your students to cause damage!"

"I was actually hoping a self-defense course would be a way for Clementine to take her energy out in a healthy way." Joseph shot her a look. If the Radys were the kind of people who winked, this would have been one of those moments.

"Not on other students, I hope."

"No! No, of course," Joseph laughed woodenly. His leg jittered.

Breathe, Clementine thought at him.

Ms. Ryans started in on his past job experience. Sunju shifted in Clementine's lap, and she winced at the sharp poke of hip bones.

"Sorry," Sunju whispered again.

Clementine shook her head. Discomfort was nothing. She'd put up with worse for less. It was actually kind of nice, if she ignored the ache in her legs: Sunju's back against her chest, warmth radiating from Sunju's knobby spine.

Clementine lowered her mouth to Sunju's ear. "Might be easier on both of us if you relax."

A low noise from Tulsi on the other side of the couch. "Good luck getting you two to relax," she muttered.

Sunju leaned carefully back into Clementine. The weight on Clementine's legs lessened.

"There," she said. "Better."

Ms. Ryans dismissed them with a promise that she'd let them know her decision tomorrow.

Clementine waited for the office door to close, then pulled Joseph down the hall. Alex caught her eye and signed clumsily in ASL: WE-GO-YOUR-HOUSE?

Clementine held up her hands. "*Wait.*"

"Thank you for doing this," she said once they were out of earshot. I know you don't like lying—"

"I'd do anything for you," Joseph said, amused.

They could have had this conversation in ASL, and the girls would've been none the wiser, but some conversations had to happen alone.

"I don't love the, uh . . ." Joseph waved a fist, "*nature* of the club, but I'm just happy you're making friends. They seem like good people."

"They are."

Clementine looked down the hall. Alex was showing the others the sign for *house*. Clementine watched their hands form a roof, and her heart swelled with huge, impossible fondness. She hadn't even known them for two weeks.

They'd come over twice now, but Clementine watched their reactions anyway. She was still waiting for one of them to come out and say it: *Your apartment is shit, and it smells.* Kids had said that about Clementine's house in first grade, and she hadn't invited anyone over since.

Nothing strange happened in the girls' faces as they piled their backpacks near the door and started for Clementine's bedroom. The first time they'd come around, there had been some surprise, Clementine was sure of it, but no one had made any comment about how Clementine didn't have a proper bed, just a mattress, or how their furniture was made up of boxes and patio chairs from the Salvation Army.

"Let me know if you need food," Joseph called as they padded down the hall.

Clementine turned. "*Thanks.*"

"*You're welcome, Clip-Clop Clem,*" he signed back.

Alex lay down on Clementine's bed. "So, what does this mean?" She held up her hand in the demented horse sign Joseph had flashed her from the end of the hall.

Clementine sighed. "It's my sign name. It's not a proper . . . it means, um, Clip-Clop Clem."

Alex stared up at her, brown eyes bright, smiling like Clementine had just told her something amazing.

"I'm . . ." Clementine fiddled with the hem of her leather jacket, losing words under Alex's bright gaze, "very heavy footed."

Tulsi barked a laugh, pulling Sunju down onto the mattress next to her. Sunju landed with an *oomph*, elbow catching Tulsi in the gut.

"Sorry," Sunju said.

"No sweat—ow!"

"Don't manhandle me," Sunju said, elbowing Tulsi on purpose this time. She tucked her hair behind her ears, turning to hide her smile. "Clem, are you sitting down?"

Clementine knelt on the wood in front of them.

Alex asked, "What's 'please'?"

Clementine looked towards Sunju, who hesitated before putting her hand to her chest and rubbing a circle into it. Alex followed suit.

"Good," Clementine told Alex.

Alex beamed. "Now I can be polite!"

Tulsi snorted. "That's your first impulse in a new language?"

"What's yours? Oh, right. Swearing." Alex shuffled until she was lying on her stomach, cheek pillowed on her hand. Evening light slanted through the tiny window onto her hair, making it glow.

Honey hair, Clementine thought.

Alex tilted her head. "What?"

Clementine cleared her throat. She'd been staring. "Nothing. Is that natural?"

Alex tugged at a stray blonde lock pooling on the mattress. "The color or the curl? Both fake. See the roots?" She tilted her head. The smallest hint of brown sat at her hairline.

"Huh."

Alex lowered her voice. On the other end of the mattress, Sunju and Tulsi had started arguing about the best kind of pencil. "Yeah, I hit high school and decided I wanted a change. Started dressing nice, doing my hair, all of that."

Alex looked suddenly shy. She didn't talk much about life before high school. None of them did.

Clementine's hand made a circle around her own face.

"What does that mean?"

Clementine's throat clicked. Too late to back down now. "'Beautiful.'"

Alex's face went slack. For a second, Clementine thought she'd ruined everything, but then Alex's face bloomed in a smile so blazing it made Clementine forget anyone who'd ever hurt her.

A loud cough. Sunju thumped her chest. "When did Ms. Ryans say she'd call Joseph's reference?"

Alex took a second to reply, flustered. "Uh, she didn't. But if she's going to tell us tomorrow, she's running out of time in the—"

Tulsi cut her off with a triumphant cry, digging her vibrating phone out with a flourish. She pressed it to her ear and cleared her throat. When she opened her mouth again, the voice of an old woman with a Spanish accent spilled out.

"Hello, this is Mrs. Jones." A beat. "Ohhh, Mr. Joseph! Yes, yes—wonderful man. Great worker. Ten out of ten, absolutely recommend—"

"Tone it *down*," Sunju whispered.

Tulsi batted at her. Sunju had been the one to suggest that Tulsi be the fake reference.

"Hands down, one of the best teachers I've ever worked with," Tulsi continued.

Alex bent close, grinning. "She sounds just like her grandma."

Clementine smiled back. The sunset was in full force now, bathing the mattress in orange and catching Clementine on the knee.

"Thank you sooo much," Tulsi said, and clicked to end the call. "Oh Jesus, that sun." She held up a hand to shield her eyes.

Clementine had never seen her wear sunglasses. How was that possible? Tulsi seemed like the epitome of a sunglasses girl. She was the kind of girl you put on sunglasses billboards, draped over a car with a dangerous smile.

Sunju watched Tulsi anxiously. "Did she buy it?"

Tulsi's mouth spasmed, trying to keep her smile cool and under control. "I think we have our gym."

Alex whooped, clambering down the mattress to drag the other two into a hug. "Good work, Tulsi!"

"Ew," Tulsi said. "Get off me." But neither she nor Sunju moved.

Alex stretched out, and Clementine moved cautiously to join the hug, nestling into the space between their heads. Someone else's hair against her forehead. Three sets of breathing mingling with hers.

Lovely. Stifling. Clementine had never good with touch. In her experience, it was always something to be wary of.

"I'll go tell Joseph," Clementine said, and stood.

Alex beamed. "See you later!"

She signed the *later* just like Clementine had taught her before their first fight. Clementine had to bite her cheek to stop a goofy smile.

She paused near the door, watching the three of them pull away. Being a witness to the hug was almost better than being in it: all the joy without the discomfort. Part of her ached for it, but it was easy to ignore as she watched the girls stained with sunset on her mattress, waiting for her to come back.

CHAPTER TEN

"**Damn**," **Tulsi said as Sunju** flung herself into the front seat. "Where's the fire?"

"Just drive," Sunju told her.

Tulsi shrugged and gunned it.

Sunju fell back against the seat, nerves draining from her with every block they passed—farther away from home, closer to her girls.

Her phone buzzed. Sunju got it out. "Alex says to hurry up. There are more than twenty girls in the gym."

"Oh, let me just run this red light—"

"Don't you dare."

Tulsi snickered. Her mouth twisted bitterly. "Quentin really came through. Surprised the whole student body didn't turn up."

Sunju was surprised at how many girls were signing up to get the crap kicked out of them. She dug her blunt nails into her phone casing. "Did you tell Alex they can start without us?"

"Duh. She said no. Said we're *important*."

Sunju scoffed.

Tulsi grinned. "What? You're important, Sunju."

"Shut up." Sunju rested her cheek against the window, a curious feeling coming over her. For most of her life, leaving her house had felt like running away. For the first time, it felt like she was running towards something.

"**This**," **Tulsi announced,** "is *way* more than twenty girls."

Sunju made a noise in agreement. They were standing in the gym doorway, the hallway dark behind them. Even the janitor had gone home for the night.

At least thirty girls stood in the gym, chatting, laughing, tying their hair back. Who were these girls who were so excited to get beat up by their classmates?

"Sunju! Tulsi!" Alex waved at them from the top of the bleachers. Other than Clementine, she was the only one not on the floor. "Come over here!"

Sunju clambered up the bleachers, sliding into place next to Clementine. "Where's—"

Clementine pointed. Quentin sat against the opposite wall, resting her feet in Yazmine's lap. A few more cheerleaders had tagged along this time, and Sunju watched their mouths curve around giggles Sunju didn't want to know the origin of. She had an alliance with Tulsi—she *liked* Tulsi—but she didn't like or trust the rest of that waspish team, especially Quentin, no matter how hard she tried to convince herself otherwise for Alex's sake.

On the other side of the gym, Quentin threw her head back in a laugh, red hair blazing.

Stay there, Sunju thought. *Keep your fire away from us.*

Alex clapped sharply. All eyes turned to her.

"Before we start the first official meeting of Girls Night . . ." Alex began.

Sunju frowned. They'd had Girls Night twice before this. Were they not official until they got out of Alex's garage?

". . . we have to go over some rules," Alex continued. Sunju waited for her to break out the binder she'd mentioned, color coding the rules into groups, but Alex just took a deep breath and listed them out.

"First rule of Girls Night: no shoes. Second rule: no eye gouging. Third: no biting, ladies! Fourth: no jewelry of any kind. Fifth: we clean up after. If you're unsure how to disinfect cuts or cover bruises, we have our resident makeup artist. Sunju?"

Sunju raised a timid hand. A few girls waved back.

"Last rule," Alex announced. "No talking about the club, IRL or online. No texting, photos, hashtags, or vague posts. *Fight Club* is a movie we watched at thirteen to feel like badasses; it has nothing to do with our lives. Got it?"

A cheer went up. Alex flushed, pleased.

She looked good up there, Sunju thought, craning her neck to see which two girls Alex would pick to fight first. A born leader. In another life, she could have led armies.

The girls were freshmen, still growing into their curves. Sunju didn't know their names. Their eyes were wide at the start of the fight and wider at the end. The only difference was the light inside: they'd slunk into the first fight nervously, bowing jokingly to mark the start. By the end, they were shaking, bellowing, slinging their arms around each other's shoulders.

Sunju felt a flash of warmth watching them lean their sweaty foreheads into each other. Then the next fight started.

Sunju averted her eyes from that first punch. "Why do so many people like fighting?"

Tulsi paused. She'd been cheering—not for anyone in particular, but for the fight itself. At first, Sunju thought Tulsi would make fun of her, maybe give her a withering side-eye. But Tulsi leaned back against the bleachers. "Don't you ever get this boundless rage?"

Sunju's pencil paused. She'd been drawing Alex's face lit from above, addressing her subjects.

"Like . . ." Tulsi fitted her tongue through her teeth and bit down, then continued. "Adults act like children, and then they tell you to grow up. Guys leer at you on the bus, and if you tell them to leave you alone, they tell you to chill out. Friends can be assholes." She nudged Sunju, a sharp elbow against the bone of Sunju's shoulder. "Don't you get mad?"

A wild cheer went up. One girl had the other in a headlock, shoving her captive repeatedly into the ground. On the other side of the gym, Quentin smiled so hard her gums showed, pale pink against her Colgate-white teeth. Sunju bet she'd never had to go to the dentist to have them pick out an infected shard of molar, her parents insisting they didn't know how her tooth got broken.

Sunju ran her tongue over the empty spot at the back of her gums where her last molar should have sat. "I'm mad all the time."

Whatever Tulsi was going to reply, it was lost in the cheers.

Menacing footsteps up the bleachers. Sunju only had to watch Tulsi's face close off to know who was coming.

Quentin caught Alex's hand and pulled her to her feet. "Alex! My team wants to ask you some Girls Night questions; come over."

"Oh! Okay." Alex shot a smile over her shoulder at the girls as Quentin tugged her down the bleachers. She even waved.

Sunju checked to see if her uneasy feeling was warranted. Tulsi was grinding her teeth; Clementine's expression was carefully blank in a way that meant she was hurt and trying not to show it. That wasn't normal, right? Sunju wasn't alone in being worried about Quentin and Alex?

Tulsi stood up on the bleachers. "AMARA, STOP BEING A LITTLE BITCH! I SAW YOU PUNT THAT VOLLEYBALL INTO STEPHANIE CHRISTIAN'S FACE LAST YEAR; I KNOW YOU CAN FIGHT BETTER THAN THAT!"

Amara raised her bloody head, dazed. She was still in the headlock, punching blindly at her opponent's chest. At Tulsi's words, her lip curled. She reached up, closed her hand around her opponent's hair, and yanked.

The girl's shriek was almost as loud as Tulsi's triumphant yell.

Sunju's gaze caught on Tulsi's ears. "Are you letting your earring holes close up?"

Tulsi startled. She'd taken them out for Girls Night last week and seemingly never put them back in.

"Yeah," she said quietly. "Guess so."

"It looks good."

Tulsi didn't answer. Sunju watched her thumb at the skin around her earlobes where all those scarlet studs had been. The skin wouldn't heal smoothly, but it would heal.

A timid cough made them look down.

"Um, hello?" A girl stood at the bottom of the bleachers, waving at Clementine. "Alex told me, um . . . you can teach me how to punch properly?"

Clementine sat very still. She leaned around Tulsi's legs to look at Sunju, as if Sunju could be of any help in this conversation.

Sunju shrugged.

"Alright," Clementine said slowly, and headed down the bleachers.

Sunju was nose-deep in her sketchbook—Tulsi lying on the bleachers, shouting biting criticisms every thirty seconds; Clementine demonstrating proper fighting stances to a growing group of girls; Alex with Quentin in her lap on the other side of the gym—when someone said, "Hi."

Sunju looked up. A freshman from the first fight stood at the bottom of the bleachers. A black ring bloomed over her eye.

"I don't know how to hide these," she admitted sheepishly. She hugged her elbows, a motion that reminded Sunju of a toddler. These freshmen got younger every year. "Alex said—"

Sunju stood up. Her sketchbook fell off her lap.

"Sorry." She wrangled her sketchbook into her bag, resurfacing with her makeup kit. She surveyed the girl in front of her: dark brown skin. She would need start buying different shades of foundation. "Do you have makeup?"

The girl nodded.

"Show me."

Most of the girls hadn't watched the necessary makeup tutorials. The fights had been over for half an hour by the time Sunju left, hands smudged with four different tones of foundation, trying to remember the names of all the girls who had introduced themselves during the night.

Alex grabbed her laundromat girls in a hug as they walked out into the dark parking lot. Quentin had left after the last fight, and Sunju had tried not to look relieved.

"This was so fun!" Alex cried. "I'm so glad you guys are here."

"Calm down," Tulsi told her, car keys jingling where her hand was trapped next to Sunju's hip.

Alex hugged them harder. She hadn't fought tonight, but Girls Night adrenaline didn't require punching. Just being there lit you up. Even Sunju felt it, dizzy with the yells and the energy.

Alex gave them one last squeeze before leaning back, glowing under the moonlight. "Next one will be even better."

Sunju thought of the timid girls shoving each other into the floorboards. A cheering crowd, hands raising at the question of *Who's next?* Alex, taller than all of them, head held high and powerful. A busted cheek turning smooth and clean under Sunju's cautious hands.

All these girls showing up to get punched. All these girls showing up for something even more than punching.

The next Girls Night was alright. More sketching, more averting her eyes from the violence and hiding the aftermath, more girls forgetting their makeup. A few from last time sat next to Sunju as she demonstrated how to cover a bruise, asking about the tutorials she'd recommended.

It was nice, being of use. Having so many people say her name like she mattered. But the highlight of the night was still the ride home in Tulsi's car, everybody singing along to a hit from SingStar that Sunju didn't remember until the chorus dropped.

The one after that was good, despite the girl who had an asthma attack. Sunju sat with her until it subsided, googling symptoms and patting her back. The fights started up again after that, and Sunju traced a pencil around the shape of Clementine's hard shoulders.

"I have better shoulders than that," Tulsi told her, and flexed.

"You're broad," Alex corrected, eyes fixed on Clementine's expert punches as she whaled on a senior. "She's got *muscles*."

"Screw you. I'm muscly." Tulsi flexed a second time. Sunju concentrated so hard on not looking at her biceps she didn't notice she was drawing Clementine's spine wonky until it was too late.

Alex joined in the next fight. On the drive home, Sunju watched them in the rearview mirror of Tulsi's car, Alex's cheek pillowed on Clementine's shoulder, Clementine stiff but smiling so softly and tenderly that Sunju had to look away.

The next one was glorious.

All this time, Sunju had been assuming she would only like slivers of Girls Night. She'd like sitting with her friends or driving home afterwards. She'd like sharing Alex's homemade snacks. She'd like people listening to her when she talked. She'd like touching girls' soft cheeks, showing them how to hold the brush, tilting their heads.

She would *tolerate* the other aspects of Girls Night. She'd put up with the violence for the sake of her new friends, and she'd keep her eyes on her sketchbook or her makeup kit or her girls.

Then, a few weeks into their strange arrangement, Sunju looked over in the middle of putting the first layer of foundation onto a sophomore's cheek and found herself breathless.

It wasn't the fight—it was the girls. It was the gym lights turning everything hazy. It was the cheer rising like a prayer, sweat like a benediction, Alex's voice an invocation above their heads.

"Next fight!" she screamed, cheeks flushed, one eyebrow bloody.

The girls screamed back, Tulsi and Clementine among them, perched on the bleachers with their fists raised.

Beautiful. Sunju still didn't understand it, still flinched away from it . . . but the weight of these girls' love for it made Sunju's chest clench. She'd been alone for so long. It was a relief to be a part of something.

"I think you're my favorite."

Sunju startled. The girl sitting in front of her beamed around a split lip.

"What?"

"Ringleader," the girl said, tilting her bruised cheek for Sunju to continue her work. "I think you're my favorite."

Sunju blinked. "What's a Ringleader?"

CHAPTER ELEVEN

Ringleaders. Four of them. No Quentin in the lineup, which Tulsi made sure to rub in her face every chance she could get. Then she got dropped three times in a single cheer practice. She brought it up less after that.

Tulsi was, predictably, the Cheerleader. Not the most original name, but half the reason Tulsi had taken the cheer gig in the first place was the status. As titles went, she could do worse.

Clementine was The Bruiser, the epitome of cool. Tulsi kind of wished she could borrow it. Clementine didn't appreciate the coolness of her title enough.

Sunju was The Artist. It was obvious—when Tulsi had heard it for the first time, she'd taken one look at Sunju's pleased blush and smiled so hard she'd had to flee to the bathroom until she could get her face under control. It wasn't even a brutal smile, sharp and proud—no, this smile was mortifyingly fond. Not the kind Tulsi could own up to, especially in front of a crowd.

Then, of course, there was The General. It made Alex sound way more badass than she was, like she was the one orchestrating this whole event, like she was in control. But Tulsi was beginning to get the sinking feeling Alex was making things up as she went along.

She felt this most strongly when Alex spoke to Quentin, and the smart, strong girl Tulsi knew melted into something Quentin could wrap around her little finger. At first, Tulsi had hoped it was all part of some master plan, but the more she watched, the more she came to a horrifying conclusion: Alex really was that naive. She really was falling for Quentin's bullshit, just like Tulsi had.

It was difficult to watch. Even more difficult to ignore. But if there was one thing Tulsi was good at, it was ignoring shit.

Case in point: keeping her eyes straight ahead as she passed Alex's locker three weeks after the first gym meeting of Girls Night. She'd been about to veer sideways and bump Alex into the wall—love taps, she insisted—when she heard Alex let out a high, desperate laugh that only occurred around one person.

Tulsi veered away from the redhead she hadn't seen behind Alex until now, but of course, she didn't tear her gaze away fast enough.

"Tulsi!" Alex sounded overjoyed, like they hadn't just seen each other last night and weren't texting this morning. "You have a free period now, right?"

Out of the corner of her eye, Tulsi saw Quentin wave, her smile a dark crimson slash. She used to leave that same color on Tulsi's neck.

Tulsi ignored them, fuming and anxious. Her stomach churned. She packed away the sick feeling until it was small enough to ignore, telling herself it would be gone after the next Girls Night.

If Tulsi packed all the Quentin shit aside, things were good. *Great*, even. Girls Night was a roaring success. It went from being once a week to twice, then three times, and after that, Tulsi stopped bothering to go to every session.

There was something so beautiful about all these girls filing into the gym to holler and spit and beat the crap out of each other. How had no teenage girl come up with this before?

"We should sell tickets," Tulsi told Alex.

Alex looked over. They were at their usual spot at the top of the bleachers, looking over their kingdom of bloody knuckles.

"That makes it inaccessible to less privileged people, Tulsi," Alex said, like she'd actually thought about it. The girl was ridiculous. Tulsi didn't know how Alex had made it through high school without her.

Alex frowned at her phone.

Tulsi leaned over. "What?"

"Someone's been breaking the rules." Alex tilted the phone towards her, showing an Instagram feed. Blurry photos of blood on wooden floors. A crimson-stained grin. Two girls with their faces hidden in each other's shoulders, their knees scraped, knuckles bright red. There were about twenty posts in total, all of them tagged *#GirlsNight*.

"They're being vague," Tulsi said. She flicked through the accounts. All anonymous accounts turned to private. "*I can't even tell who they are.*"

"Still," Alex said. "I'll have to give another talk about keeping it off socials."

"Gotta keep the girls in line." Tulsi grinned.

Alex grinned back. For a second, the worry lingered in her face. Then Tulsi leaned into her and said, "Right, General?" and Alex's face melted into the same brilliant joy she got whenever anyone addressed her by her new title.

The next night, Clementine asked Tulsi why she didn't just quit the cheer squad if she didn't like Quentin.

Tulsi scoffed. "Uh, because cheerleading is awesome, and I'm good at it?"

Clementine eyed her. Scissors slid into a stack of bandages, cutting a long line. They cut them in groups nowadays—too many girls needed wrapped knuckles.

Tulsi took a bandage, twining it around her fingers. She might not fight tonight, but she needed a reason to avoid Clementine's gaze. She saw too much sometimes. She rarely called Tulsi on her shit, which Tulsi appreciated, but she *saw*. Tulsi didn't like anyone seeing past the sharp mask she'd constructed. She'd put a lot of work into it.

"I don't know what she'd do to me," she admitted, rolling white around her healing knuckles. "If I quit."

Clementine's gaze was like a brand. Tulsi was relieved when Alex climbed up the bleachers, asking for Clementine's expertise.

"You do it better than me," Alex said, holding out her hands.

Clementine's jaw clicked shut. She got up and took the bandage. Tulsi had a theory: she went silent when she got nervous.

Tulsi shot Sunju a look. Sunju was already looking at her, hiding a smile behind her sketchbook. They hadn't talked about it, but Tulsi was pretty sure the looks meant, *Alex/Clementine 4eva; Alex/Quentin can go suck rocks.*

Put that *in the Girls Night hashtag,* Tulsi thought.

"You do it really well," Sunju said. "Alex talks about it all the time."

"Oh." Clementine's grip faltered. "Thank . . . you."

"You're a bandage expert!" Alex grinned. A little shy, but nothing compared to the giddy nerves she had around Quentin. Was that good? Was being more comfortable around Clementine good or bad?

A yell went up. The next fight was about to start, and a girl wanted Ringleader permission to wear her purity ring.

"No jewelry," Alex called back.

The girl groaned. "I promised my dad I won't take it off until I'm married!"

"Ew," Tulsi muttered. Sunju and Clementine nodded in agreement.

Alex glanced up. "Not even for a shower? Not even when you're kneading dough?"

"No!"

For a moment, Tulsi thought she wouldn't turn away, that she'd stay here with them and shoot the shit like they did during so many fights. But Alex squeezed her newly-wrapped hands around Clementine's, glowing with delight.

"Duty calls," Alex chirped, and flounced down the bleachers to bestow the General's wisdom.

A month after the first official meeting of Girls Night, Sunju caught Tulsi in the halls between classes and handed her a set of stapled pages. It took Tulsi a second to realize what was happening.

"Cutting it real close, Park." Tulsi slid the papers into her bag. Sunju had put them in a clear file—considerate of her.

"It's not due until 3 p.m.," Sunju replied. "It's 1. You have *ages*."

Tulsi laughed. Sunju was getting better at this—making her laugh. She was also getting better at not looking shocked at the result. Tulsi got the feeling Sunju hadn't gotten many chances to be funny before, too busy being Sunju Park, wallflower extraordinaire.

Tulsi slung her backpack over her shoulders with a wince. She really had to start spacing out Girls Night and cheer practice. Having them one day apart wasn't enough. Her back was one big bruise.

"Thanks," Tulsi said, "for the essay."

"Thanks for the blackmail," Sunju said.

Tulsi laughed. This one was wooden. She still wasn't sure how mad Sunju was about that, and how much was teasing.

Sunju hesitated. Then she clapped Tulsi on the elbow, feather-light. "Well! Friendship over."

For a moment Tulsi was struck dumb, caught between dumb panic *(holy shit, is she serious?)* and delirious affection (*she's messing with me, oh my god, I like her so much*) until Sunju finally cracked a smile.

Tulsi wet her lips. "Good luck getting rid of me, asshole. I'm a goddamn fungus."

Sunju laughed. It was a rusty laugh, like Clementine's, the type that didn't get brought out that often. She wavered, and for a horrifying, wonderful moment, Tulsi thought she might step into Tulsi's space. Tulsi felt herself sway back on instinct.

Sunju's smile twisted. Her head ducked. She hadn't ducked it before the smile—when had that started happening?

"See you later," she said, and hurried into the stream of girls changing classes.

Tulsi's cheeks burned. She watched Sunju's dark head disappear into the crowd, unable to decide if she was disappointed or relieved.

Six weeks after the first gym meeting, Tulsi watched a sophomore called Jem beat the living shit out of a student librarian. She'd never been in a fight, she'd told the crowd before laying into her opponent with the delighted violence of a hungry toddler beating a pinata.

Tulsi knocked Alex's knee. "Kid's good."

Alex snorted. "Kid? We're *one* year above her."

"Don't disrespect your elders," Tulsi said. She was one month and three days older than Alex.

Alex laughed, distracted. The view was better from up here, on the bleachers. Tulsi kept expecting girls to climb higher than the first rung, but they never did. A few newbies tried, but they were always yanked back by the others. And there were always others— more and more every night. Every time Tulsi went into the changing room after gym class nowadays, there was always a bruised thigh, a split lip, a busted eyebrow.

Girls grinned at Tulsi in the halls, and wasn't that a trip? They still avoided her path, but not out of fear she'd snap at them. Their lowered gazes were heavy with reverence.

#TheCheerleader had appeared in the Girls Night hashtag, accompanied by blurry photos of Tulsi's knee on someone's back, Tulsi's black hair arcing out behind her as she charged—all faceless, of course. Someone had made a Pinterest board with pictures of blood and glitter, pompoms and bloody elbows, mean grins and dark hair, and captioned it with *The Cheerleader aesthetics*. Alex had given the social media talk twice in the last week, but the posts were only gaining momentum.

Jem pinned her opponent to the ground, bashing her head against the floorboards—once, twice, three times. The girl tapped out, shrieking.

"She never talks to anybody at school," Alex said. "Never raises her hand in class. Now look at her."

Jem raised her fists, flushed and beaming as classmates came over to slap her on the back and shake her shoulders. Jem laughed through bloody teeth, one eye swelling, skirt ripped. Her eyes shone with the fight: revelation.

Tulsi felt her mouth stretch into a smirk. "Look at what we can do."

Jem wobbled over to the bleachers, sweaty hair falling out of her face as she tipped it back to watch Alex.

"I want . . ." she said, and swallowed. The usual Girls Night chatter quieted as everyone turned to look at the sophomore taking audience with the General.

"I wanted to say," Jem called up at Alex, "thank you for creating this. I didn't want to come tonight, but I . . . I didn't know how much I needed it. Thank you."

Alex stood. Tulsi waited for her to say something, but she just nodded.

Jem nodded back. Almost bowed. It was a joke, but part of it was true. There was true devotion in Jem's eyes as she backed away and the chatter started back up.

"Hey, do you think—" Tulsi looked over, words dying in her throat. Alex had that same revelatory look in her eyes, only growing bigger as the cheers subsided.

Alex's head jerked towards her. "What? Sorry, you said . . . something."

Tulsi had been about to ask if they wanted to stop at McDonalds on the drive home. It seemed like a pointless question with Alex full of wonder and hunger, staring into space. She got like this sometimes during Girls Night, but this seemed . . . intense. Like she really did have a plan, or at least the start of one.

"Look at what we can do," Alex said, dazed.

"Stealing my line," Tulsi muttered, watching her cautiously. "Alex. Seriously. What are you thinking?"

Alex shook her head. Not a refusal: a delay. She'd tell Tulsi when the thoughts were ready. She glowed under the gym lights, looming tall and gorgeous over the room.

"Like she could lead armies," Sunju whispered, and Tulsi shivered.

CHAPTER TWELVE

There was a girl crying in the first-floor bathroom.

Alex paused. She'd been fixing her lip liner when a choked sob sounded from the furthest stall, the occupant unable to keep quiet any longer.

Alex's first thought was, *I hope she's alright.* Her next was, *Maybe it's hot gossip,* before she remembered she was no longer gossip queen of Sterling; she'd handed in the mantle to become the General.

Alex turned, filled with bright purpose. *Ringleader.* Girls gazed at her with devoted eyes and open ears, waiting for her words. Jem had panted at the bottom of the bleachers, calling up in thanks.

Look at what we can do, Alex mouthed. She cleared her throat. "Hello?"

More stifled sobbing.

"Are you hurt?"

"No," came the croaky reply, clogged with tears. "Please go away."

"Do you want to talk? I'm Alex. What's your name?"

A low sniffle. The door creaked open to reveal a girl hunched on top of a toilet, high heels scraping the lid. Her smudged mascara was so winged it was becoming ambitious, and her brown hair was cut in a way that would've been fashionable in the 80s. Somehow, it suited her anyway.

The girl raised her chin, trying to look haughty. "I'm Becca."

"Hi, Becca." Alex crouched down in the stall. "What's up?"

Becca snorted, swiped a hand down her face. "Just . . . guys being dicks."

Alex nodded sympathetically, trying not to let boredom seep into her expression. Some part of her always closed off when girls talked about their boy troubles. "Boyfriend stuff?"

"*Ugh.*" Becca grabbed a wad of toilet paper, blotting furiously at her makeup-streaked cheeks. "I'd rather die. No, they're just . . . they're calling me and saying shit. Messaging me and saying shit. Driving past my house and throwing shit."

"Shit," Alex said.

Becca barked a laugh. "Yeah."

"Can I ask what it's about?"

Becca eyed her warily. "Aren't you . . ."

"I won't tell anyone." Alex took her damp hand, smiling encouragingly. She meant it. She'd never meant anything more. Alex had a new cause, and it was righteous.

Becca looked disappointed. "So, you don't trade favors for favors?"

"Secrets. And no, not anymore."

"Huh. Shit." Becca sniffed. "The guys are, um, from my old school. Sterling Boys."

"Oh," Alex said. Then, as the implication sunk in: "*Ohhh.*"

Becca nodded. "One of them thinks I stole his girlfriend. That I, like, *turned* her."

Alex closed her mouth. She'd assumed the problem was Becca being trans. Going off Becca's judging eyes, she absolutely knew it.

"Can't steal someone who wants to leave," Alex tried.

Becca's gaze softened. "She's . . . we're not even together. And she's not gay! She's bi! It's not that she can't like guys; she just doesn't like *him.* But try to tell *him* that—"

"I will," Alex said.

Becca stopped. Her hand loosened on the wad of paper. "What?"

Alex stood. It was hard to feel like a righteous angel in a toilet stall, but she managed it. "I'll make him leave you alone."

"Oh. Um, thanks?" Becca squinted. "Is this a . . . a Girls Night thing? Beating guys up? Do you have, like, hitgirls?"

"Nope! Special service, just for you." Alex led her out of the stall.

Becca scuffed a shoe against the floor and stopped halfway through the motion, probably because if those shoes were as expensive as Alex thought they were, they shouldn't be going through any amount of scuffing.

"I'll pay you back," Becca said. "Like . . . I'll owe you."

"No payment necessary."

"Seriously, I'll—"

Alex waved her away. "Sometimes I'd just tell girls whatever they wanted to know, whether they had a secret to trade or not. I didn't actually care about, like power. I just wanted to talk to people, you know?"

She cringed internally. *Oh my god, that's sad. I thought it'd be comforting, but it was just sad. Change the subject!*

She shot Becca her sunniest grin. "Anyway! Give me your number, and I'll get all the details."

Becca's smile was uncertain, probably because Alex looked way too eager to go on this errand for a girl she didn't even know.

They traded phone numbers. By the end of it, Becca's sniffle was gone.

"Let me know when you want that favor," she said, and turned to leave.

Alex beamed at her reflection, reaching once more for her lip-liner.

The door swung open. A pause.

THWACK!

Alex turned. Becca was a heap on the floor, struggling to get her knees underneath her. Two girls stood above her, giggling. They'd come in, seen who was trying to get to the door, and shoved her.

Alex was moving before she realized it, fists clenched, ready to . . . what, punch them? Alex had never punched anyone outside of Girls Night, but there was a white buzz in her ears and a hot rage in her gut.

The girls' smiles died as Alex surged towards them.

Becca held up a hand. "I'm fine."

Alex stopped. Her march had put her right at Becca's side. "Are you sure?"

Becca nodded. Her cheeks were flushed. She wobbled to her feet, high heels unsteady on the linoleum.

The girls stared. Alex had seen them at Girls Night, teeth bared, baying for blood.

Alex peeled her lips back from her teeth. "If you think—"

Becca's hand shot out and closed around her wrist. Her eyes were pleading. *Don't*, she mouthed.

Alex's lips thinned. She jerked her head at the girls. "Pee somewhere else!"

They fled.

Alex turned. "Why—"

"It's a new school." The words seemed like a struggle. Becca wiped at her clammy cheeks. "It'd be—it'd be awesome, watching you yell at them. But not worth it. I don't want . . . it's a new school," she repeated, shoulders slumped, face set in angry lines.

Alex nodded. "I'll stop those guys from harassing you," she said. It didn't feel like enough. Alex touched the back of her hand. "You should come to Girls Night sometime."

Becca's throat bobbed. She brushed her 80s hair out of her face with a short, sharp shake. "I'll think about it."

"You look weird," were Tulsi's first words to Alex after she stormed up to their study session and announced they were taking a walk.

Alex stared at her.

Tulsi flipped her off but obligingly pushed her chair back. "Walking," she said. "Whatever our leader says. Come on, girls."

Alex led them to the parking lot where all this had started.

"Aw, memories," Tulsi said flatly. "What's so important that you—"

She stopped. At the end of the parking lot was an abandoned warehouse. The door used to bear the words HARTBURN CANDIES, the paint old and peeling. The words were gone. In their place was a painted hand towering over them, white and gleaming, nails painted coral pink, fingers clenched into a fist.

Underneath were the words, LOOK AT WHAT WE CAN DO. Despite Alex's warnings about keeping Girls Night off socials, it was already a hashtag. This graffiti was already in a dozen posts, and now almost every Girls Night post came with a *#lookatwhatwecando* hashtag. Alex scrolled through it late at night, cycling through all her apps with a spark growing in her gut.

Alex stood under the fist and announced, "Girls, I think we can do more."

The others looked at each other with less enthusiasm than Alex would have liked.

"Girls Night started out as this fun little thing to let off steam," she continued. "But now it's . . . it's *helping* people. Don't we have a duty to make this bigger? To help even more?"

No one met her eyes, which was fine. She could see the start of something in their imaginations. Even Tulsi looked thoughtful, though she was trying to hide it by examining her shoes.

Wrapped knuckles, eyes going from dull to glowing. Girls helping each other to their feet. A shouting crowd turned into one organism, mouths opening as one . . .

"We can really *do* something," Alex stressed. Her throat was tight. She couldn't help it, not with the graffiti so bright and clear behind her, the memory of Becca on the floor fresh in her mind.

Up on the bleachers, all eyes on her. She had to *deserve* it, right? She had to give all those girls something worth following.

"How would you guys like to take a trip during lunch tomorrow?"

"Uh, sure," Clementine said slowly. Sunju was soon to follow.

Tulsi rolled her tongue in her mouth. "I'm assuming you just did that thing where you offer up my car without asking."

"I did."

"Thanks for letting me know."

Alex braced for her to say something cutting.

Tulsi flicked her dark hair away from her sharp cheekbones and sighed. "Where're we going?"

The boy went to Sterling Girls' sister school.

In the car, Clementine admitted she hadn't known Sterling Girls *had* a sister school.

Alex twisted around in the passenger's seat. "Whose games did you think we cheer at?"

Clementine shrugged. "Our volleyball team or something."

Tulsi laughed, loud and surprisingly unguarded. It made Alex smile.

Sterling Boys High was as disappointing as its sister school, with the added stomach kick of being packed with teenage boys. There was something disheartening about watching them in groups.

Tulsi pointed. "There."

Alex cupped her hands around her mouth. "BRYCE!"

A trio of boys looked up from a set of concrete steps. The boy at the front twisted his cap around and grinned, freckles creasing. The freckles made him look friendly. Everything else—backwards cap, the aggressiveness of his sprawl, the hot-shitness of his grin— made Alex's skin crawl.

Sunju exchanged a dubious look with Clementine as Alex hugged him.

"Footballer," Alex explained.

"Don't forget middle school!" Bryce laughed as he pulled back. "You always had the best snacks. Never stingy about sharing, either." He slapped Alex's shoulders, ignoring how it startled her, then turned to Tulsi.

"Tul-*si*." He said it like most people said Tulsi's name: like she was trouble. Unlike some people, though, he phrased it as if he'd prefer his life to have more trouble in it.

"Bryce," Tulsi said, clipped. She had a faint smile, but only because Alex had promised she might get to watch him get punched. She kept eyeing Clementine like she wanted her to go for it.

Bryce wavered towards Tulsi, then stopped.

Wise, Alex thought as he turned back to her.

"What brings you to the bigger and better Sterling? Please tell me you brought more cheerleaders."

"No cheerleaders, Bryce."

"Yeah." Bryce eyed Sunju, who gave a strained smile, averted her eyes, and started picking at the thumbholes in her cardigan. "No shit. So, what's up? Who're these ones?"

"Who're your ones?"

"Hm?" Bryce looked over his shoulder like he had forgotten about the other two boys at all. Both were pointy and scruffy, and everything about them screamed of exactly how profoundly stoned they were. One of them was doing up one of his shirt buttons with the care one would usually put into arming a missile. "Oh, I rotated my group since we hung out. This is Chester and Wong. Say hi, guys."

Both of them grunted.

Tulsi muttered, "I give it two months."

"Huh?"

Alex beamed. "Hey, Bryce! Heard of anyone called Becca? She used to go here?"

Bryce's smile ticked, then faded.

"You're here for *her*?" He groaned and held up his hands, placating. "Okay, look. Once I've explained, I know you'll be on my side."

He took a steadying breath. "She stole my girlfriend. You know Jessica H.? Things were great between us. Then Becca came along with her . . . with her poetry nights and evening coding classes. She totally turned Jessica against me. Suddenly, Jessica's picking fights for no reason, saying I'm an asshole over such *weird* shit, like 'get back in the kitchen' jokes. Who cares, right?"

Tulsi made a noise in the back of her throat.

Alex touched her elbow. "So, she broke up with you and got with Becca?"

"Right."

"That's so weird!" Alex laughed. Every instinct she had told her to keep it as nonthreatening as possible . . . but that spark was still in her gut, burning hotter and hotter. "Becca and Jessica aren't together. I asked their friends."

"Well of course *they're* going to say that," Bryce said sullenly. He spat on the ground. Some of it splattered up onto his sneaker. "Anyway, Jessica will come to her senses eventually. I just have to get Becca to give her up."

He finished with a proud smile, as if waiting for congratulations.

Alex clicked her tongue. "I have to say, Bryce, I'm relieved you're using her pronouns."

"'Course I use them. I'm not an idiot."

Tulsi looked over at Alex, who had to look away to hide her grin.

"Your ex isn't gay," Tulsi said. "She's bi. Just not into *you*."

Bryce laughed.

Tulsi's glare intensified.

Bryce stopped laughing. His gaze darted to Clementine, who was standing stock-still, staring into his lackluster soul.

"Alex," he said, "come on. You . . . you get me, right?"

Alex's smile was fixed in place. It was doing strange things; she could feel it. No more of that peppy friendliness she tried to broadcast at all times. "You're going to stop messing with her."

"You're serious?" Bryce twitched, like he was about to step forward. Alex was surprised to find she wasn't scared. Even though Bryce had two inches on her, even with his classmates starting to pay attention.

Alex stepped forward. "Ask me again how serious I am."

Bryce stared at her, appalled. "I thought you were cool, Alex."

"Oh?" Alex cocked her head. "I always thought you were a loser, Bryce."

Bryce's chin flexed. His shoulders broadened as his cronies came to flank him. "Yeah?"

"Yes!" Alex leaned up, lips skimming Bryce's cheek. "You're never going to mess with Becca again. You're not going to get anyone else to. Want to bitch about her to your friends? Go for it. But you're never messing with her again."

More boys joined them. It wasn't a crowd yet, but it could turn into one, and a crowd could easily turn into a fight—especially if there was testosterone and pride involved.

Alex checked behind her. Sunju looked like she was ready to start apologizing. Clementine's fists were clenched, eyes darting with cautious glances at the boys, taking notice. Alex expected Tulsi to look eager, but her shoulders were tense, almost frightened.

Alex shot her a look. *Chickening out on me?*

Tulsi smirked, but it was too fast—there and gone.

A month ago, it would've made Alex back off. If the mighty Tulsi was freaked out, Alex should be, too. If the dangerous Clementine was wary, Alex should be running for the hills.

I fear no gods or men or scruffy high school boys, Alex thought. It sounded cool. It would make a good post, but she had promised she wouldn't contribute to the Girls Night chatter online. She couldn't betray her own rule. She'd have to settle for writing it on her bedroom wall.

Bryce looked disappointed that his big shoulders and skinny friends weren't making her back down. "I'm . . . going to pretend you didn't say any of that."

"I can repeat it for you!"

Bryce swallowed. He glanced back at his friends. "What is with you, Veck? You got your period or something? Is it that time of the month?"

Light pinpricked into existence and exploded. Alex felt herself grin. "Oh, wow. Say that again."

He showed his teeth and did.

Without breaking eye contact, Alex reached down. She shoved her hand down the front of her skirt. Everyone watched, stock-still, as Alex shifted, as if she was trying to pull on skinny jeans that were a size too small.

"Um," Clementine said.

Sunju made a noise of agreement.

Alex removed her hand. Three of her fingers were streaked with dark, clotted red. Bryce hardly had enough time to drag up a horrified expression before Alex punched him in the face.

"Oh, shit," Tulsi said in a high, strangled voice Alex hadn't heard before.

Bryce stumbled backward onto the concrete steps. Alex was on him before his body even absorbed the impact, smearing her period blood over his face, his lips, forcing her red fingers into his mouth and curling them into his tongue. She felt drunk. She felt righteous. She regretted not doing this to the bullies in the bathrooms.

Bryce screamed, thrashing wildly and making garbled noises for help. It didn't take long for his stoned cronies—*stonies*, Alex thought deliriously—to break through the shock and weed enough to move for Alex, but she was already climbing off him. She moved to wipe her hand on their clothes. Both boys instantly jerked out of range.

Bryce struggled to his feet, gasping. "What . . . what the fuck!" He spat on the deck and wiped his mouth desperately, eyes wild. "What the *shit*, that's *disgusting*, you're *insane*—" He doubled over, gagging.

Alex wiped her shaking hand on her skirt. "You're never messing with Becca—*or* your ex—again. Okay?"

"What?" Bryce choked, his hands braced on his knees. "I—"

Alex started forward.

"God! Okay!" Bryce flung up his hands. "I'll leave them alone!"

Alex beamed. Triumphant sweat beaded under her armpits. Her hands trembled in ecstasy. She felt like she was standing on the bleachers, all eyes on her.

"Thank you," she said sweetly, and turned to go. Three pairs of footsteps followed her, and the sound of them falling into perfect step made Alex want to turn and hug them, punch the air, kiss them all on the lips.

"Security," Clementine said. A harried middle-aged man in a security uniform was advancing on them unhappily.

"Right," Alex said. "We should—"

"Yeah," Tulsi said.

They ran.

By the time they had climbed into the car, Tulsi was laughing so hard, she could barely speak.

"You just . . ." she managed, and then fell back into it. "He was so *scared!*"

Alex dug her forehead into the car seat. She was rapidly approaching the silent stage of laughter, complete with an aching stomach and tears rolling down her face. She wiped her cheeks. Her fingers were still stained faintly with red, and she made a face.

"Don't," Tulsi said, still managing to be threatening through her laughter.

"I wasn't," said Alex, who had absolutely been about to wipe her fingers on Tulsi's car. "I can't . . . I can't believe I *did* that. Oh my god."

She almost wished Quentin was here, but they were more of a one-on-one hang. Anytime she brought these girls into it, things got awkward fast.

Sunju spoke up from the backseat. Alex hadn't seen her laugh like this since that first night in the parking lot. "Did you hear what he asked someone as we were leaving?"

Alex caught her breath. "What?"

Sunju beamed. "He asked if it was toxic. He was worried about getting poisoned—"

The girls burst into laughter so intense, the car vibrated. Alex leaned over to press her head into Tulsi's shoulder. Tulsi just laughed harder. In the backseat, Clementine and Sunju fell against each other.

So close so fast. Alex wanted to be wary of the intensity of this four-way friendship, how fast they'd dived into it, but she couldn't bring herself to feel anything but gratefulness, a shine so deep, it almost surpassed her excitement.

This laughter hurt her chest, her stomach. It was the best thing she'd ever felt, sitting in the car with her friends as they laughed themselves into pain.

CHAPTER THIRTEEN

Look at me, **Alex thought,** and everyone did.

On Tuesdays, Wednesdays, Thursdays, and Saturdays (with the possibility for future expansion), Alex stood on the bleachers and delivered the rules. A growing horde of Sterling girls gazed up at her with glittering, eager eyes.

They stared at her in class—well, at *them*. The Ringleaders. Their titles were known before Alex had even gotten wind of it, which would've been disconcerting before. Nowadays, Alex couldn't care less about her old role as gossip queen of Sterling. She'd only done it so people would talk to her, and *everyone* talked to her now. Girls swarmed her in the hallways to proudly flash their bruises, tell her about winning a fight, demonstrate their new makeup skills. The *#GirlsNight* and *#lookatwhatwecando* hashtags grew by dozens of posts every night, and Alex looked at each and every one, never liking, never commenting, making sure the accounts were anonymous and private, nothing they could track to anybody.

There was one downside to no longer being gossip queen: Alex couldn't figure out who had come up with the Ringleader names. It was annoying.

"I want to thank them for it," she told Sunju as another Girls Night finished up. "Like . . . the *General.* Makes me sound like I should have an eyepatch, but, like, a *sexy* eyepatch. Ow!"

"Sorry." Sunju smoothed a bandage over her eyebrow. Couldn't bury all your injuries in makeup.

Alex looked over her kingdom: girls trickling out, sweaty and satisfied; Clementine showing stragglers how to kick someone's feet out from under them; Tulsi admiring her squadmate's split lip.

Cady caught Alex's eye and skipped over, wiping blood from her mouth. Flecks stained her pink hair. "Alex! I caught some good gossip yesterday if you want to trade?"

A flash of red behind her. Quentin's hair was a bright pile on her head. She flickered her fingers. Alex waved back.

"I'm good," she said, "thanks, Cady. How go the protests? It looks like you're getting more people carrying those signs."

Sunju tilted Alex's head, curving a brush down her cheek.

Cady politely moved with Alex's eyeline. "Yeah, it's great! I've been getting way more people coming up to me in the halls saying they want to help. I think we're really making a difference. Actually, we're thinking of getting all Girls Night up in our protests."

"Getting . . . what?"

"You know." Cady punched the air.

Alex laughed.

Quentin caught her eye again, raising a brow. *Something funny?*

Alex shook her head, careful not to dislodge Sunju. *Tell you later.*

"We'll help with your protests," Alex said. "But don't go getting arrested for assault, alright?"

Sunju snorted, covering it hastily with a cough. They still brought up Bryce's bloody punch at least once a week. Alex made sure to laugh along with them, caught between pride and embarrassment. She still couldn't believe she'd done that.

Cady looked surprised. Then she wilted. "Oh. Okay. I thought . . . okay."

"We'll do something," Alex promised, trying to think of the words that would make Cady stop wilting but also make her go away. "It'll really make people notice. Something bombastic. Talk later, okay?"

Cady nodded and left, pink ponytail bouncing.

Sunju held up a small mirror for Alex to examine her reflection. Other than the bandage over her eyebrow, everything was hidden under a pristine layer of makeup.

"Excellent work as always, Artist." She squeezed Sunju's slender wrist in thanks.

Sunju's hand faltered on her makeup bag. Alex got the feeling she hadn't gotten touched much either before Girls Night.

Another flash of red. Quentin was striding over. She was leaning into brighter reds nowadays, less of the dark lipstick she'd shared with Tulsi. This lipstick was . . . pinker. More like Alex's. "You're coming to my party, right? You didn't text me back."

"I'm sorry, I got distracted! We're totally coming."

Sunju grimaced, zipping up her makeup bag. "I should get home soon."

"Your curfew is ages away! Come onnnn." Alex cast a look at Clementine, who had let a girl out of a headlock to watch Quentin's approach. Tulsi was watching too, though she was pretending not to notice, staring at her squadmate's split lip with an intensity it definitely didn't deserve.

"We're coming," Alex confirmed.

Tulsi's groan was audible from the other side of the gym.

Quentin flicked Alex's bangs. "Looking forward to it, General."

Quentin's house was disappointingly normal. For some reason, Alex had pictured a mansion, complete with a waterslide and crystal chandelier. There was no one with a house like that at Sterling, but it didn't matter—Quentin gave off the air of champagne in gleaming flutes.

There were no waterslides, no crystal. Just a one-story house in the suburbs with fairy lights covering the wallpaper and a scratchy speaker above the drinks table blaring Carly Rae Jepsen.

Sterling girls swarmed around them, taking cups from a plastic sleeve on the ground. Alex led her girls through to the drinks table, hand in hand like a kindergarten class. As they finally reached the table, a senior crouched underneath it and vomited like a cat.

"Jesus," Tulsi said, stepping away from the growing puddle. She poured a shot of vodka into orange juice and passed it to Alex. "It's only 9. Is it a full moon?"

Alex took a sip and wrinkled her nose. She hated vodka. Going off Tulsi's smug look, she knew it.

"We were with Quentin a few hours ago," Sunju added. "How did it get so crazy so fast?"

Clementine tapped Alex on the shoulder. She signed something, and at Alex's blank look, she just pointed. Alex turned to see a smeared window, and beyond it, a glowing full moon.

Alex snorted and pointed this out to Tulsi, who groaned.

"Don't do anything crazy," she warned.

"No, that's your job." Quentin appeared at Alex's elbow. She was sweating, gleaming hair sticking to her forehead in a way that reminded Alex of Girls Night, of Quentin on top of the cheer pyramid, teeth bared, arms wide.

Tulsi nodded at the pool of vomit under the table. "Have fun cleaning that up tomorrow."

Quentin laughed. She had a peculiar laugh when it came to Tulsi: bright and edged, a fruit with a razorblade instead of a pit.

"Your hair looks great," Alex chirped.

"Of course." Quentin scraped her sweaty hair back. Light bounced off her tooth earrings, a shockingly realistic-looking molar hanging from each ear. "Want to dance?"

Alex looked over at her laundromat girls. Sunju and Clementine didn't look excited about the prospect. "I don't know, I think—"

"Not them." She reached up for Alex's bangs, sliding them slowly between her fingers. "Just you."

Alex chugged her drink, feeling her cheeks heat. Was this flirting or a power play? Did she *want* it to be flirting or a power play?

Quentin held out a hand.

Tulsi took it, turning it flat.

"What?" Quentin smiled, all surprise and pleasure. "You want to come?"

"No. Just looking for a joy buzzer."

"You know I'm not that obvious." Quentin took Alex's arm, smearing sweat down her wrist, and dragged her towards the dance floor. Alex turned, tried to sign something at her girls, tell Sunju and Clementine to *talk* to people, but they were immediately swallowed by the gleaming partygoers.

Quentin pulled them into the warm center of the throng. An elbow dug into Alex's side. Quentin stepped on her shoe. She danced like she'd never apologized for taking up space, moving fast and careless. Alex felt lost, and then everything melted away as Quentin's hands found her hips, making them sway in time.

Quentin leaned in close. Her breath was so minty, Alex's eyes watered. "I've watched you, you know, during Girls Night. Tulsi won't spill the beans, but you're *planning* something, right?"

It was hard to think among so much noise, vodka hazing her head, Quentin pressing against her front. "Girls Night can be so much more than a place we go to beat each other up, you know?"

Quentin nodded. This close, you could see the green in her eyes, gleaming like the bottom of a pool. Alex watched her blink and thought of drowning.

"I want it to be bigger than the gym," Alex said. "I want girls to take it home with them. I've been thinking about giving assignments—"

A harsh voice behind them. "Move."

"Sorry—" Alex was already moving when she noticed who it was. "Hey!"

Tulsi took them both by the hands and spun them. Alex went with it, pulling herself in as much as she could. She wasn't the biggest girl on the dance floor, but she came close.

Tulsi spun her to a stop, slotting herself between Alex and Quentin. "You look constipated."

Alex pushed back a wave of irritation at how bothered Tulsi looked, like Alex was some annoying puppy who Tulsi had to untwist from a trap.

"Are the others coming?" Alex craned her head, but no Sunju or Clementine appeared through the crowd.

"Give them a second," Tulsi said. "*Oof.*"

Quentin fluttered her lashes. She'd just shoved her way into the middle of their little dance, a mirror of what Tulsi had just done to them. Alex missed Quentin's hands on her hips telling her what to do.

The song changed over, even faster than the last one.

I'm so cool
Don't need you to save me
I'm free like you
Baby, baby, baby . . .

Quentin and Tulsi's eyes went wide.

"This is just like—" Quentin started.

"*Yes.*" Tulsi grinned.

Quentin took her hands, and for a second, you could mistake them for their freshman selves, orbiting each other like twin moons.

They danced very similarly, Tulsi and Quentin, arcing their bodies in tandem despite their closed eyes. Two vibrations humming on the same wavelength. It made Alex too aware of her own limbs, like she was the only dancer in the lineup who hadn't learned the choreography. Tulsi and Quentin danced like they knew every movement by heart, bodies fitting together almost intimately. Once, they had looked at each other like they were the only two girls in the world. Whatever had happened to break them apart . . . it couldn't be worth the separation. Alex would forgive anything if it meant she could have what Quentin and Tulsi had had in freshman year.

A low voice in her ear. "Alex?"

Alex turned. Sunju and Clementine stood awkwardly among the dancers.

Relief filled Alex's chest. The longer she tried to dance with Tulsi and Quentin, the more she felt like she was interrupting something.

"You came!" She threw her arms around them. The vodka was really hitting. Alex didn't drink much.

Both girls were stiff against her. Clementine bent down. "Everyone's wasted. Not great for talking. Can we go somewhere quiet? I can't hear."

Tulsi grabbed Alex's wrist. "You heard the woman. Let's go."

Alex frowned. A moment ago, Tulsi had been dancing with Quentin like they were best friends again. What was Alex—a bartering tool? A child of divorced parents, weaponized to hurt each other?

Quentin laughed, reached for Tulsi's hair.

Tulsi slapped her hand away. "Don't be one of *those* white girls, Q."

"I can't help it. You look so pretty tonight. Who are you showing off for?"

"I'm just naturally gorgeous." Tulsi tugged once more on Alex's wrist. "Let's *go*, Alex. Q can have her plaything back later."

Don't call me a plaything. Alex opened her mouth to say it, but Quentin talked over her, scraping a finger down Tulsi's cheek.

"You did fancy eyeliner patterns. You want someone to *notice*."

Music throbbed around them. Tulsi's grip was a vice, but she didn't look at Alex. She only glared at Quentin, who gazed back with a brilliant smile, like she was pleased Tulsi had cut into their dance. Like Alex had never been there at all.

Something hot and ugly bubbled up Alex's throat. "Maybe Mr. Keener's around."

Sunju made a low noise. Tulsi's mouth dropped open. Quentin's gaze finally snapped over to Alex, smile freezing in place.

Clementine signed to Sunju: "*What'd she say?*"

"*Later*," Sunju signed back.

Clementine looked annoyed and nodded.

Sunju signed, "*Sorry*," and started fingerspelling, fast and clumsy.

Tulsi's mouth closed into a thin line. "Thought you weren't spreading rumors about me anymore."

Alex ripped her hand back to her side. "It was *one* rumor, ages ago, and it wasn't even that bad!"

"You said I fucked a grown man. When I was *fourteen*."

Sunju winced, her fingerspelling faltering.

"*Ew*," Alex said. "I never said that; I said you *liked* him. It's not my fault people took that and—"

"Don't pretend the mighty Alex Veck's gossip empire didn't have casualties." Tulsi's voice was whip-sharp and shaking. "Don't stand there all high and mighty with your new goddamn empire and pretend you never hurt people."

Tears pricked the edges of Alex's eyes. *Oh god, please, not now.* She blinked hard. "It . . . it wasn't that bad. You handled it."

The bullying had only lasted for a few weeks at the start of freshman year. Alex had tried to stick up for her, tried to make up for her mistake, but every time she'd come close, Tulsi had given her a molten, betrayed look and stormed off. One day, she'd dragged Alex into the bathroom and started yelling.

Don't talk to me anymore, got it? We're not friends. A friend wouldn't pull this shit.

Alex had tried to apologize, but Tulsi had just kept giving her that look, more disappointed than devastated. Like she should've seen this coming.

Alex stayed away after that. It wasn't long before Tulsi had made a senior burst into tears in the middle of the cafeteria. And then came Quentin and the cheer squad, and years had passed, and no one dared to make fun of Tulsi outside of her squadmates, and Alex avoided her in the halls just like everybody else.

Tulsi's eyes were mortifyingly bright in the fairy lights.

Alex started, "Look, it happened a *million* years ago—"

Quentin cut her off. "It was *funny*, Tulsi. You should know how to take a mean joke by now." She dug a newly blunt fingernail into Tulsi's chest. "Sharp heart."

Whatever *that* meant, it was brutal. Tulsi's face screwed up, mouth opening like she was going to start screaming loud enough people could dance to it.

Alex tensed, waiting.

Tulsi slumped. She turned, girls parting to let her leave, until her tall, bobbing head vanished from the room.

Sunju checked her watch. "It's getting late."

"Late," Clementine echoed, not looking at anybody.

Alex opened her mouth to plead, but she didn't want to piss them off any more than she already had. She could feel it, how much they wanted to leave.

She pulled up a desperate smile. "Alright. See you on Monday?"

They vanished into the party. Alex watched the space they left get filled up by girls twisting to the beat.

An arm snaked around her neck. Quentin's many earrings pricked her cheek. "Look at that. Got you all to myself after all."

Alex tried to smile. It fell flat.

Quentin nosed at her cheek. "What?"

"Q, come on. That was messed up. Even if Tulsi was being a dick—"

"She'll get over it! Come with—" Quentin stopped, digging out her phone. Her face lit up in the bright light. "Um . . . one second! Stay there."

She strode off through the crowd, phone at her ear.

Alex craned her head, watching her disappear down the hall towards the back of the house.

"Staying here," Alex said to no one. "Right."

She got another drink. Drank half of it. Felt sick. Tried dancing. Felt more sick.

Five minutes passed, and girls came up to her or conspicuously *didn't* come up to her; whispers from all four corners of the living room, excited glances from the dance floor. Alex yearned for Quentin's hands on her hips, guiding her. She couldn't get Quentin's expression out of her head, the white screen reflected in her surprised, nervous eyes. Alex had never seen her nervous before. Who was on the other end of that call?

The hallway was long, but there weren't many rooms to check. It was a small house. Strange art installations hung on the walls, a riot of color and impossible angles. No family photos.

Just the back porch left. Alex pushed the door open into the dark.

Strained sobs choked to a stop.

Alex froze.

A snatch of noise, like someone trying to muffle a wet gasp.

Alex leaned out cautiously. "Quentin?"

A low croak. "What?"

Alex turned on her phone's flashlight and pointed it towards the voice. Quentin flinched as it revealed her curled in a ball in the corner of the porch. Her face was blotchy, her cheeks wet, mascara running glitter down her face.

Alex's chest tightened with dread. Last year, she'd seen Quentin stumble. Three of her team members had laughed. Quentin had straightened up, eerily calm, and turned to them. Within thirty seconds, the squad members were crying as Quentin pointed out everything they'd done wrong in the last year. Alex trembled to think what she would do to the person who caught her crying in her own home.

"Sorry," Alex said. "I'm . . . I can go . . . I didn't see anything!"

She stumbled back, fumbling for the back door.

Quentin sucked in a gasp. "My mom *sucks*," she said, and collapsed into sobs.

Alex hesitated. Her chest was still twisting, but she couldn't leave *now*.

"Your mom sucks?"

Quentin sniffed hard, sucking snot. "My mom . . . she won't stop taking *trips* since my dad left. Like, *every* excuse she gets. She met this guy last *week*, and he invited her to his beach house, and"— she slapped a hand into her own thigh, dug her nails in—"it's for a whole month! And she keeps saying we'll do more stuff together; she won't run off like Dad! And then she pulls shit like this!"

Another smack to the thigh. Alex thought of punches, the hard wet snap.

"She can't just leave you alone," she heard herself say. "You're sixteen."

"She'll transfer me food money." Quentin let go of her thigh. Five nail marks stood out, deep and dark. "I can handle myself. She's been doing this for years. I just . . . she said we'd start having dinners together!" She crumpled in on herself.

Alex inched down the porch and sat down next to her.

"I have maybe five conversations with my parents a year," she said. "They're too tired for anything else."

Quentin's feet twitched towards her—shiny kitten heels, diamonds along the back. "Yeah?"

"Yeah," Alex said. "Sometimes I want . . . I wanna just grab them. Scream into their faces to just . . . *look* at me."

"Yeah," Quentin whispered. She sniffed again, wiping her face on her sheer shirt. "It's stupid that I'm so upset about this. She does it all the time. But, like . . . I was really looking forward to our dinners. We were going to make beef stroganoff."

She stared at her hands, bruised at the knuckles. She'd never looked younger, not even in freshman year. Had they gone to the same middle school? Alex didn't remember.

"Don't tell anyone about this," Quentin said, and *there* was the threat Alex had been expecting. It was almost a comfort.

"I won't," Alex said. "I . . . we could make beef stroganoff."

Quentin looked at her.

Alex stammered. "I mean, if you want—"

"I'd like that," Quentin said. She rubbed at her vulnerable pale scalp.

Alex never had, and never would, relax in her presence. But in that moment, she'd never felt closer to anyone as the two of them sat on that dark porch, Alex staring at Quentin's skinned knees, Quentin wiping glitter off her own cheeks.

CHAPTER FOURTEEN

Tulsi stalked around the bus stop, vibrating with rage, for barely two minutes before Clementine showed up and punched the glass wall out.

Shards glittered on the ground. Clementine wiped her bloody knuckles on her leather jacket.

"Jesus," Tulsi heard herself say. She nudged a boot against the silvery pile. "That . . . looked fun, actually."

She turned to the other wall and slammed her elbow into it. *Crack!* Not enough. Tulsi brought her elbow down again. Glass spilled onto the concrete.

A delighted laugh climbed Tulsi's throat. She whirled to face Clementine, who was standing strangely still. "Wanna go?" She raised her fists.

Clementine's fingers twitched. Blood dripped off her pinkie. There was none of the savage determination Tulsi had come to recognize, no rage. If anything, Clementine looked . . . disappointed.

Tulsi sat down. "Whatever. Why are *you* pissed, anyway? She wasn't a dick to *you*."

Clementine shifted in the shadows, a stocky silhouette with acne scars. "I caught some of that. Sunju explained the rest before her bus. Alex picked Quentin."

Tulsi wanted to make fun of her. To jeer, poke at her wounds. *You thought you could trust Alex Veck?* Then Clementine turned enough for Tulsi to see her face in the streetlights. That pain was old and reserved and had nothing to do with her ragged knuckles.

Tulsi was not made to comfort, but she could pretend.

"Tonight, sure. I'm sure she'll be back to her regular bullshit self on Monday."

But Tulsi wasn't convinced. Even at Alex's worst, she hadn't lashed out like she had at the party. She didn't know what would be waiting for her on Monday. Another one of Alex's weak apologies? A polite, tight smile? An upturned nose and a middle finger?

Clementine sat down on the bus seat next to her, careful not to let their legs touch. Tulsi snorted. They'd bled on each other, and the girl didn't want to touch her leg.

"My therapist would be disappointed in me," Clementine said, and sighed. "Not disappointed. Just 'wanting me to jump back on the right path.'"

"Path to what?"

"My best self."

Tulsi laughed. "Man, she would *hate* Girls Night."

Clementine shot Tulsi a sideways look, like she had said something weird.

Cars passed in the night. Tulsi kept her eyes on the end of the street, waiting for the bus to come around the corner. Would Clementine ask her about Keener? She hoped not. She had just climbed out of that trembling anger; she didn't want to dive back in.

"How's your car?" Clementine asked.

"Still in the shop."

"Which shop?"

"Not your brother's," Tulsi said.

The bus emerged from around the corner. They stood in unison, glass crunching under their shoes.

It was almost empty. Clementine sat down first, Tulsi in the seat behind her. The back of Clementine's head was scruffy, just like the rest of her. She'd missed a patch shaving her hair. That too-short square of stubble made Tulsi's fingers itch. When she was growing up, she'd feel her big brother's stubble, pushing it back and forth for that satisfying rasp.

She reached forward and felt at the unshaved square.

Clementine stiffened. "Don't."

"You don't make this fun at all," Tulsi told her, and lay her head on the rumbling window to distract from the guilt.

The bus pulled over. Infuriating stillness against Tulsi's forehead.

She sighed. "You missed a spot."

"What?"

"I said you missed a—"

A man's voice echoed down the aisle. "Tulsi!"

Tulsi's jaw clicked violently shut. *Speak of the devil, here he is in khaki pants.*

Mr. Keener patted his slick hair, smiling that stupid, trustworthy smile as he strode down the bus. "Two run-ins in as many months. What are the chances?"

Pretty high. We live near each other. Also, get the hell away from me. Tulsi wanted to spit venom, make use of her sharp heart, but she couldn't open her mouth.

Mr. Keener pointed at the empty seat next to her. "Is this seat taken?"

Oh god, no. Tulsi nodded.

Mr. Keener chuckled. "You always were a funny one."

"Seat's taken," Tulsi mumbled. She still couldn't meet his eyes. Her cheeks burned. She hoped Clementine wasn't paying attention to this shit. If all those girls who posted badass pictures with *#TheCheerleader* hashtag saw this, they'd delete their posts.

"Oh," came Mr. Keener's disappointed voice. "Sorry."

"'S fine."

Clementine slid into the seat. Tulsi hadn't noticed her getting up. Her jean-clad knee pressed into Tulsi's.

"Good to see you, Tulsi." Mr. Keener took a seat a few rows down. Clementine's red knuckles must've put the fear of God into him.

Tulsi lay her head on the window. Rumbling cascaded through her forehead, down into the balls of her feet. As they got closer to her stop, she snuck a look over at Clementine. The girl hadn't looked at Tulsi once since she'd sat down, like she knew Tulsi couldn't take it.

Neither of them spoke until Keener got off. Tulsi watched him out of the corner of her eye, hoping with all her heart that Clementine wouldn't ask.

The doors closed. The bus pulled into the street. Clementine continued staring straight ahead. Maybe she hadn't even noticed he got off?

Clementine said, "He was weird."

"Who?" Tulsi dug her nails into her palms. Houses blurred outside the window. She frowned. "Wait, we're in the suburbs. You missed your stop."

"Right." Clementine hit the stop button, then got up and stood there for the full minute it took for the bus to get to the next stop. Tulsi kept wanting to make fun of her—*just sit down, you weirdo*—but bit her tongue.

The bus pulled over.

"Bye," Clementine blurted.

Tulsi watched her hunched form cross the road, a lump growing in her throat.

She was taking the bus back the way they'd come. She'd stayed on the bus until Keener got off because she knew Tulsi was freaked out. And she didn't even ask why.

Tulsi blinked back awful, mortifying tears. She couldn't remember the last time somebody had done something so sweet for her. She squeezed her tongue with her teeth until heat stopped building behind her eyes and her stop was approaching.

She ran the whole way home.

The light was on. Tulsi stood on the porch until her breathing calmed down, listening to laughter drifting through the screen door and wondering if she should turn around and keep running. But she was tired, and she wanted the day to be over. She pushed open the door.

The laughter paused. A hoarse yell from the living room: "Who is it?"

"A burglar, Auntie." Tulsi threw her boots in the shoe corner. It was even more untidy than usual.

"Oh, good. Take the microwave before one of us electrocutes ourselves with it." Aunt Mags twiddled her long pink fingernails in a wave as Tulsi trudged into the room. Her face creased up in a smile, more wrinkles than her years suggested, and Tulsi fought equal urges to slap her and to rub her face against that warm, papery cheek.

Ingrid and Louis waved from the floor. All three of them were holding bowls of chocolate ice cream. Special bowls, too: Ingrid had I SCREAM, Aunt Mags had YOU SCREAM, and Louis propped WE ALL SCREAM on his hairy knee.

Tulsi lingered warily near the couch. "What are we celebrating?"

A collective gasp went up. Tulsi braced herself.

"My boss promoted me," Aunt Mags stabbed her spoon—a soup spoon, because she was a freak who ate ice cream with big spoons—at Ingrid. "*She's* getting proposed to—"

"For real, or he just teared up at an engagement scene in a movie again?"

Aunt Mags gave Tulsi a dry look. "A woman knows, love. And Louis is getting a callback!"

Louis bowed. It was difficult to do while sitting on the floor, but he managed.

"Nice," Tulsi said. "What for, another toothpaste commercial?"

Three pairs of rolled eyes, all the same shade of brown. Tulsi was just glad her eldest brother, Henri, was on the other side of the world on a fishing boat. Tulsi was the baby of the family. She was determined to move out as soon as she turned eighteen, and unlike the rest of her siblings, she would never move back in.

Tulsi turned to leave. She'd shower, then crawl into bed. She wanted to wash the night off her.

Ingrid hummed around her ice cream. "How was the party?"

"Who says I was—"

"You're *very* dressed up."

You look so pretty tonight. Who are you showing off for?

Tulsi bit her tongue until she tasted blood. "It was shit."

"Oh, Tulsi." Aunt Mags tugged her fraying dressing gown tighter around her body. They bought her a new one every year, just as the old one was falling apart. This one was getting close. "Why is it every time we talk to you, there's another tragedy?"

That old anger rose inside Tulsi like a wave. Why hadn't Clementine taken her up on that fight at the bus stop? If she'd stumbled in bleeding, maybe they'd take her seriously. "You don't know! Maybe someone *died* at the party."

Ingrid rolled a dark curl around her finger. "Did they?"

"Shut up."

Louis flipped her off and examined his eyebrows in the reflection of his spoon. He had the best brows in the family, with zero effort. Tulsi cursed him every time she bent towards a mirror with a tweezer.

Aunt Mags caught his middle finger and lowered it. "Louis, really. Don't encourage her."

"Oh no," Tulsi seethed. "Too late! I'm encouraged."

Aunt Mags sighed. Tulsi was sucking the fun out of the room, she could feel it, and yet she couldn't stop.

"If you knew how hard I've worked—" Aunt Mags started, and Tulsi groaned so loud she had to stop and glare.

"If you knew how hard I worked," she repeated, "you'd know just how privileged you are, having this life. A roof over your head, good food on the table, a loving family—"

Tulsi made a fart noise.

Aunt Mags steamed on, undeterred. Her hand slipped into her dressing gown pocket, and Tulsi imagined the sobriety chip warm in her palm. Fifteen years this December. "—and yes, we all struggle! But you know what else we do? We *pick ourselves back up*, like proper Ortizes. We don't wallow like a pig in shit."

Pig in shit. Sharp heart. Tulsi gritted her teeth, tasting copper.

"Whatever," Tulsi snapped. "I'll just go screw myself then."

They started laughing again before she could get to the end of the hall, bright and flashy. The Ortizes were a birthday cake, and Tulsi was a fly wriggling around in the frosting.

What was so bad about acknowledging when things were awful? She wanted to storm in and lay everything out: the fistfights, her new Ringleader title, Quentin's machinations, Alex's betrayal, running into Mr. Keener on the bus. But she was so tired of that *look*—that long, tired look that meant the room was a better place without her in it.

Halfway through cheer practice, Tulsi had to go to the bathroom and spit blood into the sink. Cady's knee had caught her in the cheek during a flip and re-opened that cut on the inside of her mouth. Every time it started to heal, she found a way to reopen it.

"I'm so sorry," Cady said, muffled from behind the door.

Tulsi swilled tap water in her mouth, spat a mouthful of pink. *Dumb bitch.* Cady apologized way too much, an antelope for the team's lions. She was mostly there to get picked on, and Tulsi always joined in.

"Watch where your spindly little limbs are going."

"Right," came Cady's voice through the door, low and sad. "Sure."

Tulsi spat again and thought about Aunt Mags: hazy, barely-there memories of Ingrid screaming at Aunt Mags after she'd found her passed out on the couch covered in her own vomit. *Why do you keep doing this?!* And Aunt Mags, slurring from sleep deprivation (among other things), had told her she honestly didn't know.

Tulsi knew why she kept doing this: satisfaction. Power. It made her feel superior for a second, even if . . . yeah, even if she felt like shit after, deep down.

What was she supposed to do, *not* tell Cady she was an idiot? Cady, who once farted into Tulsi's face when Tulsi was holding her upside down in a desperate attempt to make the squad like her?

She swung open the bathroom door. Cady shrank back.

"I'm so—"

"Move," Tulsi said.

Cady moved.

Tulsi swiped her with her shoulder on the way past, loving and hating the gasp Cady made. She could've just waited for Girls Night, swung a fist into Cady's nose and called it quits. It didn't even have to be Cady; it didn't even have to be her own fight. Tulsi could've held onto this shit and watched a fight and had that anger loosen like a cramped muscle. She really could've.

The rest of the girls were doing stretches. Quentin had her legs out in front of her, touching her toes.

"You left blood on the floor," she told Tulsi, not looking up.

Yazmine sniggered. She was doing the splits. "Ohhh, *that's* why she's breaking out so bad this week. There's this big ugly zit right in the middle of her face—oh, wait! It's just your nose."

Just wait, Tulsi told herself. *Just wait until Girls Night, or you'll regret it . . .*

Yazmine raised her voice. "What's the problem, Ortiz? Is your rat nest clogging your ears?"

It would be so easy. Tulsi turned, reply at the ready: *Remember in middle school when you got your period during camp, and you were afraid we'd see pads in the trash, so you kept them in your bag all week and stank out the place? Remember how we didn't catch on 'cause you* always *stink that bad, Yaz?*

Her tongue caught on the side of her cheek. It tasted like copper. She was so tired of reopening this damn cut. She was tired of Quentin's friendly menace and people avoiding her in the hallways. Tired of her sharp goddamn heart.

Tulsi sank her teeth into her injured cheek. Blood flooded her mouth, sharp as a punch.

Yazmine's smile shrank, confused. Her squadmates looked at each other—Tulsi Ortiz without a cutting retort? What was the world coming to?

Tulsi swallowed. "See you later."

She walked out to shocked silence in her ears and blood in her teeth.

CHAPTER FIFTEEN

Somebody was calling her.

Clementine groped for her flashing phone. Who the hell was calling her at 10:02 a.m. on a Sunday morning?

She fumbled her hearing aids in. "Hello?"

"Hi, sorry," Alex said in a rush. "I'm at your apartment. I knocked! And I texted, but then I figured you wouldn't have your hearing aids in—"

Clementine sat up. "You're here?"

"Is that okay?"

"Um," Clementine said. "Sure. One second."

She crept silently through the house. When she and Joseph had lived with their parents, a knock on the door had meant turning off all the lights and hiding. You never knew who it might be: debt collectors, social workers, someone Clementine beat up wanting a rematch . . .

She stretched to look through the keyhole. A distorted version of Alex peered back, clutching a bag of takeout. Her nervous expression collapsed into sunny relief as Clementine pulled open the door.

Clementine swallowed, fighting back the surge of emotions that had been raging in her since the party. "Are we doing something?"

Alex shook her head. Even under the unflattering apartment building lights, she was gorgeous: sleek ponytail, pink eyeshadow, and a pastel button-down. A neat white headband kept her hair back. She looked like those good girls Clementine never bothered to talk to, those good girls with clean nails and decent parents and futures. One time, in grade school, Clementine had gotten in trouble for smearing dirt in a girl's hair. She'd had a headband just like that, hair pulled back in that same shiny ponytail. The girl had asked Clementine to pick dust off her bangs, and the next thing she knew, the teacher had dragged her up to the front of class to berate her. She'd held up Clementine's hands, dirt under the nails, and shook them. *Dirty girl*, she'd hissed.

Clementine went to put her hands in her pockets, but she had none. Her sweaty palms slid against the boxers she'd slept in. Shit.

"I did text you," Alex said. "I didn't want to do that old person thing where they just drop by unannounced, I would've waited until you answered, but these were getting cold."

She held up the takeout bag. On it, a panda and a snake were curled together with cartoony smiles.

Clementine's chest squeezed. This was an apology, right? It had to be. Making up for choosing Quentin over them at the party. That logo was from that fancy fusion place Clementine had said she wanted to try when she and Joseph could afford it.

Alex tucked a blonde strand back into her headband. "Did I wake you?"

Clementine watched the strand fall back onto her cheek. Her fingers twitched against her boxer-covered thighs.

"No," she lied. "Come in."

Alex set them up in the kitchen. They huddled over the patio table—an upgrade from the box that had served as a table for the first few months.

Alex rubbed her wooden chair arms. "These are new. Salvation Army or street?"

"Street."

"They're nice."

Clementine scanned her for insincerity. Alex's smile was soft and a little pleading. These were definitely apology noodles.

Clementine lifted the chopsticks to her mouth. Lemon burst over her tongue, tangy and sticky and wonderful. She chewed as slow as she could, making it last. "You didn't have to do this."

Alex made a happy noise around her mouthful and put her hand over her lips (she had a thing about talking with her mouth full). "Oh, this is more for me. You made it sound so great, I just had to try it."

Clementine tried to remember if Alex had ever told her what her allowance was. Her parents worked themselves ragged—not typically the sort who could provide their kid with spending money. Then again, Alex's clothes were always so impeccable, and not just well kept. The material was *fancy*. Fancy meant expensive, right?

"Actually"—Alex swallowed; her hand dropped from her mouth—"I found something out. Thought you'd want to know in person, not just text."

Clementine's grip tightened on her chopsticks. *Anything can be a weapon*, Joseph had told her once, a bruise fresh on his brow, the two of them huddled in the bathroom with all the faucets running so they wouldn't be overheard. *A dish towel, your teeth—anything, Clip-Clop.*

Her old therapist's voice came next. *You're not on a battlefield. Your first instinct doesn't always have to be a fight.*

Alex continued, "Olive Barnes is back from her 'mental health stay' at her cousin's place in Ohio. She'll be back at Sterling tomorrow."

Clementine sucked in a deep breath. Sun on the floor. Lemon in her mouth. Alex across the table, oil gleaming at the corner of her pink lips.

Clementine forced her fingers to loosen. "Oh."

Alex brushed her finger through her pile of noodles to pick up stray shards of peanut from the side of the carton. She still hadn't brought up the party, or Quentin. Maybe these weren't apology noodles after all. Maybe they were Bad News Noodles.

Alex glanced up. Whatever she saw made her chopsticks pause. She reached out and held Clementine's wrist.

"Whatever you need," she said, "I'm there. I'm sorry I didn't find out sooner—you would've had more time to prepare."

"I'm fine," Clementine said, wrist tingling under Alex's touch. Alex's hands were warm and soft and solid, and Clementine missed them when Alex went back to her chopsticks.

They ate in silence for a while. Then Alex's phone buzzed on the table. It buzzed and buzzed so much, Clementine thought she was getting a call, but when Alex checked it, all the notifications were texts and Instagram DMs. More updates in the *#GirlsNight* and *#lookatwhatwecando* hashtags.

Alex didn't go to the hashtags this time. She tapped into the most recent texts.

"I'm trying something new with Girls Night," she explained when Clementine gave her a questioning look.

"Oh," said Clementine, unsure if she should be offended. She was a Ringleader, after all. Shouldn't she be consulted?

"It's just a test run," Alex hurried to say. "I'll tell you guys all about the assignments next time we're together."

Assignments? Clementine thought about asking. She took another mouthful of noodles instead.

Alex silenced her phone. "Um. While I'm here, I also wanted to say sorry for what happened at the party. That was super weird, and I'm sorry you got caught up in it."

Clementine blinked. They were Apology Noodles after all.

"It's fine," she said. She thought about asking why she was telling Clementine and not Tulsi, but Alex's smile was so relieved, she couldn't bring herself to say it.

Clementine didn't have any classes with Olive on Mondays, but that didn't stop her from sweating the whole day. More whispers than usual: girls stealing glances, passing notes. No fear in their eyes—

people said hi to her in the halls now; they even made small talk. Last week, someone had asked her for a pencil and hadn't looked scared at all. Tulsi had shown her a new hashtag, *#TheBruiser,* filled with scrapes and boots and wrapped knuckles, ripped jeans and shaved heads and, for some reason, cigarettes.

It fits your aesthetic, Tulsi had told her. *They think you're cool.*

No fear. Just . . . caution. Strange excitement. It set Clementine's teeth on edge.

She was still on edge during Girls Night, fists up.

Across from her, Jem beamed. One of her incisors was missing. Every time Clementine came to Girls Night, Jem was there, asking for tips on her stance, her hand wraps, her right hook.

Clementine sucked in a breath, adjusting her footing. She hadn't been trained in a martial art—no gloves, no technique. She'd learned rough and messy, with all the stupid, avoidable scars to prove it.

"Don't go easy," Jem told her. She beamed, and that gap drew Clementine's gaze like a fish eyeing a hook.

"I won't," she promised. She gestured at Jem's raised fists. "Bring them closer. Guard your face, remember? Like we practiced. I don't want you getting distracted by some cute guy's Insta post this time."

Jem groaned. "That was a special case, Bruiser! Now come on and hit me!"

A soft hand on Clementine's shoulder. Clementine's arm stuttered mid-pullback, and she turned around to meet Alex. Of course it was Alex, her pink lips stuck in a grimace, her hair still in that neat headband. Nobody else would touch Clementine right now. No one would dare.

"Olive's almost here." Alex clutched her phone anxiously, voice low and hushed. "I'm sorry, I was texting people all day, but no one would give me a definite yes until now, and that's only because I threatened to tattle on a freshman for smoking on campus—"

Clementine cut her off. "It's fine. It's fine," she repeated, looking up at Tulsi and Sunju, who were both watching from high in the bleachers. Tulsi was off to the side. She and Alex were talking, at least, but they hadn't sat in their usual clump tonight.

Clementine clenched her fists, loosened them. Wood polish and sweat. Girls Night chatter around them. Alex smiling tightly at her side.

Clementine asked, "When is she here?"

The gym doors swung open. There stood Olive Barnes, everyone's favorite class president, back from her mental health stay in Ohio. She'd done homework by email, Alex had told her. Her mom was a lawyer, a childhood friend of Principal Ryans, otherwise they'd have had problems.

The swelling wasn't gone, not all the way. There was the slightest bloom in her right cheek, the flushed shadow of bruises under her eyes. Her nose was crooked. Clementine could remember the harsh snap as it had broken under her knuckles.

She walked towards Clementine, chin lifted high and haughty. For a moment, Clementine's insides shriveled—she looked just like she had when she'd confronted Clementine in that classroom, smile tilting, teasing and terrible as she asked Clementine what was wrong with her. Raising a hand. Touching her ears . . .

Then Olive arrived in front of her. Her jaw twitched. She blinked just a little too fast.

Clementine dropped her hands. "You can break my nose."

Alex choked off a whine. The hushed chatter around them grew louder. *What's she doing?*

Olive blinked again—surprise this time, not terror.

On the other side of the makeshift ring, Jem made a disappointed noise in the back of her throat. She'd been waiting to fight Clementine since last week.

"Excuse me?"

"My nose. You can break it." Clementine braced herself. "Go ahead."

Alex whispered, "Clem—"

Clementine shushed her.

Olive was wearing mascara. Most girls gave up on makeup before Girls Night, but some got up from the ground with eyeliner running down their cheeks, lip gloss smudged stickily over their chin, imprinted on the other girl's palms.

Olive's fingers closed into fists.

Clementine closed her eyes. She hadn't done that in a fight in years, but she didn't want to scare Olive any more than she already had.

"Okay, this is just depressing."

Clementine's eyes opened.

Olive shifted from foot to foot, uncomfortable. "I'm not going to beat you up while you just stand there," she said. "I want to get good at it. *Then* we can have a rematch."

She flounced off towards the bleachers.

"Thank you for not pressing charges," Clementine called after her.

Olive flipped her off. Fair.

Fists still raised, Jem cleared her throat. "Um, are we still on?"

Clementine didn't answer her.

Alex was stepping close again. "Are you—"

"I'm fine," Clementine said. She signed it at Tulsi and Sunju, who halted in their walk down the bleachers. *Fine, fine, fine.* Wood polish and sweat, Alex hovering at her shoulder.

"Hello!" Jem clapped. "I have a curfew here! I'm running the clock! Are we good to go, or do you want to stand there while I beat the crap out of you?"

A chorus of laughter. Somebody whooped. Jem shot a grin around the room. She was a showboat until the fight started—then you couldn't tear her away from her opponent with a stun gun.

Alex still hadn't moved from Clementine's side.

"You should get back," Clementine told her quietly.

"What? Oh!" Alex shuffled back into the crowd. It parted for her, automatic and awed. "Go get her."

Clementine nodded, turned to Jem, raised her fists—a gesture she'd done so many times in fear, anger, adrenaline. The rush was easy. The rush was familiar. The rush was the only thing that had made sense for so long, and it was a relief to sink back into it.

"I'm gonna give it all I got."

Jem grinned.

"Good," she said, and lunged.

They ended the night at Clementine's house, with an ice pack on Clementine's cheek, bean bags from a thrift store, and *Star Rangers* on Clementine's laptop. *Star Rangers* was Tulsi and Sunju's favorite cartoon when they were kids. Clementine liked the monotony: superhero high school girls fighting bad guys and doing homework. Evil plans and exploding buildings and boyfriend troubles. Everything would be okay by the end of the episode.

Tulsi passed around a bowl of microwaved popcorn. She had dropped off a battered microwave last week.

"This is for *me*," she'd insisted when Clementine tried to say no. "I need my microwave popcorn when I watch *Star Rangers*, Clem! Do I look like the person who does things out of the goodness of my own heart?"

It was free, she'd said. Her sister's friend was going to throw it out, and Tulsi had stepped in. If Clementine or her brother tried to "pay her back" for something she'd gotten for free, she'd slash Joseph's tires. It was the sweetest threat Clementine had ever received.

Alex cleared her throat as they were scraping the bottom of the popcorn bowl. "So, I thought it could be a good idea to move Girls Night out of the gym."

Tulsi huffed. "You want us to . . . what, start beating up randoms in the street?"

"No, like—" Alex pushed her hair behind her ears, then frowned at her buttery fingers. Clementine watched her wipe her fingers neatly on a dish towel and tried not to feel worried.

"I was thinking assignments," Alex continued. "Like in the movie."

"Like *start a fight and lose*," Sunju said dubiously. She'd watched *Fight Club* for the first time a few weeks ago. Tulsi and Alex had quoted along. It had been one of their go-to movies in middle school.

"Sure," Alex said. "But, like, *empowering*. Or useful. My first assignment was for everybody to draw over a piece of hateful graffiti. Small steps."

Tulsi nudged Clementine and signed *crazy*.

Clementine didn't laugh. Covering up hateful graffiti was a net good in her book. She asked, "What's next?"

"I don't know!" Alex beamed at the laptop, *Star Rangers* reflecting pink over her face. "But I'm excited. Do you guys have any ideas?"

"Write Tulsi's essays," Tulsi said.

"Oh my *god*," Sunju said. "You're not actually that bad! You do fine when you put effort in!"

She threw the last popcorn piece at her. Tulsi caught it in her mouth and crowed, victorious.

Clementine watched Tulsi laugh and tried to quell the discomfort in her gut. Alex wouldn't drag them into anything dangerous. She wasn't like the girls Clementine used to hang out with. Alex flirted with danger, but she never went all the way.

Sunju's phone rang.

Clementine checked the time. They had two hours before Sunju had to get home.

Sunju dug in her pocket, fumbling out her phone so fast she nearly dropped it. "Hello, Mom. I'm at Clementine Rady's house. Yes, I—oh."

Her mouth flattened. "Yes," she repeated, meek in a way Clementine hadn't heard lately. "I'll be home right away."

Clementine shot a look at Tulsi and Alex. They were watching Sunju as closely as she was, both of them trying to look like they weren't.

Sunju stood.

Tulsi nudged her foot, like all the fun hadn't been sucked out of the room when Sunju had accepted that call. "Back to the salt mines?"

"Aw," Alex said over her, too sweetly. "Going already?"

Sunju nodded, not looking at any of them. She pulled her hair into a ponytail. "Sorry, guys."

Tulsi picked at a popcorn shard between her teeth. "What's at home?"

"Nothing," Sunju said, too fast. Rookie mistake. The silence that fell was heavy and awkward. "I have to clean my room."

Tulsi snorted. "Come on, you can lie better than that."

"I'm not lying."

"Why'd they go into your room?"

"They didn't. I don't have a door." Sunju checked her watch, bit her lip.

Clementine ached for her in an old part of her chest she'd kept numb for a long time. *It'll be okay,* she wanted to say, even though she hated when Joseph used to say that. It was never true fast enough.

Tulsi laughed. "What, did someone steal it?"

Clementine tried to meet her eyes, but Tulsi was too busy standing up and following Sunju out of the room.

"Jesus, fine," Tulsi called after her. "Alex, you're bussing home. Let me get my shoes."

"Um," Alex said. "Okay."

Sunju talked over her. "It's fine, I can—"

"Don't make a big deal out of it," Tulsi said, half-snarl, forceful enough to make Clementine's fingers twitch. Sometimes, Tulsi's sharp edges were a strange comfort, like scratching an itch. But usually, they just stung.

Sunju stopped in the hallway, shoulders pulled straight. Her eyes were as dull as they'd been since she'd answered the phone.

"I mean . . ." Tulsi sighed. "I have something to do on that side of town anyway."

Sunju hesitated, a spark in her eyes. "What?"

"Hmm?"

"What do you have?"

"A drug deal. Are you getting in my car or what?"

Clementine and Alex watched them peel away from the window, Tulsi honking as she pulled into traffic, nearly taking someone's side mirror off.

"That was nice of her," Clementine said.

Alex leaned on the window frame. Her smile was strained. "She can actually be kind of soft under all that sharp."

Joseph had said that to somebody once about Clementine, though he hadn't said *sharp*—he'd said *hard*. If Tulsi was sharp edges that people cut themselves on, Clementine was hard armor for pummeling.

The next morning, Joseph paused at the trash can. He picked up the takeout carton and tilted the hugging snake and panda towards the kitchen table.

Clementine took another mouthful of cornflakes. "*Alex got it for me.*"

"*Nice of her.*" Joseph dropped the carton back into the trash and returned to the table, coffee in hand. "*I was listening to you guys last night. What do they call you?*"

Clementine cocked her head.

"*Not your friends,*" Joseph continued. "*The Girls Night disciples.*"

Oh. "*The Bruiser.*" Clementine brandished her spoon.

Joseph whacked it with his toast, laughing. He bit out the dent Clementine's spoon had left in it, and Clementine took the opportunity to look him over. The bags under his eyes were as dark as ever. Even before he dropped out of high school to work, he didn't get enough sleep. He had nightmares. He never told her what they were about.

Joseph bit the crusts off and said, "*Bruiser. How do you feel about that?*"

Clementine mimed a monocle, evoking her old therapist.

He zapped her in the cheek with a piece of crust. "*Yeah, yeah. But really?*"

Clementine thought about it. "*Fine.*"

"*Yeah?*"

"*I don't know. I was hoping . . .*"

Her hands stilled. Joseph chewed, waiting. When they were younger, half their conversations were Joseph waiting for Clementine to figure out what she wanted to say.

"*. . . to be different? Someone who didn't hurt people. But maybe I'm doing something good? I teach more than I punch. I'm less angry, I think. I don't need it like I thought I would. I like it, but I also like hanging with my friends.*"

Joseph nodded. He rubbed a crumb into his hands—stubby, just like his sister's. He didn't look at her, but that didn't mean he was ignoring her. He had to look away from something to think hard about it.

"*We're giving out assignments now,*" Clementine continued.

Joseph frowned. "*Like what?*"

Before she could answer, her phone buzzed. As Clementine reached for it, it buzzed twice more.

Three texts. All from Sunju.

Good morning. I have two questions.
One: how did you get out of your parents' house?
Two: can you teach me how to fight?

CHAPTER SIXTEEN

Sunju piled yet another shade of foundation into her makeup kit. Not enough—they were still getting more girls every session. She was surprised there was anyone at Sterling who hadn't at least *tried* Girls Night.

"You're heading out already?"

Sunju whirled. Her mom was standing in the doorway, fingering anxiously at the holes where the hinges used to be. Sunju's bedroom hadn't had a door for a year. *Privacy is earned*, her parents assured her.

"Are you sure you don't need a ride?"

"No," Sunju said hastily. *Act like a loving and grateful daughter*, she reminded herself. "Thank you. My friend is picking me up."

"Which one?"

"Tulsi."

Sunju's mom nodded. She'd said she was happy Sunju was making friends, but whenever Sunju said one of their names, her mouth would pinch.

"Well. Call if you need us to pick you up early." Her mom walked up for a hug.

Sunju opened her arms automatically, trying not to look surprised. They didn't hug goodbye when her mom was mad, and she'd been mad a lot recently. Sunju had been expecting a low, angry hum and no eye contact. Instead, she was wrapped up in her mom's embrace, tight and getting tighter.

Loving and grateful; oh god, I hope you die; no, loving and grateful—

Sunju couldn't help it. She flinched.

Her mother drew back, lips caught in a sharp frown. "Sunju, what did I tell you about flinching? It's very hurtful."

"I know," Sunju said. "I'm sorry."

Her mom pulled her sleeve up. Sunju made sure not to wince as her arm was inspected. Another bruise, this one on her upper arm. Sunju had done her best, but she wasn't a professional—she was a kid with a lot of YouTube tutorials under her belt.

Sunju's mom tugged the sleeve back down, tutting. "You need to cover this better. People will think we're animals."

Sunju nodded, watching the doorframe. If they were planning on giving her door back, why had they painted over the hinges during renovations?

"Have a good night, Sunny-bun."

"You too, Mom." Sunju's heart rate started to calm as she reached the stairs.

"Say goodbye to your dad!"

Sunju's heart thudded once more into overtime.

Michael was her stepdad, technically. But her biological father had moved back to Korea when she was one, so Michael was the only father she remembered. He was an amateur artist and birdwatcher. His family had lived in Ohio since the Civil War. He wore shoes around the house, no matter how many times his wife tried to convince him otherwise. He was very quiet, except when he wasn't. Then he was shockingly, explosively, violently loud.

Sunju paused at the opening to the living room. "Bye, Dad."

He grunted from his favorite armchair. "Sunju."

"Yes?"

He raised his eyebrows.

"Right." Sunju reached behind her head to draw her hair into a ponytail with the hair tie that was always on her wrist. Her hands moved in fast, practiced motions. "Sorry."

"Good," her dad said, turning back to his bird book. They hated her hair down unless she was hiding a bruise.

"Bye, Dad."

"Sunju." He held up his sketchbook. A swan arched, as if trying to escape the pages.

"Their damn necks," he said. He was always complaining about bird proportions, and yet they were the only thing he drew. He was the one who'd taught her how to draw. When Sunju pictured good times in her childhood, she pictured Saturday mornings in her parents' room, scribbling silently with her dad.

"Their damn necks," Sunju agreed.

They smiled at each other. He went back to his sketchbook.

It may have been a good night, Sunju told herself as she ran to Tulsi's car, makeup bag clinking at her side, *but the good nights don't make up for the bad ones.*

There were always stragglers at Girls Night. Sunju was patient with them, answering their questions and making impressed noises at their bruises as she covered them up. Her impressed noises became shorter and shorter until Tulsi appeared over her shoulder and started clapping at them.

"Ringleader business," she yelled. "Move it!"

Sunju fought a smile as Tulsi herded them towards the door, absurd fondness curling in her gut.

"Great job, girls. Don't forget this week's assignment!" Alex called from the top of the bleachers, a bruise blooming on her brow. Tulsi had kneed her in the face twice in the past week. Sunju got the feeling she hadn't moved past the mess at Quentin's party.

The gym doors slammed shut. Girls peeked through the windows.

Tulsi slammed on the glass. The girls vanished down the hall, giggling.

"Vultures," Tulsi muttered.

Clementine cleared her throat and offered Sunju a roll of elastic wraps—the proper ones with Velcro at the ends.

Sunju took them gingerly. The blue material was surprisingly smooth. "You hate the Velcro wraps. You said they were for rich kids who take kickboxing lessons."

"Yeah," Clementine said. "Well."

She jerked her head. Sunju got up from the bleachers and followed her to the middle of the gym floor, which was still misty with sweat. Sunju's bare feet stuck to the wood. She grimaced.

At the top of the bleachers, Alex clapped. "Go, Sunju!"

Tulsi whooped, sitting down heavily next to her. She didn't look as excited as Sunju had expected. If anything, she looked . . . worried. Like Clementine. Even standing in front of her with raised fists, Clementine looked at Sunju the same way she'd looked at her all day: like she was giving Sunju a chance to back out. Like she hoped Sunju would.

Sunju strapped the blue Velcro into place. "I won't pass out if you hit me. I'm not *that* pathetic."

Clementine blinked. "O . . . kay?"

"I'm just saying. You look really worried. You don't have to worry about me."

"I'm not worried about *you*. I just . . ." Clementine's shoulder rolled, as if shaking off a thought. Her voice lowered. "Do you want to talk about the other thing you texted me about?"

"Later." Sunju shivered. The gym was surprisingly cool, like the Girls Night crowd had sucked all the heat out with them. "Thanks for the links."

"Joseph picked up a pamphlet. It's in my bag."

Sunju's mind raced with terrifying possibilities. She held up her fists, trying to feel like the girl in the *#TheArtist* hashtag, which Alex had shown her a few weeks back. That girl was badass, strong. She led a simple life of foundation and assistance and funny memes. More and more girls posted before and after photos of a shard of a cheek or chin, bruised and then normal looking, no hint of the hurt underneath it.

Making #TheArtist proud, the posts said.

"Right." Clementine's posture changed—head up, limbs pulled in, knees bent.

Sunju copied her. She'd seen Clementine prepare for a fight dozens of times—how could she not make her body follow suit?

"You want to start moving in the direction of the punch," Clementine said. "Away from the punch. You'll catch less of it."

"Okay."

Another whoop from the stands. Alex was on her feet, giving them a double thumbs-up. Next to her, Tulsi looked almost bored, but the boredom didn't fit her body: all coiled limbs ready to strike.

Clementine's fist shot out. White bandages from a box, the same brand she'd been taught to use as a kid. *There's something comforting about it,* she'd told Sunju when she was bemoaning Velcro.

Sunju's head emptied. Her body locked. Pain exploded in her chin, familiar and awful.

It doesn't hurt, Sunju told herself, even as her head snapped sideways. *You won't even bruise.*

Clementine's fists dropped. "Are you—"

"I'm fine." Sunju smiled thinly. "Really. Jem wasn't kidding about your private sessions—you're a good teacher. I'm just a bad student."

Clementine eyed her dubiously. "Do you want to stop?"

"No."

"Are you sure?"

Sunju clenched her teeth together. Her head was ringing. Why was it ringing? She hadn't been hit that hard.

She probed at her jaw. The throbbing was already fading. She'd had worse—so much worse. It was just Clem; they were safe. Why had she reacted like that?

Clementine lowered her hands. "Sunju—"

Sunju lurched forwards, fist outstretched. Her knuckles clipped Clementine in the ribs.

Clementine moved with it obligingly. "Okay. So, um, move in the direction of the punch."

Sunju nodded. She was trembling. She clenched her hands, trying to make them steady—

Clementine hit her in the shoulder.

Sunju stumbled back. It wasn't hard, it *wasn't*, but Sunju still gasped, her heartbeat climbing, her cheeks hot with blood and panic.

"Okay," Clementine said. "I'm calling it."

Sunju wrenched open her eyes. She hadn't realized she'd closed them. "Wait, I can—"

"I could show you how to get out of holds," Clementine said. She eyed Sunju's trembling hands. "Later."

Sunju sighed, disappointment washing over her in a bitter wave. "Fine."

She slunk back towards the bleachers.

Alex waved from the middle rung. "Clem, if you aren't going to fight Sunju, could I interest you in a quick one? I haven't fought anyone except Tulsi in two weeks."

"Your sacrifice is greatly appreciated by the devotees of Girls Night," Tulsi said flatly. Was she relieved? Freaked out? Sunju couldn't tell, Tulsi's face was obscured by her hair and hands, biting her cuticles so roughly, Sunju made a note to check later for blood. Tulsi didn't take care of her open wounds.

Clementine paused. She'd been about to undo her wrappings. "I can do a quick one."

Alex beamed. She caught Sunju on the way down the bleachers—Sunju was heading up—and held her in a hug.

Sunju hugged back. Alex gave the best hugs, warm and all-encompassing, with a small squeeze at the end. They never made Sunju feel trapped. She waited for the caged feeling every time and was always surprised when it didn't come.

"You'll do better next time," Alex chirped, but there was something behind her eyes: that same worry Tulsi and Clementine kept denying was there.

Sunju joined Tulsi on the top bleacher, sitting closer than she'd usually dare. Their knees didn't touch, but it was close.

The fight started down below. Sunju started undoing the blue elastic around her hands. Her fingers were shaking. Sunju lowered them, hoping Tulsi was watching the fight instead of her stupid trembling—

"Ugh," Tulsi said. "Give it here." She didn't take Sunju's hand, or even look at it, until Sunju gave it to her.

Below them, Clementine slung her knee into Alex's ribs.

Tulsi worked silently, with none of the complaints or quips that Sunju had been expecting. Her hands were warm. Sunju tried not to think of it, like she didn't think of the girls' skin she touched after every Girls Night, helping them to apply their makeup. It helped to pretend it was happening to someone else, that Sunju's hands weren't her own, that it was some other girl rubbing foundation on a girl whose cheeks were smooth except for that new, lumpy bruise.

I am not here, Sunju thought as Tulsi freed her hands with fast, efficient fingers. *Tulsi is not touching my skin.*

Tulsi dropped the bandages in her lap. "You're getting desensitized."

Sunju bundled the blue pile into her pocket, squeezing her shaking fingers into a fist. "Sure."

Alex ducked a punch, kicked Clementine's legs out from under her. Clementine's back hit the floor. She wasn't trying. Alex was a good fight, but not Clementine "Bruiser" Rady good.

"Come on," Alex panted. "Give me something!"

Clementine muttered something under her breath and grabbed her, wrestling her to the ground.

Tulsi snorted, derisive. It used to set Sunju's teeth on edge until she realized that half the time, Tulsi only did it to fill the silence, grab some kind of power. She did it when she was nervous.

"We should grapple," Tulsi said, too fast. "If you want to learn how to get out of holds."

Sunju's mind raced with terrifying possibilities. Tulsi's black hair hanging in her face. Hot breath on her neck. She'd lain in bed last night sketching the lines of Tulsi's back muscles from memory. Then, even more illicit, the blade of her cheek. Her dark eyes, caught in those rare moments of softness . . .

Sunju's throat clicked. "Clementine's more experienced. But sure, if you want."

Are you excited for it? Sunju wanted to ask. She didn't, of course. Hopefully, Tulsi wasn't as disappointed with her as she was in herself.

Tulsi hummed in acknowledgement, picking at her nails. Her thumbnail was torn and bloody. Sunju wanted to go find a band-aid, but she didn't want to come back and find Tulsi with her walls up. Any sudden movement might spook her.

"Who was your favorite *Star Ranger* character?"

Tulsi laughed. "What kind of question is that? Rockstar."

Rockstar was the wild child of the group, always ready with a quip or an insult.

"What about you? No, let me guess—Sirius."

Sirius was shy and quiet. She was also the character who died the most, though it never stuck. There were a lot of resurrections in that show.

Sunju opened her mouth to agree. She did like Sirius, but she liked all the Rangers. And there was only one character who she'd drawn over and over in her My Little Pony notebooks all throughout elementary school.

"No," she admitted. "Mine's also Rockstar."

Tulsi blinked. Suddenly, she looked less like something you could cut yourself on, eyes as butter-soft as they were in Sunju's sketchbook.

CHAPTER SEVENTEEN

Tulsi was listening to Clementine explain what the hell a muffler was when Alex sped up to her desk.

"Wow," Tulsi said. "Hi?"

"Ms. Ryans wants you to come to her office," Alex said. She held up her phone. It had a text from Yazmine, who worked in the office for extra credit:

ms ryans wants tulsi to come to the office lmao good luck bitchhhh.

"Have you done anything untoward?" Alex asked, her face twisted in regret as Tulsi went into immediate mocking mode.

"*Untoward?* What are you, a 19th century nun?"

"I'm speaking fast, and it was the first word I thought of." Alex shoved her phone back into her skirt pocket. She wasn't wearing tights today. She'd once told Tulsi she didn't like baring her legs in public, which was a waste—Alex had nice legs, wide and flush.

"Maybe it's some other Tulsi," Tulsi suggested. She looked to Clementine, who nodded despite her raised eyebrows which were blatantly calling Tulsi out on her bullshit.

Alex stared at them both and then turned to Sunju, who was reading at her desk. "Sunju, come tell Tulsi to stop being difficult!"

Sunju didn't look up from her book. "No one is big enough for that job."

Tulsi grinned.

The PA buzzed on. "Tulsi Ortiz, come to the principal's office."

Tulsi sucked her cheeks in. "Hey, Clip-Clop, what's 'I didn't do it' in ASL?"

Clementine showed her.

"Great," Tulsi said, executing the worst copy she could manage. "Got it covered."

Alex followed her out into the hall. Her worried look was back, even if it was masquerading behind her Everything Is Okay look, one of Tulsi's least favorites. "If she has anything on you—"

"Fold like a cheap stack of cards and blame it all on you?"

Alex's laugh set her on edge—too fast, too high. She caught Tulsi's arm before she could turn around. "Hey . . . we're okay, right?"

That same stupid, hopeful smile she'd given Tulsi in freshman year, girls whispering around them about the rumor Alex had spread. She hadn't meant it to catch fire, she'd insisted. It took years for Tulsi to believe her. It was easier seeing Alex as a backstabbing, social ladder-climbing bitch than what she really was: a girl with a pit of loneliness at her center, hungry for anyone who would fill it and damn the consequences.

Tulsi flashed her teeth. "Why wouldn't we be okay? I'm friends with Alex Veck—I made room for some bullshit."

Alex's smile fell.

Tulsi rapped her on the arm. "Thanks for the tip," she said, and charged down the hall.

It's not about Girls Night, she told herself as she neared the office. When that fell flat, she tried, *she doesn't have anything concrete on us.*

Unless she did, and she'd marked Tulsi as the one most likely to screw them over for personal gain. Some of those social media posts were getting less vague. A girl had posted a *#GirlsNight* photo of her skinned knee that showed people's faces in the background. Another girl had made a text post talking about how her latest assignment had gone on her public account: sneaking out to play drums in her new punk band. Alex had made them take both of them down, and the next Girls Night, she'd given an impassioned speech about not posting anything on socials you wouldn't want your mother to read in front of your whole family.

No talking about Girls Night, she'd begged. *No assignment talk, no showing off bruises, and for the love of God, no face pics.*

Yazmine tilted side to side in a roller chair, high heels up on the admin desk. She hit Tulsi with a lazy peace sign as she entered. "Good luck, bitch. Hope your new school sucks."

Tulsi flipped her off and knocked.

Ms. Ryans's voice floated through the door. "Come in."

Tulsi sat on the couch and slouched down as far as she could get away with. "What's up?"

Ms. Ryans's weariness was showing through her concealer. Her eyes drifted down to Tulsi's thigh, where a bruise poked out from under her skirt's hem.

Tulsi sat up.

Ms. Ryans smiled tightly. "How's your family doing?"

"Great. We're always great, us Ortizes."

"And you're still writing your own essays nowadays?"

"You know it," Tulsi said. They hadn't caught on to Sunju's one. She'd been starting to think she was in the clear.

"Good," Ms. Ryans said. Her smile was brittle in the way it was around most students she had in her office. Tulsi often got the feeling she regretted her career choices.

Ms. Ryans nudged a pencil back into its perfect place. All straight lines on her desk.

"Let's not beat around the bush," she said. "We've been noticing some worrying injuries since this self-defense course started."

I bet, Tulsi thought. Skin splitting open on knuckles or floorboards. Bruises turning black. A gouge mark from someone who hadn't listened to the "no long nails" requirement. Last week, someone had spat out a tooth and giggled. There were so many girls at Girls Night nowadays that most attendants only got the chance to fight once every few weeks, and when they did, they unleashed a month's worth of shit.

Tulsi waited. "And?"

"And," Ms. Ryans said, sighing, "we would like to know if the rumors of a . . . of a *fight club* are true."

There we go. They'd have to get more people on lookout.

"A *what?*" Tulsi barked out a harsh laugh. "No. *Shit*, no."

"Are you sure?"

"If there was a *fight club*, we'd know about it."

"Mm. How's Joseph been as a teacher?"

"Joseph? He's fine. Good guy."

Ms. Ryans's eyes narrowed. Maybe Tulsi should've been more dismissive. She didn't go around calling people *good guys*.

Tulsi picked at her blunt black nails. Her cuticles were bloody, hidden under the band-aids Sunju had layered on last week. "Look, whatever 'worrying' stuff you've been seeing, none of it's happening in those classes."

"What about outside your classes?"

"Alex would know about it. Something that big? She'd know."

"And she'd tell you."

"She'd tell *you*."

Ms. Ryans stared at her for a long time. Tulsi glared back, trying to look like her time was being wasted and she wasn't sweating bullets under her crop top.

Finally, Ms. Ryans dropped her gaze, shifted her perfect pencils laid out in lines on her desk, out of place and then back in. "You can go."

Tulsi resisted the urge to run, and also the urge to ruin the perfect line of pencils. She entertained a brief fantasy of swatting them to the floor like a cat. Then she got up and walked at a totally normal pace out into the admin office.

Yazmine watched, amused, from the front desk. She raised her hands in another peace sign, questioning.

Tulsi strode out, closing the door on Yazmine's cry of, "Oookay, screw *me* then!" Her armpits were sweating. Paper towel time.

Tulsi headed towards a bathroom, rounding a corner to find Alex standing motionless a few feet down the hall, staring at Becca's retreating form. Becca had only been to a few Girls Nights, and she couldn't punch for shit, but Tulsi admired her retro fashion sense. Eighties was *back*, baby.

Tulsi slunk up behind her. "Couldn't just wait *two* minutes for me to get back?"

Alex jumped, hand going to her chest. Sometimes she did these old woman gestures. Tulsi told herself it was lame, but she couldn't stop the smile.

She put her hands on her hips. "And *where* is your hall pass, young lady?"

Alex held up a keychain wrapped in brown duct tape, the tape adorned with the words HALL PASS. She was staring past Tulsi at nothing, slowly turning red.

Tulsi snapped her fingers. "What is your face doing? Becca ask you out or something?"

"What? No." Alex let out the fakest laugh Tulsi had ever heard. "She's . . . she told me about the favor."

"The one she insists she owes you?"

Alex nodded distractedly. "She's going to start up an LGBT club."

"Oh," Tulsi said. The sweat was back. "You mean a gay-straight alliance?"

"No," Alex said weakly. "An LGBT club. It's more of a favor to Sterling, since we don't have one. I think it'll be great! For Sterling."

Tulsi waited, lips pressed together tight enough to hurt. Against laughter, sure, but mostly, she was afraid a smile would give something away. Not that she was worried about that. It was just nobody's business, especially not the former gossip queen of the school.

"She thought this was a favor to you because . . ."

"Oh! She thought . . ." Alex coughed, folded her arms. It was like watching a fifth grader do an "aw, shucks" routine, trying to convince the teacher they definitely hadn't looked over at their partner's answers. "It doesn't matter." She gave Tulsi a desperate smile.

Tulsi almost let it go by. She really thought about it.

"Are you gonna go?"

"To the LGBT club?" Alex's voice hit a high and then crashed back down. She coughed again. "I'm so busy lately, I can't fit in another club. You?"

"Same," Tulsi said, watching Alex closely.

Alex had to . . . *know* about Tulsi, right? Tulsi wasn't parading around in rainbow flags, but Alex wasn't an idiot. She had to know.

But Alex just nodded.

Tulsi nodded back.

They stood there, making direct eye contact and nodding, Alex's blush getting bigger and bigger as Tulsi struggled to force back her smile.

Alex's mouth started to twitch.

Okay, Tulsi thought, Now *she knows*. She let out a giggle.

"What?" Alex said, squeaking all over the place, flushed with embarrassment.

Tulsi covered her mouth. "Nothing." Her giggles increased.

Alex raised a hand in front of her mouth, a mirror image of Tulsi.

There was a video Tulsi had watched at the start of high school, a "how to make friends" tutorial. She hadn't watched much. Her aunt had walked in halfway through, and Tulsi had switched to her porn tab—less embarrassing. Anyway, one of the tips had been to mirror people's body language. Alex seemed too overwhelmed for this to be anything but unconscious.

Alex started hiccuping with laughter.

"Quit it," she managed. "It's not . . . this isn't even . . ."

She shook with it, clamping both hands over her mouth so they didn't attract a teacher. It was unlike her to hide her laughter. Tulsi didn't understand until she noticed the deep relief in Alex's face, almost entirely obscured by how hard they were both losing it in the hallway.

Relief. Yes. Alex was muffling her laughter so they could keep this moment, just the two of them. Relief and recognition.

Once the laughter had died down enough for them to speak, Tulsi slapped Alex in the shoulder. "You should've said something!"

"I didn't even know back then," Alex admitted. She beamed, nervous, like she didn't have a bunch of dirt on who was in the closet at this school. Probably. Tulsi had never asked. There were queer girls at Sterling, but there had to be more—*so* many more—who were keeping it quiet or hadn't yet realized.

"But yes," Alex continued, "it would've been . . . nice. Not being alone."

For a moment, Tulsi pretended they hadn't gone years without talking to each other. That she had gotten to call Alex at 11 p.m. stressing about what Quentin had done, what did it mean, does she like me or does she *like* like me, and Alex could've . . . what? Hosted movie nights of *Jennifer's Body* and *But I'm A Cheerleader* until one of them got a clue? Waxed poetic about Halsey? Suggested some practice kissing? Tulsi almost wished she had. It would've been sweeter than her real first kiss: Quentin lunging so hard she cut Tulsi's lip with her front tooth.

"What?"

Tulsi blinked. "What, what?"

"You're staring."

Tulsi thought about brushing her off. Thought about making a joke about how they could've been each other's first kiss. She could ask about Clementine. She could ask if Alex knew about Tulsi's mortifying, soul-destroying crush on Sunju. She could say they should head to class. It wouldn't be long before someone was sent to find them.

"I missed you," she said instead.

Alex's face collapsed, just for a second. Then the smile came back, shining and open, a bruise barely visible under her foundation. Tulsi had put it there last week with her sharp fist. At the time, it had felt like forgiveness, making things even. But here it was, forgiveness in spades, no blood necessary.

CHAPTER EIGHTEEN

"Are you *sure* you don't want to come?"

"With you and Q? Hmm, let me think." Tulsi tapped her car keys on her chin, barely audible over the fight noises raging through the gym. "No."

Alex whined, digging her chin into Tulsi's shoulder. She got like this during Girls Night sometimes, strange and clingy. She'd be embarrassed later, but for now, her girls were around her on the gym floor, waiting for the last fight to end so Tulsi could peel off with Clementine and Sunju, and Alex could walk off wherever Quentin was taking her.

Tulsi ground her keys into Alex's cheek.

"Ow."

"You've got dirt on Q, right?"

Alex thought about it. "Not really."

"Seriously?"

"Seriously," Alex said. Tulsi didn't look happy about that. "Why?"

"I don't know, she thinks you do. And you might want leverage."

"Leverage?"

Tulsi ground her teeth. Her voice was backlit by yells, a wet, hard punch ringing out through the gym. "Look, just be careful, alright?"

"Aw," Alex said. She poked her knuckles against Tulsi's cheek like Tulsi had done to her with the car keys. *You caaare about me*, she wanted to say. But Tulsi looked annoyed, even a little hurt. And behind her, Clementine and Sunju looked . . . relieved, almost. Like Tulsi had said something they all wanted to say.

Alex deflated. "Thanks."

Tulsi surveyed her, searching for sincerity.

"I'll be careful," Alex said. "I promise."

Tulsi shrugged. "Your funeral if you don't."

Quentin appeared at Alex's side, looping an arm around her neck. "You ready, Alex?"

"Yeah!" Alex chanced another look at the girls. Clementine and Sunju were talking in low tones—something about Sunju sleeping with a teddy bear—and Tulsi was examining her own nails, turning her hand over and over.

Quentin tugged. Alex followed. She had to unless she wanted to duck out from Quentin's hold. In one of Clementine's earliest fighting lessons, she'd demonstrated how people will move in the direction their head is pushed. *If you control the head*, she'd told them, *you control the whole body.*

Quentin took them for a walk. When Alex asked where they were going, Quentin said she would see. The way she walked—chin high, red hair in a glowing pile, her knuckles newly-bloodied—Alex wanted to follow her to the end of the world.

She also wished the others were here. If Quentin would just stop playing with them, show them how fun and interesting she could be, they'd love her.

She and Quentin led the pack. Behind them, Yazmine and Cady tried to trip each other. Sometimes they succeeded, and the laughter increased.

Quentin didn't look at them. But every few seconds, she'd glance over at Alex, as if making sure she was still there, and she'd smile.

Alex smiled back. When Quentin was looking at her, her need for her laundromat girls went from a roaring forest fire to a low smolder.

Quentin still had her arm around the back of Alex's neck, and the night was bright and eternal. Something dark curled in Alex's stomach. She liked it the same way she liked getting punched: it was satisfying for one shining minute. In that minute, she wouldn't care how much it'd hurt later.

"Here we go," Quentin said, coming to a stop outside a small, squat building.

They were at an indoor public pool. Alex used to swim in it over the summer when she was a kid.

Quentin led them down the side of it, then around the back. Alex thought briefly of Tulsi breaking into the laundromat.

Quentin produced a key with a flourish. "I used to volunteer here," she explained when Alex gave her a questioning look. "I had a copy made."

The lobby was cool and quiet. There was tile that hadn't been deep cleaned in a long time, a front desk, and behind it, glass doors leading to the pool.

Alex waited, mind spiraling—she didn't have a bathing suit; she couldn't jump in with her clothes and take a bus home soaking wet; she had *very* mixed feelings about jumping in in her underwear, even with all this vivid night around them making everything possible—but no one headed towards the glass doors.

Cady sat down on the bench that spanned the wall. Quentin sat down behind the front desk and threw another set of keys to Yazmine, who headed for the vending machine.

"Oh," Quentin said when she saw Alex near the glass doors, "I don't have the pool keys. Just that door and the vending machine." She sighed longingly at the pool, which glimmered under the railing lights. "I *wish* I had the pool keys. There's something so romantic about a night swim."

Alex stared up at a security camera.

"It doesn't work," Quentin assured her.

Yazmine clicked the vending machine door open. "Okay, who wants what?"

"Oooh, could I have a Three Musketeers bar?"

Yazmine snorted. "Yeah, I *bet* you want a Three Musketeers bar, Alex."

Cady tittered.

It was stupid, but it still stung. Not many people brought up Alex's weight nowadays. She checked to see if Quentin was going to say something, but she was busy frowning at the cash register.

Yazmine threw the bar. Alex caught it, tossing back an uncomfortable smile, and went over to Quentin.

"Good," Quentin said as Alex arrived at her side. She pushed a bobby pin into her hand. "Try and pick that, would you?"

Alex stared at the bobby pin clutched uselessly in her hand.

"Um," she said. "Sure!" She went to pull up a WikiHow article on her phone.

Quentin scoffed. "You don't need that—the lock sucks. Just do it!"

Alex fumbled ineffectually at the tiny lock, scratching the metal. "I can't . . . I can't. Sorry."

She put the pin on the desk and stepped away fast. The dark curl in her stomach had retreated, replaced by something much less satisfying—cloying, grasping. Who did she think she was?

But Quentin looked so disappointed, like she had expected Alex to break out some lockpicking master skills, Wikihow be damned. Even as she said, "Never mind," Quentin's gaze was suddenly disinterested, looking around the room for something other than Alex.

She swallowed.

The pool glimmered in the corner of her eye. Across the room, Yazmine flopped down on Cady's legs, both yelping with laughter.

"Hey," Alex said. "Quentin."

Quentin looked over.

Alex picked up the trashcan and smashed it through the doors.

Glass burst onto the tiles, dusting Alex's boots. Cady's yelp was pure this time, no laugh in it. On top of her, Yazmine was pure laugh, high and cackling.

Alex turned back to Quentin, who stared. Alex rearranged her face so it wasn't broadcasting all that deep want.

Slowly, and then all at once, Quentin's face lit up. She grinned at Alex like she'd just done a magic trick.

"What are you waiting for?" Alex asked.

Yazmine sprung up. "Last one in's a dumb bitch!"

"Guess you're sticking behind—" Cady doubled over, wheezing. Yazmine had thrown an elbow into her stomach.

Alex stepped back to let everyone in. They crunched past the glass, ducking away from the shards that were still attached to the doorframe.

Quentin was the last one up, smiling in a way that made Alex want to break a hundred glass doors.

"You amazing creature," Quentin said.

They couldn't find the main lights, so they had to make do with the railing ones. When Alex took off her clothes and dived into the pool—thinking very hard about the water and not how her entire stomach and thighs were exposed—she opened her eyes in the dark. Pinpricks of light drifted down from the surface.

Alex stared up at them, blurry lighthouses. Then a shape appeared above her, blotting them out. It swam down and stopped in front of Alex, red hair clouding around them.

Quentin, Alex thought.

Tulsi's hair would do this, darkness drifting around them like a storm. Sunju's would be a crown around her head. Clementine's would stay the same, her buzzcut barely getting fuzzy before it was shaved down again. Alex imagined it: wet stubble, the stark shape of Clementine's skull bordered by water on all sides.

She swam up, broke the surface. As she breathed deep, Quentin emerged, keeping her chin low in the water. Alex thought fleetingly of sirens singing from the rocks. Anything and everything you want.

"You are such a surprise," Quentin said, illuminated by the railing lights.

Alex laughed. "Thank you."

Yazmine piped up from the other side of the pool. "Whale sighting ahead!"

Quentin pursed her lips, eyes widening pointedly.

Alex turned. "At least my eyes are a normal distance apart, and I don't smell like fried crap after walking up one whole flight of stairs!"

Quentin giggled. Yazmine followed suit.

Cady resurfaced, wiping water out of her eyes. "What? What'd I miss?"

Alex propped herself up on the side of the pool.

Quentin followed, floating next to her. She was wearing a matching red bra and panties. Of course they matched. Alex didn't own any matching underwear, despite color coding everything else in her life. Color coding her underwear felt like too much hope that someone would see it. She didn't want to jinx it.

Quentin asked, "How are the assignments going?"

"Good!" People had been sending Alex photos of before-and-after graffiti pictures all week. "I've been thinking of giving people, like, personalized assignments, like volunteering, or protesting, or dying your hair crazy colors."

"Oooh, crazy *hair*. Come on, Alex, you can do better than that." Quentin splashed her and held up her hands against the return assault.

"Some parents get really weird about dyed hair!" Alex's laughter faded as Quentin swam closer, brushing water from Alex's brow.

"What's my personalized assignment?" Quentin whispered.

Kiss me. It burned like coals behind Alex's lips. She could feel her cheeks turning red. Alex liked to think she'd do it if they were alone. She was confident, right? She'd started a fight club. But there was a terrifying difference between throwing a punch and asking the girl you liked to kiss you.

"Um, I've been meaning to ask," Alex said instead, resolutely not glancing down again at Quentin's bared body hazy under the water, "what happened with you and Tulsi?"

Quentin blinked, ducking chin-deep into the water.

Alex expected her to evade the question, like every other time Alex had tried bringing it up. But Quentin resurfaced and sighed.

"It's . . . complicated. I accidentally injured her shoulder in sophomore year, and . . . I don't know. She just doesn't trust me anymore. Sharp heart, you know?"

"Sure," Alex said, ignoring the sting of betrayal in her at the agreement, remembering how Tulsi's face had broken open at Quentin's party.

Quentin ran a hand through the dark water. "Why, what did Tulsi say?"

"She hasn't said anything."

Quentin looked bitter, just for a second. Her eyes flickered over her shoulder, and her smile returned.

"Oop," she said. "There goes Yazmine's underwear."

"What?" Alex looked over her shoulder and then back again immediately, cheeks flushing.

"She's underwater," Quentin said. "You can't even see anything!"

"Still," Alex said weakly. She wished sorely for that deep wild from when she was walking here. It had flared up when she broke the window, but only for the moment of shattering. Then she was self-conscious again, embarrassed, waiting for everyone to announce that she was a weird loser and kick her out of the group.

Quentin often made her feel like that, she realized. She would just have to try harder.

Her arm sat slick on the tiles. Alex tilted it until she could see the healing bite mark Quentin had left on her in her garage. It would fade, Sunju had assured her. The wound wasn't deep enough to scar. Soon there would be nothing but skin.

She took a deep breath. "Sometimes I want Tulsi to bite me."

Quentin lit up again. *Oh, thank God.* "Yeah?"

"Clem, too," Alex admitted. "Kind of Sunju? I think she'd be the least into biting me. I want it to scar."

Quentin stared, her gaze tilted questioningly at Alex's arm.

Alex showed her the healing skin. "You won't be able to see it soon. You didn't go deep enough."

"Aw," Quentin said softly. Her smile was shark-wide as she gripped the edge of the pool and hauled herself up.

"Look," she said, and held up her leg. It was bristly, but only a little, like Clementine's head. A silvery half-moon scar sat at the soft back of her knee.

Alex nudged it with her fingertips, then she drew back. "Sorry."

"No, go ahead." Quentin angled her leg closer.

Alex ran her pointer finger around the semicircle. It was faded. "Who—"

"Tulsi. Freshman year," Quentin said. She slid her leg back into the pool. "We were wrestling at a sleepover. She won."

Alex tried to imagine a situation where wrestling would end up with Tulsi at mouth level with the back of Quentin's knee. Her cheeks went red again.

"Soft spot," she said.

Quentin hummed. "She almost hit a tendon," she said quietly. Her mouth twitched to one side, and she bowed her head. Embarrassed. Alex hadn't known Quentin could be embarrassed.

The next day was a high. Alex strode through the school with her Ringleaders at her side, Quentin flitting in and out, girls whispering and glancing her way at lunch. The whispers only increased once Alex started calling girls over for personalized assignments.

She rode that high all the way into the evening, right up until she was in a fight with some senior who had a crappy right hook.

Alex was winning. She spat blood and glowed. Everything glowed—the crowd glowed; the gym floorboards glowed; Sunju and Tulsi and Clementine and Quentin all glowed from the sidelines where they were watching her win.

Her opponent tapped out. Alex stood, arms raised, as the cheering crescendoed.

"LADIES OF GIRLS NIGHT," she yelled breathlessly, "FOR YOUR NEXT ASSIGNMENT—"

A horrified hush fell over the crowd. A voice rang out through the gym. "What the *hell* is going on here?"

Alex turned, fists still aloft. Ms. Ryans stood in the gym doorway with her hands on her hips, face frozen in shock and fury.

Oh, Alex thought. *I lose.*

CHAPTER NINETEEN

Heading into the Principal's office the next morning was almost a relief.

Sunju already knew fragments of what was coming. Clementine had texted late last night to let them know that Joseph had been fired from a volunteer teaching position he'd never actually worked. Alex had had a very stern talk with the girl who was supposed to be on lookout last night.

No one's parents had been called yet. Sunju didn't need to be told that. She had avoided her parents coming home last night and leaving that morning, sure they would catch the guilt coming off her in waves.

No, not guilt— the knowledge that bad things were coming. Since Ms. Ryans had walked into the guts of Girls Night, Sunju had been clenched in a perpetual wince. The sword of Damocles hung over her as she squished next to Tulsi, Alex, and Clementine on the principal's couch. Sunju wished it would just fall and skewer her already. Whatever was about to happen, she wanted it over.

Idiot, she told herself as she slumped into the office, friends at her side. *You let yourself be happy and look what happened.*

Ms. Ryans clasped her hands together, nails digging into the skin.

Before she could say anything, Alex launched into the story she'd circulated: they'd heard about the Girls Night rumors and wanted to have some fun during a self-defense session while the instructor was running late.

Ms. Ryans didn't speak for a while after Alex finished. She looked over them all, and Sunju did her best not to cower under her gaze. It was easier than she'd expected to meet her eyes.

"I want to believe you," Ms. Ryans started, in a tone that suggested otherwise. "You do realize someone could've gotten seriously hurt."

"We know," Alex said hurriedly. "It was a momentary lapse of judgment—"

"Momentary."

"Yes! We swear."

Ms. Ryans held up her hands in a stiff approximation of Alex's triumph. "'For your next assignment?'"

Alex laughed thinly. "Out of context, ma'am. I was quoting a movie. Joking around."

Ms. Ryans gave her a flat look. "Humor me: are you four the leaders of this whole thing? The 'Ringleaders?'"

Sunju stiffened. How much did she know?

Alex shook her head vehemently. "No. As far as I know, they don't exist."

Please don't know about the hashtags, Sunju thought. The latest one was a text post, posted this morning: *good luck girls, sending u strength,* cocooned by heart emojis. Below it was something about setting fire to old diaries, which might have been in the wrong tag—Alex hadn't set any assignments involving fire.

Ms. Ryans sighed. "You know, I thought it was strange that the four of you started spending time together."

Tulsi asked, "What are you going to tell our parents?"

Ms. Ryans blew a hard breath through her teeth. "Since we have no real evidence—other than the *senseless* and *stupid* actions I witnessed last night—I'm going to tell them everything I know for sure. Then I'm going to tell them things they could watch out for."

Sunju closed her eyes and conjured up the four of them at the laundromat. In the library, bent over their textbooks. Sitting on beanbags in Clementine's house, watching *Star Rangers.*

She opened her eyes. Ms. Ryans was still talking.

"You are aware that if I find any definite evidence," she continued, "I can and will go to the police."

"Ms. Ryans," Alex said, and her desperation sounded a lot like *you're too smart for this*, "do you really think we could orchestrate something like this?"

"I *think* . . ." Ms. Ryans paused. "I don't know if that question is useful right now."

Sunju zoned back out and waited for the sword to fall.

The office door closed. Alex's polite smile dropped in the empty hallway.

"Okay!" She breathed a long, thin stream, pinching the bridge of her nose. Sunju thought of a general preparing their troops for battle—armor on, sword lifted high. Imaginary Alex could fend off armies. Here, in the real world, she couldn't protect Sunju from jack shit.

Alex clapped. "First!"

Tulsi pinched her.

Alex flinched, lowering her voice. "Oh my god, right, sorry. Um, first! We need a new location for Girls Night."

Clementine frowned. "Is that . . . is that the most important thing right now?"

She wasn't looking at Sunju, but conspicuously so. Tulsi, too—staring at her nails like they owed her an essay. Only Alex looked at her, eyes widening in realization.

"Right," Alex said. "Right."

Sunju started, "It's not—"

A flash of red. Sunju jumped as an arm fell around her shoulders.

"I know a place," Quentin said. She gave Sunju a little squeeze, and *there* it was: that panicky, trapped feeling she always expected when Alex hugged her.

Sunju stepped away. Quentin's arm didn't even pause, raking her fingers through her bold locs, like that was what she'd brought her arm up for in the first place and Sunju had only been a convenient place to rest it on.

"Um," Alex said, in that shrill, syrupy voice she used when Quentin was being a dick to her friends. It was always paired with a smile that reminded Sunju of a TV host whose guest was getting out of control. *The show must go on!*

Alex gestured down the hall. "Let's talk over here!"

Quentin followed her down the hall.

Tulsi watched them, but not for as long as usual.

As soon as they were out of earshot, Clementine stepped in close to Sunju. "Have you looked into a lawyer?"

Sunju averted her eyes. "I don't have money, Clem."

"You can apply for legal aid. Have you been taking photos?"

Sunju stared down at her loafers, wishing Tulsi had slinked off with the others. "They go through my phone. Not a lot, but—"

Clementine cut her off. "I can take them on my phone."

"Okay. Okay, when I—"

An earsplitting ring cut the hall in half. Sunju got her phone out of her pocket and stared. Down the hall, Alex and Quentin's conversation had paused.

A strange new part of Sunju screamed to let it go to voicemail. She watched herself click ACCEPT.

"Hello—"

"You get home right *now*," her mother hissed, and the force of it was enough to make Sunju flinch. Her mother continued, but Sunju didn't take it in, just nodded dully and felt her fate click into place.

"School hasn't even started yet," Sunju tried. "Did you not go to work?"

"Don't talk back to me," her mother snapped. "I'm coming home. So is your father. If you aren't home in twenty minutes—"

Sunju let her mother yell herself out. Then she said, "Yes, Mom. I'm sorry, Mom," and waited until she was allowed to hang up.

Sunju pocketed her phone. She waited until her hands stopped shaking, then she started putting her hair into a ponytail. "Could one of you take notes for me today?"

Clementine nodded.

Alex called down the hall, "Are you okay?"

Next to her, Quentin watched with curious eyes.

Sunju's skin crawled. She leaned into Clementine. "When I get back," she told Clementine, "you can take photos."

Clementine jerked her head in a nod. "Sunju—"

Sunju turned to Tulsi. "Could I have a ride? You'd miss first period—"

"Screw first period," Tulsi said, even though it was gym, which Tulsi hated the least out of all her subjects. "Let's go."

A buzzing, familiar dread kept Sunju's eyes trained out the window as Tulsi drove. She didn't notice they'd pulled over until Tulsi nudged her.

Sunju tuned in. They'd barely moved—they were idling beside the parking lot where the first fight had happened.

Tulsi leaned back in and made expectant eyebrows at Sunju. "Well?"

Sunju got out of the car.

Tulsi led her to the door of the Hartburn Cadies warehouse. "Thought you'd need it. Give you something to . . . I don't know, hold onto when you walk into . . . whatever you'll walk into back at home."

The graffiti had grown since Alex had brought them here before their trip to the boy's school. That had been a pep talk, an inspirational talk about where Girls Night could go, the implications of which Sunju still worried about. Alex kept making noises about potential. *We can really* do *something*. This, with Tulsi, was . . . what? A comfort talk? *Something to hold onto.*

The start of a wrist. A hand curled in a fist. The hand had shading now, outlines of tendons, light glinting off the nails. Lines making it clear the fist was clenched tight.

Sunju's gaze fell to the words painted underneath: LOOK AT WHAT WE CAN DO.

It was beautiful. Sunju tried to feel moved.

Beside her, Tulsi made a flat noise. "This isn't helping."

"It's a picture," Sunju said. "It's all over the hashtags. Someone photoshopped it onto the Statue of Liberty last week."

"It's more the idea than the picture—"

"It's not going to do anything for me," Sunju said. "It can't . . . it's not going to be there with me when I get home."

Tulsi was silent.

Sunju waited for her to throw up her hands. *Forget about it, then! I try to do something nice . . .*

Tulsi blurted, "We could sneak into your house, after your parents leave you alone. Or we could come in with you—"

"No," Sunju said, "you can't."

She watched Tulsi struggle against it, the lack of power that came with being sixteen.

They got back into the car. It rumbled to life. Sunju waited for them to pull out into the street, but Tulsi just sat there, glaring out the windshield.

Sunju said, "Come on. I'm on a schedule."

Tulsi laughed, but there was nothing behind it. The car lurched into the street.

Sunju closed her eyes.

CHAPTER TWENTY

Ms. Ryans stood on the stage, examining the crowd for black eyes as everyone avoided hers.

"I'm sure you all know why we're here," she said. Her clothes were as rumpled as ever, but her chin was higher than Alex had ever seen it. She smoothed her hands down her creased skirt in a movement that reminded Alex bizarrely of herself.

"I've been hearing some disturbing accusations these past few months," she continued. "Your gym teacher in particular has been noticing that girls are moving like they're in pain. Not to mention the sudden influx of my students showing up with visible bruises. Do you know how many girls have told me they walked into a door?"

Beside Alex, Tulsi shifted. She'd just gotten back from dropping Sunju off when the PA had instructed everyone to head to the gym. She was silent and twitchy and paying even less attention than usual to Ms. Ryans.

Alex closed her eyes and sent up a quick prayer. *If I have any strength in me, please give it to Sunju. Please, God, make sure she's okay, or that she'll be okay soon. Thank you, God.*

"I implore you," Ms. Ryans said, "if any of you have information about . . . about this fight club . . . you *have* to come forward. You'd not only be helping yourself, but the whole school."

Alex squirmed with guilt. Ms. Ryans had always been good to her, even if it was a purely circumstantial kindness—Ms. Ryans hadn't been good to *Tulsi*. She hadn't been mean, just . . . careless. Tulsi had told her that when she got brought in for cheating on a test for the third time, Ms. Ryans barely looked at her, too busy with something on her laptop. When she had looked at Tulsi, she'd sighed.

Another one falling through the cracks, she'd said, which Alex thought was pretty dramatic. Tulsi wasn't doing coke in the bathrooms or mugging classmates in the parking lot (both things Sterling girls had done since Alex's freshman year). She had just cheated on some tests.

When she'd suspended Clementine, she'd barely looked at her, either. Clementine said she'd glanced at Ms. Ryans's laptop on the way out to find her playing Solitaire.

It was a vast contrast between that woman and the one who stood in front of them all, hauling them out of homeroom so she could stare pleadingly into the crowd.

"Please," she said. "Come forward."

Girls shifted uncomfortably. No one spoke.

Ms. Ryans sighed.

Falling through the cracks, Alex mouthed. Was that what they were doing? Alex was turning Girls Night into something to be proud of, something empowering, something *good.* Right?

The bell for first period ran through Alex like a gong.

"She could be getting beat up as we speak," Tulsi hissed as they huddled on the way to history. "Like, right now—*boom*! Kick to the stomach."

"We could go over," Clementine said slowly, her brow furrowed like she was thinking hard. "But that—"

"Might just make it worse," Tulsi agreed. "We can't really—"

"We can't do anything if she's just going to go back to that house."

Tulsi squeezed Clementine's wrist. "Exactly! Thank you. So, what do we do?"

The last part was directed at Alex, who brought her hand up to her forehead and then swiped it away, turning the palm outward. "*I don't know.*"

"Gotta do the facial expression with it," Tulsi reminded her.

Both of them looked at her.

"Aw," Alex said. "You've been watching the ASL videos we sent?"

"No. I . . . Clem must've said something at some point, I don't know." Tulsi dropped back to a whisper. "Guys, Sunju is getting the *shit* kicked out of her right now."

Alex clapped. "Let's keep this positive!"

"Sure," Tulsi said flatly. "I'm *positive* something bad is happening to Sunju right now. Clem, you guys were talking about getting her out—"

"We need a lawyer."

"I know lawyers," Alex said. "I mean, the daughters of lawyers. Olive Barnes's mom is—"

Tulsi shushed her. Alex winced. Too loud again, and the girls passing them in the hallway weren't being subtle about eavesdropping. They respected their Ringleaders, sure, but in the way you respect a celebrity.

"I'm just saying," Alex continued, hushed. "We could ask—"

"Alex!" Cady jogged up, twisting her pink hair anxiously. "I wanted to talk about my, um, assignment?"

They were getting too close to history class. Alex reached for Cady's arm to pull her away.

"Uhhhh," Tulsi hissed after her. "Hello!"

"One second," Alex called back. She pulled Cady out of the flow of students and snapped her fingers. "Talk as fast as you possibly can."

Cady made a noise like a pinball machine announcing you lost. "I . . . sorry, you said Girls Night would help me make my assignment more, um, bombastic?"

Right. She *had* said bombastic. She'd been riding high on Girls Night adrenaline and too many painkillers at the time.

Alex looked back at the classroom doorway. Clementine and Tulsi stood to one side, heads bent together—hopefully discussing state laws on emancipation or legal aid. Maybe Girls Night could set up a GoFundMe?

"I'm surprised you want to help," Cady said. "I almost thought you were brushing me off earlier."

"I'm not," Alex said distractedly. She forced herself to focus. Girls Night was a force for good. This was her chance. "I mean . . . I've been busy."

Think of something! Come on! Bombastic, what could make it bombastic . . .

"Do you know Jem?" Alex blurted.

Cady blinked. "With the rainbow hair? Sure, she kicked me in the ribs last week. She's super good."

"Jem's family owns a fireworks company. We're, uh, sorting something out. I'll get you your people; I'm just kind of busy at the moment."

"Right, of course." Cady's face went grave behind her pink bangs. "What are we going to do about the gym?"

"Oh," Alex started, "actually, Quentin had this great idea about—"

The bell rang. Walks turned into brisk jogs as the hallway cleared.

"Shit. My class is on the other side of the building. See you." Cady took off sprinting, ponytail flouncing.

Alex watched her go. As soon as Cady was out of sight, she dug her phone out of her pocket and scrolled furiously until she reached Jem's number.

Hey Jem :)))) How are you girlie??? Clem says your punching is getting so so good!! Wanna help out on an assignment later?? Hmu <3

"Alex!" Tulsi yelled. "Move your ass!"

"One second!" Alex called. She glanced up. At the end of the hallway stood Quentin, leaning against the wall like she didn't have anywhere to be. She didn't look stressed about the assembly they'd just been let out of. She looked . . . excited. Even with Ms. Ryans breathing down their necks and threats of cops, when you walked with Quentin, you were always one step ahead.

Quentin grinned.

Alex felt her own mouth stretch in response.

"Alex," Clementine said from the doorway.

All her nerves flooded back—Ms. Ryans, the gym, getting Sunju out of her house. And, Alex remembered as she followed her friends into class, they had history homework due. Alex had been too busy coming up with her own assignments, imagining the admiring faces of each girl as she bestowed them.

Alex was taking off her shoes when the impossible happened: her mom walked into the lounge in pants and a shirt. No pajamas. No scrubs. Hair in a sleek blonde knot on her head, which she only did when she wanted to look nice.

"I covered someone's shift last week," she said when she noticed Alex staring in clear confusion. "Got a day off."

Alex didn't bother asking how this must've messed up her sleep schedule.

Her mom nodded at the backpack next to her feet. "What're you up to?"

"I'm . . . I'm . . ." Alex was at a loss. This was the first conversation past hello/goodbye that she'd had with her mom in months. There was so much to say!

She opened her mouth to say she was still acing her classes—no, that was a lie: she'd dropped down to a B in two classes. Study sessions with her girls were good, but she'd been doing much less homework . . .

Alex beamed at her mother. Friends! That was what she could tell her. She had real friends now, not just people she texted all the time! She studied with them after class, she had sleepovers her parents seemed very unsurprised by, she went to parties and stuck around with the same people instead of flitting aimlessly between groups!

Alex started, "I have f—"

Her mom cut her off. "While I have you here, I wanted to ask—I got a call from your school. Anything I should worry about?"

Alex squeaked, "What? No."

"I thought not," her mom said, scanning the room, then going over to the laundry table to get her phone. She glanced up at Alex as she scrolled. "I can't see you getting involved in anything like *that*," she scoffed. "We've seen a few Sterling girls at work. Awful. We had to put five stitches in one girl's face. Why would they do this to themselves?"

Alex shrugged jerkily. Neither of her parents had noticed the bruises, covered in foundation but still visible through the layers. If she'd had a visible band-aid, she'd avoided them until it came off.

Her mom sighed, still scrolling. "In my day, we just snuck a drink or wrote bad poetry, played a contact sport."

She looked up. Alex pulled her shoulders back and tried to look innocent.

"You'd tell me if you were part of an underground fight club, right?" A laugh. "Or the . . . what did Ms. Ryans say . . . the *Ringleader*?"

Alex laughed with her. It was wooden. "Sure."

Her mom nodded, frowned down at her phone. "Smart girl," she said distractedly. "How've you been?"

"Great! I've been great. Mom, I have—"

Her mom groaned at her screen. "Goddamnit!" She winced. "Sorry I swore. I gotta go, baby."

Alex moved automatically out of the way as her mom headed for the door. "Bye."

Her mom was already on the phone. "Are you sure you need me *now*?"

The door swung shut.

Alex stared at it for a long time, her hope folding in on itself like a star forming a black hole, ready to consume everything in its path.

Hartburn Candies had a sliding door; even wide open, the graffiti was visible on it: a clenched fist, bright in the moonlight. Pulsing veins. Pink nails. LOOK AT WHAT WE CAN DO.

Alex held up her own nails—pink, like the spray paint. She turned to her Ringleaders, who were waiting behind her.

"How does everyone feel about pink nail polish?"

Sunju considered. Clementine made a face.

Tulsi glanced dubiously at Alex's nails. "*That* pink? Hard pass."

"I just want us to match," Alex said, and turned back to the open door, the gleaming fist towering above them. She'd bring it up again later.

"Look at what we can do," she murmured, and stepped into the warehouse.

Bare lightbulbs hung from the tall ceiling, barely enough to light the cavernous space, the corners turning into shadows. The warehouse was twice as big as the gym, which was good—they'd been starting to run out of room. Maybe being forced to move was a blessing in disguise.

The warehouse was already full of girls chatting and giggling, comparing bruises, snapping photos.

Alex inhaled. Already the stench of sweat; they would put so many coats down on this cool concrete. Something sweet hung in the air—this was a candy warehouse before it was a husk. Alex looked out over the sea of girls and thought of hard candies, gleaming neon and cracking between her teeth. Sweet, sour, coated in prickly sugar.

Alex wanted to bite someone.

She clapped hard, cutting through the din. "Alright! Your Ringleaders are here!"

A cheer went up. The crowd parted, forming a line for them to walk through.

Alex led the others into the middle, which had been hollowed out in preparation. Girls waved as she passed, and Alex waved back. There were so many of them, and some of them were strangely unfamiliar. Did they even go to Sterling?

Alex stood on her tiptoes in the middle of the crowd. She missed the bleachers, where everybody had to look up at her. She waited for the others to file in with her and clapped once more.

"So! Girls Night has a brand-new space. Who's excited?"

A whoop went up. Her laundromat girls joined in.

Alex paused to beam at them, delighted, before turning back to address the crowd. "Hands up if you're new!"

A dozen hands flew up.

Alex sucked in a breath. "FIRST RULE OF GIRLS NIGHT!"

"NO SHOES!" the crowd screamed back. Some of the newcomers laughed in relief, while others looked around curiously, wondering what joke they'd missed.

Tulsi whispered, "Who comes to a fight club without watching the movie?"

Alex continued: "SECOND RULE!"

"NO EYE GOUGING!" the girls yelled.

They went down the list: *no jewelry; no biting; we clean up after; no talking about the club, IRL or online.*

"And if you *do* post online," Alex continued, glaring into the giggling crowd, "use a burner account. Do *not* put anything identifiable in your posts—no faces, no addresses, no grandmother's necklace you've had since you were eight. You want your family to be able to look at the posts and not know who, where, or what anyone is. Got it?"

"YES, GENERAL!"

"Good. Now"—Alex grinned and stepped to the side—"my girls!"

Alex introduced each Ringleader with a flourish, pride rising in her chest as Sunju smiled and Clementine nodded easily and Tulsi shot a quick punk rock sign, flashing her tongue. Alex's chest squeezed. *My girls, my girls, my girls!*

"Now," Alex finished, "who wants to christen this place with me?"

Hands flew up.

Alex looked through the excited faces, eyes catching on a snatch of crimson hair.

Quentin beamed, her lips bright red. Gasoline to a fire.

Alex burned.

"The lady with the hair!" she called.

Quentin strode up, hands already wrapped in pristine white elastic. She fluttered her fingers at the other Ringleaders as they joined the crowd, leaving Alex and Quentin in the makeshift ring.

Alex crouched. "Ready?"

"For you?" Quentin kissed her wrapped knuckles, leaving a lipstick print like a blood spot. "Always."

Quentin won. As usual, Alex couldn't bring herself to be annoyed. She was rarely annoyed at losing a fight, too caught up in the adrenaline. And it was never a chore, losing to Quentin Scarhill.

Quentin pulled her into the crowd and pressed a kiss to her bleeding eyebrow. "A pleasure as always, my General."

Alex laughed. Her scalp stung from Quentin yanking at it, trying to get Alex off her. Another fight was starting up in the ring, but

Quentin had pulled her to the fringes of the crowd. They couldn't see it from here, only hear it: a low gasp at the first punch, the scrape of fabric on skin, the yells gaining traction as the fight started in earnest.

Quentin chinned herself on Alex's shoulder. Quentin's hair bled over her face. It always came out of its bun, no matter how tightly she coiled it.

"Remember when I said you can thank me later for the warehouse idea?"

Alex nodded.

"It's later, Veck."

Alex nudged their foreheads together. "*Thank* you, Q."

Quentin giggled. Up this close, she didn't look like anything, just a crimson blur.

The lack of light made the warehouse feel dreamlike, a liminal space outside of time. The gym, Alex realized, was too bright, as well-lit as a classroom. *This* was how Girls Night should be: dim, grainy, lit up by a few scant bulbs and the teeming energy of a hundred girls packed into one space.

Quentin sighed in satisfaction. "Good turnout for the first night here."

"Right? I don't even recognize some of them."

"Other schools are trickling in." Quentin pulled back, Alex's eyebrow blood smudged on her hairline. "Want to go somewhere?"

CHAPTER TWENTY-ONE

The party was in full swing: girls falling off staircases, cannonballing into the pool.

"Later," Quentin said into Alex's ear, pointing at the glistening water, "we should dive off the roof."

Alex nodded. The motion was fun, so she did it some more. Quentin had snuck her wine on the bus over here. She wasn't sure what neighborhood they were in, but the house was fancy enough to not be anywhere near hers.

Alex squinted at the girls around them. Some were from Sterling. "Whose party is this?"

"Who cares?" Quentin's teeth flashed in the dim hallway. "At least it's not mine. I hate parties at my house. Feels like my guts are hanging out for show."

Alex thought back to Quentin's unassuming house, plain wallpaper and strange art on the walls. "Then why host?"

"I don't know. Don't you do stuff you hate sometimes? Just to see how bad it makes you feel?"

She grabbed them beers from the kitchen and dragged Alex to the dance floor. Alex watched her bare hand as she was dragged— Quentin had taken off her wraps. Alex missed the lipstick mark on Quentin's knuckles. It had felt so intimate slamming into Alex's cheek.

Quentin swayed her hips, her arms, all cheerleader strength and grace. Alex raised her hands, buzzing with adrenaline and the wine she'd had on the way here. The music was loud enough that the pain became background noise. Her thigh would bloom with bruises soon, just like her ribs. Her cheek was already going purple. Her body sang with the impact of skin on concrete, a song that vibrated in time with the music.

Someone had taped a speaker to the ceiling. A woman crooned:

Kiss me
So gently
With your fist
Embrace me
Embrace me—

A girl dug her elbow sharp into Alex's side in a dangerous dance move, turned around and gasped. "Shit, sorry Alex!"

"It's okay, Zoe."

As Alex was falling back into the dance, a girl yelled, "ALEX!" from across the room and waved.

Alex waved back, desperately grasping for the girl's name. She'd given her a personalized assignment the other day: stand up to her deadbeat dad. "Hi, Jess!"

Quentin put her face close to Alex's ear. "I don't know how you do it! You've always known everyone's names since you became gossip queen of Sterling."

"Jess is in your AP Bio," Alex said. She had to lean in close so Quentin could hear her. "Zoe's—"

"How did that start, anyway? The Tulsi thing, right?"

Alex stopped in the middle of the dance floor. Around her, girls writhed.

Alex put her mouth next to Quentin's ear so she didn't have to yell. "Um. Not really? That was, like, the third gossip I got. I overheard someone telling their friend about someone getting suspended for swearing at a teacher, and later, I heard someone else asking their friend why she got suspended. I told her, and she called all her friends over. She—"

A girl stepped on Alex's foot. She didn't wince. If anything, it made her intimately aware of how close everyone was, all of them moving together to the music, with purple light shimmering over them from a disco ball.

Love me
so gently
with your eyes . . .

Alex wet her lips. "She got me to tell them everything I knew. And then they went away, but for a minute, they were all looking at me."

Quentin blinked. Her eyelashes skimmed Alex's bruising cheek.

So gently
with your fist . . .

"So, when somebody asked about Tulsi—"

Alex's stomach squirmed. "Nobody asked. I just . . . I just said it. Everyone started looking away, and . . . I shouldn't have. It was stupid."

Quentin's blunt nails dug into Alex's wrist. "I don't think you're stupid, Alex. I think you wanted people to pay attention. It's normal, needing attention."

Need. Alex wished she'd said "want". *Need* made her feel like a toddler screaming for her parents at the dinner table. *Pay attention to me!*

"Hey." Quentin tilted her chin up. Warm fingers. She'd cleaned Alex's blood with those fingers. She'd caused the blood in the first place.

"Hey," she said again, softer. Her gaze dropped to Alex's mouth.

Music pounded in Alex's ears. Sweat dripped down her spine. Girls all around, elbows and knees. Somebody stepped on Alex's foot again. Alex made a noise that had nothing to do with pain and everything to do with Quentin leaning in.

Alex's eyes fell closed, waiting for the softness and fireworks the movies promised.

No softness. No fireworks. Just a sting in her bottom lip. Quentin had bitten it.

"Wait here," Quentin whispered.

"Okay," Alex croaked.

Quentin gave her another nip and vanished into the crowd.

Alex stood there, dazed, her pinched lip pulsing in time with the music. She touched her mouth and grinned, doing a little shimmy.

Many shimmies later, Quentin was nowhere to be seen, and the elation was turning into worry. What was the holdup?

Yet another girl stood on her foot.

"Ow," Alex said.

"Sorry—" the girl stopped and gaped. "Oh my god, hi! You're her!"

"I'm her," Alex told her. She stood on her tiptoes. Still no sign of Quentin.

Alex beamed at the gaping girl. "Excuse me."

The girl rushed to get out of the way. She was from another school and still recognized Alex enough to stare. Alex tried to feel flattered, but all she felt as she escaped the dance floor was . . . lost. Alone. All these girls staring as she passed, and she still felt alone; what was *that* about? Where was Quentin? What was so important that she had to run off instead of giving Alex her first kiss?

Quentin wasn't in the kitchen. Alex got another drink—whiskey this time—and asked if anyone had seen Quentin around. No one had.

Alex got another drink. Then a lemonade, because whiskey was truly the worst. No one had seen Quentin.

Alex found a quiet bedroom and got out her phone. She did a quick scroll through the hashtags, a knee-jerk response at this point.

Blurry shots of blood on concrete, harsh light on sweaty hair, a vague tweet about falling in love with drunk women in bathrooms, several mid-tier memes, a text post about the boiling point of metal (what did *that* mean?) . . .

Alex sighed and went into her contacts.

It rang seven times.

"Come onnnn," Alex whined.

Click.

Clementine's voice was bleary and worried. "Alex? What time is it?"

Alex checked her watch. "*Barely* 1 a.m. How are you?"

Clementine didn't reply.

Alex sank down onto the bed. Her head was spinning. "I'm really, really sorry if I woke you up. I just wanted to talk. Wait, shit, you said deaf people hate phone calls. Do you want to FaceTime?"

"This is fine," Clementine said slowly. "Is something wrong? Joseph can come and get you."

The pillows on this bed were boring: white and pillow-shaped. Alex took a boring pillow and held it to her chest.

"I'm fine," she said. "I'm at a party in . . . alright, I don't know where. But I'm at a party."

"Okay."

Alex waited. Static crackled over the line.

"Did you want to talk about anything in particular?"

Alex dug her teeth into the divot Quentin had left in her bottom lip. "So . . . say I like a girl."

"Oh," Clementine said, strained. "Okay?"

"But I can't get a read on what she feels about me. I'm pretty sure, but . . . sometimes I get mixed signals?"

"Okay."

Alex imagined lying in Clementine's bed, a bed Alex had sat on top of as her girls crowded together watching movies. Clementine's weekly planner blu-tacked above her pillow. Cool concrete, peeling wallpaper, a window with a view of a brick wall. It was a terrible room. Alex was so fond of it.

"Are you asking for . . . advice?"

Alex snapped her fingers. "Yes! What do I do?"

"I mean . . ." Clementine said, and laughed. It was a short, huffy laugh, one Alex rarely heard. Clementine didn't laugh much. "I'm not good at this, but . . . I think you should ask her how she feels."

Alex hummed. For a moment, she felt weird about asking Clementine about this. Sometimes, she looked at Clementine during class—that lovely stubbled head in the fluorescent lights—and ached. But Clementine had never kissed her fist before slinging it into her face. She'd never dug her chin into Alex's shoulder or sunk her teeth into her arm. Clementine wasn't *hungry* for Alex. Not like Quentin.

"Alex?"

"I'm here." Alex rubbed the boring pillow against her face. It was too warm in here. Or maybe she was too warm. She couldn't tell the difference. "I'll . . . I'll do it, Clem."

"Okay." Clementine sounded nervous.

At a Girls Night last month, she'd signed, *Get me out*, and Alex had run over to find that a group of girls had roped Clementine into talking about their love lives.

I never know what to say, Clementine had confessed. *Even when it's not about me, I just don't have the right replies.*

"You did good," Alex said. "Good romance talk."

"Oh," Clementine said again. "Okay." Another laugh. This one was happy, almost bubbly. "Do you want Joseph to come pick you up? You can stay here, if you want."

"No, it's fine. I'll find my way home. See you later." Alex flicked the sign aimlessly above her head. "I'm signing 'later'. You can't see it."

Clementine laughed. "Later, Alex," she said, sounding the kind of fond Alex always wanted to coax out of her.

She grinned as she hung up.

A knock on the door. "Alex?"

Alex's heart leapt into her throat. *Speak of the devil* . . .

She ran over and flung the door open. "Hi, sorry, you took ages, and I wanted—"

Quentin dove in and pressed her nose into Alex's collarbone.

"Got lost. Missed you," Quentin said, muffled against Alex's chest. "Tell me something good?"

Alex's head swam. Quentin's breath was hot on her neck.

Got lost? The house wasn't *that* big.

Dizzy with booze and this strange, raw version of Quentin clinging to Alex like a spider monkey, Alex said the first thing that came to her head. "We're getting Sunju out of her house."

Quentin made a questioning noise. Alex told her about the bruises, the phone calls, the no door thing.

"We're going to get her emaciated. *Emancipated*," she corrected. "Out of that house."

"Huh," Quentin said softly. She sat back, considering. She barely talked to Sunju, but for a moment, Alex thought she was going to offer to help.

"It's good she has you," Quentin said softly, and scrubbed a hand down her face. For a moment, she looked like she had crying on her back porch, all her armor stripped back to expose naked skin.

Alex frowned. "Where'd you go? Are you okay?"

Quentin gave her a look like the question was offensive. "Am I *what*?" She laughed, and the odd, vulnerable Quentin sloughed back into the sharp, brilliant girl Alex was used to. "I am *amazing*, Alex, as always. Now, I seem to remember somebody promising to jump off the roof with me."

Alex blinked, confused. But Quentin was smiling again, and it seemed real enough, and she was here. *Here*, with Alex, wanting to pull Alex into another adventure.

Alex took a breath. "Sure! But, um, before we do, I want to tell you—"

Quentin took off running, pulling Alex out of the room and down the hall.

"Come on," Quentin kept saying. "Come on, come on, come on!"

Up the stairs, into a bedroom with an open window that led out onto the roof. Alex squeezed out and stood, wobbling, on the roof tiles.

Quentin went to the edge and waved her over. "Come on!"

The pool shone below them, girls clamoring around the edges. It was a dizzying drop.

Alex sucked in a breath. "Quentin? I really like you."

Quentin looked over so fast, her hair smacked Alex in the cheek. For a moment, her smile froze, and Alex's stomach plunged to her feet . . .

Then Quentin grinned, blazing. She reached down and linked their fingers.

"Secret for a secret," Quentin murmured, and leaned in. Her lips brushed Alex's ear. "I really like you too."

Then she yanked.

Alex yelped as they tumbled off the roof. A series of gasps from down below. Someone yelled, *Incoming!*

Quentin cackled. She was still laughing when they hit the water.

Alex's eyes stung. *Chlorine*, she thought, and then, *I'm still wearing shoes.* She kicked towards the surface, but a tug on her hand stopped her.

Quentin floated close, a bright scarlet blur. Their noses bumped. Quentin rubbed the back of her neck. Alex breathed a cloud of bubbles and closed her eyes.

Kiss me, she thought.

Quentin leaned in. Her mouth was a hard burn in the cool water. Her tongue ran over the seam of Alex's lips, her hands tight on

Alex's hips. She was so warm, Alex wouldn't have been surprised if the pool had started bubbling around them.

Alex's lungs ached, but she didn't kick for air until Quentin did. They broke the surface in one, panting, foreheads bumping.

"Hi," Alex gasped.

Quentin pushed her wet hair away from her forehead.

"Hi," she said, gaze bright and trained right on Alex's face like nothing else existed.

Alex would do anything for it—jump off a hundred roofs, get left on a thousand dance floors. Quentin could rock up to Girls Night in brass knuckles and Alex would present her cheekbone for shattering if Quentin would just keep looking at her like this, luminous in the blue light, her hands hot on Alex's waist.

Alex's hangover was brutal. By the time Monday rolled around, she was still walking slowly so she didn't make her stomach lurch. She hobbled towards her usual lunch table, flipping Tulsi off as she got up from her seat and cradled her stomach in a mocking impression.

Tulsi sat back down. "You look like shit, Veck!"

"Don't listen to her," Clementine called. "You look nice."

Alex smiled. Clementine smiled back, so wide and warm that Alex felt her own smile grow in response.

A voice volleyed over from the cheerleaders' table. "Alex!"

Alex turned. Quentin had drunk as much as Alex, but she didn't seem to be affected at all, waving her over with an enthusiasm that made Alex jealous.

"One second!" Alex turned to her own table, gesturing for them to follow. "Come on, guys."

Sunju and Tulsi looked at each other dubiously. Clementine began to scrape her chair back, hesitant.

"There's no room," Quentin called. "Just you, Alex."

Clementine lowered herself back into her seat. Alex wavered, torn.

Quentin said her name again. "Are you going to stand there all period?"

She raised her hand to her mouth, playing at biting her cuticles. Her knuckle skimmed her mouth in the smallest kiss.

Alex's heart spasmed in her chest. She glanced back at her table.

"*Later*," she signed, and headed for the cheerleaders' table. She glanced back, but Clementine didn't look charmed the way she usually did when Alex signed *later*, just confused.

Quentin pulled back the seat next to her, where Tulsi used to sit. Alex couldn't help but think of thrones as she sank down into the plastic chair.

Quentin leaned over, hot breath tickling Alex's cheek. "You look like death warmed up. You know what would distract people from your eyes, the bags on bags on bags?"

"What?"

Quentin tugged her earlobes. "More earrings." Her own earrings glinted in the fake light, ruby and rhinestones all the way down. Tulsi's ears used to look like that. Alex would watch them walk down the halls and wonder what it was like, being *marked*. Quentin's girl.

Her stomach twisted—hangover or nerves, she wasn't sure.

A cool gaze on the back of her neck. She glanced back at her table. Sure enough, Clementine was staring right at Alex, face fallen, as if trying to talk herself out of a horrible realization.

CHAPTER TWENTY-TWO

There was a car in Tulsi's neighborhood that hadn't moved in five years. The windshield was cracked. The hubcaps were stolen, battery gone. There was a dent in the passenger door from Tulsi backing into it during her first driving lesson.

The car was good for scrap metal and nothing else. Tulsi had never seen anyone touch it, until she was heading back home after a boredom-induced walk, thinking idly about how she would beat up Sunju's parents, and spotted a girl bending to peer in the window.

Tulsi would've kept walking if the girl's hood had stayed in place. But a breeze blew, and the light hood tugged away to expose a rainbow loc.

"Jem," Tulsi said before she could stop herself.

Jem startled and turned, hand whipping cleanly out of a jagged hole in the window. "I . . . Tulsi! Hey!"

She stood in front of the window hole and smiled, like this would distract from the shifty shit that was obviously going down. "What's up?"

"Nothing much." Tulsi craned her neck. "You live around here? Clem said you live on the other side of town."

"No, yeah, I do." Jem tugged at a loc. She'd been maintaining them less since she'd started coming to Girls Night. Her roots were growing in black.

"Jem. Seriously. Is something up?"

Another pause.

"What? No," Jem said, but swallowed hard. Her smile went apologetic. "It's just . . . we should probably run."

"Run?" Tulsi thought of cop cars, suspicious neighbors. She glanced over her shoulder. No one was peeking out a window right now, but that didn't mean much.

"Yes," Jem said. "Now."

She started off at a fast walk, tugging Tulsi along until she went with her. Then she started jogging, Tulsi keeping to her side as she flung wild glances over her shoulder.

They got to the end of the street.

Tulsi asked, "Why are we—"

A sharp *bang* rang out.

The girls whirled around. The car was on fire. Smoke leaked out of the car's blown-out windshield. Sparks faded on the sidewalk.

Tulsi gaped. "Did you *bomb* the—"

"No! It was a firework." Jem stared, a wild smile growing on her sweaty face. "Do you think we'd have gotten hurt if we were in that car?"

Tulsi decided this situation required swearing. "Jem, what the shit?"

Jem's smile guttered as someone came out of their house to check what was going on.

"Oh, shit," Jem said, and took off.

Tulsi followed, heart pounding.

Do you think we would've gotten hurt if we were in that car? What the hell was Jem doing? Was this a family rite of passage: use the family fireworks and light up some unsuspecting public property . . .

Tulsi went cold.

There were more posts in the Girls Night hashtag than ever, and Tulsi kept finding ones that she didn't understand. Vague posts, sure—wanting to punch a boyfriend or stressing over homework or about parents who just didn't understand why their daughter stood up for themselves nowadays—but there were also danger signs. Posts that got flagged for explicit (meaning gory) content. DIY stitches. DIY *bombs*. Before it got taken down, a comment under that bomb post had read, *I know an easier way.*

Tulsi dragged Jem to a stop outside a gas station.

Jem panted. She looked nervous, but she also looked . . . expectant. Eager. Like she was waiting for Tulsi to say something. She was a Ringleader, after all.

Tulsi gritted her teeth. "Was this one of Alex's assignments?"

Jem's smile twitched into a confused frown. "What?"

"Did Alex tell you to—" Tulsi gestured at a cop car as it streaked past, lights blaring. "Please tell me you're not that stupid. Please tell me *she's* not that stupid."

Jem stared at her. Not for the first time, Tulsi felt like she was missing something.

"No," Jem said finally, "Alex didn't tell me to do this."

"Well, Clem definitely didn't, so what the *hell*—"

A shoulder rammed into Tulsi, cutting her off. Jem reached out to steady her, but Tulsi was already straightening, whirling around to face whoever had almost taken her out. "Watch where you're—"

"Jeez, Tulsi, I'm so sorry." Mr. Keener blinked down at her, slicked hair falling down his loathsome face.

Tulsi balked. She still couldn't meet his eyes, and she hated it. *Nothing happened*, she told herself. *Why are you like this?*

"That was totally my fault," he continued, all neat, sorrowful brows. "Let me make it up to you."

Tulsi stepped out of the way of his comforting hand.

"Tulsi," he said, and laughed that chalky laugh that only came out when he thought you were being unreasonable. "Did I hurt you? I didn't think I ran into you that hard."

"Didn't hurt," Tulsi mumbled. "Come on, Jem."

But Jem was gone. Tulsi looked over to see her retreating back. *So much for solidarity*, Tulsi thought as Jem's rainbow locs vanished around a corner. Alex had been harping on about it at Girls Night—

girls stick together; no girl left behind—and there went Jem, leaving Tulsi with this creep.

"Fast one," Mr. Keener said conversationally, like they were making small talk. Like this wasn't a hostage situation, with Tulsi numb and cowering like a child and not the badass fist fighting cheerleader she was.

People cheer when I fight, Tulsi thought as she stared at his scuffed shoes. *People wait for weeks for my knuckles on their face.*

"Tulsi." Mr. Keener frowned. "Seriously. You okay?"

Tulsi thought about punching him, running her nails down his face. Blunt or not, if she applied enough pressure, that would do the trick. She thought about kicking his knees out from under him, getting him on the ground. A foot in his stomach, to the nose. Blood on the ground, Mr. Keener coughing red onto the asphalt.

She wanted him to choke. But more than that, she wanted to get away.

When he reached for her again, she ran.

"Tulsi, hey! You're early." Alex looked her up and down, tightening her neat dressing gown. She was wearing hair curlers, a blackhead strip over her nose. "Out for a run?"

Tulsi nodded, hands on her knees and breathing hard. She couldn't talk yet.

"Okay." Alex tweaked a hair curler. "Well, we'll need the car to get to school. Unless we're taking the bus, in which case, you're still early."

Tulsi straightened, swayed forward. Alex leaned back.

"Nope." Tulsi took her chin. "Look me in the eyes, Veck."

"Um, alright."

Tulsi jabbed a finger in her face. "Did you tell Jem to blow up a car? Was that some stupid assignment shit?"

Alex blinked. Her cheeks squished in Tulsi's grip. "Jem blew up a *car*?"

Her eyes were big and blue and guileless. Alex was a great distracter, but she was a shit liar, especially when you looked her in the eye.

"Jesus. Fine." Tulsi let her go and bent over, wheezing. "I need to run more."

"Clearly." Alex patted her hair back into place. A pale strand had fallen out when Tulsi had grabbed her. "Tell me more about our little pyro. Nobody got hurt, right?"

"Not yet."

"What?"

"I don't know. She said some weird shit."

Tulsi watched Alex's bare feet leave her line of sight. She looked up to find Alex holding out a glass of water. Tulsi took it, condensation dripping down her wrist. She drained it in three large gulps, thinking that when Alex finally did screw her over, it would probably be unintentional. Just like last time.

The warehouse was strangely silent as they approached. Usually, it would be buzzing with overlapping voices. But there was just one voice rising over the concrete as they edged through the door.

The voice was in the depths of the crowd. The three of them recognized it as soon as they stepped into the building.

Quentin stood in the warm center of Girls Night. There was no podium, but you couldn't tell with the way she stood, everyone listening raptly as she announced, "We're taking that power for ourselves, and it looks however you want it to."

Alex *excuse me'd* her way through the throng of girls, which parted easily as soon as they realized who it was. Tulsi shouldered in after her, Clementine following in her wake.

"Everybody did so well last week," Quentin continued. "Now—"

Alex hit the front of the crowd.

Quentin cut off. There was a moment of fear on her face that thrilled Tulsi, but then the fear was covered by a broad smile.

"Alex, hey! Didn't think you were coming tonight." Quentin bounded over and kissed her cheek.

Clementine averted her eyes. Tulsi narrowed hers.

Alex reached up to touch the lipstick mark Quentin had left. "So you thought you'd get started without me?" Alex laughed, but her eyebrows were furrowed.

Quentin shrugged happily. "You know we don't always have a Ringleader! Girls Night is on *every* night nowadays. Someone has to take charge, right?"

"I guess," Alex said slowly. "But . . . Q, what was that about?"

Quentin laughed. "I was giving a pep talk, babe. You know—girl power, yay!"

Alarm bells rang in Tulsi's head. *Babe, babe, babe.* Quentin only used pet names for Tulsi when she felt like she was losing ground.

Someone has to take charge, right? Shit, had *Quentin* told Jem to blow up a car? What good would that do?

"Quentin—"

Quentin pulled Alex into the middle. "Your General is here, everybody!"

The crowd cheered. More of them were from other schools. Some of them were new—they had that nervous energy—and even they were staring at Alex like she had the answers.

Alex's shoulders shot back. Her smile came up, beauty-queen ready. Tulsi used to watch her practice it in the mirror, middle-school cute with her socks pulled up to her knees.

Alex raised a fist. "Let's fight!"

Another cheer. Someone yelled, "Can I fight you, Alex?"

Tulsi yelled back, "She's out of commission tonight!" and motioned for Alex to follow her to the fringes of the group.

Alex followed, troubled. She kept twisting to watch Quentin, who was being talked to by six girls at once.

Tulsi wanted to shake her. *Can't you see she's not good for you?! I told you! I wish someone had told me!*

She pulled Alex out of earshot of the crowd. "You haven't asked about Sunju yet."

Alex hummed distractedly. "Why, what happened?"

"Nothing I know about," Tulsi said. "But usually you ask."

"Is she okay?"

"I don't know," Tulsi said, and let go of her. Rage simmered in her gut. She felt . . . pointless. Ineffective. *Stupid.* She entertained the idea of shaking Alex into her senses. It was less satisfying than she'd hoped.

A bark of laughter drew her gaze. Quentin was still surrounded by eager girls, head tilted in a way that made Tulsi's hackles stand up. It was the head tilt of an animal luring something small into its trap. *Come closer. Almost there . . .*

Tulsi gritted her teeth. "Q, YOU UP FOR A FIGHT?"

She pushed back through the crowd—or tried to, because it parted. Annoying. Tulsi wanted to elbow people. The downsides of being important.

She came to a stop in the makeshift ring. In the time it had taken to march through the crowd, Quentin had started wrapping her knuckles with the remains of a tie-dye shirt.

Great minds, Tulsi thought.

"May the best man win," Quentin said, and threw Tulsi two thin straps.

Tulsi caught them. "Got it, coach."

The shirt scraps were soft between her fingers. Tulsi tucked the ends in. "Are we doing a countdown, or do we just—"

Quentin lunged. Tulsi caught her, tumbling them both onto the concrete. Fighting Quentin felt like a sick victory.

Is this what you've always wanted? she thought as Quentin cracked her cheek against her teeth. She couldn't tell if she was thinking about herself or Quentin.

Blood streamed down her throat. *That damn cheek cut.* Tulsi had been hoping this time, it would finally heal for good. That was what she got for asking Quentin for a fight.

Tulsi scrabbled.

Quentin grabbed her hair and bent down. "Hope I don't pull your hair out. Keener would be disappointed."

Tulsi dug her nails into Quentin's scalp.

Quentin growled and slammed Tulsi's head into the floor.

Tulsi saw stars. She sneered, spitting blood, pushing herself up onto her elbows to drag her back down—

Quentin was faster. She stood up and brought her bare foot down hard on Tulsi's shoulder.

Tulsi's sneer gave way to a scream. The pain was bright and deep, deeper than cutting her cheek with her teeth, deeper than her ears ringing. This was deep in a way she'd never claw out.

A gasp rose over the audience.

"Shit," Tulsi choked. She froze on the floor, pain paralyzing her. "Shit, stop, stop—"

Quentin kept her there, pinned by the foot on her shoulder. The heel dug in.

Tulsi screamed again.

"STOP THE FIGHT!"

They looked up at Clementine's ragged voice. She and Alex had shoved to the front of the crowd, eyes blown wide in a way that nobody's ever were after Tulsi took a spill in trust falls. Clementine was staring, tense and dangerous, at Quentin, but Alex didn't look at her. She was staring in horror at Tulsi.

Clementine started, "Get—" but Quentin was already relenting, stepping off and away.

Tulsi collapsed. She didn't dare touch her shoulder, throbbing like fire.

Alex knelt down next to her, hand held out.

Quentin followed suit. "Are you okay?"

Tulsi ignored her. She grabbed Alex's hand and let herself be hauled up.

Alex asked, "Do you need to go to the—"

"I'm fine," Tulsi gasped. Sweat dripped into her eyes, down her cheeks. Familiar. It was too familiar. She'd screamed at cheer practice when Quentin first stomped down on this same shoulder. And just like last time, Quentin had stomped harder, just for a second, before letting Tulsi go.

Quentin twisted her hands, uncharacteristically nervous. "I didn't realize," she said.

Tulsi let out a shard of a laugh. She'd almost believed it back then.

Clementine flanked her. "Come on."

It took a second. Alex was stock-still at her side, staring back at Quentin with an expression Tulsi was intimately familiar with. She'd seen that face in the mirror: doubt was creeping in about Quentin Scarhill.

CHAPTER TWENTY-THREE

"There's no excuse," Alex whispered as they crouched in the backseat of a van. "Quentin feels terrible about it."

Oh, Clementine thought. *We're actually talking about it.*

"Right," she said, muffled by the car seat. She sat up to look out the window.

They were parked on the street across from a supermarket loading dock. A cluster of Sterling girls loitered outside the gates, fidgeting with their hoodies. Clementine had coached them all on how to throw a punch; now she was regretting not teaching them how to not look suspicious. The workers inside the loading dock weren't looking their way, but only because they didn't get paid enough to care about a bunch of shifty teenage girls skulking around the open gates.

"How are they doing?" Alex asked.

Clementine leaned back down. "Why are we here, again?"

Alex had the gall to look disappointed, like Clementine was in the wrong for not paying attention to Alex when she'd shown up at Clementine's door at 6 a.m. on a school day. Clementine had only had one hearing aid in for most of Alex's explanation and had still been shaking off a disturbing dream about breaking a piñata open and realizing she'd just beaten Sunju black and blue. She'd only caught the end of Alex's speech: *Are you coming?*

The sun wasn't even up yet. Alex had spent every available minute of the last few weeks with Quentin.

Of course, Clementine had said. Then: *Wait, is Quentin coming?*

Alex had shaken her head no.

And here they were, 7 a.m., no breakfast, crouched in the backseat of Becca's van. At least Becca had the right idea about looking normal: she was scrolling lazily through her phone and humming, like any normal person killing time in a van.

"Yazmine bled through her uniform on Friday," Alex explained. "Did you know our state doesn't legally require schools to keep sanitary products in the bathrooms? Anyway, obviously, I started thinking of an assignment."

"Obviously," Clementine muttered.

"One of the cheerleaders works at a chain supermarket," Alex continued. "And Girls Night is, like, anticapitalist—"

"We are?"

"Yes! Anyway—" Alex winced, massaging a crick in her neck.

Clementine rolled her eyes and sat up.

"Hey!" Alex tugged at her belt. "Get back down! We don't have hoodies—"

Clementine shushed her. "Yaz is coming out."

"Wait, really?" Alex peeked.

The other girls needed a class on how not to act suspicious. Yazmine, Clementine thought as she watched her slouch out the back of the supermarket with a hand truck stacked with boxes, could *teach* that class. Same bored expression as ever. She even yawned as she pushed the hand truck through the loading dock, scratching idly at her borrowed uniform.

The hooded girls waiting outside the gates perked up. One of them jumped on the spot, as if preparing for a race.

Clementine sighed. "Why are we getting them to do it for us?"

"It's an assignment. We can't take their girl power away from them." Alex held her breath as Yazmine reached the gates. Almost in the clear.

Yazmine yawned again, setting the hand truck down. The hooded girls started hauling boxes into their arms.

"What?" Alex hissed. "No, just wheel the whole thing over—"

Clementine nudged her. "You should yell that."

Alex glared.

In the driver's seat, Becca blew a gum bubble.

Yazmine bent down to pick up the last box. A tired-looking twenty-something slowed as he passed her.

"Oh, shit," Alex whispered as the guy stopped and said something to Yazmine.

Clementine nodded. She couldn't hear anything from across the road, but whatever the guy said made the girls freeze like baby deer in headlights.

All except for Yazmine. She fiddled with her nose ring, meeting the guy's gaze head-on as he pointed at the boxes the girls were carrying.

Come on, Clementine thought. She reached for the door handle, just in case. Was this why Alex had wanted her to come along—not Tulsi, not Sunju, but Clementine? So she could be the muscle in case things went south?

If so, she needn't have worried. The second the man's expression slid from weary confusion to shock, Yazmine slammed into him with all her strength, box-first.

"GO!" Yazmine shrieked, and took off sprinting across the road.

Alex scrambled out of the van. "Doors!"

Clementine followed her around to the van's back doors, yanking them open just in time for Yazmine to dump the first box. The other girls were in hot pursuit, the boxes thudding to an uneasy stop on the carpet.

"Van, go," Alex chanted, slapping each girl on the back as they dropped their boxes into the backseat, "van, go, van, go—"

Shouting drifted from the other side of the road. The guy from before was pointing, a few more guys blinking blearily in the early morning light. One of them started jogging towards them.

The last box landed. Alex and Clementine climbed in after it and pulled the back doors closed.

"Floor it!" Yazmine blurted from the passenger's seat.

Becca grinned. The car jerked into the street.

A man in a supermarket uniform banged on the back windows and then was gone, the van picking up speed and careening around a corner.

It was a long drive to school. Sterling was on the other side of the city.

"So we don't run into those workers again," Alex explained as they carted the boxes up to Sterling's fourth floor. "None of us shop at that supermarket. Box cutter?"

A cheerleader handed her one. Alex ripped into the first box and peered over the stairwell. Ten minutes until homeroom. Girls were still filtering in, glancing excitedly at their General opening boxes at the top of the fourth floor stairs.

Alex beamed at them. Then she looked at Clementine, and her smile died.

"Look," she said. "About . . . Quentin. I know you don't . . . *like* her . . ."

Like she could lead armies, Sunju had said once about Alex addressing the crowd from the top of the bleachers. Now here she was, toying with a boxcutter so she wouldn't have to look Clementine in the eyes.

The tide of girls became thicker. Clementine pressed against the stairwell to stay out of the way. "I really don't. How do you?"

Quentin was dangerous. She'd known it since that day in MeatLovers, Alex and Tulsi having some secret discussion in the bathroom. Quentin kept *looking* at Clementine, sizing her up. She had this uncanny ability to watch you like she saw you, down to your bones, and you should be concerned about what she saw.

Alex sighed, flipped her hair over one shoulder. Clementine couldn't remember her doing that before she'd started hanging out with Quentin, who had the hair flip down to an art.

Rage and disappointment boiled in Clementine's gut. She'd been so *sure* that night Alex called her. She'd lain in bed after she hung up, giddy and grinning. And then Alex had snubbed her at the cafeteria, and hadn't sought her out after school, and hadn't returned any of Clementine's sneaky glances.

There's this girl I like. Maybe Alex hadn't been talking about Clementine at all. Maybe Alex only ever had eyes for Quentin, and Clementine was desperate and stupid, making things up in her head. It was pretty ballsy, calling up your crush to talk about your crush. Clementine had always thought Alex was brave. Watching her rip into another box so she wouldn't have to look Clementine in the eyes made her reconsider.

"Tulsi's shoulder was an accident," Alex said. Did she believe it? Clementine couldn't tell. She was definitely *trying* to believe it.

Alex handed her a box. Clementine stacked it with the others.

"Things are complicated between those two," Alex said, "but she'd never hurt Tulsi on purpose."

"I've hurt—" Clementine lowered her voice, all too aware of the curious stares coming from every girl who passed. "I've hurt a lot of people, and I've been hurt by a lot of people. I . . . I *recognize* Quentin."

It did nothing to convey the way her skin crawled the first time she'd seen Quentin marching down the halls with her hair in a bright red crown around her head, eyes bright and cruel and terrifyingly keen. *That girl knows how to hurt.* She knew to fear Quentin the same way she knew to fear her parents' footsteps: marrow-deep, animal-deep. *Fight or flee, Clip-Clop. Which is it gonna be?*

She had to stop herself from flinching as Yazmine leaned on the stairwell next to her.

"Almost time," Yazmine told Alex with an easy grin. "Ready?"

Alex flashed a peace sign. Yazmine snorted and did one back, then grabbed a box from the pile.

"Look," Alex whispered as the girls lined up against the stairwell, boxes at the ready. "You don't have to be happy about it. I'm friends with Quentin, but I'm friends with you, too. Those two things won't stop being true."

There was the General her subjects had come to expect. Clementine had never had it directed at her before. She wanted to be reassured. Instead, she felt like a secondhand salesman was trying to sell her a car.

Alex glanced over at the boxes. "Aren't you grabbing one? You *were* in on the assignment."

I didn't know what I was agreeing to, Clementine wanted to say. *I just said yes because it was you.*

She picked up a box.

Alex smiled and turned to the stream of students heading up the staircase. "HEY, GIRLS!"

All eyes on Alex, who raised her arms. "LOOK OUT BELOW!"

"Heave-ho, bitches," Yazmine muttered.

Clementine heaved. A dozen boxes emptied into the staircase shaft. The lighter pads drifted, floating in the air-conditioned breeze. The heavier ones fell straight down, hitting first-floor girls with upturned hands.

The staircase dissolved into laughter and whoops. Clementine shook her box empty as girls shoved pads into bras and backpacks. She knew so many of these girls now. They smiled at her in the halls.

Alex leaned over, flushed and triumphant. "Totally worth getting up before dawn, right?"

"It's pretty cool," Clementine allowed.

Her gaze caught on a pile of rainbow locs pressed against the third-floor banister. Jem had bent down to scoop pads into her pockets, giggling like a kid. Clementine tried to feel uplifted, but all she could muster as she watched Jem playfully wrestle a girl to the floor and take her pads was slow, creeping dread.

The bus was most of the way to Sterling when a flash of rainbow locs caught her eye.

Jem slid into a seat at the front of the bus. She had industrial-sized headphones, head swiveling to the beat. It had been a few days since Yazmine's pads assignment.

I think Jem wants to hurt someone, Tulsi had told her when she'd caught Sunju and Clementine up on Jem's pyrotechnic extracurricular activities. Clementine imagined Jem's face, half-scared, half-exhilarated in the firework lights. The hard *bang* of sparks on metal. The hot sizzle of flame on flesh. Jem falling into whatever pose Clementine demonstrated, brows pinched in concentration. *It does something to me,* she'd said about the fight, bruised and bloody and *young* in a way Clementine had never been. *I like it.*

Clementine waved a cautious hand beside Jem's face. She hated it when someone walked up behind her and tapped her on the shoulder.

Jem looked over. Her face split into a grin, and she shuffled over. "Bruiser, hey! Come sit."

Clementine sat, careful to leave space between them. "Haven't seen you lately. I was getting worried."

Jem pouted. "Aw, sorry. I did mean to text you back! Remember that show I keep telling you to watch? Forget everything I said; it's a trash fire. Anyway—" Jem unzipped her backpack, flashing two rolls of elastic wrap. "Look! I finally found rainbow. Matchy-matchy."

She shook out her colorful locs, and Clementine didn't have to force her smile. Jem was lovely, small and sweet and full of fight. Clementine hoped Jem's fight was born from something good, bright and fun and electric, rather than the cautious, dark terror Clementine's had been born from.

"Matchy-matchy," she agreed.

Jem lowered her voice. "Are you heading to Girls Night? I thought you always got a ride with the Cheerleader."

"I'm on my own."

Jem nodded knowingly. "Gotta get the hit even when the friends are busy. I got you." She giggled. "*Hit.* Get it?"

This was the girl who'd had Clementine over to her house to watch reality TV and meet her elderly dog, Ludo. The girl who cried at sad commercials and gave Clementine DVDs of all the TV shows she wanted Clementine to watch. The girl Clementine had taught in too many one-on-one sessions to count, and even with all the punches Jem had landed, it was hard to picture her hurting anybody. Even if they'd had to remind her three times about the no biting rule.

I get carried away, Jem would say, her teeth bloody, her face sorrowful. Sure, she hurt people, but that was Girls Night, under Clementine's watchful eye. Could she really hurt someone in real life?

"Ha ha." Clementine glanced around. Their half of the bus was empty except for the driver, a bored middle-aged woman humming along to the radio. It would still be safer if they could sign. "Jem. Tulsi told me about the car."

Jem's face twisted—excitement and nerves. "Aaaand?"

"And what are you planning?"

Jem's face fell. It was almost adorable. "Um. Nothing?"

"Jem." Clementine did her best *I'm not angry; I'm disappointed* look, which Joseph excelled at.

Jem picked at the pink foam around her headphones. "If you're gonna act like that, then *definitely* nothing."

"This is serious. You could really hurt someone."

"Good." Jem bit her lip. "I hope I kill him."

Clementine fought back a shudder. This wasn't something Jem would invent on her own—not without help, without someone whispering in her ear. Someone like Quentin.

Who would Quentin even want to kill?

Clementine kept her voice even, trying to channel Joseph's calming tone. "I don't have to tell you why that's a bad idea."

Jem shrugged, picked some more at her headphone foam. A shred of pink crept under her fingernail. "Some things are worth getting in trouble for."

"*Trouble*, sure. Lifelong imprisonment"—Clementine checked; the bus driver was humming along to Joan Jett, oblivious—"not so much."

Jem pouted. She hugged her backpack to her chest. She was a freshman. And she'd gone up a grade in middle school. She was younger than everybody else at Sterling. Her dog, Ludo, was six months older than she was.

"Jem," Clementine tried, "tell us what's going on, and we can help."

Jem eyed her hopefully.

"*Without* hurting people," Clementine added, wishing Joseph was here. He'd get Jem to stop. He'd stopped her from doing so much stupid shit. And here she was, trying to keep some hotheaded teenage girl from doing something that would ruin her life, something he'd talked her out of so many times, and she was bombing it.

Jem scowled. "You guys beat up that asshole from Sterling Boys! Becca told me about it. She said he even called her to apologize."

Clementine was surprised Bryce had bothered. Maybe Alex's period blood had knocked some sense into him. "That was a one-off."

Even as she said it, she was unsure how true it was. Alex had all these *plans* for Girls Night. Maybe Quentin had even more. What would the Ringleaders be called to do?

Jem's mouth wobbled. "You really won't help me kill him?"

"No."

Jem sniffed. "He really deserves it."

Clementine's heart pounded in her chest. *They deserved it.* How many times had Clementine spat those very words at her brother, her teacher, her parents? She'd said it to Principal Ryans, even, when she was dragged into the office for beating up Olive Barnes. She'd remembered Olive's cruel smirk as she reached to touch Clementine's hearing aids and believed she deserved Clementine's fists with every fiber of her being. Broken nose? She deserved it. Black eyes? Deserved it. Deserved *worse*, even.

Clementine's throat clicked. "What did he do to you?"

Jem's face turned bitter. "Like you care. Get up."

"Hey. Of course I care—"

Jem stabbed the stop button. "Get *up*."

Clementine got up.

Jem shoved past her as the bus jerked over to the side of the road.

"Don't text me again," she croaked. "And don't bother giving me my DVDs back; those shows suck. *You* suck."

"Wait," Clementine said. "Come on. We can still help."

Jem stormed off the bus without looking back. The bus pulled away.

Clementine watched Jem walk from streetlight to streetlight. Even after the bus turned the corner, Clementine kept watching the last spot she'd seen Jem yanking her headphones back up, swiping furiously at her cheeks, emotion making her chin tremble.

Betrayal, Clementine realized. She was becoming familiar with it.

Clementine's hands shook as she walked into the warehouse. Any other night, walking into Girls Night in full swing would get Clementine twitching in a good way. But now the whoops and cries and smacking noises had her fighting down flinches.

Nothing happened. You're fine. Clementine breathed in through her nose and out through her mouth, like her old counselor had told her. *You're safe. You might have ruined Jem's life by not talking her out of whatever she's planning, but you're safe.*

A girl yelled in pain. Clementine wrenched open her eyes.

You're safe, she thought again. She squeezed her hands into fists. They wouldn't steady. Maybe she should just head home—

A hand closed around her shoulder. "Can I get a rematch after these guys finish?"

Clementine turned. Olive Barnes was grinning at her, cheeks flushed and eyes bright. The bruises were gone. She looked almost as if Clementine had never gotten her down onto the floor and beaten her until her nose broke.

It took a while for Clementine to speak. "Maybe next time."

Another hand on her shoulder, this one sliding so an arm was around the back of her neck. Clementine flinched hard before Tulsi came into view.

"It's Clip-Clop Clem. Didn't expect to see you here." Tulsi's smile was lopsided, her hand over her injured shoulder. *Fake having fun until you're actually having it,* Tulsi had told her at a party once. Sometimes, Tulsi tried too hard.

Clementine unstuck her tongue. "Didn't expect you, either. I thought we appointed Yazmine as leader on Thursdays."

"She's still here. Just not in charge. Ringleader privileges." Tulsi hooked a thumb over her shoulder at Yazmine scrolling through her phone on the fringes of the group.

Girls Night was on too often now for them to attend every meeting. Yazmine got Thursdays, Cady got Saturdays, Quentin got Tuesdays. They weren't Ringleaders—Alex was sure to stress that—they were temporary group leaders, wrangling the girls when the actual leaders weren't present. It made Clementine nervous.

"Homework was boring. I decided to come along," Tulsi said. Her smile became more solid. "And it's good I did—guess who else is here."

Clementine turned to where Tulsi was gesturing. Sunju appeared. People were always appearing out of nowhere when Clementine got like this: it was hard to focus on anything that wasn't directly in front of her.

Was she hurt? Clementine couldn't see anything, but that didn't mean much. Sunju's cardigan sleeves went down to her wrists, her jeans baggy against her shoes. She could be hiding anything under there.

Tulsi kept talking, but Clementine didn't hear it. She nodded at Sunju and hoped it counted as a hello, one of their wordless communications Clementine was so fond of.

Clementine took her shoes off on autopilot. Tulsi started pulling her towards the circle. Olive followed.

Right, Clementine thought. *The fight.*

"Not tonight."

"Why?" Tulsi said. Her gaze turned scrutinizing. "You hurt?"

"I'm fine—"

"Then go!" Tulsi pushed her into the ring. The other fight must have ended.

Clementine bit her cheek to the blood. Girls Night had this effect on people: it put them in a dazzlingly clear space where things were fast and fun and the world was a hot, exciting place, with them in the center. Consequences were on hold, and nothing could cause lasting damage.

I'm a consequence, Clementine thought at her. She couldn't make her mouth move. *I'm hurt; I'm a hurt; don't brush this off as nothing—*

Olive stood in front of her, bouncing from foot to foot and punching the air like boxers did in the movies.

Tulsi was holding her hand out. Clementine stared at it as Tulsi said something she didn't catch.

"What?"

"Hearing aids," Tulsi said, in the tone that suggested she'd repeated it more than once.

Not tonight, Clementine thought, but the thoughts were very far away. They could never reach her mouth from how deeply they were in her head. She took her hearing aids out, and things were a little easier, the world falling into muted static. She dropped the aids into Tulsi's hand and turned to Olive on autopilot.

Olive was still jumping. It was both too slow and too fast at once.

It's just a fight, Clementine thought. She could fight. Maybe it'd fix her. Maybe this was what she needed. How many times had she gone looking for a fight? How many times had she *needed* a fight, blood burning in her veins, aching for the crack of knuckles on skin?

Clementine raised her fists.

The first punch caught Clementine in the forehead. She moved with it, thinking vaguely about the talk she'd given multiple groups about avoiding the face when punching. Everyone always aimed for the face. It was dramatic. It was movie material. It was dangerous, bone on bone. Better to aim for the stomach.

The next punch came. Clementine caught it. Her hands were getting steadier.

Olive said something. Clementine watched her mouth move. Watched her smirk, like she had before she touched Clementine's hearing aids. Watched Olive's arm cock back—

Clementine drove her fist into Olive's gut. It felt more real than anything in the last ten minutes.

Olive doubled over. Clementine rammed her elbow into her back and followed her down to the floor.

You deserve this, her dad said to her once. Just once, so young that Clementine couldn't reach the kitchen sink to get herself a glass of water. They'd been in the kitchen, actually, Clementine huddled against the fridge with blood running down her throat, her dad huge and horrible as he stomped out of the room. *You deserve this*, tossing the words over his shoulder like an afterthought. It became a mantra. Hitting or getting hit. *You deserve this, you deserve this.*

Smack. Clementine hit her in the jaw.

Smack. Olive had given up on punching; now she was flailing blindly.

Smack. Tears streamed down Olive's face, one eye already swelling. When had Clementine caught her in the eye?

Clem. A distant call, someone yelling from a faraway mountain she could never visit.

Clem!

A hand on her back.

Clementine whirled, snarling, ready to pounce.

Sunju stood back, hands up. Her stance was strong, feet not too far apart, just like Clementine had shown her. Tulsi hovered behind her, finally looking horrified, just as she should have when Clementine walked in. Clementine was a consequence; Clementine was a hurt; she was—

Sunju signed, *"You OK?"*

Clementine got up and walked out. The walk from the ring to the warehouse door was so long and so short.

Cool night air on her cheeks. Cracked asphalt, fading paint. She found a corner and sat down, dropping her head against her knees. There was a breathing thing she was supposed to be doing. Big breath in through the nose. She held it until her head swam. Breathe out through the mouth . . .

A hand waved beside her face.

Clementine looked up. Sunju was framed by a halo of streetlight.

She didn't say hi or nod, but she did look at Clementine for many seconds before sitting down next to her. She held out a hand. Tulsi must have given her the hearing aids.

Clementine fitted her hearing aids in but did not turn them on. *"Thanks."*

"You're safe," Sunju tried.

She didn't say it again. Whatever Clementine's face had done in reaction to that, it must've been bad. When somebody told

Clementine she was safe, she didn't think of friends coming to save her. She remembered adults telling her that her parents could never have done what Clementine said they did, and that she should stop lying. Doctors telling her something wouldn't hurt right before it did.

"*You're outside the warehouse,*" Sunju said. "*It's cool. It's dark. You're clenching your hands. Can you feel them?*"

Clementine sucked in a breath, squeezed her fists tighter. Yes, she could feel them.

Sunju kept narrating the space around them—the glare of the streetlights, the scratchy material of Clementine's shirt—until Clementine's breathing evened out.

"*Thanks,*" she said again.

"*No problem,*" Sunju said.

Clementine let her knee shift sideways so it pressed into Sunju's. This, too, was comfortable.

"*How are you?*"

Sunju shook her head. "*You?*"

Clementine wiped sweat from her neck. "*Worried.*"

"*About?*"

Clementine wanted to tell her about Jem. *You really won't help me kill him?* Jem's betrayed eyes, gleaming with tears. Whispers in the hallways turning reverent. Quentin's watchful gaze making the back of Clementine's neck prickle. What had they gotten themselves into?

Big breath through the nose. Out through the mouth.

"*Alex is spending too much time with Quentin. It's not good for her.*"

Sunju's nod was too knowing. It had been too knowing back at that cafeteria table, watching Alex leave them for the cheerleaders' table. She knew what Clementine felt.

They lapsed back into silence. It had taken Sunju a while to figure out that Clementine's silence wasn't a plea for conversation, that they were both comfortable just sitting in quiet. Clementine got the feeling Sunju had been raised to believe her preference for silence was rude, so Clementine had made it clear she didn't mind. It was nice, this not talking together. Lately, she'd been thinking about the parts of herself she recognized in the others. Tulsi's venom, her carefully hidden softness. Alex's loneliness and her fascination with the fight. Sunju's underlying hurt, but mostly her quiet. Clementine and Sunju were suited for the quiet. They'd built it into a defense so long ago, neither of them could picture themselves without it.

Sunju looked down. Her phone lit up on her knee. *MOM*.

"*You're getting a call*," Clementine signed when Sunju didn't move.

Sunju rested her chin on her knees. "*I know*."

They sat there until the screen went dark.

CHAPTER TWENTY-FOUR

Sunju watched the tight line of Tulsi's shoulders and itched for a sketch pad. She'd fill out the coiled posture first, Tulsi pacing barefoot across the concrete. Her thumbnail was in her mouth, gnawing her cuticles. Any moment now, the blood would show up, and Tulsi would make that same face she always did: resignation, brief regret. Then she'd bite harder to rip the shred off her finger.

A call rang out through the warehouse. "Sunju! What are the makeup colors, again?"

Sunju turned towards the door. There were still a few stragglers putting their shoes on. The room had cleared out pretty fast once Yazmine had given Olive a ride to the hospital.

"If it's purple-toned, use a yellow concealer," Sunju told the girls. "Green for red bruises, peach if it's going yellow."

The girl grinned. A bruise the size and color of a grapefruit swelled on her cheek. "Thanks, Sunju!"

"You're welcome," Sunju called. It echoed around the empty warehouse, getting one more good ring as the three girls squeezed out the crack in the warehouse door.

Tulsi swore. Blood beaded at the edge of her thumb. Sunju watched her teeth close around the offending piece of flesh.

"Clem won't be mad you made her fight," Sunju told her. Clementine had gone home not long after Sunju had found her under that streetlight.

"What?" Tulsi swallowed her cuticle and looked up. "I know."

Sunju wrinkled her nose. "That's disgusting."

"This place has seen grosser." Tulsi rubbed blood spots into the ground with her bare foot. "How was home?"

Sunju curled a hand over her side. One big bruise all down her ribs was going yellow. "Why do you like the fight so much?"

Tulsi hesitated, rubbed her thumb. Sunju tried to imagine how she'd draw the blood smear.

"The rush."

"And?"

Tulsi shrugged, still pacing, scraping her heels into the concrete. "And that's it."

Sunju ducked into her way. "Does it make you feel safe?"

"Uh," Tulsi said. "Safety isn't really why I do this." She tried to step around.

Sunju stepped in front of her. "Does it make you feel in control?"

Tulsi didn't answer. Sunju watched her face. Tulsi watched back, each of them waiting for the other to look away.

Sunju was so tired of waiting.

"Let's grapple."

Tulsi blinked. Her mouth twitched, like Sunju was telling a strange joke and she was trying to figure it out.

"You said we should," Sunju said, "so let's."

"Grapple," Tulsi said slowly. Her pupils were dilated, giant pools of black with a thin circle of brown penning them in.

"I can practice the moves Clem has been showing me."

"The last time I saw you two doing that, she was teaching you how to headbutt."

"It's an effective way to get out of a hold," Sunju recited. She got into the stance Clementine had shown her. "Are you coming at me or what?"

Tulsi folded her arms. They flexed. Sunju was 90 percent sure she wasn't doing it to draw her eye.

"Come on." Sunju butted her knuckles against Tulsi's flexed arm. "Don't be a—"

Tulsi lunged. Sunju's butt hit the floor, then her legs. Tulsi was still holding her head, protecting it from the concrete. Sunju's bruised side barely twinged.

"Okay." Sunju patted Tulsi's elbow gingerly. "We probably should've started on the ground."

"Probably," Tulsi agreed. She moved so she was braced over Sunju, legs pinning Sunju down, hands circling Sunju's elbows. "So, how are you gonna—"

Sunju headbutted her. Not hard: just enough to shock Tulsi into yelping.

"Holy shit!" Tulsi yelled, jerking back.

Sunju used the surprise to rip her hands from Tulsi's grip and shove her sideways, pushing into the momentum to roll them over.

Tulsi's back hit the floor, shaking with laughter.

"You *asshole!*" she crowed, grinning.

Sunju slid her hands around Tulsi's wrists, knees pressing into Tulsi's thighs. They were both wearing jeans, the denim rasping.

Sunju leaned up. "How am I doing?"

Tulsi laughed again. Sunju waited for that look she often got at the start of a fight—the spark in her eyes, smile turning razor blade mean. Her eyes sparked, but it was a different kind of spark than Sunju was used to. This one was adrenaline, sure, but there was no promise of hurt. No sharpness. Just light.

Sunju shifted on top of her, redistributing her weight. Tulsi moved with her, getting comfortable, and Sunju's mind flickered with unmentionables. Things she'd scribbled in a hurry in her sketchbooks and immediately crossed out, sometimes so hard the pencil tore the paper.

Whenever Sunju looked at Tulsi like this, it was all stolen glances: a glimpse of collarbone, a flash of thigh under a skirt. More and more, she'd let herself look while Tulsi fought. It was safe— *everyone* was watching Tulsi, and Sunju could pretend she was admiring the fight instead of the way Tulsi's dark hair fanned out around her head.

It was doing it now, that hair. Dark with a hint of curl, splayed out like a net. Her cheekbones, sharp and dangerous. Her chin, which Tulsi once dug into the back of a girl's neck until the girl let go. You could cut yourself on everything when it came to Tulsi.

But Tulsi's voice was soft as she said, "You have freckles."

Sunju swallowed. Her throat was dry, her cheeks hot. "What?"

Tulsi nodded up at her. She hadn't tried to get out of the hold while Sunju held her down. She hadn't even strained.

"Freckles," Tulsi said. "Across the bridge of your nose."

Sunju swallowed again, watched Tulsi watch her, eyes dragging over the line of Sunju's throat as it worked.

What the heck, Sunju thought, *am I doing?*

She rolled off of Tulsi onto the concrete. It was still warm from all the hot bodies that had pressed into it. She lay on her back and stared up at the ceiling.

Next to her, Tulsi was very still.

"My forehead hurts," Sunju said.

Tulsi made a noise of agreement.

"I didn't even hit you in the right place," Sunju continued. "I'm not supposed to get you in the forehead. It's the strongest part of your head. I'm supposed to get you in the nose."

Tulsi hugged her own hips. "You're welcome to try again."

"How's your shoulder?"

Tulsi rotated it. "Fine."

"Alex said Quentin really—"

"I said it's fine," Tulsi said. "How's . . ." She trailed off.

Sunju sighed. She could change the subject again. For all Tulsi knew, it wasn't that bad. She could say she was healed up.

She rolled over and pulled up her shirt. Fading yellow all down her ribs, half-hidden by her bra.

"Jesus," Tulsi said. "They should be in jail. Is it both of them?"

Sunju pulled her shirt down. "Kind of. It . . . um. Actually, I don't want to talk about it. Change the subject."

"As you command." Tulsi doffed an imaginary hat. "What subject are we changing to? I can't think."

"What do we think about our General letting Yaz and Cady supervise Girls Night when we aren't there?"

"Who gives a shit about Yaz and Cady? Q's the one we're worried about. I *shudder* to think what a Quentin-led Girls Night turns into." Tulsi rubbed her temples. "Alex *will* step in, right? If it gets really bad? She won't, like . . . let Quentin introduce brass knuckles?"

"Sure."

"Sure," Tulsi said, half-mocking. She waved a hand conductor-style. "Subject change. Go."

Sunju paused. There was a question she'd been wanting to ask for a while. It had never seemed appropriate. It still didn't feel right, but she'd shown Tulsi her bruises; Tulsi could show Sunju hers, if she wanted.

"What's the deal with the Keener guy?"

Tulsi twisted away. Sunju watched the curve of her shoulder, the concrete cooling underneath them.

"Um . . ." Tulsi said. "I . . . he . . ."

"You don't have to say—"

"Oh my god, shut *up*." Tulsi kicked her in the shin. "It's not a big deal."

"Okay."

"He's just some creep." Tulsi turned back, gaze tracking the ceiling. Her face creased, a silent conversation she was having with herself. Sunju imagined it: *This is stupid. Just say it. Not a big deal. Just—*

"He didn't touch me," Tulsi said in a rush. "He just . . . he said some stuff. And he was . . . I thought he was good. We were, like . . . friends? Or kind of . . . dating. But obviously not, because he was, like, 20-something, and I was fourteen. Thirteen? Anyway, I thought he was nice. Good dude. Cute. You know?"

Sunju nodded. She didn't know what to say. Nobody had admitted this kind of thing to her before. She'd heard about it, of course. She knew it happened. Statistically, a third of the girls in every class she'd ever been in had experienced something like this. But no one ever said anything.

Tulsi blinked. Her eyes were wet.

"I almost let him," she whispered. "I almost . . . I kicked him and ran out. But I almost . . ."

Sunju reached for her hand.

Tulsi sat up too fast and grabbed her injured shoulder.

"Shit," she spat. Her eyes squeezed shut, a vein throbbing near her hairline as she massaged her injury. Sunju watched her knead at the skin and imagined the muscle beneath, sinew and veins and the nerves that Quentin had forever damaged.

"You should really go to the doctor."

Tulsi grunted. "Sunju?"

"Yeah?"

"How much does your head hurt?"

Sunju felt her forehead. The throb was almost gone. "Not much."

"Ugh. You're not seeing halos?"

"What?"

Tulsi blinked hard, like someone trying to adjust to the light. Then she said, slower than Sunju had ever heard her speak, "I think I have a concussion."

CHAPTER TWENTY-FIVE

Joseph leaned out of the window, peering across the street at the dark parking lot. "*I don't see—*"

Clementine pointed. Sunju and Tulsi were standing at the parking lot entrance, melting into the shadows.

Joseph waved them over. Clementine fitted in her hearing aids just in time for the back doors to snap closed.

Joseph twisted to look at Tulsi. "Are you—"

Tulsi cut him off. "Why are *you* here? You should be . . . recovering."

"Back at you," Clementine said. Dried sweat crusted her armpits, her neck, sliming up her back. She'd been about to get in the shower when Sunju had called her. "Are we going to the hospital?"

"Yes," Sunju said.

Tulsi shook her head. "I've been concussed before," she said, slow and careful in a way that reminded Clementine of Tulsi drunk, without all the laughter. "This one's not bad. Just need to get woken up every . . . yeah."

"Every two hours," Sunju recited. She'd probably looked it up while waiting. Or maybe she just knew about concussions from personal experience, like Clementine.

She twisted to face Sunju. "Your head's okay?"

"Yes!" Sunju kept tugging at her hair, making motions like she was going to tie it up, and then dropping her hands. "I don't know how this happened! My head is fine! It's sore, but I'm not seeing halos!"

Tulsi stared up at the car ceiling, eyes tracking lazily. "Sunju needs to get home."

"*You* need to go to the hospital."

"Are you paying for it?" Tulsi went to scratch her nose. It took two tries.

Joseph tapped a beat on the steering wheel. "So, where are we headed?"

Tulsi opened her mouth.

Sunju talked over her. "She doesn't want to disturb her family. Said they'd never let her live down a 'come get me' call this late."

Clementine turned. Joseph was already looking at her. He raised his eyebrows. Clementine raised hers back. They nodded in time.

"What was that?" Tulsi asked flatly. "What's happening?"

Sunju wasn't happy about being dropped off. She fidgeted the whole way home, throwing cross, worried glances at Tulsi. Clementine watched in the rearview mirror. There were other glances, too—soft ones Clementine didn't want to intrude on.

"Every two hours," Sunju reminded Tulsi, leaning against the backseat window. Her house loomed behind her, dark and silent except for one pinpoint of light: the living room was still alive. Her parents were waiting. They had ten minutes before curfew.

"I'm not the one to tell that to," Tulsi said.

Sunju lingered. The anger faded. Another soft look.

Clementine averted her gaze towards the street. Carefully maintained backyards could be seen through the fences. Sunju wasn't the only one with a fishpond—several houses had big ones. If you put a goldfish in a big pool, the fish gets big.

Clementine loved big goldfish. She'd seen them twice in real life, both times when she was ten. Puppy-cute, with their tiny mouths opening and closing. Joseph had had to stop her from sticking her hands in the water and petting them.

"I'm sorry," Sunju said from the backseat.

"This isn't even the first concussion I've had this year," Tulsi replied. "At least you did it by accident. Yazmine missed my trust fall because I made fun of her nose ring."

"Really?"

"I don't know. Maybe." A pause. "Have a good night, Sunju."

"You too. Thanks, Joseph, Clementine."

Joseph waved.

Clementine nodded, still thinking about big goldfish.

They pulled away from the curb. Clementine watched Tulsi watch Sunju unlatch the gate. Sunju disappeared down the driveway.

Clementine asked, "They're letting her out now?"

Eyes closed now, head tilted into the seat, Tulsi recited, "She's allowed out this weekend if she stays home for all of next week."

"School?"

"Yeah, she can go again."

Joseph asked, "Is she okay?"

They didn't answer. The car rumbled underneath them as smoothly as Joseph could make it. Mechanics only went so far before reality set in: it was a shitty car.

Tulsi didn't talk again until they were in the apartment. She lay down on Clementine's mattress. "I can take the sleeping bag."

"No," Clementine said. She unrolled it. It was bright orange, which meant it was Tulsi's. Alex's pink bag sat coiled in the corner. *You're the only place we have sleepovers,* she'd said when she'd suggested this. *It's easier than lugging them to school.*

Both of them had asked if it was okay, taking up space in Clementine's room when they weren't there. Clementine had tripped over her words, she was so fast in telling them it was alright. She liked to look over at the sleeping bags, at the promise of the two of them coming over, of Clementine waking in the night and rolling over to find them there in the dark.

Sunju had a sleeping bag too. She had yet to use it. It was small and blue.

"How are you?" Tulsi asked. She closed her eyes, motioned at nothing. "After . . . Olive."

"I'm fine," Clementine said.

Tulsi hummed. Her eyebrows were pinched.

"Do you want Tylenol?"

Tulsi shook her head, winced.

"You sure?"

A nod.

"Okay. I'm going to shower. Don't die while I'm away."

Tulsi snorted, winced again. Clementine switched the light off, and her face began to smooth out.

It was a relief to wash off the sweat. Clementine's cheek smarted with Olive's punch, but not enough that she had to be careful of her face when she soaped it up. She checked in with her body, something her old therapist had taught her. Other than the cheek, nothing else hurt.

Joseph was waiting for her in the hall. "*Sure you don't want me to stay up with her?*"

"No. Thanks."

Joseph twitched, itched at his ear, his forehead, the inside of his cheek. He always tried very hard not to get angry.

"*This is dangerous,*" he signed.

"*We're fine.*"

"*No, you're not. I could've gotten into real trouble pretending to be a teacher. I shouldn't have encouraged this. Tulsi should be in the hospital right now.*"

Clementine swallowed. Her hands were still for a moment.

"*We have it under control.*"

Joseph didn't look comforted. He put his hands on his hips, but only for a second. That was something their mom used to do. It had meant bad things were coming, and Joseph didn't want to be a bad thing.

"*I don't like it,*" he told her.

Clementine shrugged. "*I do. And all my friends are in it.*"

Joseph fixed her with a wary look.

Clementine puffed out her shoulders, tried to look confident. Like she hadn't felt that stab of weariness when she'd told Joseph she liked Girls Night. It wasn't a lie. But it wasn't fully the truth.

Joseph sighed. "*You can tell me anything, you know that?*"

Clementine nodded, but they had never been that kind of family. Joseph was her protector, her soldier next to her in the trenches, and sometimes her confidant. But there would always be things they didn't tell each other.

I sent a girl to hospital tonight, she imagined telling him. *I didn't even mean to. I just shut down. There's this other girl who wants to kill someone with her family's fireworks. I thought Alex liked me, but it turns out I'm just an idiot.* Even the idea of that conversation made Clementine impossibly tired.

When she got back to her room, her phone was lighting up on her pillow. Clementine fumbled in her hearing aids and grabbed for it. Unknown number.

"Hello?"

"I had to talk my mom out of pressing charges," a slurred voice said.

Tulsi groaned. "Turn off the light!"

Clementine crept out of the room.

"I *did* ask you to fight me," the voice continued.

"Olive?" Clementine eased the door closed behind her. She checked the hall. Noise from the kitchen: Joseph making a late-night snack. "Did you tell your mom—"

"No, I didn't tell her about Girls Night. *God.*"

"You can have a free shot," Clementine offered. "Hurt me all you want."

"Ugh. It's not fun if you just stand there."

Clementine's hand shook. She tightened her grip on the phone. "I don't want to fight you again."

Olive blew a raspberry. "What was with you, anyway? Everybody said you aren't usually like that."

"That was—" Clementine craned her head. The microwave was on in the kitchen. Tulsi's microwave popcorn. They'd have to restock. "It just happens sometimes. PTSD . . . thing. I'm really sorry."

A long pause.

Clementine wondered how bad it was. She should've asked. That was what you asked when someone got hurt.

"How are—"

"You're really messed up, huh?"

Clamor in the background. The staticky buzz of a PA. Clementine hated hospitals.

Olive sighed. "Should've known better than to mess with The Bruiser, I guess."

"I guess," Clementine echoed, something deep inside her cracking. "Yeah."

Olive hung up.

Clementine stood there trembling until the microwave beeped in the kitchen. Then she FaceTimed Alex.

"Hi," she said. "Sorry if I woke you."

"'M awake," Alex rasped, in the voice of someone who had been asleep until very recently. Her hair was mussed, her cheek bunching against her pillow. She aimed the screen down so Clementine could see her mouth. "Everything okay?"

Clementine picked at her bruised knuckles. The pain was dull and familiar. Anything could be comforting if it happened enough.

"Something's going on," she said. "Jem might try to kill someone. I think it's an assignment. I think Quentin gave it to her."

Silence down the line.

Clinking from the kitchen. Joseph was putting away the dishes.

"Clem," Alex sighed. "I . . . she might kill someone? What *happened?*"

"Jem said she wanted to kill someone. The fireworks were a trial run. She expected me to help—*us* to help. The Ringleaders."

"Well, yeah. They look up to us." The screen tilted as Alex sat up, hugging a heart-shaped pillow to her chest. If there was a pillow around, Alex was going to hug it.

"I know Q's a *lot*," Alex said, and Clementine's heart sank. "And I know you don't like her—"

"This isn't about—"

"—but that's intense, Clem. I mean, *murder?* Are you sure Jem wasn't exaggerating?"

"I'm sure."

"Why do you think Quentin's involved?"

"Because who else would tell Jem to firebomb someone?"

"Who says she got told to do it?"

"I don't know! I just—" Clementine lowered her voice. The kitchen was quiet. "It fits. I'm not saying definitely; I'm saying we should look into it."

"And by we—"

"You. You should look into it."

More hushed rasping. Alex rubbed her cheek on her fuzzy pillow. *When I die,* she once told Clementine as she lay in her sea of heart-shaped pillows, *I want to be buried with these.*

Clementine had watched her sprawl out over a rainbow of hearts and thought a number of stupid things, like how beautiful Alex was and how she'd like to be buried with her when the time came.

"I'll look into it," Alex said. "But . . . Clem, I don't think—"

"Alex."

"Quentin would never do that. Even if she's giving out assignments—which we don't know if she is—she'd never ask someone to do that."

"Sure," Clementine said. "Right. Yes. Bye."

"Clem, I—"

Clementine hung up.

Joseph rounded the corner into the hallway, cradling a bowl of popcorn. He tilted it towards her.

Clementine took a piece, thinking of apology noodles. "*Thanks.*"

Joseph nodded, stood there across from her in that thin hallway, scooping popcorn with one hand. For the second time that night, Clementine thought about telling him everything.

He rapped her forehead with his thumb. "What's going on up there?"

"I'm going to check on Tulsi." She ducked back into her room.

Tulsi was awake, watching Clementine blearily from her thin mattress. "Clem, if you could fight any celebrity, alive or dead, who would you fight?"

Clementine thought about it. "Woody Allen."

"Oh." Tulsi snorted, closing her eyes. "Good answer. I was going to say Marilyn Monroe. That girl needed an *outlet.*"

She fell asleep in seconds, snoring loudly.

Clementine took her hearing aids out, and the snores fell away. Joseph's retreating footsteps in the hall fell away. Clementine climbed into bed and wished there was a life version of that— everything falling away—that didn't hurt.

Girls Night felt good, she'd told Joseph. And it did. It felt good to fight for fun; it felt good to teach; it felt good to get whispered about in the halls out of admiration, to look over and see people smiling, not flinching.

But beating Olive's face in didn't feel good. Watching Jem walk away crying didn't feel good. Lying in bed worrying over Quentin's plans didn't feel good.

Alex, she thought as sleep dragged her under fifteen minutes before her alarm would wake her for Tulsi, *what did you drag us into?*

CHAPTER TWENTY-SIX

They were an hour into Girls Night, and Alex was still no closer to finding out anything about Jem she didn't already know. Every time she'd sidle up to a girl and find a way to nudge Jem into the conversation, the reaction would be one of the following:

1. Oh, the girl with the rainbow hair?
2. Oh, the girl whose family owns that firework factory?
3. Oh, that girl who kicked my ass last week and left me with this gnarly bruise? Want to see it, General?

Jem was younger than the other freshman. Jem got decent grades, but she wasn't going to get into any AP classes. Jem's parents were still together, and she had an older sister who went to college out of state. Jem cried last week because she stepped on a butterfly. Useless, useless.

It didn't help that Alex had to do all this out of Quentin's earshot. Every time Quentin came over, Alex would have to change the subject, and she was running out of subjects. But she was still getting away with it.

Or at least, that was what she thought until Quentin asked, "What's so interesting about Jem?"

Alex's smile froze in place. She glanced over at her laundromat girls leaning against the opposite wall. Tulsi was shielding her eyes from the dim warehouse lights, still recovering from her concussion. Sunju was sketching, determinedly not paying attention to what was happening across from her. Only Clementine was watching them, a frown creasing her brows.

What? Alex wanted to ask her. *I'm doing what you wanted! Quit it with the annoyed face!*

Quentin cocked her head, expectant. She was smiling, but it was that sharp smile she usually reserved for her cheerleaders when they'd executed a move incorrectly. Alex felt like a pinned butterfly.

Then Quentin's smile softened, and she reached out to rub a soothing circle into Alex's bruised knuckles. "Just making conversation, Veck. Didn't know it was such a sensitive subject."

"I've been asking around," Alex said. "She hasn't been at Girls Night for a week, and she's missed a few days of school."

Quentin hummed, turning Alex's hand over and tracing a line in her palm. Her nails were too sharp. Alex kept meaning to ask Quentin to file them down—she couldn't fight with nails that sharp—but even with all the time they'd spent with each other, practically glued to each other for the past few weeks, every time Alex went to bring it up, she'd lose her nerve.

Quentin asked, "Is she injured?"

"That's what I'm trying to figure out," Alex said, relieved for the excuse. Now to find some slick way to ask Quentin if she'd been handing out assignments.

"Do you know much about her?"

"Jem?" Quentin shook her head. "Freshman. That cool hair. *Vicious* right hook."

"Nothing else?"

"Not really. Why?"

"Nothing, I just—ow." Quentin's nails were digging in.

"What? Oh, sorry." Quentin pressed a kiss to the indent in Alex's palm. "Better?"

"Better," Alex said, unable to keep the giggle out of her voice. She averted her gaze towards the fight in the middle of the warehouse. It was hard to concentrate with Quentin watching her like that, her hand still stinging from the kiss.

What are we? she imagined asking. No, not the time. Clementine wanted her to put her suspicion to rest. And honestly, so did Alex. If it was just her, she would bury it, convince herself she was being paranoid. But all her friends were giving Quentin the side-eye. She could ignore her own worry, but she couldn't ignore theirs.

It would be a relief, clearing Quentin's name. Alex just . . . wasn't totally sure it would scrub clean so easily. She didn't think Quentin would instruct someone to commit *murder*, but she could definitely be keeping things from Alex. Alex would be surprised if she wasn't.

She glanced over at the wall, hoping to find Clementine's approving face. But Clementine wasn't paying attention to them at all—she was staring at the fight with a stormy expression that made Alex's chest twist.

Quentin's grip tightened around her hand. Alex barely noticed, too busy searching for Clementine's gaze. *I'm doing what you wanted! Look at me, damnit!*

Tulsi appeared at her side, still shielding from the light. "Hey! I'm going home. Last chance to ride the Tulsi-mobile."

"Is your head okay?"

Quentin made a sympathetic noise. "What happened?"

Tulsi rolled her tongue around her mouth. "Concussion."

"Oh, no!"

Tulsi gave her an amused look only slightly tinged with bitterness. "You were way less worried when *you* gave me a concussion."

"It wasn't that bad; you just liked making a fuss." Quentin tugged at Alex's hand as Alex stood. "Wait, no, come on. The bus isn't that bad. I'll ride with you."

Alex paused.

A yell from the ring. A girl waved through the crowd. "General! Watch my fight!"

"You got it," Alex said automatically. "You look great!"

The girl whooped.

Alex stood on her tiptoes. It had been easier to watch when they'd had the bleachers.

Sunju and Clementine appeared at Tulsi's side, Sunju bundling her sketchbook into her backpack, Clementine still watching the fight with a sour expression.

Look at me, Alex begged silently. *I'm doing what you wanted; just look—*

Another yell from the ring. The fight had started.

Alex craned to look, catching the whites of people's eyes in the bare warehouse bulbs as they alternated between watching the fight and watching Alex watch it—

Tulsi shook her shoulder as she passed. "Last chance. Walking out now."

"One second," Alex said.

Quentin tugged on her hand. "Alex."

Alex stopped. Her laundromat girls were heading for the door, not even looking back to check if Alex was following. Quentin stood behind her, clasping Alex's palm tight enough to make it tingle, the way she'd grasped Alex before she'd dragged them into the pool and kissed her.

And yet . . . and *yet.* They hadn't kissed since the pool, not properly. Quentin had never asked her out, never said *girlfriend* even though Alex had spent so much time with her lately.

Alex missed her girls. They'd been holding off on watching *Star Rangers* for weeks, waiting for Alex to join them.

"I'll see you tomorrow," Alex told Quentin. Then, in a rush of bravery and desperate hope not to piss Quentin off, she raised Quentin's hand to her mouth and kissed it.

Quentin's lips parted. She looked pleased, shocked, and Alex had to bite her cheek to stop herself grinning as she followed her girls out of the warehouse. It was nice to finally get the upper hand.

The others were halfway to the car when Alex made it out into the dark parking lot. Thankfully, they hadn't seen the hand kiss.

Alex caught up to Clementine. "Should Tulsi be driving?"

Clementine took a moment to respond. She held up Tulsi's car keys. "I'm driving."

"Oh, cool! She must really trust you."

"It's called having no other options," Tulsi said, opening the passenger's seat grudgingly.

Alex hummed. "No, I think she really trusts you. Sunju?"

"With her life," Sunju called, sliding into the back seat.

Alex beamed. "See?"

Clementine's mouth gave way into a small smile.

Alex felt her cheeks heat. For a second, she almost didn't miss the warehouse and all those eyes turned to her.

Things were good for almost an hour. Forty-five minutes, maybe fifty, of good times and easy laughter and no one bringing up Quentin or Jem or Tulsi's concussion or how Clementine sent Olive to hospital or how Alex kept ditching them to hang out with Quentin.

Alex didn't know how much of it was genuinely not wanting to talk about any of it and how much was not wanting to talk to *Alex* about it. Clementine had been particularly tight and snappish about the Jem situation whenever Alex tried to ask about it—which, granted, had only been twice, but still. Alex didn't think she'd deserved that leveling glare and the, *Why don't you ask Quentin?* That was just cold.

Almost an hour of good times watching *Star Rangers* on their allocated beanbags. (Alex didn't care which beanbag she got, but everyone else did.) Then Sunju pointed out that the exploding buildings onscreen reminded her of the ending of *Fight Club*.

Tulsi laughed through a mouthful of popcorn. "Yeah, here's hoping Girls Night goes out with less of a bang."

And Alex—like an idiot—latched onto this like a dog with a bone. She sat up, watching Tulsi pick a kernel out of her teeth. They'd never brought up the idea that Girls Night would end. Did they want it to end? When it did end—*if* it ended—obviously, it wouldn't go *that* badly. They weren't hurting anyone who hadn't signed up for it.

But she couldn't say all that. At the very least, she had to hide it in a joke.

So she let out the fakest laugh she'd ever heard and said, "I mean, with the way things are going with Jem, who knows? Maybe Girls Night will rack up a body count."

She laughed again.

Nobody joined in.

Alex's smile shrank as her friends traded looks.

"What?" Alex said. "That's not . . . nobody's *dying*. We're not *dangerous*."

Tulsi made a noise in the back of her throat.

"We're good," Alex tried. "We're . . . we're a force for good. Like *Star Rangers!*"

"But less stylish," Sunju said, waving at the screen full of leather-clad teenage superheroes gasping in horror at their burning city.

Alex looked pleadingly at Clementine. She would understand, right? She'd helped so many girls with their stances, their punches, but she'd also helped out on assignments and listened to so many stories about how it made them feel *stronger*—able to stick up for themselves, try new things, join the movement. With Girls Night, they were a *part of something*. That wasn't nothing.

"Um," Clementine said, rolling the Styrofoam through the beanbag material. "Sure, yeah, I guess."

"You guess?" Alex stood, looked around. Tulsi was impassive, chewing her popcorn like this conversation didn't matter. Sunju looked encouraging but . . . apologetic?

"I think it's good," Sunju said. "I just . . . I never really thought about it that way before you started talking about it? For me, it was mostly a social thing, not . . ."

"A movement," Tulsi said, licking salt off her fingers.

"Well, it is." Alex had never said it aloud before. "It is a movement. We're the leaders of a *movement*, guys."

They looked up at her. Clementine paused the episode.

"And it's good," Alex continued. "It's a force for good."

Tulsi crunched her popcorn. "Maybe if we were the only ones in control."

"What? We are."

Tulsi sighed. "Alex, have you seen the hashtags lately?"

"Every night," Alex said. "They're being vague, like I told them to be."

"They're being *secretive*, because Q *told* them to be secretive, because she doesn't want you finding out whatever she's got going on. Someone posted about trashing an anti-abortion clinic. That's awesome, but it *obviously* wasn't us. Quentin and Cady and Yazmine—"

"They're not Ringleaders! They just stand in for us when we aren't there."

"Quentin gives out *assignments*. She's telling these girls—"

"We don't know that for sure!" Alex dug out her phone. "*We're* in control. I'll prove it."

Yazmine didn't pick up. Alex didn't blame her—probably staring at her phone like, *Who calls without texting first?*

Cady picked up on the third ring. "Alex, hiii! Is this about the MeatLovers protest? I'm so excited—"

Alex punched the speakerphone button. "Tell me everything you know about Jem."

Cady made a high-pitched sound not unlike a kitten. "She's . . . badass? And weirdly sweet? And young—I think she went up a grade in middle school. And, um, I haven't actually talked to her that much. Why are you asking me this?"

"Because you used to be *useful* when I was gossip queen," Alex gritted.

Clementine snorted.

Sunju held out her hand. Tulsi shook some popcorn into it.

"I'm still useful," Cady said, hurt. "When Quentin asked, I— uh."

Sunju stopped, popcorn halfway to her mouth. Tulsi started slapping her knee like a football fan whose team was finally winning.

"Quentin asked . . ." Alex repeated. "About Jem?"

"Uhhhh," Cady said, voice pitching so high, Alex winced. "No?"

"Why does she want to know about Jem? What's she planning?"

"I didn't ask," Cady said quickly. "Hey, just forget everything I said. Seriously, I'm so tired; I don't know what I'm saying; bye, Alex—" She hung up mid-fake yawn.

Alex stared at her screen. She scrolled furiously through her contacts until she got to *Q*, followed by a crown emoji. Her thumb hovered over the CALL button.

Three pairs of eyes burned into her cheek. Alex squirmed. However this conversation went, she didn't want to have it in front of these girls. She still hadn't told them about the kiss in the pool. And she didn't like talking about Quentin in front of them, or vice versa. Everyone got . . . weird. Alex tried to distract them from each other, but it was getting worse. Like one day Alex would walk in and find all of them sitting in a room waiting to give Alex a choice: her laundromat girls or Quentin. Pick one; burn your bridges with the other.

I can have both, Alex imagined saying. But even in her mind, the protest was getting weaker.

She put her phone in her pocket. "I'll . . . ask her tomorrow."

Tulsi snorted. "Good luck."

Quentin's smug expression was hastily covered with excitement as Alex slid into the cafeteria seat next to her. "Aw, I get you today?"

"You do," Alex said. She bumped Quentin's ankle under the table.

Quentin paused. Then there was an answering bump, and she dragged her chair so their thighs were touching.

Alex didn't dare look over at her usual table. The girls always looked uncomfortable watching them cozy up together.

Quentin leaned over, mouth brushing Alex's ear. "I know I've been coveting you lately. I just can't help it. Are they jealous?"

Alex tried to think of something to say that wasn't *hfhghhh*. Quentin's hand was on her thigh, lips almost touching her ear. They were at *school*.

"They miss me," Alex managed.

"*I* miss you," Quentin said, pulling back. Her eyes were amused, but there was something behind it, a tenderness that made Alex want to forget about what she'd told her friends about Jem's plan, about all of it. Quentin looked at her, and Alex wanted to ignore everything that wasn't Quentin's heavy gaze, watching Alex like she was the world.

Quentin's mouth spasmed. It did that sometimes when she thought she'd given away too much.

Alex sucked in a breath and pressed her foot harder into Quentin's ankle. "Q."

Quentin twisted Alex's hair around her pinkie. "Mmmm?"

"I've been hearing some weird whispers. About Jem."

Quentin stopped twisting. "Is she injured?"

"No. She's . . . she wants to hurt somebody. With fireworks. Do you . . . know anything about that?"

Quentin dropped her hair and looked out across the cafeteria, the world seeping back in. Cheerleaders whispering down their table. A girl with a black eye and staples in her cheek bending to pick up a juice box.

"Why would you think that?"

I'm just covering my bases, Alex wanted to say. *I know you didn't have anything to do with it. Let's just forget about it. Play with my hair again?*

"Q," Alex said. "Quentin. It's . . . it's dangerous."

Quentin laughed, a short, sharp thing that reminded her of Tulsi in her peak mean era, sophomore year, derisive and menacing. The kind of laugh that promised some very unfunny things.

Quentin took her hands. "I watch you, you know. At Girls Night. The fire in your eyes. The fire you *give* to these girls. And everyone knows you're my girl, so some of them started looking at me like . . . "

She sighed, laughed again. No sharpness in it, just . . . resignation. "I didn't think she'd *do* it. I just . . . she needed a push. So I gave her an assignment. She didn't actually hurt anyone, right? I didn't tell her to. I just said to . . . plan."

"No. She didn't hurt anyone."

"Oh, thank God." Quentin raked her hands through her hair, relieved. "That would've been . . . ugh. This is so stupid. I'm so sorry, Alex. No more assignments from me."

Alex nodded, dazed. She could count on her hand the number of times Quentin had apologized to her. She'd have been less surprised if Quentin had kissed her in the middle of the cafeteria.

"Was it . . ." Alex hesitated. "It was just one, right? You only gave out one assignment? Because the socials—"

Quentin gave her a strange look. "Of course it was just one. Everyone gets weird on socials; you know that."

"But—"

Quentin ran a hand through her hair. "If anyone else comes to me, and I think they need a push, I'll send them to you."

"Thank you."

"Of course," Quentin repeated, fingers running gently through Alex's scalp, catching a tangle and pulling until it broke, ignoring Alex's wince. "Anything for my girl."

CHAPTER TWENTY-SEVEN

The new chair in front of Ms. Ryans's desk was hard and uncomfortable. The kind of chair that, even if you were as determined as Tulsi, made it impossible to slouch.

Ms. Ryans steepled her fingers. "What are your plans for after high school?"

Tulsi took a second to adjust, another to come up with something meaningless. "I hear the gas station down the road is always hiring."

Ms. Ryans, as always, didn't laugh. "No college?"

"Not really my thing."

"No? You're smart."

Tulsi squirmed. Since when?

"At least, you're not stupid," Ms. Ryans continued. "You're a B student. That's decent."

Tulsi waited. This had to be going somewhere.

"What if your fees were fully paid? Would you be interested in college then?"

"You just said I'm a B student. Pretty sure they don't give full rides to B students."

"They might," Ms. Ryans said. Her fingers were pressed together so hard, her nails would leave marks on her fingertips. "If someone were to arrange something."

She opened a drawer and pulled a slim clear file filled with documents. She held it out.

Tulsi checked. Sure enough, her fingertips had deep nail impressions, repeated half-moons, like she'd been doing it long before Tulsi had walked in.

Tulsi eyed the clear file. Ms. Ryans shook it gently, as if tempting a dog with a stick. When Tulsi didn't take it, her lips thinned. She set it in front of Tulsi on the desk.

Tulsi stayed where she was. "What is it?"

"It's a cheerleading scholarship. UCLA."

Oh. Shit.

She folded her arms tight across her chest. "You're gonna need to spell this one out for me, teach. Like I said, I'm a B student."

Ms. Ryans paused, steeling herself. Tulsi did the same. *Shit, shit, shit, shit, shit.*

"I would gladly make sure this happens for you," Ms. Ryans started. "All you would need to do is confirm the existence of Girls Night."

Tulsi bit the inside of her cheek. The mostly-healed cut throbbed but didn't spill over. Six months ago, she would've sold out anyone and anything for a full ride to college. Christ, *three* months ago, she would've agonized over it for a while and then given in. But three months ago, she hadn't been to Clementine's apartment. She hadn't helped Sunju carry patio chairs up five flights of stairs so they'd have somewhere to eat dinner, or gone thrift shopping to find things to tack on the apartment walls. Three months ago, she thought every one of Alex's niceties were barbed, that she had a master plan, that she didn't have that gooey caramel center. She didn't have a handle on Clementine, couldn't tell her stressed silences from her excited ones. And she hadn't noticed Sunju's freckles.

Tulsi put a hand on the clear file, let it linger on the plastic, gliding over the letters in SCHOLARSHIP, imagining it. Her aunt's excited scream, her brothers dogpiling her in a hug, her sister kissing her cheek, all of them left in the dust for Tulsi to visit on Thanksgiving. *Independence.* A new city. Shitty dorm. Campus life. Maybe her new cheer squad would be her second family, like on the TV shows she pretended not to watch . . .

She pushed the file away.

"Wish I could help you," she said, "but I don't know what you're talking about."

A vein in Ms. Ryans's forehead twitched. The last time Tulsi had set that off, Ms. Ryans had told Tulsi to be quiet, and Tulsi had called her a bitch in front of the entire assembly.

"You're not betraying them by telling me anything," Ms. Ryans said. "I won't say it was you. I can tell them it was somebody else."

"Oof," Tulsi said. "Who's the lucky girl?"

Before Ms. Ryans could respond, Tulsi pushed up from the chair.

"See you around," she said, and started for the door.

"Please."

It was so desperate, it jerked Tulsi to a stop. When she turned back, Ms. Ryans was steepling her fingers again, pressing almost hard enough to break skin.

"Please," she repeated. "Help me stop this before something worse than a black eye happens."

Tulsi looked at her blankly.

Finally, Ms. Ryans let out that sigh.

"I don't know why I offered," she said. "You're the most likely one, but even *you* . . . you're obviously their girl now."

She sighed into her hands. "If Quentin is here, send her in on your way out."

Tulsi was glad Ms. Ryans's gaze was hidden behind her hands. Otherwise, she would've seen Tulsi's impassive expression slip into one of deep dread.

Quentin was leaning on the wall just outside the office, examining her nails. They were long again. She'd been ignoring that rule lately. Every cheer squad member had been a victim of Quentin's long nails.

She smiled like a shark. "Hi, Tulsi. How's—"

Tulsi backed her into the wall.

Quentin laughed, delighted. "You have my attention!"

"Shut up."

Quentin grinned and shook her hair out of her face.

All through freshman year, Tulsi had lived for those times when Quentin shook that red waterfall from her face. She did it like she did everything else: like she was being watched. Slow, languid, shampoo commercial style. It had made Tulsi's fourteen-year-old heart spasm in her chest. Now it made her jaw tighten. *Annoyance*, she told herself, and it was mostly true.

Tulsi hadn't seen her this excited in a long time, not even when she was standing on Tulsi's shoulder. She looked like a kid with a new toy. No, an *old* toy. An old toy she'd thought was lost to her, a beloved ragdoll she'd ruined and cast aside. Now it was back, shiny and new.

Quentin pushed her back. "If you'll excuse me, I have an appointment—"

Quentin stammered to a stop, pupils swelling as Tulsi leaned in. Her eyes flickered to Tulsi's mouth.

Once, Tulsi would have burned the world down for her.

"You can mess with me," Tulsi said, "but don't mess with Alex. I thought she was putting all that shit on, but she really is that sweet. And stupid."

"It's very interesting you'd say that," Quentin said slowly. Trying to twist her into knots, grabbing for the upper hand.

Quentin opened her mouth to spew more bullshit. Tulsi grabbed her arms.

"I know some part of you actually gives a shit about me," Tulsi whispered, "past all the manipulative thorny crap. If I ever meant anything to you, cut Alex free. Okay?"

Quentin's smile died. It was real—no bullshit in sight. This was Quentin, undiluted and unmasked, bleeding all over the place. It should've felt like victory. It felt like picking thorns out of her hand.

"Okay?" Tulsi repeated.

Quentin swallowed. She was shorter than Tulsi, even in heels. Tulsi had barely noticed even in the depths of their friendship. Quentin gave off the irrevocable vibe of being taller than everyone she met. Tulsi had never felt taller until that moment, watching Quentin blink back surprised tears.

Tulsi turned.

"Wait!" Quentin barked. "You're . . . you're coming to cheer practice after school, right?"

Tulsi slammed Ms. Ryans's door open. It banged off the wall. "Quentin's here!"

Tulsi stalked out of the office, smiling wide at Quentin's pure startle, her confidence slipping for yet another precious second before hastily being dragged back up.

Quentin called after her. "Tulsi!"

Tulsi stopped. "What?"

Seconds passed. Tulsi turned to find Quentin staring, mouth twitching like she wanted to say more.

"I lined something up for you girls," Quentin said finally. "For lunch. I hope you like it."

Tulsi started to ask what the hell she was talking about, but Quentin was already gone.

Tulsi stared at the closed door as long as she dared, then stormed towards the cafeteria.

Sterling Girls' cafeteria had one window. It was in the middle of the wall. You could see the sidewalk, the street, and the MeatLovers parking lot. As far as entertainment, it wasn't much. But sometimes you got lucky.

Tulsi didn't think to look out the window until she'd piled her tray with food. She turned towards her table, still deep in thought. *I lined something up for you? What the hell is she up to?*

She glanced out the window.

Then she stopped. Stared. Booked it over to her table, shoving her tray down with a clatter. "Alex."

All three girls looked up from their essays on the table. Alex was trying to reverse engineer her own thesis statement from the other girls' essays. She'd really been falling behind on homework and had asked Tulsi what she would do. A cry for help if Tulsi'd ever heard one.

"You got Cady all that stuff to help with the protest," Tulsi said, "right? Girls, megaphone, banners, fireworks?"

Alex bit into an apple. "We ditched the fireworks to make room for a blood paint demonstration. They're going to pour it on a giant plastic lamb."

"Did you tell her to beat up everyone who's walking through the door?"

"What? Why?"

"Oh, shit," Sunju said, leaning past Tulsi to look out the window.

Tulsi stabbed a finger at her. "*Oh, shit* exactly. Come on."

"Wait, what's—" Alex turned and stuttered to a stop.

Across the street, the MeatLovers parking lot was in chaos. There was the inflatable lamb, dripping with red paint. Girls in ski masks ran around, streaked with crimson, battering anyone who got near the door, including anyone who was trying to escape the fast food chain. Customers milled at the windows. Too many of them had their phones out filming or, more likely, on the line to the cops.

And in the middle of the parking lot stood Cady on a stool, with a bubblegum pink ski mask and her fist raised. Her yells were audible even from across the street: "LOOK AT WHAT WE CAN DO!"

Beside Tulsi, Alex winced.

The MeatLovers door swung open. A man in sweatpants streaked out, hands over his head.

Cady shrieked. "GET HIM!"

A gang of girls descended, flinging paint and smacking him with their signs. The man reached his car and immediately dropped his keys onto the asphalt. Tulsi watched him bend down and fumble on the ground, signs and screams flurrying around him.

A middle-aged woman escaped next.

"Jesus shit," Tulsi said as the woman was tackled to the ground by a girl who, as far as she knew, wasn't even a vegetarian. The woman reached out to defend herself and got bit on the wrist for her troubles.

"No biting," Alex said weakly.

Sirens wailed in the distance. Red paint splattered over the MeatLovers windows, and customers moved to the next one to get a clear shot. They weren't the only ones filming—there was a Sterling girl with a sign and a phone held aloft, filming her friend bashing in a taillight with a sign that said THE CONSEQUENCES ARE NOW, BITCHES.

Tulsi could already imagine the hashtags.

"We should . . ." Sunju said.

Alex nodded. "Yeah."

Clementine caught her by the back of her shirt. "Cops."

"But—"

The sirens grew louder. The cowering man struggled into his car and drove off, almost running over the inflatable lamb on his way out of the parking lot. Cady tried to start a chant, but the incoherent screaming quickly drowned her out. A passing jogger tried veering around them and then started sprinting, pursued by screaming girls.

Tulsi couldn't watch. She turned away, Ms. Ryans's words circling in her head: *Before anything worse than a black eye happens.*

She cleared her throat. "Alex."

Alex looked at her, dazed.

Tulsi tongued the cut in her cheek. Blood ran into her mouth. "I ran into Quentin. She said something I think you should know."

CHAPTER TWENTY-EIGHT

Quentin wasn't answering Alex's texts.

Which was fine. It was totally fine. It was absolutely, totally, completely fine, because *other* people were answering Alex's texts, and every one of them said Quentin was at Girls Night.

Alex stormed into the Hartburn Cadies warehouse, Sunju and Clementine in tow. Tulsi was at her sister's birthday dinner, which meant they'd had to take the bus. It was hard to make a badass exit off a bus, but Alex's righteous anger had carried her through.

Let me know how it goes, Tulsi had said. *Every little detail. Girls Night is* yours. *Take it the hell back.*

Alex pushed through the cheering crowd, which tried to part when they realized who it was but not fast enough. Alex threw elbows until she reached the makeshift ring.

Yazmine and Cady were circling each other. Cady shrank back under Alex's burning gaze.

Alex sneered. "Where's Quentin?"

"Bathroom," Yazmine said. She raised her wrapped fists. "Uh, wanna fight? You look like you need it."

Behind Alex, someone said her name. The crowd was too loud—she couldn't tell if it was Clementine or Sunju. It might've been both, Alex's name tripping in unison from their worried mouths.

Alex ignored them. Take it the hell back. She couldn't think of a better way to start that than with a fight.

She strode forwards. "Nose ring out, Yaz."

Yazmine rolled her eyes. "Just avoid my face, man."

"Done." This was usually the time for Alex to announce the Girls Night rules—no jewelry, no long nails, no biting, no *goddamn* socials, guys, come *on*. There were new faces in the crowd; there were always new faces in the crowd nowadays, girls from other schools and, if the whispers were to be believed, other cities. The number of posts using the hashtags grew and grew. Every day, they got stranger, darker, more confusing.

Yazmine's nose ring gleamed under the bare bulbs. Too many girls had wounds from Quentin's ever-sharpening nails. And Alex had caught more than a few bite marks in the gym changing rooms. Who cared about rules, really? The answer was usually Alex. But crouched in front of Yazmine, dozens of girls baying for blood, it was hard to care about anything but the need singing in her veins.

Avoid her face? Alex would avoid her face.

She sprang forward and dug her knee into Yazmine's gut. Yazmine doubled over, breath knocked out of her in a choked noise.

Alex kneed her again. Yazmine collapsed. Alex rammed her foot into her ribs once, twice, three times.

Yazmine tapped out, hand curled in a shaking peace sign.

Alex panted. It wasn't enough.

She turned to the crowd. "WHAT'S MY NAME?"

"THE GENERAL!" they screamed back.

Standing too still in the front lines, Sunju and Clementine's mouths moved around something else. Part of Alex wished the crowd was following suit, but some of these girls had never heard of Alex beyond her Ringleader title. Did they even know her name?

Alex waved at them like a conductor. "WHAT'S MY NAME?"

"GENERAL!"

She had them do it three more times. Each time was louder, and each time, Alex needed it more. She missed the bleachers. The warehouse was dramatic, but there was nothing like standing tall above them all, everybody's chins tipped up to stare at her.

"WHAT'S MY—"

Alex stopped. Quentin emerged from the throng, all her teeth showing. She looked at Alex like she was the most exciting thing she'd ever known.

"Looks like a good night," Quentin laughed as Alex ran over. "What's the occasion?"

"Did you tell Cady to start hitting people at her protest? Tulsi said you admitted you set it up. You gave Cady an *assignment!*"

Quentin's smile didn't change. "Alex—"

"What? Don't you dare blow me off; I *know*. The Girls Night posts are getting really weird, and they're talking about things I know nothing about. Bombs, and . . . boiling metal. Someone made a meme about a guy catching fire. What are you *doing?*"

"I'll tell you if you fight me."

Alex dragged her into the ring as Yazmine stumbled out. Quentin went laughing, tying her hair above her head, jumping from foot to foot like a little kid. Alex almost didn't want to bloody that smile. Then she remembered Quentin's contrite face when she'd said, *I'm so sorry, Alex. No more assignments from me.*

Quentin hit her in the cheek. "That wasn't an assignment," she called as Alex's face snapped sideways. "We were just *talking*, I said it would be cool. I didn't tell her to *do* it."

"Yeah? Tulsi says otherwise. *Cady* says otherwise. The socials—"

"Cady's a little bitch; she'll say anything if she thinks it'll make you like her. And Tulsi . . . well. You know our ol' sharp heart!"

Alex ducked the next fist, slammed her pointed fingers into Quentin's ribs. Quentin backed off, hissing and giggling.

"Ouch. Nice." Quentin shook her hair out of her face. It always escaped its bun, always bled over her forehead. There was nothing like Quentin Scarhill, a hundred shades of red, beaming underneath the warehouse lights.

Alex grabbed Quentin's wrists, yanked them into the small of her back. Quentin kicked behind her, catching Alex's legs, but Alex held fast.

"Did anybody get hurt?" Quentin gritted.

"Do you care?"

"I care," Quentin said.

"The socials—"

"I don't know what the hell they're doing on socials." Quentin twisted to meet Alex's eyes. "Alex. You *know* me. I just want to have fun. I don't want anybody to get hurt."

Alex thought of Tulsi's shoulder, Quentin baring her teeth as she stomped on it. Cheerleaders limping around after being dropped in practice. The healed bite on Alex's arm.

Quentin jerked, wrists slipping out of Alex's grasp. She turned. Their noses brushed. Alex braced herself for a headbutt.

It didn't come.

Quentin kissed her. Her mouth was sweat-slick, blood-hot, hard enough to bruise. Alex made a noise against her tongue, eyes falling shut. It didn't feel like a kiss, exactly. It felt like a punch to the mouth.

The crowd's roar took on a different pitch, high and a little confused.

Alex pulled back. Quentin was panting, flushed, her smile strangely hesitant, like she didn't know what Alex would do next. All eyes on her.

Alex sank her hands into Quentin's hair and pulled her in again.

The cheers exploded. Alex's ears rang with whoops, shrieks, triumphant laughter. There was something she was forgetting, but it was hard to think with Quentin's warm fingers on her jaw, tilting her head for a better angle, teeth catching her bottom lip, nails scratching the nape of her neck. Only after did it kick in what she was forgetting—chest heaving, sweat pooling on her lower back, Quentin's hand crushing hers as they raised them towards the wailing crowd.

There, standing on the front line, was Clementine. A statue among the cheering spectators. Alex only got a glimpse before

Clementine pushed into the crowd, Sunju trailing after her, but the betrayal in Clementine's expression was enough to yank Alex down from her adrenaline high.

She moved to chase after her—*it doesn't mean I'm picking her over you guys; I wouldn't; I'd never*—but Quentin held her fast.

"Quit worrying," Quentin said in her ear. "Just bask, General."

Her breath was so warm against her cheek, eyes so bright and promising, the crowd so loud and lovely. What else was Alex to do but stand there with Quentin, their joined hands raised, until everyone was finished clapping?

Every girl in English class waved hi to Alex the next day except for Clementine and Sunju. Alex even stood next to their desks for a few seconds longer than necessary, just in case Clementine's hearing aids were off and Sunju was too immersed in her sketching, and neither of them noticed.

It had been like this all day. She'd sat at Quentin's table during lunch, but whenever she looked over, Clementine and Sunju were deep in conversation, not looking anywhere near her. They hadn't told Tulsi about the kiss yet. If they had, Alex would know—the whole tristate area would hear Tulsi yelling.

A girl had posted a meme this morning, a screencap from an old TV show with the caption, *WHEN YOU THINK SHE'S GOING IN FOR A PUNCH BUT ACTUALLY IT'S A KISS.* Alex got her to take it down. Just to be safe.

She was about to lean closer to Sunju's desk when the girl next to her caught her eye. Yazmine slumped over in her chair, clutching her stomach.

"God," Alex said. "Yaz, are you okay? Do you need the nurse?"

Yaz raised a weak peace sign. "Period troubles. Nurse already gave me pain meds. Nothing else to do."

Tulsi slouched into the classroom mid-yawn. She took her seat next to Alex and frowned. "Holy shit, Yaz. Are you *dying*?"

"I hope so," Yaz croaked, wiping her sweaty hair from her forehead and shooting Tulsi a shaky smile.

Becca passed by Alex's desk, fluttering her fingers in a wave. Her 80s hairdo had only gotten more intense over the past few months, her eyeliner even wider than when Alex had encountered her crying in the bathroom.

"The room got confirmed," Becca told Alex. "Just wanted to keep you in the loop."

Alex was still whirling with her first kisses, her still-smarting cheek, and her friends being mad at her. It took a second for her to do anything but stare blankly.

"Right," she said finally. "For the gay-straight alliance."

"LGBT+ club," Becca corrected.

"Right. Yes."

Becca eased into her seat at the back of the room. "Any of you girls want to join?"

She directed it at the other Ringleaders, all of whom glanced up from what they were doing—Clementine hunched over her backpack, Sunju bent over her sketchbook so close her nose was touching paper, Tulsi slinging her feet up onto the desk.

Alex made her face politely interested to cover the burning desire that had begun to boil in her stomach. Girls had sent her so many knowing looks last night, after the kiss. And her chat with Tulsi after they'd come out to each other . . . there was a comfort, an understanding, a *solidarity*. Alex wanted that again.

Sunju closed her sketchbook. "I'll join."

Becca beamed at her. "Great! Anybody else? Yaz?"

"Not gay," Yazmine moaned.

"That wasn't a gay question; that was an 'oh my god, are you dying' question."

"Not dying," Yazmine whispered, not lifting her head from her arms. A bead of sweat ran down her hairline and dripped onto the desk.

Mrs. Garibaldi walked in, frazzled as usual. The bell rang.

"Not late," Mrs. Garibaldi blurted. "Okay. Who's finished Act 2?"

Half the class put up their hands, Alex included. Hers always went up high. It was a lie, but she'd read the SparkNotes.

"Good enough," the teacher said. "So, *these violent delights have violent ends.* What's the friar talking about? Becca?"

Becca straightened up in her seat. She hadn't put up her hand. "Romeo and Juliet's relationship."

"And?"

"And . . . it's really intense. Something that intense, it's bound to blow up in your face."

Fire and powder, Alex thought. She touched her bottom lip.

Yazmine struggled to her feet.

"Yes, what?" Mrs. Garibaldi said, and stopped. Her eyes widened. Yazmine was pale and shaking. Behind her, the desk was damp with sweat.

Yazmine wrapped her arms around her stomach. "I . . . gotta . . . go."

Alex eyed her stomach. Was she pregnant? Miscarrying? She'd read that Jacqueline Wilson book where a teenager didn't know she was pregnant and then gave birth in a bathroom.

Mrs. Garibaldi stared. "Oh," she said faintly. "What's—"

Yazmine tried to take another step and collapsed. Her knees hit the floor, then the rest of her. Her elbows shook on the linoleum as she tried to push herself up.

Becca knelt next to her, hand hovering. "Just stay there, okay?"

She glanced back at Alex, and she wasn't the only one. As the shock started to wear off, Alex became aware that everyone was staring at her.

"Alex," gasped the girl to her left, "what do we do?"

How should I know? Alex thought.

"Call an ambulance!" Alex crouched down next to Yazmine, who was whimpering and clutching her side. Alex eased her T-shirt up to expose the side the girl was clutching.

"Oh *god*," Becca said.

Alex flinched. The skin over Yasmine's ribs was distended, one big lump of purple. Something was pooling under the surface.

A memory emerged through the panic: Alex ramming her foot into Yazmine's torso, again and again, until she tapped out.

Alex cleared her throat. "Somebody google what that means."

Silence. Alex looked up at the girls typing hesitantly into their phones.

"Call 911 and *then* google what it means!" Alex yelled.

Mrs. Garibaldi finally burst into action, fumbling at her pocket. "I'll call—"

Tulsi barked into her phone, "Hi, could we get an ambulance to Sterling Girls High right the shit now?"

Someone came up next to her. Alex looked up at Sunju, who hunched into her shoulders.

"I . . . I think she's bleeding internally."

Alex blanched. "What do we do?"

Sunju joined her on the floor. She reached out as if to touch the distorted skin over Yazmine's ribs, then dropped her hand. "Wait for the ambulance."

Alex nodded, tried to stop shaking.

A prickling sensation crawled up her neck. She looked up. Twenty-five anxious gazes were fixed on Alex, waiting, expectant.

All eyes on me, Alex thought, and shuddered.

CHAPTER TWENTY-NINE

"I still think it's down the hall."

Sunju shook her head, pulling Clementine back when she started following Tulsi down the hospital hallway. "You read the sign wrong; it's—"

Alex walked into the nearest room and waved. "Hi, Yazmine."

Yazmine shot them a goofy thumbs-up. She was eating green Jell-O, the only pop of color in the sterile white room. The thumbs-up sloughed into a crooked peace sign, her frown hazy with painkillers. "Hiii!"

Alex sidled up to the bed. "How're you feeling, bud?"

"Feeling goooood." A spoonful of Jell-O slipped off the spoon and splatted onto Yazmine's chest. She frowned, scooping it up again with great care.

"Great," Alex said. "We're so happy you're on the mend."

"So happy you won't go to jail," Tulsi muttered.

Alex forced a laugh. She really wasn't looking forward to Tulsi finding out about that kiss. It had to happen soon—Clementine and Sunju had been weird and silent around her all day, and Tulsi's suspicion was only sidetracked by Yazmine collapsing in class. The last few hours in the hospital waiting room had been torture, the conversation so stilted and awkward that everyone had given up and started watching the cooking show in the corner, which had no sound and German subtitles.

It doesn't mean I love you any less, Alex rehearsed in her head. *I can have friends who aren't you. Friends who I kiss. I don't know if Q is my girlfriend; we haven't had that conversation. Anyway . . .*

"Think I'll just watch for a while," Yazmine said, garbled around her Jell-O.

Alex blinked. "You're . . . still going to Girls Night after this?"

A sluggish shrug. Yazmine on pain meds was a lot like Yazmine after five beers, her slow, lazy movements dialed up to eleven.

"You don't want to stop going? You needed emergency surgery. You were in there for *hours*." Alex winced, imagining the horror show underneath the plastic gown.

They had to cut her open, Alex had thought on a loop on the way over. *You hurt her so bad, they needed to cut her open, take the hurt out. They cut her open.*

"I like fighting," Yazmine said simply.

"This isn't *fighting*. This isn't a wrestling class or taekwondo. This isn't boxing. This is meeting secretly and getting the shit kicked out of you by your classmates, and none of them know the difference between a punch that doesn't do damage and a knee to the stomach that'll make you bleed out internally!"

Yazmine gazed up at her, confused and distant. She put her hand over her side, and Alex imagined the blotchy row of stitches. Would the bruising have gone down by now? The discoloration, surely, if it had been caused by all the blood massing under her skin.

Alex shivered.

Yazmine burped. "Am I a meme?"

"No," said Alex, who hadn't checked the hashtags yet. If someone had made a meme about this, it would be taken down by the end of the day. Even if it was very, *very* funny.

"Alex," Clementine said. The first word she'd said directly to her all day. "We should go."

Alex looked back at her, relieved and questioning. All that time stuck in the waiting room and now they were leaving after not even a minute of conversation?

Clementine hadn't complained once in that small plastic chair. Alex had been too busy stressing to examine her properly, but looking at her now revealed the bags under her eyes, the defeated slump of her shoulders. She was tired and ready to go the hell home.

Alex sighed. "I'll call you later, Yazmine."

"Cool," Yazmine said, sounding much more concerned with her Jell-O. She reached up to twirl her nose ring in her nostril.

There was a WikiHow article on Alex's phone detailing the consequences of internal bleeding. The last, of course, was death.

It was dark outside. Alex squinted at the eye-watering brightness of her phone screen as it lit up in an incoming call. *Q*, with a crown emoji.

"I'll catch up," Alex told the others, and put the phone to her ear. "Hello?"

"Hey! How's my third favorite cheerleader?"

"Yaz is fine." Alex watched Clementine, Tulsi, and Sunju's retreating backs and ached. "She'll make a full recovery."

"Awesome," Quentin said. "That's awesome."

Music in the background. A cacophony of chatter. "Where are you?"

"Are you coming to the party tonight?"

"Party?"

"I'm repurposing the warehouse for the night."

"What?"

"I know I told you."

Someone laughed too close to the phone, and Alex winced away from it. "That's not . . . it's not a *party* warehouse."

"Right, it's a *meeting place for various extracurriculars*." Quentin made a fart noise. She sounded drunk. "Are you coming? You have to come, get some normal into your weird day."

The others stood around the car, chatting over the hood. They looked just as tired as Alex felt—bone-tired, like she wanted to sink into bed and not get up. They could go to Clementine's place, lie around in the beanbags. That sounded like heaven. Alex and her girls, breathing in time.

"Q—"

"Everyone's been complaining you're not here. We need our General."

Alex sighed. The image of everyone turning to watch her walk into the party was . . . tempting. But she really just wanted to curl up in one of Clementine's beanbags.

"I need you here," Quentin continued. There was a whine in it, but there was also a soft undertone that Alex had only started to hear recently.

"I'm really tired. We all are. We were in the waiting room for a long time."

"Bring them along," Quentin said instantly. "Come on, it'll help you unwind, all of you. Please. You're my girls."

Alex made a face. Alex was her girl, sure. But *all* of them?

"You can leave after, like, forty-five minutes," Quentin begged. Her voice dropped, low and sultry. "I'll make it worth your while."

Alex's mind blurred with memories—Quentin biting her lip; Quentin kissing her knuckles and driving them into Alex's cheek; Quentin slick with chlorine, her hands in Alex's hair. The idea of seeing Quentin only made her more tired, but in an adrenaline crash way. More excitement before the night was over.

Alex touched her bottom lip. "Forty-five minutes."

"You're the *best*," Quentin said, then Alex was talking to a dial tone.

"No," Clementine and Sunju chorused.

"I'd rather be dragged through the streets by my hair," Tulsi said.

Alex kept her smile on. "It's just what you guys need to unwind. And we'll only be there a little while."

Three tired faces stared back at her. Tulsi dropped her head against her car window.

"It'll get some normal into our weird day," Alex tried.

Nothing.

She sighed. "Please? Just for forty-five minutes. I'm going, and I want . . . I want you there with me. You're my girls."

Was that why Quentin had said it—giving Alex ammunition for later? Alex didn't know if she loved or hated that idea.

Tulsi groaned.

Clementine signed something to Sunju so fast that Alex missed it. Judging from Sunju's blink, it took her a second to understand it, too.

Sunju tugged Clementine off to the side, their backs to Alex. Clementine was signing, Sunju whispering in reply.

"What the hell?" Tulsi said.

Alex shrugged, heart pounding. Was now the moment they told Tulsi about the kiss?

More signing, more whispers. Clementine's shoulders were tight under her muscle tee.

Sunju shook her head. Her voice rose loud enough for Alex to catch a snippet.

"Something's gotta give," Sunju said. "We can watch *Star Rangers* after."

Clementine paused. Her hands moved.

"Fine by me," Sunju said. When she turned, her blank gaze made Alex's hope wilt.

"Forty-five minutes," Sunju said. "Then we go."

Alex nodded. "And then we can go and watch *Star Rangers*."

"You're not coming," Sunju told her, and got in the car.

Alex stood there for a moment, fighting back tears. Then she pulled up a tight smile and climbed into the passenger seat, dread building in her gut.

Someone had fixed a disco ball in place of Hartburn Candies' three lightbulbs. Pink and purple light cascaded over the gray warehouse walls, over the hundreds of bodies dancing, drinking, comparing bruises.

Alex poured herself a drink and realized that here, right here, was where she'd kissed Quentin to a stampede of cheers. It had been twenty-four hours. It felt like a thousand years.

An old stain lay under Alex's shoes. She rubbed at it. Layers of blood and sweat. Some of it was her own.

She hadn't found Quentin yet. She told herself she wasn't relieved and turned to Clementine, who was clutching a plastic cup of orange juice and glaring into the sea of dancers. They'd lost Sunju and Tulsi on the way to the drinks table.

Alex drained her drink and signed, "*Dance with me.*"

Clementine blinked. Her mouth came open.

"*Please,*" Alex said, fingers hard and clumsy against her own chin. "*My girl. Please.*"

Clementine ducked her head. Her fingers flexed around her juice.

Alex held out her hand.

Clementine eyed it like Alex's hand was an animal you loved that wouldn't stop biting you.

Alex led her onto the dance floor. A familiar song came on as they weaved their way into the writhing mass of girls.

I want you
To want me

Alex's scalp tingled. Bodies pressed into her at all sides, and Alex ignored all of them except the one in front of her.

Clementine swayed her shoulders stiffly. Her feet shuffled. She blinked hard anytime a light touched her, as if trying to shake it from her eyes.

Alex laughed. She put her hands on Clementine's jean-clad hips.

"Like this," she said, and rocked them slowly from side to side.

Clementine moved with her, eyeing Alex's hands.

Alex kept them there. She didn't squeeze, but suddenly, she wanted Clementine to do the same to her and hold hard enough to leave marks. Not bad ones like the ones on Sunju's shoulders—*wanted* marks, ones you ran your fingers over later and smiled at. Sometimes when Alex and Clementine were hanging out, Alex would find herself wishing that a look could leave a mark. If looks could bruise, Alex wanted to be covered in them.

She slid her hands around Clementine's back, stepping closer so they were chest to chest.

Clementine blinked faster, lips parting, but she didn't move away.

I want you
To want me . . .

Alex rested her head on Clementine's shoulder. After a moment, there was the weight of Clementine's broad chin on her collarbone, Clementine's hands coming up to press tentatively into her back.

She let out a harsh puff of breath against Alex's neck. "What are we doing?"

"Dancing," Alex replied. "Why, what does it look like?"

"I'm not good at this," Clementine said, and pulled back. Purple light flowed over her shaved head. She'd been letting it grow out, soft fuzz instead of stubble. "Alex—"

Behind her, a glimpse of Sunju and Tulsi through the dancers. Tulsi was bending down, Sunju yelling something in her ear. Tulsi's face was twisted up in a way that sent panic thrumming down Alex's spine. Oh, shit.

A hot hand dug into her chin, jerking her around.

Quentin glowed with glitter. Red and gold in her hair, down her tight dress, even studding her boots. Crimson studs in her sunglasses, which were so reflective, Alex could see her whole face in them, shocked and squished in Quentin's rough grip.

Quentin smiled. "Hi," she said, and sank her teeth into Alex's shoulder.

Alex screamed. It was a tiny scream, but a scream nonetheless. The pain was incredible and terrible. As soon as the scream fell out of her throat, Quentin was there to swallow it. She kissed Alex hard and unforgiving, and Alex heard herself grunt.

The taste lingered as Quentin pulled back, panting. Copper and salt. Blood and sweat. Her hand was still around Alex's chin, holding her fast.

"Um," Alex squeaked. "Hi? Ow?"

Quentin laughed. Her teeth were pink. Her gaze flickered to Clementine, and Alex's jaw ached with the effort it took to follow her eyes.

Clementine looked devastated. Other emotions seeped through—concern for Alex and the hard hand on her face, exhaustion, disappointment—but mostly, it was devastation, bone-deep and awful. She looked up at Alex and flinched, like . . . like she . . .

Oh, Alex thought. *She* likes *me.*

The realization hit her like a punch, like a kiss, like a balm on a wound. Clementine *liked* her. She'd thought the party phone call was about her; of *course* she had; Alex was an *idiot*. Those looks of betrayal in the cafeteria, then last night, after the kiss—she wasn't friendship jealous; she was *girlfriend* jealous . . .

Dancers parted like a drunken sea. Alex twisted just in time to watch Tulsi charge through and drive her fist into Quentin's nose.

Alex screamed again. "Tulsi! Jesus Christ!"

Quentin stumbled upright. Her sunglasses were gone, a red mark on the bridge of her nose where they'd dug in during Tulsi's punch. She grinned, teeth still pink. Alex's blood? Quentin's?

"You jealous too?" Quentin crowed, raising her hands. "Let's go."

Tulsi sneered, lunging forward. Her fist glowed with glitter from Quentin's cheek.

Clementine jerked like she was about to grab Tulsi's shoulder.

Alex beat her to it. "Cut it *out!* This isn't Girls Night!"

Tulsi shoved her away. The four of them were hastily making a small spot in the middle of the dance floor that was . . . not *unlike* the ring at Girls Night.

"Are you two together?" Tulsi hissed.

"I don't know. I don't know what's going on—"

"Of course you don't; she keeps it vague so she has the power, you DUMBASS!" Tulsi smacked her in the boob.

Alex hunched protectively. All this fighting and she'd never been boob-smacked before.

"Are you an idiot?" Tulsi raged. "She's no good! She's poison; she's toxic *waste*; she *hurt* me—"

"Well, maybe you deserved it!"

Tulsi fell silent, purple light over her cheeks. A slow song was playing, barely enough to keep their shouts caged off from the rest of the party.

"Come on, I know what you can be like. You guys had this weird, twisted . . ." Alex gestured uselessly between them, the two sharpest girls at Sterling. "You hurt her, she hurts you!"

"I never hurt her."

"She has teeth marks in her leg!" Alex's shoulder stung. She rubbed it absently, smearing blood. "Hanging out with you, sometimes it's a string of these constant little jabs—"

"I've been better." Tulsi's throat clicked. Her eyes were shockingly shiny in the disco ball light. "I've . . . I've gotten better."

"You have," Alex said. "I'm sorry. I just . . . I always thought you were leaving something out with Q! She can't have done all this to you without you earning it."

Tulsi stared down at her. Alex had seen her bleeding and bruised, seen her clutching her shoulder in agony. She'd seen her spit out two teeth: once in grade school, a baby tooth coming loose during a game of catch, and last month, spitting out a grown molar onto the concrete of this very warehouse. But Alex had never seen her cry until tonight.

The tear barely leaked out of Tulsi's eye, gleaming pink in the disco light, before Tulsi swiped it away.

Quentin looked just as surprised as Alex. "Tulsi—"

"You're an idiot," Tulsi spat, ignoring her. Sunju emerged into the circle, and Tulsi ignored her too, shaking off the hand Sunju put on her arm. "And a coward. You sprint full-speed at whoever's showing you attention at that exact second without thinking about how it's gonna screw over everybody else."

Alex shrank back. Her arm knocked into Quentin's. She hadn't noticed her getting so close.

"Come on," Quentin said, "that's not fair."

"*Fair?*" Tulsi opened her mouth like she wanted to unhinge her jaw and crunch her to pieces.

Clementine stepped in front of her. "We're going," she told Alex, barely meeting her eyes. "Are you coming?"

Quentin hummed. "Off to go plan how to get Sunju out of that house?"

All eyes on Alex, like Yazmine on the floor of that classroom, bleeding out from Alex's blows. *Stop looking at me.*

Alex hoped the party was too loud, that Clementine hadn't heard. But Clementine's face was even more horrified than Sunju's, who looked . . . resigned. Like she'd expected this.

Tulsi sucked in a breath. "You told her?"

"I—"

"You are *such*—"

Sunju touched Tulsi's elbow at the inner hinge, where the skin was softest. Tulsi glared at her. Sunju looked impassively back.

"Fine," Tulsi gritted. "Let's go."

"Wait!" Alex pushed in front of her. "Quentin won't tell anybody!"

Tulsi looked at her like she was the biggest idiot at Sterling.

"She's my friend," Alex tried.

Quentin nodded. "Your secret's safe with me. I can even help if you want. We can get Girls Night to—"

Tulsi whirled on her. "*Don't* talk to me again. Either of you. We're done."

She pushed through the dancers. Clementine and Sunju hesitated.

"Wait," Alex croaked at the two remaining girls. "I—"

She stepped forward.

Quentin caught her arm. She tipped her head back and yelled: "SPEECH! Your General wants to make a speech, everybody!"

The news shimmered around the room. Someone turned the music down, replaced by excited whispers. *Speech, speech!* Everyone was staring; everyone was close. Too close. Penning her in. Alex's breath came thinner and thinner.

Clementine's face closed off. There had been a shred of hope that Alex hadn't even noticed until Clementine's eyes went dull. She turned and followed Tulsi through the crowd.

"Alex," Sunju said. Not expectant—more like she wanted to be expectant but knew better.

Something yanked behind Alex's ribcage. *I'll go with you.*

Around her, the crowd waited breathlessly. Quentin's hand on her shoulder, slick with blood. Her nose streamed red, dripping down her chin and onto the floor.

When Alex looked back, Sunju was gone.

Quentin's wet lips brushed Alex's ear. "Your audience awaits."

CHAPTER THIRTY

Alex swallowed and swallowed. The lump wouldn't go down.

The silence stretched. Pink and purple light drifted over the heads of a hundred girls waiting to hear the head Ringleader's speech, and Alex couldn't get one word out.

Quentin cut in.

"Looks like your Ringleader has had too much to drink!" she yelled. "We just wanted to say how wonderful the revolution is going!"

The crowd shouted. Alex was lost in it. Revolution?

Quentin called for Cady, who appeared immediately and got down on her hands and knees. Alex watched, mute, as Quentin climbed up onto Cady's back with her kitten heels. Towering over a crowd, with her hair flaming down her back and blood streaming from her smashed nose, she looked not unlike Boadicea.

"We see you," Quentin continued. "All you screwed up little weirdos waiting to explode. We're going to do such beautiful, burning things! The fire begins TONIGHT!"

More shouts. A cheer caught fire, spreading through the crowd. Alex fought the urge to cover her ears.

Quentin climbed off Cady, who stood. Quentin brushed her off and patted her cheek. "Thanks, bud."

Cady gave a wobbly smile, glanced at Alex, and then retreated into the mass of girls who were falling back into the dance. Music had started up again, thumping, groaning.

Quentin put an arm around Alex's shoulders. "Just you and me." Her smile was desperate; her arm trembled where she held Alex close. She sniffed blood back into her nose.

Alex's shoulder throbbed with her new bite mark. "Let's go somewhere else."

"No! Let's dance."

Alex gently pried her arm off. "Please? I need some air."

Quentin's newly-empty arm hung at her side. Her fingers twitched, curled into her palm. And then the smile was back, blazing.

The parking lot was empty except for one car and a girl peeing in the corner. Alex and Quentin stood opposite her, Alex facing away so she wouldn't have to look. Quentin seemed unbothered, glancing around every few seconds like she was waiting for something.

Alex blinked hard. It was difficult to focus, even without all the noise. "How is there a car here? The road's cordoned off; we have to jump that chain to get in."

"Guess somebody cut the chain," Quentin said.

Alex shook her head, trying to clear it. "Quentin . . . what *was* that back there?"

Quentin's voice was empty, and then it wasn't. "Remember that rumor you told everybody in elementary school?"

Alex had to take a second. "We went to the same elementary school?"

"Oh, yeah," Quentin said. Her heel scraped against the parking lot. Someone had been smoking—an old cigarette butt crumpled under her heel, grinding back and forth. "Do you not remember your origins?"

Alex shook her head.

The girl finished peeing, smoothed down her skirt, and went back into the warehouse.

Quentin laughed. It went on and on into the night. "'Henry the gerbil' ring any bells?"

"Oh." She remembered Henry, small and sweet and snuffly. They'd shift him around from class to class to make sure everyone got a turn to take care of him. "He died, right?"

"He did," Quentin said. "I didn't want to go home one day, so I put Henry in my pencil case, told everyone he escaped. The class stayed late to look for him."

A memory trickled back.

"You went to put him back in his cage," Alex said, "but he'd suffocated."

"Yeah," Quentin said. "Oops, right?"

"I don't remember telling everyone that."

"You saw me from the window," Quentin said. Her voice had gone empty again. Above them, the sky was dark, the cityscape drowning out the stars. "You told a few people. That was all it took."

A name bubbled up from the depths of Alex's mind. "Killer."

"That's the one." Quentin dragged her palm over her face. Nose blood smeared down her chin, trailing down her neck. She looked like a Halloween monster.

"Wasn't this in second grade?"

Quentin hummed. "But it didn't end there! I didn't shake off that nickname until middle school. I was head cheerleader there, too, remember?"

"Sure," Alex said, though she didn't. She wet her lips. Salty. "So you . . . did you want to hurt me because of it? Is that . . . back there, with my friends—"

"I didn't *make* you do anything."

"Taking over Girls Night, then."

"Taking over?" Quentin finally turned to face her properly. "Alex, I want us to rule it *together*. That gerbil story was just . . . something I wanted to check. I wanted to see if you thought you had something on me."

"I don't."

"I know that now!" She clasped Alex's shoulders. Alex gasped at the pain, but Quentin held fast. "Maybe at the start, I wanted to humiliate you a little. But that's all over now. I really care about you, Alex."

Alex stared at her, bewildered. Quentin wanted to rule Girls Night together. Quentin wanted the other girls shunted aside. Quentin wanted a revolution. A revolution of what?

"Quentin," she started.

Then she had to step out of the way for Cady and Jem as they stalked out of the party. Cady was giggling; Jem was grave and holding a bundle close to her chest. They headed for the car, which, now that Alex looked at it, shouldn't have made it here. It had three tires and looked like the sneakers Tulsi wore to cheer practice: scuffed, with holes in the bottom.

Jem put something in the car, hunching over it so Alex couldn't catch what it was. "We should go inside," she told the others, only hesitating a moment when she noticed Alex.

Alex waved numbly. She'd been asking people to put her in touch with Jem for weeks.

"Shut up, Jem," Quentin said. "The car's a million miles away."

The fizzing continued. No, not fizzing—sparking. *Burning.* Something was on fire inside the busted car sitting in the middle of the parking lot.

Alex said, "What's—"

A huge green firework spiraled up into the car roof, denting it upward. The second firework hit the engine.

"Oh," Quentin said. "Shit."

The car exploded. Alex ducked. The noise was almost loud enough to drown out Quentin's maniacal laughter, louder than Alex had ever heard it.

Sparks danced in Quentin's eyes. "Tonight," she told Alex, "is the *night.*"

The car burned. Jem was gone; Alex hadn't seen her leave. Cady was fleeing into the party, glancing nervously back at Quentin, who was still giggling like this was all a fun joke, stealing Girls Night out from under Alex, isolating her from her friends, blowing up a car in an empty parking lot . . .

The fire begins tonight. A cold feeling washed over Alex, temple to toes.

"Quentin," she said slowly, "what are you planning?"

Quentin bent down and pressed a kiss to Alex's shoulder, right over the bite mark. "I'll tell you. I'll tell you everything, all the assignments. It's going to sound like a lot, but—"

Alex pulled away. "Why are you *doing* this? This isn't what Girls Night is about!"

Quentin laughed and took Alex's face in her hands. For a moment, her expression was warm and open, like this was some inside joke they were both in on. Then she saw the obvious horror in Alex's face, and the smile died. Her nails dug into Alex's jaw.

"Why am I doing this," she echoed, lip curling into a snarl. "Why am I . . . because I want to scream all the time, every second. I'm sick of being this plastic little cheerleader who has everything under control; I want to be *out* of control. I'm sick of this narrow little world where I can't . . . where *we* can't show everybody how tired and scared and messed up we all are—"

"That's what Girls Night is," Alex begged. "We're changing things! We're fixing them!"

Quentin shook her head. The smile was back, but it was shaking. "Too little too late, Alex. Girls Night was always a powder keg; I'm just bringing the spark. You can't shove a bunch of repressed teenage girls together, tell us we don't have to be quiet or small or nice, give us attention, adrenaline, release, say we're *powerful,* and then expect us not to blow shit up. That's not how this works."

Her eyes were wide and shiny and pleading. She wanted Alex to understand, Alex realized in dazed terror. She really wanted Alex to know her, to join her.

"You thought Girls Night was about building, but it's not. It's about destruction." She twisted Alex's face towards the burning car. "This is what we need. You know that, right? You get me. You see me."

Acrid smoke burned Alex's throat. Burning diesel, metal, plastic. Alex imagined ten little fingernail cuts to match her bite mark.

"Please," Quentin said, voice cracking. "Please see me. We can do this together. You and me, we can burn it all down. The ultimate release, pure destruction—"

"Are people going to get hurt?"

Quentin dragged her in until their noses brushed. "Are you with me or not?"

Her breath was hot on Alex's cheek. Unshed tears glittered in her green eyes. Even raging, even shaking with betrayal, she was beautiful. Devastatingly so. Forest fire beauty, leaving destruction and death in her wake.

Smoke in the air. Sirens and firework sparks in the distance. This was Girls Night, Alex realized—at least, this was what it had turned into. There was no saving it.

Slowly, carefully, she reached up and unpicked Quentin's nails from her jaw. "Who are you going to hurt?"

Quentin stared at her in disbelief.

Alex swallowed. "Are you going to tell me what you have planned, or will I have to find out the hard way?"

Quentin stepped back. A hard look flickered over her face, ready to pull the shield back up.

"I think Tulsi was right about you," Alex said. "You are poison."

The hard look dropped. A tear ran down Quentin's cheek. Boadicea was gone. In that moment, she was just a sixteen-year-old girl in a parking lot, offering up her smoldering heart and being profoundly rejected.

Alex ran.

Quentin didn't call for her.

Past the smoking husk of the car she ran, stepping over pieces of sizzling metal and burning rubber, over the chain at the border of the parking lot—

"Whoa, hey," a voice said as Alex almost tripped over the chain. "You okay?"

Alex stood. Becca's eyeshadow was blue and went up all the way to her eyebrows.

She nodded behind Alex at the parking lot. "What's up with Quentin? Looks like a storm cloud took a crap on her head. Wait, is that a *car*?"

Alex grabbed her shoulders. "Do you have your van tonight?"

"Uh, yes?" Becca eyed Alex warily. "What do you need?"

A punch to the face, Alex thought. *A time machine. A kiss that doesn't hurt. The hole in my soul to fill, finally.*

"I need to get to Clementine Rady's place."

Becca was a good driver. Hands at nine and three, coming to a complete stop at stop signs. She used her turn signal well in advance, and she politely ignored Alex's breakdown for most of the way.

"This is important!" Alex yelled over Clementine's *leave a message at the beep.* "This is serious Ringleader shit! Pick up your PHONES!"

"Okaaaay," Becca said. "So, about that . . . should I be worried? Like, should I go home after this?"

"Probably." Alex pressed her head against the window. Tulsi always said it calmed her down during car rides. Alex lasted thirty seconds before leaning back with the start of a headache.

What the hell was Quentin planning? How many girls were involved? Had she really told Jem to kill someone? How long had these plans been brewing quietly behind the scenes, with Alex none the wiser?

None of Alex's usual contacts were answering her texts. The hashtags were more confusing than ever: violent memes and personal text posts and empowering quotes over photos of sunrises. An argument over Susan B. Anthony. Snapshots of bloody skirts and cigarette burns. Ski masks, nail tutorials, DIY hair bleach. A girl laughing in the dark with the top half of her face covered.

Boom boom, read the caption.

Fireworks exploded in the distance. Alex winced. *Please don't let that be the murder.*

Becca pulled into Clementine's street. Alex craned her head, trying to see if Tulsi's car was there.

Please, she prayed, *if you're up there, please let them have gone to Clem's like they said. Let them have needed each other as much as I need them, the beanbags and* Star Rangers *and Tulsi's microwave popcorn. She shares if you ask her nicely.*

More fireworks. Alex thought of signal fires. Maybe it wasn't even a signal—maybe it was a distraction. Maybe it was just chaos. Maybe it was Quentin, drunk and raging, taking that burning inside her and making it external.

Becca pulled up behind a black car parked haphazardly in front of the apartment building, blatantly disregarding the fifteen-minute parking sign.

Alex's heart leapt into her throat. She knew that beat-up paint job. She knew those fuzzy pink dice hanging from the rearview mirror—Sunju had bought them for Tulsi as a joke, and Tulsi kept saying she'd throw them out but never did.

"I owe you one," Alex told Becca, and charged out of the car.

"Get more people to come to LGBT+ club, and we're even," Becca yelled after her.

Alex shot back a wave and bolted up the lobby, up four flights of stairs—the elevator was always broken; this night was no exception—and down the faded yellow carpet that led to Clementine's apartment.

Three knocks did nothing to bring them to the door. Neither did five knocks. Eighteen knocks, one after the other, a flurry that had Alex's ashy knuckles smarting—

The door flung open. Sunju stared out at Alex, eyes wide. It was, Alex noted automatically, five minutes past her curfew.

"Hi," Alex panted. "Can I—"

Sunju dragged her into the kitchen by her shirt.

"Oof," Alex said. "Thanks. Hi," she added to Tulsi and Clementine, who were not as glare-y as Alex had expected, though Tulsi was getting there. Both of them looked unsettled, Tulsi clutching her phone like a bomb, Clementine's eyes tracking in a way that meant she was thinking hard.

Alex sucked in a breath. "I'm not here to apologize. I mean, obviously, I'm going to apologize, but we don't have time right now. Quentin has some serious shit planned. Jem's murder plan is happening tonight. We have to figure out who it is and where—"

"Keener."

Alex blinked. "What?"

Tulsi huffed bitterly. "He taught Jem drums in middle school. Sunju talked to her at the party. She said I'd be *happy* about who it was, and"—Tulsi shrugged—"he's the only person I'd wanna see die."

"Oh," Alex said weakly. "Well, we should—"

"Sure you don't want to go back to your girl?" Tulsi sneered, the sting only undercut by her puffy eyes. "Maybe if you bat your eyes enough, she'll get Jem to call it off—"

"I'm not her girl!"

It rang too loud through the quiet apartment. Alex's shoulder throbbed. Blood on her sleeve, soaking into her shirt. Each throb made her feel more and more stupid.

"I'm yours," Alex continued. "All of you. Look—" She got down on her knees.

Another bitter laugh from Tulsi. Sunju and Clementine didn't say anything.

"I will grovel," Alex said, "as long as you want. But later. We need to stop this—*I* need to stop this. Tulsi, do you know where Keener lives?"

Tulsi paused. When the reply came, it was slow, reluctant. "Yeah."

"We need to go *now*."

Sunju stepped forward. "Get up, then." She held out a hand.

Alex took it, choking back the lump of gratefulness growing in her throat. "I—"

"Not now," Sunju reminded her. She wasn't smiling, Alex realized. This wasn't forgiveness.

"If you screw us over one more time," Tulsi warned as they ran down the stairs, "I will punch you in the boob so hard, your ribs will cave in."

Alex rubbed her freshly-punched boob. It still hurt. "Got it."

They sprinted out onto the street. A few blocks over, fireworks blossomed.

Please, Alex thought as they fell into Tulsi's car, *let us get there in time to stop the shitstorm I started.*

CHAPTER THIRTY—ONE

Red sparks glowed over the next suburb.

Alex grimaced. "Tulsi, can you—"

"I'm going as fast as I can!" Tulsi snapped as they sped through the streets. "Anyone answering?"

Alex checked her messages. No one had texted her back. Last night, they'd cheered her on, all pride and wounds and excitement. Had Quentin invented a new rule? *Thou shalt not speak to the girl formerly known as the General?*

She checked her socials. More strange memes, DIY gun mufflers, blurry photos of sparks. The captions were all the same: *All hail the Q.*

Something clinked in the backseat.

Sunju cleared her throat. "Clem, did you bring brass knuckles?"

"They've gotten me through some bad times."

"Right," Sunju said. "Good."

Alex twisted to watch Clementine turn the metal over in her hands the way you'd rub a lucky penny in times of crisis. Clementine had never talked about brass knuckles before. She didn't go into her past much. Alex hoped she'd get to hear about it.

Tulsi hissed. "Shit, there he is."

"Oh my god," Sunju muttered.

Oh my god was right. A man was being dragged into the road, his wails muffled by the burlap sack over his head. His hands were tied behind his back. Cady and Jem had one arm each, yanking him towards a Toyota Camry, where a third girl held the door open.

Quentin's hair was a crimson crown, glowing under the streetlight. Her face was a mess of glitter and mascara and blood, all of it paling in comparison to her wild grin as the girls shoved a screaming Keener into the driver's seat.

"Tulsi," Alex said, "pull—"

The car jerked to the side of the road. The girls spilled out.

Quentin shoved the Toyota Camry's door shut with a flourish and turned to them, no surprise or worry like the other girls. She watched them, impatient and eager, as they sprinted up.

"Hi," she said brightly. "Took you long enough."

Jem shifted from foot to foot, flighty. She had a ski mask on, but her rainbow locs bulged out the bottom. "Q—"

Quentin shushed her. "Get the spark."

Jem hesitated, her eyes dark and heavy on their new arrivals. She reached into her jacket and pulled out a cherry bomb.

"Cady," Quentin said, not looking away from Alex's flushed face.

Cady hit the back window with her elbow. "Ow."

Quentin rolled her eyes. "Do it harder, or I'll use your head."

"Sorry," Cady whispered. She adjusted her pink ski mask and raised her wobbly elbow once more. Beyond the glass lay a huge stack of fireworks, enough to blow up a car. Enough to burn a man alive.

"Jem," Alex tried. "Don't do this. You'll go to jail—"

"I don't care." Jem hunched into her shoulders. Mr. Keener slammed his covered head against the window, and she flinched back. "You should get out of here."

Sunju spoke up, surprisingly sturdy among Mr. Keener yelling and Cady still bashing ineffectually against the glass. "We're not doing that."

"We won't let you do this," Clementine added. "It isn't worth it."

Jem stared at her, eyes full of tears. "I'm not just doing this for me. He can't hurt anyone if he's dead. Tulsi . . . you really want me to stop?"

Tulsi's face twisted.

The silence stretched. In it, Alex heard that long pause in Clementine's apartment before admitting she knew where he lived. She could see the choice in Tulsi's head. *Should I stand back? Let this happen?*

"No," Tulsi gritted. "But I don't want you to torpedo your life, either. Quentin will come out of this clean, like always, but you'll go down. Maybe Cady, too."

Cady made a sad puppy noise from around the back of the car.

Quentin sighed and stormed over.

"Useless," she spat, and slammed the window out with one brutal swing. "Jem!"

"Jem," Clementine tried.

Jem didn't look at her, making a beeline for the back of the car. Quentin held out a lighter. Jem held out the cherry bomb.

Mr. Keener screamed. His words were jumbled. Had they shoved something into his mouth?

Sweat beaded under Alex's armpits. "Quentin, this is crazy."

Quentin paused, the lighter terrifyingly close to the cherry bomb wick. "I thought you said we weren't *hanging out* anymore. I think this counts."

"This isn't a bite mark," Alex tried. "This isn't . . . this isn't nerve damage or internal bleeding. This is *murder*, you could go to *jail*. You can't want—"

"How about you don't tell me what I want?" Quentin jeered. "I'm *poison*, right? But you know what? I think people will cheer for me. Getting rid of this stain. Taking sharp heart Tulsi down a peg—"

"Tulsi didn't deserve *any* of the shit you did to her!"

"Since when?" The flame wavered ever closer. "Better run, girls."

The cherry bomb caught. Quentin tossed it through the back window and started sprinting.

Alex opened her mouth, but Tulsi was already on it, the longest-limbed of them all, running past her to shove her hand through the hole in the rear window.

"Sonofabitch threw it pretty far in," she said as she stretched her arm farther and farther, groping for the cherry bomb as it burned down.

Clementine yelled, "JEM!"

Jem didn't look back. She rounded the corner, Quentin and Cady on her tail as they vanished into the night.

Oh god, Alex thought. *Please don't let us go to jail. You don't even have to get me into a good college; just don't let us go to jail.*

"Ow," Tulsi said. Her face pinched.

Alex thought of glass shards. "What is it?"

"Ow." Tulsi gritted her teeth. "*Shit—*" She whipped her arm out of the hole, groaning.

"What, what!" Alex grabbed her arm and turned it around, checking for lacerations.

Tulsi pulled it away, clutching her shoulder. "Something's . . . it's like someone has pliers around my nerves."

Beyond the glass, the wick burned down.

"Over here!" Sunju called.

Alex ran around the front. Clementine was perched on the hood of the Toyota Camry, sliding her brass knuckles on. She punched out the windshield in a flash of silver and reached in, grabbing Keener by the shirt.

"Come on," Clementine gritted. "Come on—"

She heaved Keener onto the car hood. He squirmed, jerked, tumbled out onto the road. The girls grabbed him and started dragging.

The cherry bomb sprayed sparks. Wick after wick caught fire and exploded, smashing the remaining windows and spiraling out into the night.

Two cop cars sped around the corner, sirens screaming.

The girls dropped Mr. Keener on the other side of the street and turned, mesmerized, as a rainbow of color and noise splintered through the roof, tearing out the window frames and shredding the tires.

The sirens were lost. Explosions took over the world. Very close to her, almost drowned out in the din, Alex heard Clementine say, "Wow."

Cops poured out of their cars.

Sunju said, "We should—"

"Yeah," Alex said.

She turned just in time to be tackled to the ground.

CHAPTER THIRTY-TWO

"One more time," Officer Elton said, pinching the bridge of his nose. "You don't know who they were?"

"It was dark," Clementine repeated. "They were wearing masks."

"And you just happened to be driving by?"

"Yes."

Officer Elton leaned back in his chair, unimpressed. His jaw worked lazily around a wad of gum. "Lucky for him."

The door opened. Officer G. Teach lumbered in and slid a plastic cup of coffee onto the table. "There you go."

"Thanks," Clementine said. She didn't drink coffee. She took it anyway, curling her fingers around the warmth. Then, as the exhaustion built behind her eyes, she took a cautious sip. It had been a long wait. She was the last girl to be hauled into the interrogation room.

Teach leaned across the table. She was smiling, but it was the kind of smile these people always gave Clementine: thin and strained and always ready to turn into a growl. *Behave*, the smile warned, *or else*.

"We just want to know what happened," Teach said, not quite soothing. They always got the women to do the good cop routine with Clementine. "That was a very heroic thing, what you girls did."

"Can I have my phone? I need to call my brother." *And ask him if the city's burning down.*

"We can do that later." Teach gave her another smile, like she was helping her out. "He'll be alright, by the way. The guy you saved. He can walk out of the hospital tonight."

"Oh," Clementine said. "Great."

Hopefully her lack of enthusiasm was passed off as exhaustion. Clementine's go-to emotion in police stations was boredom. Anything else you showed would be picked apart.

"The thing is," Teach started, "that man you saved? He wants to press charges. If we think you had anything to do with this—"

"We were just walking by," Clementine repeated, hoping like hell they were lying about the charges. "We *saved* him."

Elton snorted. "Sure. Or maybe you got cold feet. You ran from the cops."

"*Everybody* runs from the cops."

"Your friend has a *bite mark* on her shoulder."

"That wasn't from him."

"Who was it from, then?"

Clementine picked at her hands. Old scars. "Can I talk to my brother yet?"

"Not until you start—"

Teach held up a hand. "It's late. Let's give the girl a break."

She said it like she was an understanding ear next to Elton's brick wall, but her smile was growing thin, impatient. Clementine would be surprised if it was before 1 a.m. She wasn't the only one who wanted to go home.

Relief flowed over Clementine in a tiring wave as she stepped away from the police landline and saw the girls slumped together across a row of plastic chairs. The cops had kept them apart during the interrogations.

Sunju had her feet up on her chair, curled against Alex like a cat. On the other side of Alex, Tulsi pillowed her cheek on her head. Their eyes were closed.

Clementine had never slept in a police station. Though she'd been in some long enough to warrant it, she never felt safe to. But watching her friends' chests rising and falling in time, Alex snuffling sleepily against Sunju's hair, Tulsi twitching in response to the movement underneath her, Clementine was tempted to sink into their laps and sleep.

She took the seat next to Sunju, who made a sleepy noise. "Clem?"

"Hi," Clementine whispered.

Alex jolted up so fast, Tulsi's head slammed into the wall.

"Ow!" Tulsi snapped. "Jesus, Alex!"

"Sorry," Alex said, but she was staring at Clementine. "Are you okay?"

"Fine."

Clementine glanced around the station. It was full of the tired, frustrated chatter of civilians stuck in a police station in the early morning—an old man with no shoes hissing down the phone; a dad and his kid over by the water cooler; a cluster of drunk teenage girls with hoodies and headphones, arguing over a crossword.

Clementine's gaze lingered on the girls. No black eyes, no bruises, no skinned knuckles. None of the telltale signs of Girls Night. And yet . . .

"They don't know who we are," Alex whispered. "But I think they know Q."

"Kept making weird crown signs," Tulsi said, and held up her hands above her head in a prickly imitation. "They won't say what they did."

"Great. That's . . . great." No one was listening in. Clementine signed it anyway. *"Plan?"*

Alex sighed. "No one's answering my calls."

Clementine nodded. No contact with The General, under pain of torture. She hadn't expected anything less from the new head of Girls Night. Quentin would love to let them rot for their crimes against her.

"But I checked the news," Alex continued. "There are a lot of fires, but no one's dead. It's mostly just . . . property damage. Vandalism that'll cost, like, millions of dollars to fix. A few reports of people getting jumped by masked teenage girls in alleyways? No idea what *that's* about."

Tulsi rubbed the imprint of Alex's hair on her cheek, watching the drunk girls giggle across the room. "Well, here's hoping this was her only murder plot. Think she's going to frame us?"

Jem wouldn't let her, Clementine thought. Then: *Like Jem has any say in what her queen does.*

Alex frowned. "What? No. This is too . . . it's too fast. She wanted me there beside her; she wouldn't have planned . . ." She stopped, touched the bite mark scabbing on her shoulder. What had she said to the cops? *I danced with another girl, and my girlfriend bit me?* Clementine still didn't know if that had been punishment or seduction. Maybe both.

Clementine looked over to see Alex climbing down onto her knees on the police station floor.

"Oh my god," Tulsi groaned. "Alex, get *up*—"

"People are looking." Clementine checked to see the teenage girls still slurring over the crossword, the old man absorbed in his phone argument, and the dad whisper-yelling at his kid, with a plastic cup of water in his hands. An officer rushed past, frowning at his watch, barely glancing at the girl on her knees in front of her friends.

"Huh," Clementine said.

"I was an idiot," Alex said in a rush. "I was blinded by . . ."

She looked around. A few feet away, a drunk girl lay down on the floor, stomach-first. Her friends didn't notice.

". . . certain people," Alex continued as another cop stormed through the room behind them, stepping over the teenager and muttering under his breath about paperwork. "And . . . certain things. And I didn't realize what I had right in front of me. But I know now. You guys are my first priority. Nothing will ever come between us again."

Red glitter gleamed on her jaw. Quentin had grabbed her chin hard enough to leave pressure marks.

"I'd offer to shut it all down to prove it," she whispered, "but I think I'm out. I think all of us are out."

"Yeah, no shit." Tulsi kicked her knee. "Get up, idiot."

"You're so dramatic," Sunju added, the last word stretching around a yawn.

Alex giggled wetly. Her shining gaze turned on Clementine, whose breath turned thick in her throat. Ever since that late-night phone call, she'd spent a lot of time avoiding Alex's eyes. Now here they were, so full of naked longing, Clementine couldn't have looked away if the building had started burning around them.

Clementine bent down and cleaned the red glitter from her jaw. "You *are* very dramatic," she said fondly.

Alex laughed again. Her lips brushed Clementine's thumb, and Clementine thought back to that very first night, Alex resplendent under the streetlight. *Fight me.*

Alex leaned into her hand, like she was going to kiss Clementine's palm right there in the middle of the police station, with their friends watching.

Clementine's heart thudded hard. She pulled her hand from Alex's face. "Later."

Alex paused and formed the sign back, smile disbelieving and hopeful.

A door slammed. Officer Teach strode in with a notepad, looking harried. She spared a glance at the teenager lying on the floor and gave the girl's friends an expectant look before heading over to the girls formerly known as Ringleaders.

"Alright." She flipped the notepad open, pen at the ready. "First, let's—why are you on the floor?"

"No reason." Alex struggled back into her seat. "Okay, shoot. Just kidding. Please don't shoot us."

Officer Teach gave them a tired look. "Explain to me one more time how you got that bite mark."

Alex swallowed. Her mouth came open.

A deep voice rang through the room. "Let 'em loose."

Everyone turned. Elton stood in the doorway, snapping gum.

"Got a call," he said to a confused Teach. "Guy isn't pressing charges. The calls are finally slowing down; I'm not wasting any more time on a girls night gone sideways. Let 'em loose."

For a moment, Clementine thought Teach was going to argue. Then she sighed. "Follow me."

The other girls watched them go. The one on the ground was wearing a crop top, tassels dangling over her midsection. As her friend shoved her onto her back, the tassels fell away and exposed a bruise, bright purple and ugly in the fluorescent lights. She flopped against her friend, giggling, raising her hands above her head. Her hands bent clumsily, her attempts fumbling as another girl bent down to haul her up. Her fingers were streaked with something, Clementine realized as Teach led them out. Red and black, blood and ash, shaking as they formed into the same symbol Tulsi had shown them before.

A crown.

It was still dark outside. Clementine checked Sunju's watch. 2:12 a.m. Clementine hadn't been up this late in a long time. The moon beamed over the buildings, half-obscured by smoke. Something was burning.

In the distance, sirens howled. *The calls are finally slowing down,* Elton had said. Apparently not enough.

Tulsi nodded at the rising plume of smoke. "Think that's us?"

"God, I hope not." Alex rubbed her bare arms. It was a cool night. Flecks of red were caught under her nails. Clementine watched them and thought of that drunk girl from before, blood and ash on her shaking hands.

Sunju looked back at the police station. They were only a few paces down the street. "When is Joseph getting here?"

"He's on his way," Clementine assured her.

Alex reached into her pocket. Clementine took her wrist before her hand could close around her phone and check if anyone had sent their old gossip queen any information.

"Not our problem," Clementine reminded her. *And no one would tell you anyway. You have no secrets to offer in return.*

Alex made a dubious noise.

Not our problem wasn't totally true, Clementine supposed. Quentin would never have stolen those reigns if Alex hadn't invented them in the first place.

Tulsi swore. Her phone was ringing.

Alex crowded around. "Who—"

Tulsi showed them the screen. Unknown number.

"I recognize it," she said dully.

Clementine didn't have to ask. The tight line of Tulsi's shoulders was enough.

The girls crowded around the phone. Keener's voice flooded out. "Hello? Tulsi, are you there?"

"What do you want?"

A harsh intake of breath. Sirens in the background. "Tell them to leave me alone."

"We're not in charge."

"Well, could you tell them I'm doing what they want?" Keener's voice was thin with fear. What had they done, ambushed his hospital room? "I swear I won't—"

"You ever talk to me again, Keener, and we don't stop them next time." Tulsi ended the call. She sounded steady, icy, in control. Like they had any idea how they'd stop the rest of them a second time. Like they weren't cut out completely, a hundred social media posts whispering about destruction none of them knew about. *All hail the Q.*

Tulsi's hands shook as she shoved them into her pockets. Sunju leaned into her side. After a moment, Tulsi leaned back into her.

Alex asked, "How are you feeling?"

"Goddamn tired," Tulsi said. "Guess they didn't want us to rot in there after all. Still got some loyalty left."

Alex paused.

"What?"

"No, just . . ." Alex got out her phone. "Becca sent me a heart emoji as we were getting out. Could be nothing, but . . ."

She trailed off, trying to put the pieces together. Girls Night was beyond them now, a network hidden beneath their feet. A hundred things could've happened tonight, and they didn't know about any of it. Maybe Becca had talked Quentin into threatening him to drop the charges. Maybe Quentin's fear had overtaken her need for revenge, and she'd put a stop to it before the cops had the opportunity to start putting pieces together. Maybe Yazmine had used her patient status to sneak into his room; maybe they'd dressed up as nurses and wheeled him out of the hospital into a white van; maybe Quentin had a hundred plans they didn't know about, and this was part of it all along, a cog in a wheel, the story still going.

It didn't feel like it, standing bone-tired in the dark, watching Joseph's car pull up beside them—it felt like an ending. Sweat cooling, bruises fading, putting your shoes back on and walking out.

Joseph waited for Clementine to climb into the passenger's seat. "*Where to?*" he signed.

Clementine twisted to look at Sunju in the back seat. "Sure you want to do this now?"

"I think I have to." Sunju hesitated. Then she reached up and undid her ponytail, dark hair splashing down around her shoulders.

CHAPTER THIRTY-THREE

Sunju's parents were asleep in the living room—Dad in the armchair, Mom on the couch. Sunju stared at them from the doorway. Two parents worried sick, waiting up for their daughter to get home safe. It should have been sweet.

A soft nudge from behind. Clementine signed, *"Where are we going?"*

Sunju led them up the stairs. The dark became more intense the farther away they got from the living room, and by the time she reached the upper floor, Sunju was feeling along the wall. She kept going until she hit her familiar, doorless room and turned on the lamp next to her bed.

"Only essentials," she reminded them, hushed. She crouched next to her bed and dragged out a suitcase.

Clementine grabbed her overflowing laundry basket. Tulsi picked up her textbooks from her desk. Alex picked up a tote bag from the floor and swept everything on her makeup table into it.

"Um," Sunju said. "Okay. Great. Done."

Joseph waved from the doorway. *"I can carry something,"* he signed.

Sunju handed him Jerry-Beary, her teddy bear.

"Aw," Tulsi whispered.

"Shut up," Sunju signed.

She led them back to the stairs, heart thumping in her throat. This was too easy. Someone had to have seen them climbing in through the kitchen window and called the cops, and Sunju would get arrested twice in one night. Her parents had to wake up. Even if they didn't make any noise, they'd *sense* Sunju.

I'm in your blood, her mom liked to say. *There's nothing closer.* In first grade, Sunju broke her arm falling out of a jungle gym, and Sunju's mom always told her about the agony that raced up her own arm minutes before she got the call. Sometimes her dad would linger awkwardly in Sunju's bedroom doorway and say, *It hurts me just as much as it hurts you.* Say, *I wish you wouldn't make us do this.* Say, *If you just—*

A soft thump.

Sunju turned just in time to see Joseph trip over Jerry-Beary, who was lying on the stairs. Joseph flailed out, catching himself on the banister, but not before he slammed into it chest-first.

"Shit," he spat, and froze.

Sunju's chest squeezed. Cold fear dampened her armpits. She turned desperately towards the living room at the bottom of the stairs.

Alex crossed herself in front of her—*Father, Son, Holy Spirit*—but it was too late.

"The *hell?*" came her dad's confused voice. "Who's there?"

Her mom's voice joined him, thin and trembling. "The . . . the police are on their way!"

I hope not, Sunju thought. It'd be a really bad look, arrested twice in one night.

Fast footsteps. It took everything in Sunju not to close her eyes as her parents appeared at the bottom of the stairs, blocking their exit. Their faces changed: fear to relief to confusion to outrage.

"Sunju!" Her mom pulled her dressing gown tight. "Who are these people? Do you know what time it is?"

Joseph waved. "Hiya! We were just leaving. Excuse us."

"Who the hell are you?" Sunju's dad barked. "Get away from my daughter!"

Joseph held up his hands. "I don't want trouble, sir. Just trying to leave."

Alex cleared her throat timidly. "Um, could you please move? You're blocking the stairs."

Sunju's dad jerked, like he was going to get out of the way and then thought better of it. "Who are you people?"

"These are my friends." It was barely audible. "They're my friends, Mom. Could you let them out?"

He jerked again.

Sunju's mom put a hand on his shoulder. Her eyes were zeroed in on Sunju's suitcase.

"Where," she said, low and dangerous, "are you going?"

Clementine stepped off the bottom step until she was nose to nose with Sunju's mom. "Move, or we will move you."

Sunju's mom shrank back, incredulous. "What . . . you . . . this is my *house*! Sunju, what are these hooligans *doing*?"

Sunju pushed at Tulsi's back. The line started shuffling forward.

"Go," Joseph whispered in her ear. "Don't look at them—just go."

Sunju kept her eyes down. Her dad's voice rose to a yell, but Sunju barely heard it. One step, then another. Her suitcase handle was slippery with sweat. They were at the ground floor now; they just needed to get to the front hall and then the door and then the driveway and then—

"What's HAPPENING?!" Sunju's mom screamed, cutting through the haze. "Sunju, what are you DOING?!"

"Just let us go," Sunju mumbled. Alex's back pressed against her shoulder. Her girls had formed a wall between her and her parents, who were grabbing for her.

Front hall, then the door. Sunju reached for the doorknob—

Nails dug into Sunju's shoulders. The girls were so focused on holding her dad back, they'd let her mom slip past.

"What have you done with our Sunju?" her mom hissed in her ear. "You used to be so *nice*—"

The sting was familiar. After a while, she would go numb. Her body moved automatically with her mother as it had done so many times before.

I'm sorry. I was an idiot. It was there at the back of her mouth, waiting. She was distantly aware of Clementine and Tulsi holding her dad back, of her mom yelling something at them, of Joseph and Alex standing there with raised hands, trying to talk them down, but Sunju didn't pay attention. Her mind was at war, old versus new. *Go limp.* No, there was something else.

Sunju drew back and headbutted her mother hard in the nose.

Crack.

Her mother screamed, reeling back. Blood flowed over her nose, her chin, her hands going red and sticky as she tried to stem the tide.

Sunju watched for two seconds. Then she turned and walked down the driveway, her parents' outraged screams echoing behind her in the night.

Sunju focused on the tiny things. A glass of water. Pumpkin soup from a can. Joseph poking his head in to say goodnight before he headed to bed to catch a few hours of sleep before work. Brushing her teeth with the neon blue toothbrush Clementine had been keeping under her sink for weeks.

It's a normal sleepover, she told herself. *Don't think about the other stuff.*

They rolled out the sleeping bags. Sunju lay down in her untouched blue bag, eyelids heavy as stones. Then they all lay motionless and awake for twenty minutes, exhaustion laced with adrenaline. It didn't help that it was four in the morning, still dark outside.

"What do you need?" Alex kept asking. "What can we do?"

They'd already unpacked. It had taken maybe five minutes. Sunju kept remembering things she'd left behind. Expensive moisturizer. Her good winter jackets. Everything on her walls.

Sunju sat up. Everyone opened their eyes. They were curled around her, a protective circle of sleeping bags.

"I want to shave my head," Sunju announced.

"We can do that." Alex pushed herself up, worrying the bandage covering her bite mark. Clementine had dabbed iodine on it and promised it wouldn't scar. "Clem, where's your electric razor?"

They shuffled into the bathroom. Clementine plugged the razor into the wall and stepped up.

Sunju shook her head in the mirror. "I want Tulsi to do it."

Tulsi paused. "Are you sure? Clip-Clop's the one with practice—"

"No. I want you."

Tulsi scratched at her face. It was shiny, freshly cleaned. She'd walked out of Sunju's house with a bloody nose and scuffed knuckles. Sunju hadn't asked.

The door closed. Sunju bent over the sink, listening to Tulsi come closer. This far into sleep deprivation, everything had an aura: the grimy tiled walls, the showerhead, the sink Sunju was braced against. Tulsi's heat was at her back, metal kissing the nape of her neck.

"Are you sure?"

Sunju nodded. Metal shifted against her skull.

"Alright," Tulsi said quietly.

The razor clicked on, filling the room with buzzing. It ran a careful line over the curve of her skull, up to the bangs. Strands of hair dusted Sunju's eyelashes. The razor vanished, then appeared again at the base of Sunju's neck. This strip was faster, more solid.

Another line. More strands landed on Sunju's eyelashes. She blinked them away, watched her hair fall into the sink, long lines of black.

Tulsi bent her ears gently out of the way. Little nudges with the razor. "How're you feeling?"

"Better," Sunju said into the sink. "You?"

"Fine. I feel fine." Tulsi's throat clicked. "Pretty badass, what you did back there."

"Didn't feel badass."

"Right. I don't know why I said that."

Sunju watched hair drift down. Tulsi's fingers were so gentle against her scalp as she revealed it to the open air.

"You are, though," Tulsi said. "A badass. You're the bravest person I've ever met."

"Not so bad yourself," Sunju told her.

More buzzing. Sunju's head felt utterly bare. She straightened, and the razor whipped away from her as she started to turn.

Tulsi laughed shakily. "Almost gouged your eye out. Warn a girl next time . . ."

She trailed off. The smile dissolved, no snark or sharpness. Just Tulsi, in all her glorious softness.

Sunju stepped close. "I don't think the rush is your favorite part."

"What?"

"Of the fight. The rush isn't your favorite part."

Tulsi's eyes were impossibly dark in the bathroom light. "No?"

Sunju shook her head. "You like the moments after the fight, when you're hugging or lying on each other."

Tulsi's lashes shuddered.

"It's nice," Sunju said. "Being close to someone."

It took Tulsi a moment to nod. Sunju had never seen her more full of longing. Sunju had never seen her more terrified.

Sunju grazed Tulsi's cheek with her fingers. "Are you scared of me?"

A desperate noise tore from Tulsi's throat. "You could destroy me. Just . . ." She mimed an explosion, a smile flinching over her face. "You know?"

Sunju pulled Tulsi's hands up, pressing a kiss to her knuckles. "I won't," she said against the bruises.

"Yeah," Tulsi whispered. "Still."

"Scary."

"Terrifying," Tulsi agreed, more breath than sound. Sunju could feel the warmth on her lips.

"Good thing we're brave," she murmured, and leaned up to seal their mouths together.

Even with all this buildup, Tulsi's breath hitched in surprise.

Sunju smiled against her, giddy and exhausted, all of her singing with it—*brave, I'm brave*. Bravery was headbutting your mom, and bravery was getting out; bravery was going to a party when you didn't want to and climbing out a bathroom window and breaking into a laundromat and saying, *Yes, I do want to form this fight club with you*. But Sunju's favorite bravery was this: standing in a dim bathroom with Tulsi's hands soft and hesitant on her newly-shaved head, kissing until her head swam.

CHAPTER THIRTY-FOUR

"Eyes on me."

The chatter died.

Alex beamed and sat back down, waving towards the head of the table. "Becca, you were saying?"

"Thanks, Alex." Becca held up a flyer. "The bowling tournament is next weekend. BYO food. There's no entry fee, but a donation is appreciated."

She handed the thin stack of flyers around their table. The LGBT+ club officially had nineteen members, but their weekly meetings usually topped out at twelve. Four of those were the former Ringleaders—Alex, Tulsi, Clementine, and Sunju were there early every single week, helping to push tables together in the art room.

Olive Barnes tapped her watch.

"Right, thank you." Becca clapped. "That's a wrap! Everybody have a good, gay week."

Everybody whooped. Alex bent to pick up her backpack.

"Tulsi," said Olive Barnes from the other end of the table, "you guys have a seat free in your car? I can pay for gas."

"Sure." Tulsi glanced over at Alex, raising her brows. Olive blew hot and cold towards them depending on the week, but Olive's mom was the lawyer who'd helped Sunju stay out of her house, and she still hadn't taken Clementine's offer to punch her.

Alex busied herself with her backpack. She had time— Clementine was asking Becca about the healing process of her new eyebrow ring, and Sunju was getting complimented on her new haircut by a shy freshman who hadn't talked for the whole meeting.

Olive lingered in the doorway. "You aren't going to ask about Girls Night?"

Alex sighed. "Should I bother?"

Olive grinned. Her face was almost healed again, nose brace gone, the shadow of a bruise fading to its normal pink. "Probably not."

Most of the Girls Night girls avoided their old Ringleaders like their lives depended on it. With Quentin in charge, who knew? Maybe it did. There was always somebody shying away from Alex's gaze in the halls, pretending not to notice her wave. The Girls Night hashtags were silent, wiped clean apart from cryptic posts once a week: a blurry photo of the graffitied fist would go up on Wednesday night with a caption written in code. On Thursday morning, it would be gone.

Not my problem. Alex almost believed it. Girls Night was spreading to other cities. Confusing news trickled in through hashtags: bombs and fights, vandalism and assaults, demonstrations with dubious motives. For every girl who dropped out, there was another girl doubling down. *All hail the Q.* There was never a shortage of teenage girls who needed something bigger than them, something to be a *part of*, and Quentin was right there to give it to them.

At a cost.

A losing game of rock paper scissors sent Clementine and Alex across the road to MeatLovers.

Tulsi leaned out her car window to scream, "DON'T FORGET TO SUB MY DRINK OUT FOR THE—"

"Nuggets," Clementine called back. "Got it."

Tulsi flashed them a thumbs-up and leaned back into the car, reaching across the center console to take Sunju's hand. Alex smiled reflexively at the easy rub of Tulsi's thumb over Sunju's knuckles, the shy delight in both of her friend's faces.

Clementine nudged her as they crossed the road. "Tulsi will yell at you again if you keep staring."

Alex tossed a grin over her shoulder, jogging to reach the MeatLovers door first. It still had cracks in the glass from where Cady's protestors had battered it with their signs.

"If she wants to yell at me, she'll have to notice me first," Alex said as she pulled the door open. "And she's too busy gazing into Sunju's—*oof.*"

Something collided with Alex's side. A flash of red sprawled back onto the MeatLovers linoleum.

"Sorry," Alex heard herself say, hand coming out automatically. "I—oh."

Quentin glowered at the hand Alex was holding out. She'd gotten even more earrings in the past few months, a curve of red spikes gleaming along her ears. Alex thought, bizarrely, of bear traps.

"Hi," Alex croaked. They hadn't talked since Alex had been arrested. "Busy weekend planned?"

Quentin bared her teeth. "Wouldn't you like to know?"

A group of teenage girls spilled out of a booth, bruised and limping, chatting loudly as they headed for the front door. All of them averted their eyes when they noticed who was lying on the floor in front of it. One brave freshman moved like she was going to help Quentin up.

"Don't touch me!" Quentin spat, and struggled to her feet. She didn't look at the other girls, who were standing stock-still—or maybe battle-ready—around Alex. She flipped her hair, narrowly avoiding clipping Alex's nose. Then she looked past Alex, and her blistering glare faltered. Her mouth pinched, eyes going shiny.

Alex had the bizarre urge to ask if she was okay. Before she could talk herself out of it, Quentin's steely gaze was back, scowl sliding into place.

"With me," she snapped at the bruised girls, and stalked off into the parking lot.

The girls rushed to follow. Alex didn't recognize any of them.

She checked behind her to see what had made Quentin act so strange. First, she saw Clementine, standing patiently. Past her were Sunju and Tulsi in the car, giggling, waiting for them to get back.

She twisted to watch Quentin's retreating figure as it vanished down the street towards the warehouse. All eyes on her and no one at her side.

A hand brushed Alex's elbow. She jumped.

"Just me," Clementine said. Her smile was stiff. "Shouldn't keep our girls waiting."

"Right," Alex said.

Our girls, she reminded herself.

"Do you miss it?" Clementine asked as they headed back to the car.

Alex thought about it. Sunju and Tulsi were waving from the front seat, making grabby hands at the bags Alex was carrying.

"Not really. I think this is what I wanted the whole time—people who know me, who have my back. My girls."

Clementine stared at her. It was nothing like how she'd stared at Olive Barnes on that first day she'd caught Alex's attention—this was so much softer—but it still made Alex's breath stop in her throat.

Alex let out a nervous laugh. She shifted the takeout bags to one hand and signed, *"What?"*

Clementine's arm lifted. For a heart-stopping second, Alex thought Clementine might take her hand, the same way Tulsi had taken Sunju's. Alex's breath caught as she thought of Clementine's calloused fingers sliding over her knuckles—

A blaring horn made both of them jump. They turned to find Tulsi slapping on the roof of her car.

"What's the holdup?" she yelled. "Sunju's wasting away here!"

"Withering away to nothing," Sunju added, draping herself dramatically over the car seat.

Clementine's arm fell back to her side. "*Later.*"

Alex signed it back and waited, hoping for more, but Clementine was already heading for the car.

Later. Alex could deal with later. She swallowed and ran to catch up, takeout bags warm against her fluttering chest. She could live with later.

Tulsi and Sunju would've seen Quentin from the car, seen the collision with Alex and her retreat with all those girls trailing behind. But none of them mentioned her as they drove towards Clementine and Sunju's apartment. Nor did they mention the graffiti gleaming on street signs, shop windows, the closed doors of bodegas: LOOK AT WHAT WE CAN DO, with that pretty pink fist. Graffiti like that was springing up all over the country.

They didn't mention the teenage girls whispering on sidewalks, passing things from backpack to backpack. Sometimes these girls would look straight at Alex with no recognition, the original Ringleaders already fading from collective memory.

It made Alex worried. It made her relieved. This thing they'd invented was rolling along, and they hadn't had the wheel for a long time. They weren't even watching from the side of the road anymore—they were watching a bright speck in the distance and hoping it didn't explode.

The car lurched forward. Alex twisted to watch the bruised girls with backpacks. What assignment did Quentin have them on?

"Alex!"

"What?" Alex tore her gaze away to find Sunju holding out a bag of fries expectantly.

Alex took them, but not before Sunju could bat the bag against her wrist. *Be here with us.* They did this sometimes, bringing Alex back from her Girls Night worries.

"We were just deciding on bowling snacks," Tulsi announced, angling her face sideways so Sunju could fit a fry into it. "Thanks, babe. Anyway, we don't want to get stuck with that slop from last time. We're getting quality stuff. What do you think, do we pool our money or—"

Alex cut her off. "Don't you feel guilty about Girls Night? We started this, guys."

Tulsi groaned.

"I think something like Girls Night would've happened without us," Sunju said evenly.

"Always going to be teenage girls who need a fight," Clementine added, too practiced, like they'd discussed it while Alex was out of the room.

Alex was touched by the idea. It didn't make her anxiety any better.

She continued. "Aren't you worried something's going to come back to bite us? What if this is only the beginning? What if something really bad happens, and we can't stop it?"

Tulsi groaned again, louder this time. Sunju and Clementine exchanged a knowing look, signing something so fast, Alex couldn't catch it.

"We'll deal with it when it comes," Sunju said. "But, like, hard to be *that* worried when you have good food and your girls."

"And *Star Rangers*," Tulsi added.

"And *Star Rangers*," Sunju agreed, feeding Tulsi another fry.

Alex looked at Clementine desperately.

Clementine shrugged. "*We're okay now. Worry later.*"

Her hand lingered on the last word, thumb near Alex's knee. Not touching. Not quite.

Later, Alex thought. She reached for that deep space inside her, the one she'd tried to fill with gossip and stares from strangers. Sitting in the car with her girls, Tulsi and Sunju laughing in the front seats, Clementine not quite touching her knee, the cavernous space was almost full. Soon they'd be at the apartment. They'd watch *Star Rangers* or do homework or go shopping for dinner, then Alex would go home, or she wouldn't. Tonight felt like a sleepover night, everybody pillbugging their sleeping bags around Clementine's mattress, which now had a bedframe they'd found at a yard sale.

She tuned back in. Tulsi was turning down Clementine and Sunju's street.

"I'm just saying," Tulsi told them, "half of us have shaved heads. What if me and Alex get in on this?"

"You love your hair too much," Clementine said.

Sunju nodded, scraping the bottom of her bag of fries. "And Alex won't do it without a reason. She'd have to donate it to a cancer fund."

"I thought about doing that!"

"Okay, hear me out," Tulsi said. She drumrolled on the steering wheel. "We start a shaved head club."

The others laughed.

Alex settled back in her seat and let it fill her up.

ACKNOWLEDGEMENTS

I wrote the first draft of GIRLS NIGHT when I was 18 years old, and a lot of people have helped me along the way. Let's go chronologically:

Firstly, to my parents. I still haven't put you guys in a dedication yet - my dedications have to thematically resonate with the book, you get it - but here's a shoutout in the acknowledgements. Thanks for nurturing my stubborn author dreams, and for staying optimistic about how I'm totally going to make enough money off of this to support you in your old age. Lower your expectations. Love you.

Thank you to Francis Cooke and Louise Wallace, who run Starling Magazine. In 2018 Starling gave me a micro-residency to work on GIRLS NIGHT (which was called FISTFIGHTS back then!) You guys are the lovely aunt and uncle to New Zealand's young writers. Thanks also to Sophie Hamley, my mentor for the 2018 Hachette Mentor Program, who told me to take out the polyamory stuff and to try getting internet famous. The polyamory stuff is mostly gone (I'm unable to write a group of friends who aren't a little bit in love with each other) and as I type this I'm a micro-influencer (second tier of influencers, in between nano-influencer and mid-tier). Lackluster high-five for a job kinda done?

To my incredible cover artist Bhavna Madan, who brought my girls to life with such light and fondness. Look at them! They're so beautiful! They're gonna fall in love AND kick your ass!

Thank you to the wonderful team at Tiny Ghost Press: Reuben Davies-Hoare, Melody Jaikes, Jeremy Gibson, Thomas Shah, Joana Podeszwicka, Jeremy Nelson, Neff Rodriguez, and Grace Park.

And to Joshua Dean Perry, founder, publisher and editor extraordinaire. It's been an absolute pleasure working with you. Tiny Ghost Press has done amazing work uplifting voices of LGBT authors, and I'm so honored to join their author ranks.

And lastly, to my readers. GIRLS NIGHT is my first traditionally published book, but so many of you joined me on my journey with ZOMBABE and its companion series BABYLOVE. For all your support, feedback, kind messages, and friendship - thank you. I'll keep the gay books coming.

ABOUT THE AUTHOR

I.S. Belle writes dark queer YA books with happy endings. She works in a bookshop and stops to pat dogs in the street. She has a Masters of Creative Writing from the International Institute of Modern Letters. You can find her on Tiktok at @i.s.belle_writes and on Instagram @isbelleauthor.

MORE BOOKS FROM
TINY GHOST PRESS

AVAILABLE NOW WHEREVER BOOKS ARE SOLD

FOR MORE SPOOKY QUEER STORIES SIGN UP FOR OUR
NEWSLETTER AND FOLLOW US ON SOCIAL MEDIA

WWW.TINYGHOSTPRESS.COM
@TINYGHOSTPRESS

www.ingramcontent.com/pod-product-compliance
Lightning Source LLC
Chambersburg PA
CBHW010550170726
48285CB00011B/2832